THE FIRST MC
PREACHER'S
SLAUGHTER

TRADE
Books & CD's

BOOK NOOK.

THE FIRST MOUNTAIN MAN
PREACHER'S SLAUGHTER

WILLIAM W. JOHNSTONE
with J. A. Johnstone

PINNACLE BOOKS
Kensington Publishing Corp.
www.kensingtonbooks.com

PINNACLE BOOKS are published by

Kensington Publishing Corp.
119 West 40th Street
New York, NY 10018

PUBLISHER'S NOTE
Following the death of William W. Johnstone, the Johnstone family is working with a carefully selected writer to organize and complete Mr. Johnstone's outlines and many unfinished manuscripts to create additional novels in all of his series like The Last Gunfighter, Mountain Man, and Eagles, among others. This novel was inspired by Mr. Johnstone's superb storytelling.

All Kensington titles, imprints, and distributed lines are available at special quantity discounts for bulk purchases for sales promotions, premiums, fund-raising, educational, or institutional use. Special book excerpts or customized printings can also be created to fit specific needs. For details, write or phone the office of the Kensington special sales manager: Kensington Publishing Corp., 119 West 40th Street, New York, NY 10018, attn: Special Sales Department; phone 1-800-221-2647.

ISBN-13: 978-0-7860-4313-2
ISBN-10: 0-7860-4313-X

First printing: January 2015

10 9 8 7 6 5 4

Printed in the United States of America

First electronic edition: January 2015

ISBN-13: 978-0-7860-3558-8
ISBN-10: 0-7860-3558-7

CHAPTER 1

One of these days he was going to just stop coming to St. Louis, Preacher told himself as he looked down the barrel of the flintlock pistol the angry black-bearded man was pointing at him. It seemed like trouble was always waiting for him every time he set foot in civilization.

Preacher dived forward as smoke and flame spouted from the pistol. The heavy lead ball hummed through the space where his chest had been a split second earlier.

Preacher landed on a shoulder and rolled over with the lithe, athletic grace of a younger man. Preacher was approaching middle age but didn't look or act like it. The life he had lived since leaving his family's farm and heading for the frontier more than two decades earlier had kept him young.

As he let the momentum of the somersault carry him back up onto his feet, he considered snatching his heavy hunting knife from the fringed and beaded sheath at his waist and plunging it into the gunman's chest.

Hell, the varmint deserved it, Preacher thought. He'd pulled a gun, after all.

But while killing this idiot wouldn't make Preacher lose a minute's sleep, dealing with the law afterward would be an annoyance. The authorities had started to frown on wanton slaughter, even in raucous riverfront taverns like Red Mike's.

So Preacher left the knife where it was, balled his right fist, put the considerable power of his body behind it, and broke the stupid son of a bitch's jaw with one punch instead.

Like a fool, the man had been trying to reload his pistol when he didn't have nearly enough time to accomplish that task before Preacher hit him. When the mountain man's punch exploded against his jaw, the impact drove him into the bar with bone-crunching force. The man's arms flew wide. The empty pistol slipped from his fingers, flew across the room, and smashed into the face of a burly keelboat man.

The redheaded whore who had started the whole ruckus by screaming in pain when the black-bearded man grabbed her by the hair and jerked her up against him now threw her arms around Preacher's neck.

"You saved me from that brute!" she gushed. She came up on her toes and planted her painted mouth on Preacher's mouth.

Preacher didn't have any objections to kissing a whore, but he knew better than to close his eyes while he was doing it, too. Because of that, he saw the keelboat man leap up from the table, blood running like twin rivers from his busted nose, and charge across the room like a maddened bull.

Clearly, the fella didn't care whose fault it was that he'd gotten walloped in the snoot. The black-bearded man had collapsed in a moaning heap at the foot of the bar, so the river man headed for the combatant who was still on his feet to take out his rage.

Preacher thought about shoving the whore at the man to trip him—after all, she'd had a hand in this mess—but that wouldn't be the chivalrous thing to do and Preacher still tried on occasion to be a gentleman.

So he took hold of the redhead under the arms, picked her up, and swung her out of the way.

"Better scoot, darlin'," he advised her with a pat on her attractive rump.

Then he turned back to the keelboat man, whose lumbering charge was practically shaking the puncheon floor under Preacher's boots by now.

Preacher lifted a foot and the fella's groin ran right into it at top speed. The shriek he let out was pretty high-pitched for somebody who was almost as wide as he was tall and all muscle. He doubled over, curling around the agony he felt, and barreled into Preacher like somebody had bowled him in a game of ninepins.

As he fell, Preacher thought again that he really ought to stay away from St. Louis in the future. There were other places to sell his furs now.

Then he was down on the sawdust-littered tavern floor and several of the keelboat man's friends came at him like a herd of stampeding buffalo.

"Get him!" one of those men cried.

"Stomp him!" another yelled.

Somebody crashed into the group from the side and with widespread arms swept the two leaders off their feet. That gave Preacher time to get his hands and knees under him and surge up to his feet once more.

He snatched a bucket of beer from a nearby table and waded into the remaining three men, swinging the bucket like a medieval flail. Two of them went down almost immediately, but the third man landed a punch to the side of Preacher's head that made the mountain man's ears ring. Working on keelboats gave a fella plenty of muscles.

One of the men Preacher had knocked down grabbed his leg and twisted. Preacher yelled more in annoyance than in pain and tried to kick the man free. The one who was still on his feet took advantage of the distraction and hammered a punch to Preacher's solar plexus that knocked the air out of his lungs.

Then he tackled Preacher around the waist and dragged him to the floor.

Preacher wound up wrestling with all three of them as he rolled around in the sawdust. A pungent blend of spilled beer, vomit, unwashed flesh, and horse dung assaulted his nostrils. He clamped a hand around the throat of one opponent and banged his head against the puncheons hard enough to make the man's eyes roll back in their sockets. He was out of the fight after that.

Another man looped an arm around Preacher's neck from behind and squeezed. The man's forearm was like an iron bar. Preacher was still mostly out of breath, and as long as the man was choking him like that, he couldn't get any air in.

Everything started to go hazy around him, and Preacher knew it wasn't just from all the pipe smoke that hung in the air inside Red Mike's.

He felt the hot breath of the man who was choking him against the back of his neck. That meant his face was right handy. Preacher drove his head back as hard as he could. His skull was thick enough that the fella's nose had no chance against it. Cartilage crunched and blood spurted under the impact.

That loosened the man's grip enough for Preacher to gulp down a breath, but the man was stubborn and didn't let go. Instead he stood up and hauled Preacher with him.

Upright again, Preacher spotted the fella who had pitched in to help him. He was part of a tangled mass of flailing fists and kicking feet a few yards away. The rest of the tavern's patrons had grabbed their drinks and their serving wenches and gotten out of the way, clearing a space in front of the bar for the battles.

"Hang on to him, Rory! We'll teach him he can't treat us that way!"

The shout came from the other keelboat man still on his feet. As his friend kept up the pressure on Preacher's throat, he closed in with his knobby, malletlike fists poised to hand the mountain man a beating.

As the man rushed in, Preacher grabbed the arm across his throat with both hands, pulled his feet off the floor, lifted his knees, and then lashed out with both legs. His boot heels caught the man in the chest with such force that he was knocked back a dozen feet before he landed on top of one of Red Mike's rough-hewn tables and lay there with his arms and legs splayed out.

Preacher got his feet on the floor again and drove hard with them, forcing the man who held him backward. Preacher always knew where he was and what was around him. His long, dangerous life had ingrained that habit in him. Just as he expected, after a couple of steps the small of the man's back struck the edge of the bar. This time it was enough to make him let go completely.

Preacher lifted an elbow up and back. It caught the man on the jaw and snapped his head around. Preacher pivoted, took hold of the front of the man's linsey-woolsey shirt, and forced him up and over the bar. A shove sent him sprawling behind it.

The man who'd helped Preacher had his hands full with his two opponents. One man had him down on the floor choking him while the other man tried to kick him and stomp him in the head. Preacher laced his fingers, stepped up, and swung his clubbed hands against the back of the second man's neck. It was a devastating blow that dropped the man like a poleaxed steer.

With the odds even now, Preacher's ally was able to cup his hands and slap them over the ears of the man choking him, causing that varmint to turn loose and howl in pain. Freed, the man bucked up from the floor and swung a right and a left that had his opponent rolling across the puncheons. The man landed with both knees in his belly and sledged two more punches down into his face.

That ended the fight.

The brawny Irishman behind the bar, the tavern's namesake, said in a tone of utter disgust, "Preacher, does this have to happen every time you come in here?"

Preacher had picked up the broad-brimmed, round-crowned, gray felt hat that had been knocked off his head early in the fracas. As he punched it back into its usual shape, he grinned at the proprietor and said, "Appears that it does, Mike."

Red Mike grunted, reached down to take hold of the man Preacher had shoved behind the bar, and heaved his senseless form back over the hardwood. The man thudded onto the floor in front of the bar.

As Mike dusted his hands off, he said, "Well, I happen to know those spalpeens just got paid, so I'll collect from 'em for the damages, and maybe a little extra for the annoyance. Why don't the two of you move on so they won't try to start another brouhaha when they wake up?"

"You're chasin' off customers?" Preacher asked, astonished. He clapped his hat on his head.

Red Mike grimaced and said, "I prefer to think of it as limitin' the potential damage to me place."

Preacher chuckled and turned to the man who had pitched in on his side. He intended to offer to buy the fella a drink in some other tavern—there were plenty of them along the river—when he realized that he knew this man.

"Simon Russell!" Preacher said. "What are you doin' here?"

"Actually, I'm looking for you, Preacher," the man said. "I want to offer you a job."

CHAPTER 2

"It never turns out well when I work for wages," Preacher said a bit later as he lifted a pewter mug of beer. "I'm a trapper. I work for myself."

"I know that," Simon Russell said. "I also know there's no finer fighting man anywhere west of the Mississippi."

They were in a somewhat more upscale drinking establishment now. The mighty river was several blocks away. The whores who worked here dressed a bit more discreetly and weren't as brazen in their behavior. The floor still had sawdust on it, but it was swept out and replaced more often.

Simon Russell wore a brown tweed suit instead of the greasy buckskins he'd sported when Preacher first met him in the mountains ten years earlier. They had seen each other at a number of rendezvous since then and had always gotten along well. Preacher considered the man a friend, although he wasn't nearly as close to Russell as he was to, say, Audie and Nighthawk.

A thatch of lank blond hair topped Russell's squarish head. His clean-shaven face bore the permanent tan of a man who had spent most of his life outdoors, like Preacher. They weren't really that different, Preacher mused, although obviously Russell had taken to civilization better than Preacher ever would.

"I heard you were in town and figured I might catch up to you at Red Mike's," Russell went on. "I wasn't surprised to find you in the middle of a brawl, either. Seems like you get mixed up in one every time you set foot in there. What started it?"

Preacher set his mug back on the table after taking a long swallow of beer.

"Oh, a fella was mistreatin' a woman."

"A whore, you mean. I doubt if a respectable woman has ever set foot in Red Mike's."

"She was still a woman," Preacher snapped. His first real love had been a whore, and he had never forgotten Jenny.

"I didn't mean any offense," Russell said. "I know how quick you are to jump into a fracas any time you think somebody is being wronged."

Preacher just shrugged and didn't say anything.

"Or when the odds just aren't fair."

"I already thanked you for pitchin' in," Preacher said, "and I paid for that beer you're drinkin', even though anybody could tell by lookin' at the two of us that you got a heap more money in your pockets than I do."

"Sorry. I didn't mean for it to come out that way."

Preacher wasn't convinced of that, but he let it

go. He sighed and asked, "What is it you want me to do, anyway?"

Russell didn't answer the question directly. Instead he said, "You know I work for the American Fur Company now, don't you?"

"I might've heard somethin' about it," Preacher replied with a slow nod.

The American Fur Company was the oldest and largest fur trading company in the United States. Founded by John Jacob Astor, the market it provided for beaver pelts had probably done more to promote the exploration of the continent's western half than anything else, no matter what the historians might say about Thomas Jefferson, Lewis and Clark, and the Louisiana Purchase. Knowledge for its own sake was all well and good, but throw in the promise of some profit and a lot more people were likely to sit up and take notice.

"The company has started sending riverboats up the Missouri to the mouth of the Yellowstone so our men can buy furs directly from the trappers up there," Russell continued. "The Yellowstone is as far as they can navigate."

"I heard about that, too. Can't say as I really cotton to the idea."

"Why not?" Russell asked with a frown.

"Riverboats are smelly, smoky contraptions, and they make a hell of a racket," Preacher said. "You've been all over that country out there, Simon, just like I have. You've seen how quiet and peaceful it is. You send riverboats up the Missouri, you're just gonna scare all the wildlife, and you're liable to spook the Indians, too."

Russell leaned forward and said, "Actually, that's exactly why I wanted to talk to you, Preacher. The last few times a boat has gone upriver, it's run into problems. Some have been attacked by Indians, and some have been waylaid by river pirates."

"Pirates," Preacher repeated. "Like the Harpe brothers over on the Ohio?" He had heard plenty of stories about those bloodthirsty criminal siblings known as Big Harpe and Little Harpe.

"That's right."

Preacher shook his head.

"I don't recollect hearin' anything about pirates on the Missouri," he told his old friend.

"That's because there was never enough traffic upriver to make it worth their while . . . until now. The company has had boats attacked on the way up, while they were carrying the money to buy furs, and they've been attacked on the way back down and had a whole boatload of plews stolen. Of course the Indians aren't interested in stealing money or furs. They just want to kill the crews and set the boats on fire so they won't come up the river again."

"I'm sorry to hear that," Preacher said. "I can make a guess what this is leadin' up to. You're in charge of one of these riverboats, and you want me to come along."

Russell clenched his right hand into a fist and lightly thumped it on the table.

"That's exactly what I want," he said. "You're

friends with a lot of the tribes out there, and the ones that aren't your friends are afraid of you."

"I don't reckon I'd go so far as to say that."

"I would," Russell declared. "They don't call you Ghost Killer for no reason."

Preacher inclined his head in acknowledgment of that point. In the past he had made war against the Blackfeet, the Absaroka, the Arikaras, and several of the other tribes.

The Blackfeet especially hated him. Russell was right about them fearing him, too. More than once he had crept into an enemy camp under cover of darkness with no one seeing or hearing him, slit the throats of several warriors, and departed just as stealthily, so the deaths weren't discovered until morning. It was a very effective way to demoralize an enemy.

It also made legends grow up around him, which wasn't something that Preacher necessarily wanted, although he had been known to take advantage of the fact.

"And if we run into any of those pirates," Russell went on, "there's nobody I'd rather have around to help me run them off than you. Anyway, if word was to get around that Preacher was on that boat, they might decide to leave it alone."

Preacher grunted.

"You're countin' an awful lot on my reputation," he said.

"Well, of course I am. You're the most famous mountain man since Colter and Bridger."

"The day of the mountain man is comin' to an

end, you know," Preacher said gloomily. "Another five or ten years, there won't be any of us left."

"I don't believe that. There'll always be a mountain man or two around, as long as there are mountains."

Preacher drained the last of the beer in his mug and wiped the back of his hand across his lips to get rid of the drops that clung to his drooping mustache.

"I hope you're right," he said.

"What about the job?" Russell prodded. "Will you take it?"

"I was plannin' to reoutfit and head back to the mountains for another round of trappin' before winter sets in."

"The *Sentinel* can get you there faster."

"That's the boat?" Preacher asked.

"Yep. Finest vessel on the Missouri River." Russell laughed. "Of course, the company only has three or four of them, so that doesn't necessarily mean a whole lot. But I'd rather be traveling on the best boat than the worst one."

Preacher couldn't argue with that logic. He said, "What about Horse?"

"That big ugly stallion of yours? Bring him along. There'll be room for him on the boat." Russell frowned and went on, "Wait a minute. Is that the same mount you had when I met you ten years ago, or a different one?"

"Does it matter?" Preacher said.

"No, I suppose not. I assume Dog's still with you, too."

Preacher just shrugged.

"You can bring Horse, Dog, and as many supplies as you want. The company will pay for them and provide cargo space on the boat for them. In addition we'll pay a fee for your help and a bonus if the boat makes it to the mouth of the Yellowstone without any trouble. Plus I can promise you top dollar for your pelts next time you sell a load of them."

"You said some of the boats had been attacked on their way back downriver," Preacher reminded his old friend. "Even if you talk me into ridin' upriver with you, I ain't sure there's enough money in the world to pay me to turn right around and come back here to this hellhole."

"Hey, St. Louis isn't that bad," Russell protested. "I've kind of gotten used to it here. But while I'd certainly like for you to make the round trip with us, I'll take what I can get. Chances are that if we have trouble, it'll be on the first half of the trip."

Preacher was torn. He liked Simon Russell, and the man *had* pitched in to help him during that fight at Red Mike's.

That wasn't the first time the two of them had fought side by side against a common enemy, either. They had been in more than one battle together against the Indians, out there on the frontier.

It was true as well that traveling as far as the mouth of the Yellowstone on the riverboat would get him back to the mountains considerably quicker than if he loaded a couple of pack animals and started out there on horseback.

On the other hand, he wasn't in any big hurry to get anywhere. That was one of the good things about being a trapper and working for himself. He didn't have to worry about sticking to somebody else's schedule.

And the thought of spending several weeks smelling the smoke spewing from the boat's stacks and listening to the roar of its engine and the clatter of its paddle wheel didn't appeal to him, either.

"Preacher?" Russell said.

"I'm thinkin', I'm thinkin'."

"Normally I wouldn't press you for an answer, but the *Sentinel* is leaving tomorrow morning. I didn't even hear you were in St. Louis until late this afternoon. So time is short. Honestly, I won't hold it against you if you say no. I understand you're not that fond of riverboats, and Lord knows you've saved my hide more times over the years than I've saved yours. We're more than square when it comes to that."

Russell really seemed to mean that, Preacher thought. It wasn't just a subtle ploy.

When Preacher still didn't say anything, Russell added, "If it's a matter of more money—"

Preacher held up a hand to stop him.

"I might haggle with you over the price of a load of pelts," the mountain man said, "but not about somethin' like this. I'll just say yea or nay." He drew in a breath. "And I'll say yea. I'll go up the river with you on that damned rattletrap steamboat."

CHAPTER 3

Once Preacher made up his mind about something, he didn't waste time brooding over whether or not he'd made the right decision.

Since Simon Russell had said that the American Fur Company would furnish Preacher's supplies for his trip to the mountains, he took the man at his word and gave Russell a list of what he wanted to take with him.

Russell wrote down the list and said, "I'll have all of it loaded on board first thing in the morning."

"Horse and Dog are at the livery stable. I'll bring them. I've got a pack horse, too, for when I leave the boat."

Russell nodded.

"That's fine. There should be room for two more horses."

Preacher wondered what he meant by two *more* horses. How many mounts did one of these fur company boats normally take along? A few, he supposed, so that fellas could leave the river and go hunting for fresh meat along the way.

With those arrangements out of the way, the two men shook on the deal. Preacher headed back to the livery stable where he'd left his two four-legged trail partners. He'd paid the liveryman a little extra to let him sleep up in the hayloft.

He could have afforded a hotel room with the money he had from selling his last load of furs, but sometimes the idea of beds and sheets and walls crowding in around him was a little too much. If he couldn't sleep under the stars like a man was supposed to, curling up in a pile of hay was the next best thing.

Preacher slept well. He always did.

The sign of a man with an untroubled heart and mind.

He was up early, settled his bill with the liveryman, and headed for the docks, leading the rangy gray stallion called Horse as well as a solidly built pack animal. The big wolflike cur known only as Dog padded along beside them, drawing nervous glances from passersby who were out early this morning.

Those glances were warranted. Dog looked like a wild animal, fully capable of ripping out someone's throat without any warning. He wasn't dangerous to anyone except Preacher's enemies—many of whom had found out what a valuable ally the mountain man had in the big cur.

Simon Russell had told Preacher the night before where he would find the *Sentinel* moored. As he approached the docks, Preacher saw smoke rising from the riverboat's twin stacks. The crewmen who worked in the engine room would be stoking the boilers, getting steam up for the boat's departure.

Russell had said that the *Sentinel* was fairly new. Its brass trim and fittings gleamed in the early morning light. The whitewash on the walls of its cabins shone brightly. The deck planks were polished. It was a sternwheeler with a draft of only a few feet that would allow it to skim over many of the obstacles it might encounter in the river. The pilot would still have to be on the lookout for snags and sandbars, though, and avoid them if possible.

Preacher was surprised to see that a flat-bottomed barge—really just a glorified raft—was attached to the back of the riverboat with heavy ropes. Rails had been erected around the sides of it so that it could serve as a floating corral. A dozen horses were already on board.

That sight made Preacher frown. He knew from talking to Russell that they were taking along a few horses on this journey, but this was more than what Preacher had expected.

For the first time, a little tingle along his nerves warned him that there was more to this trip up the Missouri than Simon Russell had told him.

Well, there was the man who could give him some answers, Preacher thought as he spotted Russell on the dock next to the thick planks leading onto the barge. Russell saw him coming, too, and lifted a hand in greeting.

Russell wasn't wearing a suit this morning. He had on high-topped boots, whipcord trousers, a buckskin jacket over a linsey-woolsey shirt, and a broad-brimmed brown hat.

"Good morning, Preacher," he said to the mountain man. "Ready to go? You can put Horse and the pack animal here with the other mounts. Dog can ride on the *Sentinel,* of course."

"Hold on a minute, Simon," Preacher said. "What's goin' on here? How come you're takin' all these horses on a river trip?"

"We'll need to do some hunting along the way for fresh meat—"

That was the same thought that had occurred to Preacher, but it wasn't a good enough explanation. He shook his head and said, "You don't need this many for that."

"That's true. The others are for the use of our, ah, other passengers."

Preacher gave Russell a hard stare and said, "You didn't say nothin' about any other passengers."

"I didn't mention them? I thought I did."

Anger welled up inside Preacher. He snapped, "Don't lie to me, damn it. We been friends too long for that, Simon. You either play it straight with me, or the deal's off."

Russell sighed and slowly nodded.

"You're right. I should have told you the whole story right from the start. It's just that I know how you feel about certain things—"

"Keepin' 'em from me ain't gonna make me feel any different about 'em."

"No, that's true," Russell admitted. "I'd tell you all about it, but it might be easier just to show you." He lifted a hand and pointed. "Here they come now."

Preacher turned and looked where his old friend was pointing. He saw several carriages coming along the street toward the docks. They were fine, fancy vehicles pulled by teams of magnificent horses. Everything about them screamed one fact.

The people riding inside them were rich and powerful.

"Aw, hell, no," Preacher said in a tone of utter disgust.

"Don't jump the gun, Preacher," Russell said. "These are good folks—"

The mountain man glared at him and said, "They're from back East, aren't they?"

"Yeah. Really east, some of them. Prussia, in fact."

"They're foreigners?"

"Some of them. Nobility. And they've, ah, got a senator traveling with them, showing them the frontier."

"A damn politician?" Preacher asked coldly. That was just as bad as a bunch of foreigners, as far as he was concerned. Maybe even worse.

"Now you understand why I didn't want to tell you," Russell said. He sounded a little exasperated now. "You've got all these ideas in your head."

"Ideas that are right. How many times have Easterners and foreigners gone out to the mountains and caused nothin' but trouble? We've both seen it happen more'n once."

"Yeah, but the company's made a deal with the government to carry these folks along on one of our riverboats, and the job's fallen to me. I don't have any choice in the matter."

Preacher said darkly, "When the damn politicians start makin' deals with the folks who run the businesses, that's the ruination of this country. Next thing you know, those blowhards in Washington City will be tellin' everybody what they can and can't do without havin' the foggiest damn notion of what actually works. I'm glad I spend most of my time so far up in the mountains that what the politicians say don't mean a damn thing to me."

"Look, I agree with you, but that doesn't help me right now. I'm still saddled with this chore. Now, I agree that I wasn't completely honest with you, and if you want to forget about our deal, I understand. But I'm hoping you'll see your way clear to giving me a hand with this, Preacher."

The mountain man was still angry, but he was curious, too. The carriages had come to a stop. He turned to watch and see who climbed out of them.

The driver of the first carriage vaulted down off the high seat and opened the door for the passengers. The man who stepped out was tall and broad-shouldered, as if he might have been a powerful gent at one time, but he was thick through the waist, too, clearly softened by easy living. His face had once been rugged as well, Preacher guessed, but lines of dissolution had appeared on it. He wore an expensive suit, and a fine beaver hat perched on a thatch of graying dark hair.

The man turned to help a woman from the carriage. She was dressed in finery to match that of the man's outfit, including a feathered hat on an upswept mass of blond curls. She was no longer young, but she was still rather attractive. Given her age, Preacher pegged her as the man's wife.

The woman who stepped out of the carriage next was equally blond but much younger, no more than twenty if that old. She was undeniably fresh and lovely. The couple's daughter, Preacher decided. The distinct resemblance between her and the older woman testified to that.

The first man out of the next carriage was whip-thin and moved with a brusque manner bordering on impatience and arrogance. He was followed by a shorter, rounder fellow with thinning fair hair that was revealed when he took off his hat to mop sweat from his forehead with a fancy handkerchief. It wasn't hot at all this morning, which told Preacher that the heavyset gent probably didn't really want to be here.

The third man who climbed out of that carriage was older, a weedy sort with a bushy brown mustache on his upper lip and a pair of spectacles tied to a string sitting precariously on his beak-like nose.

That left the third carriage. A young man with red hair and prominent ears climbed out, then climbed out again. Preacher blinked, taken aback for a second by what he had seen before he realized the two young men were twins. Two peas in a pod, in fact, as the old saying went. They were both excited and enthusiastic, too, chattering to each other in a language Preacher didn't understand but recognized as German. These weren't the first Prussians he had encountered.

That left one final passenger in the last carriage. The redheaded twins turned to help her, each taking an arm as she stepped down to the cobblestone street. She had red hair, too, but it was a rich auburn rather than the carrot tops of the twins. She lacked their pleasant, freckle-faced, jug-eared ugliness, too.

Instead she was lovely. Damned lovely, Preacher thought.

And on the frontier, a woman who looked like that was nearly always trouble.

CHAPTER 4

Simon Russell must have seen where Preacher was looking, because he said under his breath, "Yeah, she's a real beauty, isn't she?"

"Who is she?"

"Her name's Gretchen Ritter. The two young fellas with her are her brothers Heinrich and Hobart. She's engaged to Count Stahlmaske."

Preacher studied the others for a second and then said, "Let me guess. That'd be the skinny fella from the second carriage."

"How'd you know?"

"Because he looks like he's used to givin' orders—and havin' 'em obeyed," Preacher said.

"Well, you're right about that. He's in charge of this bunch. Count Albert Stahlmaske. The young man with him is his brother Roderick, and the older gent is their uncle Gerhard."

"You don't expect me to remember all these names, do you?" Preacher asked.

"Oh, you'll get to know all of them. If you make the trip with us, that is."

Preacher still hadn't made up his mind about that. He nodded toward the man who had gotten out of the first carriage and said, "That leaves that fella to be the politician."

"Senator Josiah Allingham of Vermont. Looks like the sort who'd get up and make a speech, doesn't he?"

Preacher just grunted. He was inclined to dislike all these people, but he supposed that wasn't fair. Some of them might turn out to be all right . . . although he thought the odds of that being true were pretty slim.

"That's the senator's wife and daughter with him," Russell went on.

"Let me ask you something, Simon."

"Sure," Russell said, although he sounded like he thought the question might be one that he didn't really want to hear.

"Are those women goin' along on this trip up-river?"

Russell looked distinctly uncomfortable, but he said, "Well . . . yeah, they are."

"Then you've lost your mind," Preacher said bluntly. "It's bad enough takin' along a bunch of pilgrims, but when some of 'em are women . . ." The mountain man shook his head. "You'll be lucky if any of you get back alive."

"I told you, it's not up to me. The company says take 'em, I don't have any choice but take 'em."

That right there was one good reason not to work for wages, thought Preacher.

A wagon full of trunks and carpetbags and crates had pulled up behind the carriages. Count Stahlmaske stalked back to it and snapped orders at the burly driver and the other two men riding on the wagon. They got down quickly and started unloading the vehicle.

"I reckon that's all the things they're takin' with 'em on the trip," Preacher said.

With a look of weary resignation on his face, Russell nodded.

"Yeah. Nobility doesn't travel light. Not like when you and me could spend six months in the mountains with nothing more than what we could carry on one pack horse."

Russell's demeanor changed then as the senator came toward him. He straightened and looked attentive.

"Good morning, Senator," he said. "It's turning out to be a beautiful day, isn't it?"

"It is indeed," Allingham said. "I take it everything is on schedule for our departure?"

"Yes, sir. As soon as we get all your gear loaded, we'll be ready to leave."

Allingham glanced curiously at Preacher. Russell must have noticed that, because he went on, "This is an old friend of mine, Senator. They call him Preacher."

The politician frowned slightly and said, "Preacher, eh? I suppose you have an actual name, sir."

Of course he had an actual name, Preacher

thought disgustedly. He just hadn't used it in a long time. He said, "Preacher's good enough."

The frown disappeared from Allingham's face and a grin replaced it. He stuck out a hand and said, "Well, if Preacher's good enough for you, it's plenty good for me. It's a pleasure to meet you."

The man was a professional glad-hander, Preacher reminded himself. It was his business to make people like him. But when he grinned he seemed a little more human instead of a soulless leech like so many to be found in Washington, so Preacher shook hands with him. Allingham had a good, firm grip, but again, that was part of his job.

"Josiah Allingham," the politician introduced himself. "Are you a minister?"

Preacher suppressed the urge to spit disgustedly and shook his head.

"Not hardly," he said. He didn't offer any explanation of how he had come by his name.

It had been here in St. Louis, many years earlier, where he had seen a man standing in the street bellowing about sinners and God's wrath. The fella's passionate spiel never seemed to slow down as the words spewed from his mouth.

Preacher, then known by his given name, Art, had thought of that man when he wound up a prisoner of a vengeful Blackfoot band that planned to burn him at the stake the next morning. He knew how Indians felt about crazy people, and it seemed like nobody was crazier than a fella who'd stand in the street for hours on end, preaching at the top of his lungs.

So Art had given it a try, since he didn't have anything to lose. He started talking, not really preaching but just saying anything and everything, although he was sure there were some prayers mixed in with the torrent of words.

The next morning he was hoarse and exhausted but still talking, and sure enough, the Blackfeet had decided he wasn't right in the head. It was bad medicine to kill a man who'd been touched by the spirits, so they let him go.

The story had gotten around, as stories do in the mountains, and somebody had slapped the name Preacher on him. He was still carrying it around, all these years later.

Russell could tell the senator about that if he wanted to. He certainly knew the story. But Preacher would just as soon not waste the time and energy on it.

"Are you making the journey to the Yellowstone with us?" Allingham asked.

Preacher saw the keen interest on Russell's face as the senator asked that question. He wanted to know the answer, too.

When Preacher didn't answer right away, Allingham went on, "I hope you do. You look like a very capable frontiersman. Is this your dog?"

The senator reached out toward the big cur. Preacher got ready to tell Dog to behave himself, instead of biting off Allingham's hand, but for once Dog didn't growl when a stranger started to touch him. Dog's muscles were stiff and the hair on the back of his neck stood up a little, but he sat there and let Allingham scratch behind one of his ears for a second.

Preacher never trusted a man who didn't like dogs. On the other hand, he put a lot of faith in a dog's opinion of a man, especially this one. If Dog didn't like somebody, chances were the fella was a sorry son of a bitch. Since Dog seemed to be tolerating Allingham, that was a pretty good sign Preacher should, too.

That was a hell of a thing to base what might be a life and death decision on, but Preacher had always been a man who played his hunches. He said, "Yeah, I reckon I'm comin' along."

A look of relief washed over Simon Russell's face.

"I'm glad to hear you say that, Preacher," he told the mountain man. "There's nobody I'd rather have along on this trip."

Allingham smiled and said, "It sounds as if Mr. Russell has a pretty high opinion of you, Preacher."

"Yeah," Preacher said with a faint scowl toward Russell. "Hope I live up to it."

Before they could say anything else, Count Stahlmaske stalked toward them. Even though his hands were empty at the moment, he looked like a man who ought to be carrying a bullwhip, Preacher thought.

"Our trunks should be loaded on the boat by now, Russell," the count said. "Instead they sit upon the dock."

Russell nodded and said, "You're right, Count.

I'll see to it right away." He glanced at Preacher. "Can you get your horses loaded all right?"

"Sure," Preacher said, adding dryly, "I reckon I can handle that, what with me bein' a famous frontiersman and all."

Senator Allingham chuckled.

Russell hurried off to supervise the loading of the passengers' luggage and supplies. Count Stahlmaske remained behind, crossing his arms over his chest and watching Preacher with a cool stare as the mountain man led Horse and the pack animal across the plank walk to the barge. He swung open the gate and took the horses onto the big raft.

This was an interesting way of transporting animals upriver, Preacher thought. Whenever horses traveled on a riverboat, they usually rode on the cargo deck. With this many, though, a barge like this seemed to be the only way of carrying them.

He unsaddled Horse and carried his possibles bag and other gear back onto the dock. The count was still standing there. He asked, "What is your name?"

Senator Allingham took it upon himself to perform the introductions.

"This is Preacher, Count Stahlmaske. Preacher, meet the count."

Preacher said, "Count," nodded cordially enough, and stuck out his hand.

Stahlmaske reacted just the way Preacher expected him to. He looked at Preacher's hand as if it were a slug that had just crawled out from under a rock and made no move to shake. Instead he turned his attention to Allingham.

"I thought that we would have departed by now, Senator."

"We should be underway soon," Allingham said.

Stahlmaske gave him a curt nod and swung around to walk back to the rest of his party.

"Don't mind the count," Allingham said quietly to Preacher. "That's just his way. He's European, you know."

"Which makes him act like he's got a tree limb shoved up his rear end," Preacher said with a nod. "He ain't the first fella I've run into who acts like that."

"Well, I'm glad you understand. If there was bad blood among the passengers, it might make for a long trip to the mouth of the Yellowstone."

"Yeah," Preacher said.

He figured the senator's comment was an understatement.

Based on what he had seen so far, he figured this trip upriver was going to be both long and unpleasant. He could still get his horses off the barge and tell Simon Russell he had changed his mind, he reminded himself.

But he had told Russell he would come along, and he considered that giving his word. Preacher wasn't the sort of man who ever went back on his word.

Even when honoring it might get him killed.

CHAPTER 5

Russell had gone up the gangplank onto the boat. He came back with several burly deckhands who made short work of carrying the trunks and bags onto the *Sentinel*. Preacher watched from the dock as the count's uncle Gerhard directed the deckhands to deliver the items to various cabins. He seemed to be in charge of that part of the effort.

Preacher stayed out of the way until everything had been loaded. The passengers had gone onboard as well and disappeared into the cabins. Russell came over to the rail and motioned for Preacher to come up the gangplank.

Dog followed closely behind the mountain man, but not without casting some wary glances at the river. A plank walk like this wasn't what he was used to.

A short, stout man in a blue coat and black cap came down the stairs from the pilot house and joined Preacher and Russell, who said, "Preacher, I'd like for you to meet Captain Benjamin Warner."

Preacher shook hands with Warner, who had a ruddy face and a thick mustache.

"Simon's told me a lot about you, Preacher," the riverboat captain said. "Plus, I reckon everybody in this part of the country has heard of you at one time or another."

"Is that a good thing or a bad thing?" Preacher asked with a grin. "I ain't never been able to tell for sure."

"All I know is that everything I've heard makes me glad you're coming with us. The other captains have told me plenty about the problems they've run into upriver. In fact, some of them have said that they won't make the trip anymore. They've even quit the company over it."

Preacher glanced at Russell. That was something else his old friend hadn't told him. From the sound of Warner's comments, he might be the only captain the American Fur Company had left who was willing to take a boat up to the mouth of the Yellowstone.

"I'd like to think that we're prepared for trouble, though," Warner went on. "I've got a couple of crates of rifles on board, and I've laid in a good supply of powder and shot, too, in case we have to put up a fight."

He pointed to a stack of small wooden kegs on the deck.

"Better spread those kegs out and put 'em in

different places," Preacher warned. "Indians shoot a couple of fire arrows in amongst 'em, you're liable to have a big blowup."

Warner frowned and said, "You know, I never thought of that. I'll have it taken care of right away, Preacher. You see, right there you've already proven how smart it was for Simon to bring you with us."

"We'll be counting on you for advice like that," Russell said. "If you see anything else we're doing— or not doing—let us know right away."

Preacher nodded. Russell should have noticed that about the powder kegs, he thought. It wasn't like the man was a greenhorn. He had survived on the frontier for quite a while.

But Russell had gone a little soft from living here in St. Louis, Preacher decided. Also, he was having to deal with a politician and a bunch of foreigners, and that was enough to make any man a mite addle-pated.

Russell turned to Warner and went on, "Do we have steam up yet, Captain?"

"Soon," Warner replied. "Give me another ten minutes or so. Are the passengers getting impatient?"

"The count is always impatient." Russell frowned worriedly, as if realizing he might have spoken out of turn. "Just forget I said that, all right?"

"Nobody'll hear me repeating it," Warner promised. He turned to Preacher and added, "Any time you want to visit the pilot house, you'll be welcome. Hell of a view from up there."

"Might just take you up on that," Preacher said.

As Warner went back to his post in the pilot house, Russell said, "He's a fine captain. We're lucky to have him commanding this boat for us."

"If there's anything lucky about this trip," Preacher said.

Russell shrugged and said, "Reckon we'll have to wait and see about that." He went off to check on some other details of the preparations, leaving Preacher and Dog on the cargo deck.

The *Sentinel* had three decks. The lowest was the cargo deck, which had a lot of open space that would be stacked high with dried pelts when the boat started back downriver after this trading trip. The boiler and engine rooms were also on this deck.

The next level up was the passenger deck, with a walkway going around a central structure divided into eight cabins, four on each side, along with a kitchen and a dining room that doubled as a salon.

Most of the larger riverboats that plied the Mississippi had another level above that called the texas deck, where more cabins and a more opulent dining room and salon were located, often with a gambling room. That wasn't the case here on the *Sentinel*. The pilot house, with its big windows on all four sides, sat directly on top of the passenger deck.

Preacher and Dog went up the stairs to the second level and along the polished walkway to the curved railing at the front of the vessel. The mountain man rested a hand on the brass rail and looked north along the mighty river.

A short distance above the city, the Missouri River flowed in from the west. Preacher couldn't see it from here but he knew it was there, having been down it many times in a canoe.

"Is that . . . a wolf?" a female voice asked from behind him.

Preacher looked over his shoulder. Senator Allingham's daughter stood there. She still wore the jacket from her traveling outfit, but she'd taken off the hat and her blond hair shone brightly in the morning sun.

"Might be part wolf," Preacher said as he turned to face the young woman, "but he's mostly dog."

"What's his name?"

"Dog."

"No, I mean— Oh. You're saying that Dog is his name."

"Seemed like the simplest thing to call him," Preacher said with a smile.

"Yes, I can see that. And no one can claim that it doesn't suit him."

She smiled back at him. She seemed to have an open, forthright manner. Preacher supposed she got that from her father.

"I'm Sarah Allingham," she went on. "My father is Senator Allingham."

Preacher lifted a hand and tugged briefly on his hat brim.

"Yes, ma'am, I know. I'm called Preacher."

"Is that like Dog, Mr. Preacher? A name describing what you are?"

"No mister, just Preacher," he said. "And I'm no Bible-thumper and sin-shouter, if that's what you're askin'. Fur trappin' is my line . . . and tendin' to varmints what need tendin' to."

"I see." Her eyes held a certain boldness as she looked over him from head to foot. "Well, I'm certainly glad that you're going with us. It'll be nice to have a rugged gentleman such as yourself to spend time with."

Good Lord, Preacher thought. This gal was playing up to him, bold as brass, even though he was old enough to be her father. With all the other problems this journey might hold, he sure as hell didn't need that.

"I'm no gentleman," he said, allowing a slightly sharper tone to creep into his voice. "Nobody's ever accused me of it, anyway."

If anything, Sarah Allingham's smile grew brighter and more alluring.

"That's fine with me," she said. "Chivalry is overrated. I'd much rather be around a man who's accustomed to . . . taking whatever he wants."

Preacher wondered if he ought to sic Dog on her and have the big cur chase her back to her cabin. He didn't consider the idea seriously, but it did occur to him.

He didn't have to go that far, however, because at that moment the young woman's mother emerged from one of the cabins, looked around, spotted her daughter standing at the railing with the mountain man, and came toward them at a brisk clip that told Preacher she meant business.

Sarah saw her mother coming, too, and a look of mingled anger and fear flashed across her pretty face. She stepped toward the older woman and began, "Mother—"

"Stop bothering this gentleman and go back to your cabin," Mrs. Allingham said in a no-nonsense tone that matched her stride.

"I wasn't bothering him," Sarah protested. "Was I, Preacher?"

"Don't be disrespectful," Mrs. Allingham snapped.

"I'm not. That's his name."

Preacher nodded, touched his hat brim again, and said, "Ma'am."

The older woman regarded him with narrowed eyes and said, "You're the man my husband mentioned. The one who's going to make sure we stay safe on this ridiculous trip."

"I'm hopin' we won't run into any trouble, so you won't need my help."

"I'm convinced we're all going to be scalped by savages," Mrs. Allingham said.

"Mother!" Sarah said.

"It's true. I'll never forgive myself for letting Josiah talk me into this, especially if anything happens to you, dear."

"I'm sure we'll all be fine," Sarah said. "We have capable men in charge, plus Count Stahlmaske is with us, too. Father said he was a highly decorated soldier in his country."

"Yes, I suppose." Mrs. Allingham sighed. "Now, please, dear, go back to your cabin. Standing out here like this, all the riverfront trash can wander by and leer at you."

She cast a disapproving glance at Preacher, as if she might consider him to be riverfront trash, too.

Sarah looked like she wanted to argue more, but then a resigned expression appeared on her face.

"Of course, Mother," she said in a dull voice. "I'll see you later, Preacher."

She went to her cabin and disappeared inside, shutting the door rather firmly behind her.

"Do forgive my daughter, Mr. Preacher. I know she can be annoying."

"She didn't bother me a bit, ma'am. I reckon she's just excited about seein' part of the country she's never seen before. And you don't have to call me mister. Like I told Miss Sarah, just plain Preacher is what I go by."

"Very well. I'm afraid it's not the country she's excited about seeing, though." The woman's lips thinned slightly. "My daughter is at an impressionable age. She tends to think with her heart instead of her head, especially where men are concerned. For that reason, I'll ask you to remember that you're twice her age, sir."

"Believe me, ma'am, I ain't likely to forget it," Preacher said. "All I'm interested in is gettin' you folks safely to the mouth of the Yellowstone."

"Besides," Mrs. Allingham went on, "Sarah's just a girl. She lacks the experience that a more . . . worldly . . . woman can provide."

Her blue eyes gazed boldly into his for a second, then she turned and walked away.

Good Lord, Preacher thought, wondering again if it was too late to back out of this mess.

It was. A shrill whistle blew, and the deckhands began casting off the heavy lines holding the riverboat to the dock.

The voyage of the *Sentinel* was about to begin.

CHAPTER 6

Preacher felt the deck vibrate under his feet as the engines engaged. An uncharacteristic whine came from Dog as he stood beside the mountain man gazing out at the water. Preacher reached down and scratched behind the big cur's ears.

"Don't worry, old-timer," he said. "It'll be all right."

He wished he believed that. Steam engines were unnatural contraptions, though, and they were harbingers of a noisy, stinking civilization that seemed intent on spreading all across the country and ruining the wilderness that was left. One of these days, a fella would have to go a long way to find a place where he couldn't hear an engine running.

Fortunately for Preacher, he figured the sort of life he led insured that he would be dead long before that day ever came.

With great splashes, the paddle wheel at the back of the boat began to turn. Running in reverse, its blades dug into the river and pulled the *Sentinel* away from the dock. Preacher turned and looked up into the pilot house. Through the open window he saw Captain Warner at the wheel, spinning it and guiding the boat into the middle of the stream.

When it was well clear of the docks, the whistle blew again and the paddle wheel came to a stop, dripping silvery drops of water from the blades that were above the surface. Slowly, they began to move again, turning the other way now, and the *Sentinel* eased forward. The vibrations under Preacher's feet increased a little as the engines pushed the boat ahead against the grip of the river's current.

They were on their way, Preacher thought.

The sound of loud voices talking in a foreign language made him turn his attention back to the cargo deck. He walked along the rail until he could look down at the three men who had unloaded the trunks and bags off the wagon that had followed the carriages to the docks. Preacher was a little surprised to see them. He had figured they were just men Russell or somebody else had hired to bring those things from the hotel where the party had been staying.

Since the men were still here, though, and since Preacher realized they were talking in German, it was more likely they were servants who worked for Count Stahlmaske.

And they weren't just talking in German.

They were arguing.

All three of the men were fairly big, but one of them towered over the other two. His shoulders were as wide as an ax handle, and they and his arms bulged with muscles. His head sat on a thick neck and was bald as an egg.

The argument seemed to be between him and the other two men. Preacher had no idea what it was about, since he couldn't follow the guttural words being thrown back and forth.

The big bruiser must have had enough, though. His right arm suddenly lashed out, and the big fist at the end of it cracked against the jaw of the closest man. The fella who'd been hit flew backward with his arms flung out to the sides.

For a second Preacher thought the man was going to topple off the boat into the river. He caught himself just in time to keep from getting soaked.

With an angry yell, the third man threw himself at the big bald fella from behind, jumping onto his back and grabbing him around the neck. He began hammering punches to the side of the bald man's head.

The bald man reached up and back, took hold of his attacker, and heaved him up and over as he bent forward. Howling in alarm, the man flew through the air and crashed among the trunks that had been brought aboard.

Preacher felt some admiration for the bald man. Clearly he wasn't afraid to take on two-to-one odds.

But then the man swung around to his first foe, slung him to the deck, dropped on top of him with both knees, and began pounding fists into his face.

If he kept that up for very long, there was a good chance he'd kill the unlucky gent.

Preacher leaned over the rail and shouted, "Hey! Stop that!"

The big bald man paused in the beating he was handing out and looked up at Preacher. His face, which reminded Preacher of a lumpy potato, contorted in a snarl as he spat words at the mountain man. Preacher didn't understand them, of course, but they sounded like cussing to him.

Then the man went back to smashing his fists into his victim's face.

At least this was a simple decision for Preacher to make. He didn't like being cussed at, and he wasn't going to stand by while some big bruiser beat a smaller man to death. He said, "Dog, stay," and headed for the stairs leading down to the lower deck.

Behind him, Dog growled deep in his throat. The big cur wanted in on the action, too. But he would follow Preacher's command, as he always did.

By the time Preacher reached the cargo deck, several members of the riverboat's crew had come up, drawn by the commotion of battle. They didn't appear eager to step in, however, even though they were big and muscular enough to have done so. They probably had orders not to interfere with the passengers unless they were endangering the boat somehow.

Preacher didn't have to worry about that. He strode up behind the big bald man and raised his voice.

"I told you to stop that, mister. Get away from that man, now!"

The bald man rose to his feet and turned slowly, menacingly. He was a good six inches taller than Preacher and probably forty pounds heavier. Up close like this, he was a damn behemoth, Preacher thought.

An ugly grin split the man's face. He waved a hand dismissively at Preacher and said, "You damn fool American . . . back off."

A moan came from the man lying on the deck with his face bloody and already swollen almost beyond recognition. Preacher nodded toward him and told the bald man, "Leave him alone. You keep hittin' him like that and you're liable to kill him."

"*Jawohl*, that is right, I kill him." The bald man's voice sounded like rusty nails being shaken in a keg. "He need killing."

"What in blazes did he do?"

"He says Gunther is . . . is . . ." The big man frowned as he searched for the right word. "Stupid!"

"And you'd be Gunther, I reckon?"

"*Ja.*" The man pounded one massive fist into the palm of the other hand. "Gunther Klostermann."

"Well, leave him alone, Gunther. You've already done enough damage."

"I take no orders from you, American. I take orders from Count Stahlmaske."

The man on the deck groaned again and rolled onto his side. He tried to get his hands and knees under him so he could crawl away. Gunther twisted toward him and with another of those strangled German curses lifted a foot into the man's midsection in a savage kick.

"Damn it," Preacher said. He sprang forward, grabbed Gunther's shoulder with his left hand, jerked him around, and crashed his right fist into the Prussian's mouth.

Preacher was lean and rawboned, not the sort of hulking bruiser Gunther Klostermann was, but the mountain man packed an incredible amount of strength in his frame. He put as much of that power as he could behind the punch, and it landed cleanly.

Gunther grunted and went backward a couple of steps, but then he caught himself. Blood oozed from his split lips, but that didn't stop him from grinning again.

"Well, hell," Preacher said.

Gunther stopped grinning. He bellowed and came at Preacher like an avalanche. Preacher tried to twist out of the way, but Gunther snagged his buckskin shirt and threw him against the structure that housed the boilers and engine room. Preacher hit the wall with tooth-jolting force that took his breath away.

The clumping of heavy footsteps warned him that Gunther was about to ram him against the wall again. This time Preacher was able to get out of the way so that the bigger man didn't crush him and probably snap some of his ribs. Gunther was the one who ran into the wall.

Preacher hit him in the back, then clubbed his hands and smashed them against the back of Gunther's neck. When Preacher hit a man like that, it usually knocked him out.

Not in this case. Gunther swung an arm in a

backhanded blow that felt like someone had smashed Preacher across the chest with a tree trunk. The mountain man stumbled backward.

Preacher tripped over the man Gunther had been thrashing earlier and sprawled on the deck. Gunther came after him. Preacher figured the big Prussian might kick and stomp him to death if he got a chance, so he rolled out of the way and swung his leg around.

The move took Gunther by surprise and swept his legs out from under him. With a crash that seemed to shake the whole boat, Gunther slammed down on the deck. Before he could catch his breath, Preacher landed on top of him, driving a knee into the big man's belly and throwing a left and a right that rocked Gunther's head from side of side.

Gunther seemed groggy now. The back of his head had hit the desk pretty hard when he fell, Preacher knew. Not wanting to waste even a momentary advantage, Preacher hit his foe again and again. He didn't let up for a second.

He knew that if he gave Gunther any chance to recover, he might not have another opportunity to defeat the giant.

The boom of a gunshot stayed Preacher's fists. He heard a ball hum over his head and saw the little splash where it hit the river beside the boat. Preacher froze with his right fist lifted over his head, poised to come crashing down on Gunther's face again.

"Stand up and step away from that man or I'll kill you!"

Preacher looked back over his shoulder and saw Count Albert Stahlmaske standing at the railing on the passenger deck. The count held two flintlock pistols. A tendril of gray smoke still curled from the muzzle of the weapon in his left hand.

The gun in his right hand was aimed straight at Preacher's head, and the mountain man could tell from the cold fury he saw in Stahlmaske's eyes that the count really wanted to pull the trigger right about now.

CHAPTER 7

Simon Russell appeared on the passenger deck, hurrying toward Stahlmaske with his hands outstretched.

"Please, Count, there's no need for any gunplay," Russell implored. "I don't know what's going on here, but I'm sure we can sort it out."

Stahlmaske didn't lower the gun he had pointed at Preacher. Without taking his eyes off the mountain man, he said, "That unwashed lout attacked one of my servants."

"That ain't exactly the way it happened, Simon," Preacher said. "I threw the first punch, true enough, but only to keep this big galoot from beatin' that other fella to death."

Senator Allingham came along the passenger deck, too, evidently summoned from his cabin by the commotion. He looked alarmed when he saw the pistols Stahlmaske was holding.

"What's this?" he demanded.

"Just another demonstration of how most of your fellow Americans are little more than dangerous, uncivilized barbarians, Senator," Stahlmaske snapped.

Gunther was starting to look a little less groggy, Preacher noticed. If the giant got his wits about him, he was liable to start the ruckus all over again. Preacher stood up and moved back a step. He didn't want to be within easy arm's reach if Gunther decided to act up again.

"I really reckon it'd be a good idea for you to put that gun away, Count," he said. "My dog's startin' to get a mite peeved about you pointin' it at me."

Stahlmaske glanced along the deck toward the bow, where Dog still waited, obeying Preacher's order to stay. The big cur wasn't sitting down peacefully anymore, though. He was on his feet, with the hair on his back standing up and his teeth bared in a snarl. Dog knew when his master was being threatened.

The count cursed in German and started to swing the pistol toward Dog. Preacher snatched the tomahawk from behind his belt. He thought he could break Stahlmaske's arm with a well-aimed throw before the count could pull the trigger.

Neither of those things happened because Simon Russell leaped forward with some of his old speed and agility and put himself in front of Stahlmaske's gun.

"Hold your fire!" he said.

"You dare give orders to me?" Stahlmaske roared, but he didn't press the trigger.

Senator Allingham said quickly, "I believe we should allow cooler heads to prevail, gentlemen. I assure you we'll get to the bottom of this incident and deal with it appropriately, Count."

Stahlmaske looked like he didn't want to agree, but after a long moment he lowered the pistol.

"Very well," he said. "But I want that man to stay away from me and my people."

He jerked his head in a nod toward Preacher.

"That ain't gonna be a problem," the mountain man said. "I'll be more than happy to steer clear of that bunch."

Stahlmaske glared at him but didn't say anything else. The count allowed Allingham to lead him away from the railing. The senator was talking and making animated gestures, but Stahlmaske didn't appear to be listening.

On the cargo deck, Gunther rolled onto his side and muttered darkly as he struggled to get up. Preacher backed away. If Gunther still wanted to fight, Preacher would oblige him, but the mountain man hoped this fracas was over.

Unsteadily, Gunther climbed to his feet. Blood still oozed from his lips and trickled down his chin. He pointed a blunt, sausage-like finger at Preacher and said thickly, "We will finish this another time, American."

"I'll be around," Preacher said, "any time you want to look me up."

Gunther turned and tried to swagger off, but he

was still a little too shaky to make the arrogant pose convincing. He had to put a hand against the engine room wall for a second to brace himself before he could go on.

Preacher stuck his tomahawk behind his belt again and went over to the man who'd been the object of Gunther's wrath. The other servant was already there, kneeling beside his friend and helping him sit up.

The second man looked up at Preacher and started saying something in German, then at the mountain man's uncomprehending expression he switched to halting English.

"Thank you . . . but you should not have . . . with Gunther interfered. He is . . . a very bad man."

"I've dealt with bad gents before," Preacher assured him. "Lemme give you a hand with your pard there."

He took one of the beaten man's arms while the second servant got on the other side. Together they lifted him to his feet. He tried to say something, but his jaw was already so bruised and swollen from the pounding Gunther's fists had given it that he couldn't get the words out.

"What'd they fight over, anyway?" Preacher asked the second man.

"Ludwig here—he is Ludwig and I am Egon—he commented to me that Gunther is a . . . a *dummkopf*. This is true, but it is not wise to let Gunther hear you say such a thing. Him it angers."

Preacher grunted.

"Yeah, I'd say so."

"For a while we stay away from him. Calm down, he will."

"I hope you're right, Egon."

Simon Russell had come down the stairs from the passenger deck. He approached the men and told them, "There are a couple of rooms next to the engine room that are being used for servants' quarters. Got cots in there so that fella can lay down for a while if he needs to."

Egon nodded.

"*Danke,* Herr Russell. Thank you."

As Egon led his friend away, Russell turned to the mountain man, shook his head, and said, "I'm sorry about that, Preacher. We've barely steamed away from the dock and already there's been trouble."

"I ain't sure a little scrap like this qualifies as real trouble," Preacher replied with a trace of a smile. "At least nobody got hurt too bad."

"Yeah, well, I wish it hadn't happened, anyway."

"You did everything you could to keep it from gettin' worse," Preacher pointed out. "And it sure as hell would have if that count fella had taken a shot at Dog."

Russell looked at Preacher and slowly nodded.

"You'd have killed him, wouldn't you?"

"More than likely." The mountain man shrugged. "Thanks to you, I didn't have to."

"Thank God it didn't come to that. If anything happened to the count, there's no telling how much trouble it would cause between his country and ours. He's not gonna forget that you stood up to him. He doesn't like that."

"Fair enough. I don't like him."

Russell grinned and said, "I've got a jug in my cabin. I know it's a little early in the day—"

"Never too early in the day to clear away the cobwebs in a fella's throat," Preacher said as he clapped a hand on his old friend's shoulder.

A short time later the *Sentinel* steamed into the mouth of the Missouri River. It would follow this broad stream known as the Big Muddy for hundreds of miles to the mouth of the Yellowstone River, where trappers would congregate to sell their pelts. Preacher knew that word of the riverboat's arrival would spread with surprising speed through the mountains.

That day was still a couple of weeks in the future, though, and if today's events were any indication, those weeks wouldn't be peaceful ones.

By evening, things on the boat seemed to have calmed down. The passengers had spent most of the day in their cabins. Preacher had spent his time on deck, not wanting to be cooped up inside four walls when he could be outside in the sun and fresh air.

He sat on a crate of supplies, smoking a pipe and watching the rolling landscape go by on both sides of the river. Dog sat beside him on the deck, tongue lolling out. The barge loaded with horses floated along behind the boat, attached by heavy ropes.

This far downriver, the Missouri was wide and deep. It wouldn't be until they got farther upstream that it would become treacherous, filled with snags that could rip out a boat's hull and sandbars where a vessel could get stuck.

As evening approached, Captain Warner turned the boat toward the southern bank where the *Sentinel* would put in for the night. Even in this more placid section of river, traveling in the dark was just too dangerous.

Like most river pilots, Warner knew the best places to stop. The boat steamed toward a tree-lined stretch of bank. Not only would the *Sentinel* tie up here, but the crew could also chop a little wood to replace what had been burned during the day. Farther upriver, trees would be few and far between, so it was good to take on fuel for the burners whenever there was a chance.

Preacher was standing at the railing watching the shore come closer when Senator Allingham approached him.

"Hello, Preacher," the politician said.

"Senator," Preacher replied, trying not to sound too curt. He didn't care for government folks just on general principles, but Allingham seemed to be a likable enough fella.

"You'll be dining with us tonight, I hope."

Preacher looked over at him and squinted.

"After what happened this mornin', I don't reckon the count would be too happy to have me sittin' at the same table as him."

"The count's not inviting you. I am." Allingham lowered his voice. "Between you and me, Count Stahlmaske is a royal pain in the rear end. I didn't ask for the job of escorting him on this tour of the frontier. The president prevailed upon me to do so."

"Ol' Andy Jackson can be pretty persuasive, all right. I fought under him at the Battle of New Orleans, back when I was just a youngster."

"Is that right? You've had an interesting life, Preacher."

"It ain't over yet," the mountain man said dryly. "I aim on bein' around for a spell yet. That is, if I don't get myself killed by agreein' to go along with somebody else's damn fool ideas."

Allingham laughed and said, "Like coming along on this riverboat journey?"

"You said it, Senator, not me."

"Well, I hope you'll join us in the dining room anyway. Count Stahlmaske claims that he came over here to learn about America, and I don't think he's going to find anyone more American than you, my friend!"

CHAPTER 8

Russell had told Preacher that he would share his cabin with him, but the mountain man had said that wasn't necessary. As long as the weather was good, Preacher intended to either stay out on deck at night or go ashore and spread his bedroll on the ground if there was a good place.

After the *Sentinel* was tied up, he went ashore with Dog to have a look around. This close to St. Louis, the chances of encountering any hostile Indians were almost nonexistent, but thieves and cutthroats could turn up anywhere. Preacher's long, perilous life had taught him that it never hurt to be familiar with your surroundings.

Shallow, rolling hills dotted with trees stretched as far to the south as Preacher's keen eyes could see. Here and there he spotted tendrils of smoke climbing into the pale blue sky. That smoke came from the chimneys of isolated farmhouses, he knew.

Once, St. Louis had been nothing more than a

primitive settlement known as Chouteau's Landing that marked the far western boundary of civilization. There was nothing beyond it but a vast wilderness populated by wild animals, Indians, and the stubborn, hardy breed known as mountain men.

Now the farmers were pushing farther and farther into the frontier. Wagon trains crossed what some called the Great American Desert, bound for new lands in the Pacific Northwest. Ships sailed around Cape Horn and on up to the Spanish and Russian settlements along the continent's western coast. People everywhere, going here, going there, pushing in, crowding those who had come before them . . . It was enough to make a man light out for somewhere new.

Problem was, there weren't many of those places left, and fewer all the time.

A step behind him made him look around. Dog hadn't growled at whoever it was, so Preacher knew he wasn't about to be attacked.

Sarah Allingham stood there smiling. The wind that blew nearly constantly over the plains stirred several strands of blond hair that had escaped and hung around her face.

"It's beautiful out here, isn't it?" she said. "So different from where we come from in Vermont."

"I ain't been to Vermont, so I wouldn't know about that," Preacher said. "It's probably pretty there, too, though."

"Oh, yes, it's lovely. Lots of mountains and forests."

"Sounds like I'd like it there."

"You should come visit sometime," Sarah said. "I'm sure my father would be happy to have you come. He'd love to show you off to all his friends and supporters. He says you're a famous frontiersman."

Preacher grunted.

"Notorious is more like it. Some folks claim trouble just follows me around."

"That's all right. I like trouble."

The smile she gave him was just bold enough to make him uneasy. He nodded toward the boat and said, "Might be a good idea for you to go back on board, miss."

"There's no danger out here, is there?" she asked. "Surely not this close to civilization"

Preacher had just been thinking the same thing, but he said, "You never know. Might be a war party of Indians happen by, or some thieves."

"Well, I'm sure I'll be safe enough with you here." She moved closer to him and looked out over the prairie. "Tell me about where we're going. What's it like out there? Will we see the Rocky Mountains?"

Preacher shook his head.

"We won't get that far west. We'll see some mountains, but nothin' like what you'd find farther on up the Missouri. This riverboat can't go that far, though."

"What if we took smaller boats? Canoes? Or horses and pack animals?"

"That's what you need to get to the high country,

all right," Preacher agreed. "That's where I'll be goin', but you and your folks will head back downriver when the *Sentinel* does, though."

"You could take me with you," Sarah said, and now the look she gave him wasn't just bold, it was downright brazen. "I think I'd like that, and I can promise you won't be disappointed by having me around, Preacher."

From the passenger deck, Margaret Allingham called, "Sarah, get back up here right now, please."

Preacher had seldom been so glad to see a gal's mama as he was at that moment. Sarah let out a disappointed sigh and said, "I have to go. But I'm sure there'll be plenty of other chances for us to be together before we get to the mouth of the Yellowstone."

She probably meant that as a promise, but to Preacher it sounded more like a threat.

Sarah sashayed across the gangplank and went up the stairs to the passenger deck. Preacher stayed where he was, but he couldn't get back into the meditative mood he'd been in before the young woman interrupted him.

A few minutes later, the count's younger brother came ashore and approached him. Preacher had to think for a moment before he recalled the fellow's name: Roderick.

"Hello," the young man said with a pleasant nod. "We haven't been introduced, but I know who you are, of course."

"And I know who you are," Preacher replied. He

stuck out his hand. "Howdy, Roderick. You won't get in trouble for shakin' hands with a commoner, will you?"

"I hope not." Roderick took Preacher's hand. His grip wasn't very strong, but it seemed sincere. "Anyway, we're in America now, and there's no class of nobles here, is there?"

"Some folks seem to think they are, but the way it's supposed to work, we're all the same in this country."

"A wonderful ideal. One that I'm afraid it will prove very hard to live up to."

Preacher nodded and said, "I've got a hunch you're right about that."

"I'm sorry about the trouble with my brother earlier—"

Preacher waved off the apology.

"Don't worry about that. It wasn't any of your doin'."

"Albert is very much accustomed to getting his own way, I'm afraid. When he doesn't, he becomes angry and blusters around a great deal. I hope he didn't frighten you too much when he pointed that pistol at you."

"I reckon I'll get over it," Preacher said dryly. "You speak mighty good English. Sound a little like a Britisher."

"I attended the university at Oxford."

"Heard of it," Preacher nodded. "I can read and write and cipher some, but most of what I've learned has been out here." He nodded toward the plains stretching away into the west.

"I'm sure it's been quite an education," Roderick said. "You'll be joining us for dinner tonight, won't you?"

"That's what I'm told."

Roderick sighed and said, "I hope it goes well. Just remember that Albert doesn't always mean what he says."

"Where I come from, a man stands behind his word."

"There was a time my brother did, too, before he became enmeshed in politics. He's very close to King Friedrich Wilhelm the Third, you know."

"Hadn't heard," Preacher drawled.

Roderick laughed.

"Yes, I don't suppose the politics of the North German Confederation get talked about much out here on the American frontier, do they?"

"You might be surprised. Good friend of mine who's a trapper used to be a professor before he gave it up, and every time he goes to St. Louis, he reads up on everything that's goin' on in the world. When he comes back to the mountains he talks about it to anybody who'll listen. When he's not quotin' Shakespeare, that is. Audie's the quotin'est fella you ever saw. He can spout that Shakespeare all day long, as well as things wrote by gents named Marlowe and Bacon and Spenser."

"Really?" Roderick said. "How astounding! I wouldn't have dreamed that such things would happen out here. And I mean no offense by that. I'm sure that you . . . mountain men, is that the proper term? . . . I'm sure that on average you're just as intelligent as anyone else."

"Smarter, I'd say. We ain't stuck in towns all the time. We get to breathe clean air that ain't full of smoke and cinders from a bunch of chimneys."

Roderick drew in a deep breath and thumped a fist lightly against his chest.

"I see what you mean," he said. "The atmosphere out here is wonderfully invigorating." He looked down at Dog, who was keeping a wary eye on him. "Is it all right if I pet your friend there?"

"I'd advise against it," Preacher said.

"Oh." Roderick's expression fell a little. "All right. I'll see you at dinner?"

"I'll be there," Preacher promised.

"I enjoyed our talk."

"Likewise," Preacher said, and he wasn't just being polite. Roderick Stahlmaske seemed to be a likable enough cuss, and Preacher figured his life probably wasn't very easy, having a stiff-necked varmint like the count for his brother.

Preacher located a good place under some trees to spread his bedroll later, then went to check on Horse. Satisfied that the stallion and the other horses were all right, he boarded the riverboat again as dusk settled down over the river.

Lamps had been lit on the boat, in the cabins and around the deck. When they got farther upstream, the travelers wouldn't advertise their presence like that, Preacher hoped. Showing a lot of light at night was just asking for Indians to attack you.

"There you are," Simon Russell said as he came out of the dining room/salon and motioned Preacher up the stairs to the passenger deck. "Come on in, Preacher. Dinner's almost ready."

Preacher pointed to a spot on the cargo deck and told Dog, "Stay."

The big cur sat. Preacher knew Dog would be there when he came back.

When he reached the passenger deck, he asked Russell, "Anybody told the count I'll be eatin' supper with him?"

"It hasn't been mentioned that I know of," Russell replied. "Senator Allingham may have told him. The senator was the one who issued the invitation, after all."

"I heard the count's some big he-wolf in politics back where he comes from."

Russell nodded.

"Yes, I don't know the details, but from some of the things Senator Allingham has said, I think one reason Count Stahlmaske is over here in this country is to carry on some sort of negotiations between his government and ours."

"That makes him pretty important, I reckon."

"It does. That's why I can't let anything happen to him." Russell smiled. "But thanks to you, Preacher, I don't have to worry about that. I've got you looking out for all of us."

That was true, thought Preacher. And it was looking more and more like he'd been a damned fool to go along with it.

CHAPTER 9

When Preacher and Russell went into the salon, the mountain man saw that all the passengers were there, seated around a long, polished table with Count Albert Stahlmaske at the head of it.

The count's betrothed, the beautiful, redheaded Gretchen Ritter, sat at his right. Her brothers Heinrich and Hobart—Preacher had no idea which one was which—were to her right.

Roderick sat across from Gretchen, and his and Albert's uncle Gerhard was next to him, across from one of the twins. Senator Allingham and his wife and daughter filled up the remaining seats on that side.

Sarah Allingham gave Preacher an expectant look as if trying to tell him to sit at the other end of the table, next to her, but he and Russell took the empty chairs on the opposite side, next to the Ritter twins, with Russell at the end.

That put Preacher beside either Heinrich or Hobart and across from Margaret Allingham. He figured the empty chair at the end of the table was for Captain Warner.

Stahlmaske gave Preacher a cold stare. Obviously the nobleman had not forgotten what had happened earlier.

Allingham said, "I asked Preacher to join us, Count. Since he's been on this journey many times, I thought he could tell us about the places we'll be going and perhaps even entertain us with some stories of his adventures."

"I'm not much for speechifyin'," Preacher said. He looked at the white linen cloth on the table, the fine china, the silverware, the glasses of wine, the fancy lamp in the center of the table, and wished he was sitting beside a campfire in the high country, roasting an elk steak over the flames.

"Come, come, no false modesty, my frontiersman friend," Stahlmaske said with a trace of arrogance that put Preacher's teeth on edge. "I'm told that you're the living, breathing embodiment of the protagonist in Fenimore Cooper's recent novels. Natty Bumppo, I believe his name is."

"Don't know the fella," Preacher said. He tried not to sound curt. "And most of the yarns that have been spun about me are just lies made up by varmints who sit around taverns all day and don't have nothin' better to do."

"Be that as it may," the count persisted, "you *are* familiar with our destination."

"That's true," Preacher admitted with a shrug.

It seemed like they were waiting for Captain Warner before they ate, so he decided he might as well fill some of the time by talking about the country through which the Missouri River passed on its way to the mouth of the Yellowstone. Most of it was rolling grassland, as he had told Sarah, but they would see some good-sized hills and even a few small mountains in the distance.

"What about *der* savages?" the twin sitting beside him asked. "Will we have to fight them?"

"Hard to say. We'll be passin' through the huntin' grounds of some tribes who don't care much for white men. It all depends on what they take it in their heads to do." Preacher smiled. "Problem is, the only thing harder than predictin' what an Indian will do is predictin' what a woman will do."

That brought a laugh from several of the men, as well as from Gretchen Ritter—but not from Stahlmaske. The statuesque redhead spoke to the mountain man for the first time, saying, "You are a philosopher, Herr Preacher."

"If *herr* is like *mister,* you can drop that part of it, ma'am," Preacher told her. "As for philosophizin', that's right up there with speechifyin' as far as I'm concerned. I don't much cotton to either of 'em."

Preacher was saved from having to go on by the arrival of Captain Benjamin Warner, who said as he came into the dining room, "Sorry you had to wait for me, folks. Just dealing with a little problem in the engine room."

"Nothing that will make us turn back, I hope," Senator Allingham said.

Warner shook his head.

"Oh, no, nothing that serious. It's all taken care of now, anyway. We'll be able to move on in the morning just as planned."

Several women Preacher hadn't noticed before came into the dining room from the kitchen, bringing bowls of food with them. Stahlmaske spoke to them in German, and two of the women responded with quick nods.

The third woman was thick-bodied and florid-faced, with graying red hair, and Preacher didn't have to hear her speak to know she was Irish. He pegged the two German women as servants with the count's party, while the Irishwoman was probably the maid for Mrs. Allingham and Sarah. He hadn't seen any of them come on board that morning. It was possible they had already been on the *Sentinel* before Preacher arrived at the docks, getting ready for the arrival of their charges.

The food was a mixture of Irish and German, stew made with dried beef, carrots, and potatoes, along with black bread, and the combination went together surprisingly well. Preacher always had a good appetite, so he ate heartily and washed the meal down with a couple of glasses of the wine that Count Stahlmaske seemed rather proud of. He would have rather had beer, but a fella couldn't have everything.

As they ate, the conversation around the table continued, and after a while Sarah Allingham spoke up, saying, "Preacher, I think you should tell us some more of your opinions about women."

"Hush, dear," her mother said with an air of it being a habitual reaction when Sara said something.

"No, I'm really interested," Sarah insisted. "Do you think women should be traveling to the frontier like we are, Preacher?"

"I reckon most of the time it ain't a very good idea," Preacher answered honestly.

"But surely there are Indian women where we are going," Gretchen said. "Squaws, I believe they're called?"

"That's right. They've spent their whole lives out here, though. They know what's expected of 'em, what they have to do to survive."

"Yes, but could they survive in Berlin?" Gretchen asked.

"Or Washington City?" Sarah added.

"You might be surprised," Preacher said. "All the squaws I've known have been pretty resourceful."

"Nonsense," the count said. "They are savages, so primitive that they are little better than animals. They could never function in a civilized society."

"The Indians don't consider our society very civilized," Preacher pointed out. "In fact, most tribes think of themselves as the only true human bein's. The rest of us are somethin' less than that."

Stahlmaske snorted disgustedly.

"Ridiculous."

"If you get to spend some time with any of 'em, you might start to feel different about it."

"I do not plan to 'spend any time' with the savages, as you put it." Stahlmaske's voice was icy. "If I even look at them for very long, it will be over the sights of my rifle." He picked up his glass of wine. "Perhaps they are good for something—hunting."

The others around the table were silent. Preacher was aware that Simon Russell was looking at him worriedly. Of all of them, only Russell—and maybe Captain Warner—were aware of the serious implications of what Stahlmaske had just said.

Preacher's first impulse was to stand up, go to the head of the table, and try to beat some sense into Stahlmaske. It probably wouldn't do any good, but he would enjoy making the effort.

Instead, with uncharacteristic restraint that he summoned up as a favor to his old friend, he said, "That'd be a mighty bad idea, Count. We'll be runnin' enough risks without you takin' potshots at folks who might not necessarily want to hurt us. I promise you, though, if you kill an Indian who's bein' peaceful, or even wound one, we'll have a war on our hands."

Stahlmaske sneered and said, "I am a soldier. I do not fear war."

"You don't generally fight it with women around, either, do you?"

The count's shoulders rose and fell slightly in a tiny shrug.

"I think you worry about those savages too much. Surely one civilized fighting man is worth ten or twenty of them. But I see no need to provoke unnecessary trouble."

"That's good," Preacher said.

He kept what he was thinking to himself: that if

Stahlmaske did anything as stupid as killing an Indian who wasn't attacking them, Preacher just might let the rest of the tribe have the damn fool.

The talk moved on to other topics, for which Preacher was grateful. Only one more bothersome incident occurred. The passengers were lingering at the table over brandy when Preacher felt something touch his leg. He knew that riverboats had rats on them sometimes, so he stiffened and got ready to knock the vermin away from him.

It wasn't a rat sliding up his leg, though. It was a human foot. A woman's foot in a soft slipper from the feel of it.

Preacher drew in a deep breath. Margaret Allingham was directly opposite him, but her daughter was beside her and Sarah was long-legged enough that she was in reach, too. Preacher studied them with narrowed eyes, but neither woman's face offered any clue as to which of them was caressing his calf through his buckskin trousers.

As he kept his own face as impassive as possible, the mysterious foot worked its way up to his knee, then went back down. He was glad the bold touch hadn't ventured any higher. If it had, he might not have been able to keep acting like nothing was going on.

The foot went away, and he still couldn't tell whom it belonged to. That didn't really matter, he told himself. He intended to steer as clear of the

Allingham women as he could, especially when no one else was around. He didn't carry on with married women, and he didn't despoil young ones.

Several of the passengers started yawning, including Gretchen.

"I am very weary, Albert," she told the count.

He took her hand, lifted it, and pressed his lips to the back of it.

"I'll bid you good night, then, my dear," he said. "And pleasant dreams."

The gathering broke up, with everyone heading for their own cabins except Preacher, Russell, and Warner, who stopped outside on the deck. Russell and Warner packed tobacco into pipes and lit them.

"I sure appreciate you holding your temper the way you did in there, Preacher," Russell said.

"I guess I'm gettin' a mite calmer in my old age," Preacher said.

"You're not that old."

"I wasn't that calm inside, either. If that tarnal idiot thinks he can start usin' peaceful Indians for target practice—"

"I'll make sure that doesn't happen," Russell promised. "I'll speak to Senator Allingham, too, and see to it that he understands."

Preacher nodded.

"That's a good idea. And I'll try my best not to pitch the count overboard."

Warner chuckled and said, "On behalf of the

American Fur Company, Preacher, I thank you for your restraint as well."

Preacher said his good-nights to the two men, then walked along the deck to the middle of the riverboat, where the narrow stairs led down to the cargo deck. The outside lights had been extinguished now, but enough illumination from the moon and stars remained for Preacher to see where he was going without any problem.

He saw Dog, too, and when Preacher was about halfway down the stairs, the big cur, who had been lying down, suddenly leaped to his feet and let out a deep-throated growl. He was looking up, past Preacher.

That was all the warning the mountain man needed. He twisted around, and as he did so, orange flame spurted from a pistol muzzle in the thick shadows next to the cabins.

CHAPTER 10

The boom of the exploding powder and the hum of the heavy lead ball past Preacher's ear came at the same time. He covered the rest of the distance down to the cargo deck in a single bound, and as he landed he whipped one of his pistols from behind his belt and aimed up at the passenger deck, where the gunman lurked.

Unfortunately, he didn't have a target to aim at. The man had never been anything except a deeper patch of darkness, and now even that was gone.

"Dog!" Preacher snapped. "Find!"

Dog leaped into action. He went up the stairs in a blur. Preacher knew there was a good chance the big cur would sniff out the man who had just tried to kill him.

Only if he got a chance to do so, however, and that seemed more unlikely by the second. Doors flew open, and running footsteps slapped the polished planks of the passenger deck. People were moving down here on the cargo deck, too, as members of the crew emerged from their cabins to see what the gunshot had been about. The confusion of scents would just make it more difficult for Dog to do his work.

With the flintlock pistol still in his hand and his thumb curled around the hammer, Preacher climbed quickly to the passenger deck. Senator Allingham hurried toward him. The politician's nightshirt flapped around his calves.

"Preacher!" Allingham said. "What happened? Was that a shot I heard?"

"Yeah, it was," the mountain man said.

Before he could explain, Russell and Warner showed up, too. The captain was still fully dressed. Russell had taken off his coat and shirt but still wore his trousers and long underwear. They were full of questions, too, and Preacher figured he might as well answer all of them at once.

"Somebody took a shot at me from here while I was goin' down to the cargo deck," he said.

"Are you hit?" Russell asked.

"Nope. The ball came pretty close, but not close enough."

"Did you see who it was?" Warner wanted to know.

Preacher pointed to the shadows where the gunman had waited for him and said, "No, it was too dark where he was. He got away in a hurry, too. Bound to have ducked into somebody's cabin."

Dog was scratching at one of the doors and growling. Preacher nodded at the big wolflike animal and went on, "That one, more than likely, judgin' by the way Dog's actin'."

"That's not a cabin door," Warner said.

Now that the captain had pointed it out, Preacher could tell that the door was narrower than the entrances to the passenger cabins.

Warner continued, "If you'll call your dog off, I'll show you."

"C'mere, Dog," Preacher said. The cur returned and sat down next to him, still growling quietly.

Warner opened the door. A lamp turned low burned inside and revealed a narrow corridor instead of a cabin. It ran straight across the riverboat and ended at an identical door that was bound to open on the other side of the deck.

"The crew uses this corridor to cut through from one side of the boat to the other," Warner explained. "Sometimes the passengers do, too, but most of them don't realize it's here. You can see that there's a door into the kitchen from here, too. We use it to bring in supplies without having to carry them through the salon."

"So all the fella had to do was run through here and then he could get anywhere in the boat pretty fast," Preacher said.

"That's right."

"Dog's got his scent, though," the mountain man pointed out. "Maybe he can track the varmint."

"It's worth a try," Russell said.

Before they could go on, Count Stahlmaske came up and said, "I demand to know what this disturbance is. I was trying to sleep."

Anybody else would have just asked a question, thought Preacher. Stahlmaske had to make a demand.

"Someone tried to kill Preacher," Allingham said.

The count looked at Preacher and said, "He appears to be unharmed."

"Yeah, no thanks to the fella who tried to blow my brains out," Preacher said. "You say you were in your cabin tryin' to sleep just now, Count?"

Stahlmaske drew himself up straighter and asked in a chilly voice, "What are you trying to imply?"

"I don't reckon I'm smart enough to imply anything. I just want to know where you were."

"In my cabin, as I said!"

"How about your brother and your uncle?"

"I assume they were in the cabin they're sharing as well. You can go ask them if you wish."

"Maybe I'll do that," Preacher said. "First, though . . . Dog, trail!"

Dog ran along the corridor through the middle of the boat, his nose to the floor. Preacher followed with the other men behind him and opened the door at the far end of the passage. Dog ran out onto the other side of the deck and stopped. He turned around a few times and then whined.

"Has he lost the scent?" Russell asked.

"Looks like it. Reckon too many folks have been up and down this deck today. Could be the fella who shot at me took his boots off, too. That'd help kill his scent."

"I guess the next question you have to ask yourself," Allingham said, "is who would want to shoot you?"

"I've already been thinkin' about that," Preacher said. He turned to the count and asked, "Where would I find that fella Gunther?"

"You believe Gunther shot at you?" Stahlmaske asked. "Bah! That is a ridiculous idea. Gunther is no marksman, I assure you. He is a brute, nothing but muscle."

"I'd still like to ask him a question or two."

"The count's servants are staying down on the passenger deck," Warner said. "I can have one of the crew roust them out."

"Just show me," Preacher said. "I'll do the roustin' myself."

The group proceeded back down to the passenger deck. Warner pointed out the small cabins next to the engine room where the servants were staying, and Preacher recalled that Simon Russell had said something about that earlier.

Preacher pounded a fist against one of the doors. When it swung open, Egon's startled face peered out.

"Preacher," the man said. "What is this?"

"Sorry," Preacher said. "I was lookin' for Gunther."

A big, hamlike hand came down on Egon's shoulder and wrenched the smaller man out of the way. Gunther glared out at Preacher and said, "What do you want?"

"Did you hear that gunshot a few minutes ago?"

"I hear very little when I sleep."

"This is true," Egon put in. "No one can hear much over Gunther's snoring."

He stepped back as the big man turned and snarled at him.

"So you've been here all evenin'?" Preacher asked.

"Go away," Gunther said instead of answering the question. "I do not want to talk to you."

Egon said, "We have all been here sleeping, all three of us."

Count Stahlmaske crossed his arms over his chest and said to the mountain man, "Are you satisfied now? Gunther could not have shot at you, just as I said."

Gunther's frown darkened as he looked at Preacher.

"You thought I shot at you?"

"You told me earlier you were gonna get even with me," Preacher said.

"By breaking your *kopf* with my fists, not by shooting at you from the dark like some coward!"

Preacher's eyes narrowed. He asked, "How'd you know the varmint was hidin' in the dark when he took that shot at me?"

"Night it is! Where else would he be?"

Preacher supposed that answer made sense, but he was still suspicious.

"Are you satisfied now that Gunther did not try to kill you?" Stahlmaske asked.

"Maybe," Preacher said. The count's attitude got under his skin, as it had ever since he'd met the man. "I reckon the next question is what proof you've got you were where you say you were."

"How dare you!" Stahlmaske said as he bristled with anger.

"Hold on, Preacher," Senator Allingham said uneasily. "The count is a guest in our country—"

"That wouldn't keep him from pullin' a trigger."

In frigid tones, Stahlmaske said, "If I were to try to kill you, it would be face-to-face, with sabers or dueling pistols or some other honorable means of settling our differences. A nobleman never hides his actions in the shadows."

"Just because a fella calls himself noble don't mean he really is."

"Enough!" Stahlmaske turned to Allingham and Russell. "I will not stand for this. I demand that this insolent lout be put off the boat now!"

Russell said, "Preacher's agreed to come along because some of the other fur company boats ran into trouble—"

"I'm sure Captain Warner and his crew can handle any problems we encounter."

The captain spoke up, saying, "I'd like to think so, but it's true I feel better having Preacher come along with us, Count. His reputation alone ought to make some fellas think twice about trying to bother us."

"His reputation as what?" Stahlmaske said. "An insolent fool?"

Preacher's jaw tightened as he struggled to control his anger. He said, "I'm gonna let that pass, Count, but don't push your luck."

Stahlmaske looked around at the other men and must have been able to tell they weren't going to agree to his demand that Preacher leave. He snapped, "Very well. I see now what I must do to satisfy my honor."

With that, he stepped closer to Preacher. In an alarmed voice, Senator Allingham said, "Count, wait a minute—"

Stahlmaske ignored him. He said to Preacher, "Even though you are no gentlemen, we will settle this as if you were. I challenge you to a duel!"

His hand flashed up and slapped Preacher across the face.

CHAPTER 11

"Preacher, no!" Simon Russell cried. He leaped forward but was too late to prevent the mountain man's instinctive reaction. Preacher's right fist sunk wrist-deep in the count's belly. A split-second later, Preacher's left crashed against Stahlmaske's jaw and knocked the man backward.

Stahlmaske probably would have fallen off the boat and landed in the river if Allingham hadn't been fast enough to grab his arm.

While the senator was doing that, Gunther exploded out of the cabin with a furious roar and slammed into Preacher from behind. He wrapped his arms around the mountain man and lifted him off the deck as he powered forward.

They went over the side and landed in the shallow water between the riverboat and the bank. Water flew high in the air from the huge splash.

Preacher's head was under the surface, and he hadn't been able to catch a breath before being submerged because Gunther's arms were wrapped around his chest like iron bands. With the big Prussian's weight on top of him, pressing him down into the water and mud, Preacher knew he wasn't far from drowning. Already a red haze began to settle over his brain.

He dug his feet into the river bottom in an effort to push himself up onto the bank, but they just slid in the slime and couldn't get any purchase.

Preacher was damned if he was going to die here in this muck and mire. He fought with the only weapon at his disposal. He arched his spine and drove the back of his head into Gunther's face as hard as he could.

The impact was solid enough to send a jolt through Preacher's brain. He almost passed out, but he clung desperately to consciousness. Gunther's grip seemed a little looser than it had been a moment earlier, so Preacher butted him again.

Gunther's brutal embrace slipped enough for Preacher to wrench an arm free. He rammed his elbow into the big man's belly. Drawing his knees up under him, Preacher heaved the upper half of his body out of the river. It was a feat of incredible strength, because he had to lift his enemy's considerable weight, too.

Preacher's ears were full of muddy water. Vaguely, he heard shouting, but he couldn't make out any of the words or determine who the voices belonged to. At the moment it didn't matter. He reached back with his free hand and clawed at Gunther's face. Back east they might hold with dandified rules like no gougin', but Preacher fought to win. If he could get a finger in Gunther's eye, he'd pop the orb right out.

Instead Gunther let go of him and shoved him away. Preacher rolled onto the bank and came up with his chest heaving as he dragged air into his lungs. He turned and saw Gunther trying to flounder his way out of the water. In the moonlight the lower half of the Prussian's face was black with the blood that had leaked from his smashed nose.

"Gunther!" Count Stahlmaske called from the *Sentinel*'s deck. "Stop this battle immediately!"

Gunther ignored his employer's command. Preacher could tell that the big man was too far gone in senseless anger to heed anything.

Stahlmaske, Russell, and Captain Warner stood at the edge of the riverboat's cargo deck. Up on the passenger deck, a number of people had rushed to the railing to see what was going on. When Preacher glanced up there, he saw the rest of the Prussian contingent, along with Margaret and Sarah Allingham. The blond hair of the senator's wife and daughter shone silver in the moonlight. They both watched raptly as Gunther stumbled ashore and charged at Preacher with his fists swinging wildly.

Preacher wasn't fully recovered from almost drowning—even a man with his iron constitution needed more time than that—but he had some breath in his body again and was able to set his feet to meet Gunther's attack. He ducked under a roundhouse swing and stepped in close to deliver a fast left and right to the big man's belly.

Gunther had some fat on him, but underneath it were slablike muscles so as Preacher hit him it was like punching a wall. The mountain man tried to jerk his head out of the way of a careening fist, but it clipped him and knocked him to the side.

Preacher caught himself, blocked the next punch, and peppered Gunther's already bleeding nose with a flurry of blows. Gunther howled in pain and rage and bulled forward. Preacher pivoted out of the way and tripped him. It might not have been the most sporting of tactics, but again, Preacher was in this fight to win.

In fact, he would have been more than happy to kick Gunther while he was down, but the Prussian rolled out of the way too fast. He slapped the ground and pushed himself up.

But as he did, his hand fell on a broken branch from one of the cottonwoods, and as he rose he gripped it like a club and swung it at Preacher's head.

Preacher had to retreat as Gunther whipped the branch back and forth. His pistols had gotten wet, so they would have to be cleaned, charged, and primed again before he could use them. Anyway, he didn't really want to kill Gunther, and for that reason he didn't reach for his knife or tomahawk, either. He wasn't afraid of the law, but he knew if he killed the Prussian, he would have to leave the riverboat. The count would never stand for having him on board. And he had given his word to Simon Russell to try to help.

The crewmen yelled, caught up in the excitement of the fight, and Dog barked thunderously. The big cur couldn't contain himself anymore. He leaped easily from the deck to the shore and bounded forward, eager to get in on the fray.

"Dog, stay back!" Preacher shouted. If Dog knocked Gunther down, his fangs were likely to rip out the man's throat before anybody could stop him.

Dog halted but continued snarling and yapping, ready to spring into action if Preacher should fall.

"I bash your head in, then kill that stupid dog, *ja*?" Gunther said as he paused in his swings with the makeshift club. "You lay a hand on the count, you deserve to die."

"Seems like a mighty foolish notion to me, Gunther," Preacher said. "I ain't sure that stiff-necked aristocrat is worth either of us dyin'."

Gunther roared again and renewed his attack.

Preacher was ready, though. He twisted out of the way as the branch descended toward his head and grabbed Gunther's wrist with both hands. Twisting even more, he used the big man's own momentum against him and hauled him forward, at the same time throwing a hip into Gunther's body. It was a classic move the Indians used when wrestling with each other for sport.

Out of control now, Gunther flew into the air, turned over, and landed on his back with stunning force. Preacher grabbed the club and tore it out of his hands. He dropped to his knees next to Gunther's head and pressed the branch into the big man's throat with enough force to keep Gunther from breathing.

"I can crush your windpipe before you can stop me," Preacher warned his opponent. "You might beat me, but even if you do, you'll strangle to death before anybody can do anything about it."

Gunther tried to growl and couldn't even do that.

"I'm gonna step back and let you up, but this fight is over, you understand? Come at me again and I'll kill you. That's a promise, mister."

Gunther lifted a hand, but instead of making a fist and striking at Preacher, he used it to wave the mountain man away.

Preacher lifted the branch from Gunther's throat, stood up, and stepped back. Gunther rolled onto his side and gasped for breath.

Preacher knew the feeling. He had been doing the same thing a few minutes earlier.

"Bravo! What a stirring battle!"

The shout from the boat took Preacher by surprise. He looked up at the passenger deck and saw Roderick Stahlmaske standing there, an excited grin on his round face.

"Roderick!" his older brother snapped from the cargo deck. Roderick suddenly looked like a little boy who had been caught doing something he shouldn't. He backed hurriedly away from the rail.

"I agree," Sarah Allingham said from where

she stood several yards along the railing. "It was a fabulous display of savagery."

"Hush!" her mother scolded her. "And what are you doing out here in your nightdress? This is scandalous! Get back in the cabin right now."

Stahlmaske jumped with athletic grace from the deck to the shore and stalked toward Preacher and Gunther. Preacher thought at first that he was going to help Gunther up, but then he realized he should have known better when the count strode past the still-gasping servant.

"My man's crude defense of my honor changes nothing," Stahlmaske said as he came to a stop in front of Preacher. "My challenge to you still stands."

"You ain't fixin' to slap me again, are you?" Preacher asked. "I wouldn't take it kindly."

"I've already issued the challenge. There is no need to repeat it. It would have been more fitting had I had a gauntlet with which to strike you, but one must make do in a backward country such as this."

"I got no interest in fightin' a duel with you, Count. It's a downright stupid idea if you ask me."

Stahlmaske trembled with anger as his hands balled into fists at his side. He said, "Are you declaring yourself to be a coward, then? That is what refusing my challenge will amount to."

Preacher glanced at the boat. He could tell from the faces of both Russell and Allingham that the two men wanted him to find some way out of this. They wanted the incident smoothed over.

Russell was an old friend and Preacher liked

Allingham more than he'd expected to when he found out the man was a politician. But there were some things he just wasn't going to do, even out of friendship.

"Nobody's ever made me say I was yellow, and it sure as hell ain't gonna start with you," Preacher said. "I accept your challenge, Count. If you want a duel, you got one."

Up on the cargo deck, Russell cursed softly.

"Excellent," Stahlmaske said. "As the challenged party, you have the choice of weapons. Will it be pistols or sabers?"

With pistols, Preacher was pretty sure that one or both of them would wind up dead. He might stand more of a chance of defeating the count in a knife fight without killing him. And a saber was just an overgrown knife, wasn't it?

"I reckon sabers will do," he said.

"Excellent!" Stahlmaske looked genuinely pleased. "Tomorrow morning at dawn we cross steel—in a duel to the death!"

CHAPTER 12

"Preacher, have you lost your mind?" Simon Russell asked a short time later.

Preacher was in Russell's cabin, along with Senator Allingham and Captain Warner. The meeting had the atmosphere of a council of war, Preacher thought. Given the evidently delicate nature of the relationship between the United States and the Kingdom of Prussia, maybe that was a good description of it.

Allingham said, "Without being quite so blunt about it, this does seem to be a bad idea, Preacher. It's going to cause trouble for a lot of people if you kill Count Stahlmaske in a duel."

Preacher was using a rag to wipe off some of the slime that had gotten on his hat when Gunther knocked him into the river. Without looking up from the task, he said, "I don't plan on killin' him. That's why I picked sabers instead of pistols. I got a hunch he's a pretty good shot, so the only way

I could be sure of him not killin' me would be to blow a hole in him first."

"But he's an excellent duelist," Allingham said. "Good Lord, he trained at Heidelberg!"

"And I've fought in scraps from New Orleans to the Pacific Ocean," Preacher drawled. Satisfied that he had gotten most of the mud off his hat, he put it on.

"But have you ever fought a duel with sabers before?"

"Not to speak of. But a saber's just a big ol' knife, ain't it? I've been in plenty of knife fights."

Russell sighed.

"You heard what the count said, Preacher. He's going to be trying to kill you. You won't have any choice but to defend yourself."

"Unless you take your animals and leave the boat tonight," Allingham suggested.

"Wait just a damned minute," Warner said. "I sort of like the idea of having Preacher along on this trip."

"So do I," Russell agreed. "I just didn't think this much would go wrong so fast. We just left St. Louis this morning!"

"Look," Preacher said, "all I've got to do is knock that pigsticker out of his hand, and the fight's over. Just because he wants to kill me, there's nothin' sayin' I have to kill him."

"He'll be insulted," Allingham warned. "He'll still be nursing a grudge against you."

Preacher chuckled.

"I can live with that."

"I don't see what else we can do other than hope for the best," Russell said. "Preacher, we're depending on you."

"Reckon I'll go ashore and turn in," Preacher said. "The count wants to have this little ruckus at dawn, and I'd like to get some shut-eye before then!"

He took his bedroll and Dog and left the boat, which was now quiet and dark except for a few lamps turned down low. He spread his blankets on a level piece of ground under the trees and stretched out on them with his pistols, rifle, knife, and tomahawk all within easy reach right beside him.

Dog lay down on his other side. Preacher knew he could sleep soundly, confident that if any enemies came skulking around, Dog would know about it and wake him.

It took a lot to make Preacher lose any sleep at night, and the run-ins he'd had so far on this trip didn't rise to that level. He dropped off quickly, falling into a deep, dreamless slumber.

When Dog growled sometime later, however, Preacher was awake instantly and completely alert. Soundlessly, he reached out and closed his hand around one of his pistols. He looped his thumb over the hammer but didn't ear it back as he raised the weapon. He kept the hammer mechanism well-oiled, but it made a sound anyway when it was cocked. That couldn't be helped. Preacher didn't want to warn a keen-eared enemy that he was awake.

He put his other hand on the back of Dog's neck, and the big cur fell silent. He wouldn't make another sound until Preacher released him.

"Preacher?" a voice whispered. "Preacher, where are you? I know you're out here somewhere."

Preacher rolled his eyes in the darkness and didn't reply. He recognized the voice and hoped that if he didn't say anything, Sarah Allingham would give up and go away.

She kept coming, though, until she was practically on top of him. She whispered his name again.

"Careful," Preacher said. "You're fixin' to step on me."

Sarah gasped in surprise, but instead of jumping back as Preacher expected her to, she rushed forward. One of her feet thumped into his leg and she lost her balance. She fell and landed squarely on top of him. He barely got the pistol out of the way in time so the barrel didn't jab her in the belly.

He had been in some pretty odd situations over the years, he thought, but this was the first time he'd ever had a nubile young woman who happened to be a senator's daughter squirming around on top of him.

From a purely physical standpoint, it was a mighty pleasurable predicament. Sarah's nightdress was thin and she didn't seem to be wearing anything else. She was a well-packed armful of warm female flesh, too.

But she was an armful of trouble at the same

time, so he rolled her off of him and sat up. She said, "Ooof!"

"Pipe down," Preacher told her. "What in blazes are you doin' out here?"

Her nightdress was tangled around her. She kicked her legs and straightened it out so she could sit up, too. The skin of her bare legs flashed in the dappled moonlight that came through the overhanging branches of the cottonwoods.

"Make up your mind," she said. "Do you want me to be quiet, or do you want me to tell you why I'm here?"

"I reckon you better tell me. Just keep your voice down as much as you can."

Sarah laughed.

"Really, Preacher. Can't you guess?"

"If I had to guess," Preacher replied grimly, "I'd say you're tryin' to get your pa to come after me with a shotgun. That wouldn't be a good thing for anybody."

"My father doesn't care what I do," Sarah said. "He just wants to stay in the good graces of the president. He has his eye on the job himself some day, or at least vice president."

"Oh, I reckon he'd be upset, no matter what you think."

"There's no reason for him to be. I'm hardly the blushing maiden he believes I am."

Preacher didn't want to hear any of this. He didn't want this brazen hussy of a girl involving him in any of her scheming. He pointed toward the river and said, "You'd better get back on the boat right now."

"I'm liable to get caught."

"You were able to sneak off of there without anybody noticin'. I reckon you can sneak on."

She leaned closer to him and said, "Maybe I want to get caught. Did you ever think about that? Everyone knows you're camping here under the trees. If they find out I'm coming back from here, what are they going to think? You know the conclusion they'll leap to." She reached up and rested a soft hand against his beard-stubbled jaw. "If you're going to be damned for something whether you do it or not, doesn't it make sense to go ahead and take whatever pleasure you can?"

Preacher took hold of her wrist and moved her hand away from his face.

"That way of thinkin' gets people in trouble. There's right and there's wrong, and you can't just argue one around into bein' the other."

"Why . . . why, you're just a stiff-necked old Puritan!"

"Not hardly. But I've got sense enough not to get mixed up in somethin' that can't end no other way but bad."

Sarah blew out her breath in an exasperated sigh. She stood up and hugged herself as if she were suddenly cold in the thin nightdress.

"All right," she said. "I'll go back to the boat. And if anybody catches me, I'll say that I was just taking a walk and that I didn't go anywhere near you. Satisfied?"

"That's fine. It'd be better if you managed not to get caught, though."

She snorted disgustedly and flounced away.

Preacher scratched Dog behind his ears and said, "You'd think a gal like that wouldn't have no interest in a hairy, smelly old scoundrel like me. Like I said, there just ain't no figurin' women."

Dog whined as if in agreement.

Preacher stayed awake long enough for Sarah to get back on the *Sentinel*. When he didn't hear any commotion from the riverboat, he assumed she had made it onboard without being discovered. He dozed off again and slept soundly the rest of the night, until the sky began to lighten in the east with the approach of dawn.

Count Stahlmaske wanted to fight the duel at sunup, so Preacher went onboard and climbed the stairs to the passenger deck. When he went into the dining room, he found a gloomy Simon Russell already there, sipping from a cup of coffee.

Preacher poured himself a cup from a pot that sat on a sideboard and joined Russell.

"I reckon we're goin' through with this fool business," the mountain man said.

"I haven't heard any different," Russell replied. "Are you sure there's no other way out of this, Preacher?"

"The count called the tune."

"I know. And I can't really blame you."

Preacher drank some of the strong, black brew and said, "I recollect a time when you would've done the same thing I'm doin', Simon. When things got rough, nobody ever made you back down."

Russell sighed.

"That was a long time ago."

"Not really. Just a few years."

"Yeah, well, even a few years of working for wages and spending a lot of your time in town will change a man."

Preacher shrugged in acceptance of that. At least Russell was wise enough to know that he wasn't the same man he'd once been.

"Where's this duel going to take place?" Russell went on.

"Don't know. Wherever the count wants to fight it, I reckon. There's room on the cargo deck right now, since it ain't full of pelts yet, or we could go ashore."

The dining room door opened and Captain Benjamin Warner came in.

"Gentlemen," he greeted them with a nod.

Preacher grinned and said, "Folks seem to keep mistakin' me for one of them critters."

That brought a chuckle from the captain as he joined them.

Preacher didn't eat any breakfast. He didn't want anything weighing him down. Although he was confident in his own ability to meet any challenge, he knew that he had never used a saber before, while Count Stahlmaske was an expert with one. The count intended to kill him, too, if he got the chance.

Stahlmaske must not have had much of an appetite, either. He didn't show up in the dining room. After a while, though, his Uncle Gerhard came in and said, "My nephew awaits you on the lower deck, Herr Preacher, if you are ready."

"Ready as I'll ever be," Preacher said as he drank the last of his coffee and got to his feet.

The eastern sky was full of beautiful reddish-gold light as Preacher emerged from the dining room. The sun hadn't quite peeked over the horizon yet, but it was close. With Russell, Warner, and Gerhard Stahlmaske following him, Preacher went down the stairs to the cargo deck.

The count stood in the middle of the large open space forward. He wore high-topped boots, tight black trousers, and a blousy white shirt. His head was bare. He held a saber that he whipped back and forth. The blade made a faint keening sound in the early morning air.

As Preacher approached, Stahlmaske replaced the saber in a velvet-lined wooden case held by his brother Roderick. The count gestured at the pair of sabers in the case and said to Preacher, "Your choice of weapons, sir."

Preacher wasn't the sort to waste any time overthinking things. He picked up the saber Stahlmaske hadn't been using, weighed it in his hand to test the balance, and nodded.

"This'll do fine," he said.

Stahlmaske took the other blade. Roderick closed the case and backed away.

Preacher took off his hat and tossed it to Simon Russell. He glanced up at the railing along the passenger deck. Gretchen Ritter and her two brothers were there. Heinrich and Hobart looked excited, but Gretchen wore a worried frown.

So did Senator Allingham, who was also at the rail with his wife and daughter. Sarah looked sullen this morning, thought Preacher. She was probably nursing a grudge against him because he'd rejected her the night before.

Gerhard announced, "Each man's second will now examine the opponent's weapon."

Such formality struck Preacher as foolish, but he was willing to go along with it if it would get this foolishness started. He looked at Russell, who sighed and went to look at the count's saber. Roderick examined the saber Preacher held. After a moment both men nodded and then got out of the way.

"Very well," Gerhard said. "This is a test of honor, so you will both fight like gentlemen." He glanced at the eastern horizon. The sun had appeared, rising into view like a garish orange ball. "The duel will commence."

Stahlmaske raised his saber in front of his face in a salute and said, "To the death."

Preacher returned the salute but didn't say anything about killing. He still hoped to avoid that.

Stahlmaske lunged forward, thrusting with his blade. Preacher parried. Steel rang loudly against steel, and the duel was on.

CHAPTER 13

The count was fast. Preacher had to give him credit for that. The saber in Stahlmaske's hand moved so swiftly it was hard for the eye to follow as it darted and slashed.

Preacher's incredible reflexes, honed by years of living a dangerous existence, were all that saved him from being run through or having his throat ripped open. The sound of the blades clashing was almost continuous as Preacher turned aside a flurry of attacks by the count.

He realized that he was being forced to give ground as he defended himself. Stahlmaske had maneuvered him back almost to the edge of the cargo deck. So far Preacher hadn't been able to launch an attack of his own. All he had done was counter Stahlmaske's moves.

That was no way to win a fight, and Preacher knew it. He had to go on the offensive if he was going to have any chance to win this duel.

Gradually, Preacher realized that Stahlmaske was

following a regular pattern. At that Heidelberg place, whatever it was, the count's dueling instructors must have taught him a fairly rigid set of moves.

Audie had told Preacher in the past about how chess masters had certain patterns of attack they followed. Those moves even had names. Preacher figured that dueling must be similar. He watched the count closely.

Thrust, jab, jab, slash, thrust, jab, slash . . . The pattern was complex, but as Preacher parried each of the moves in turn he began to get a sense of their rhythm. When Stahlmaske got to the end of the sequence, he started over. Knowing what was coming made it easier for Preacher to block the count's saber—and to start thinking about some moves of his own.

The possibility that Stahlmaske might be trying to lull him into thinking that occurred to Preacher when it was almost too late. Just as he thought that he needed to be on the lookout for the count changing things up, the blade flashed at him from an unexpected direction.

Preacher twisted his wrist just in time to catch Stahlmaske's weapon with the tip of his own blade and send it sliding off to the side. The point burned a line across Preacher's ribs rather than penetrating his heart.

One of the women cried out. Preacher didn't know which one and at the moment didn't care.

Stahlmaske stepped back and lifted his saber to proudly display the smear of crimson on the tip. He grinned and boasted, "First blood to me."

The shallow cut on Preacher's side stung, but he was able to ignore the pain. He had ignored plenty worse in his life, like the time he had tangled with a grizzly bear.

"First blood ain't as important as last blood," he said.

"True," the count said. He lunged forward again and resumed his attack.

This time there was nothing predictable about his movements. Preacher knew he had narrowly escaped the trap Stahlmaske had baited for him. His inexperience at this kind of fighting had almost cost him his life.

But he had a few tricks of his own he could try. The next time Preacher caught the count's blade on his own and shoved it hard to the side, he took a quick step forward that brought him within reach of Stahlmaske. He balled his left hand into a fist and smashed it against the Prussian's jaw.

The blow took Stahlmaske by surprise and knocked him back several steps. From the passenger deck, Roderick shouted, "I say! That's not fair!"

Stahlmaske caught himself. His lips twisted in a snarl as he said, "I should have known you could not do battle as a gentleman. You are a savage!"

"Was that against your fancy rules?" Preacher drawled. "Sorry, I only go by one rule: stay alive."

With his face darkening in fury, the count came at him again. Preacher had his hands full just blocking all the thrusts and slashes. Stahlmaske was so angry that for a moment he got careless. He put so much power behind one of his strokes that when he missed, he stumbled a little.

Preacher had been waiting for that. He moved quickly, using sheer power to batter the count's blade down. Then as he withdrew, a flick of his wrist sent the tip of his saber raking up Stahlmaske's forearm.

Stahlmaske yelled in pain as he sprang back. Blood stained the sleeve of his white shirt.

"Reckon we're even now on the blood-drawin'," Preacher said.

He didn't mention that for a split-second, he'd had the opportunity to plunge his blade completely through the count's body. Stahlmaske had to know that, though. If he was the experienced duelist he claimed to be, he would be aware that he had been wide open.

"I'm willin' to call this thing quits," the mountain man went on. "With blood spilled on both sides, don't that mean your honor has been satisfied?"

"Hardly," Stahlmaske said through clenched teeth. "I said this was a fight to the death, and I meant it!"

"I don't want to kill you, Count. Your sword arm's wounded. Better just let it go."

"Never!"

Stahlmaske tossed his saber from right hand to left and attacked again. Preacher hadn't expected that at all, even though he had seen men do the same thing during knife fights in the mountains. Not only was he surprised, but having the count's line of attack change so drastically was disorienting. Preacher had to retreat again as he barely blocked several thrusts.

He had refrained from killing Stahlmaske once

already when he'd had the chance. He didn't know
if he could afford to do that again without putting
his own life at too much of a risk. All Stahlmaske
needed was an opening, a split-second during
which Preacher's guard was down, and the mountain man would find himself with a foot of cold steel
lodged in his body.

He heard Heinrich and Hobart Ritter shouting
encouragement to the count. Oddly enough, neither Gretchen nor Stahlmaske's own brother were
cheering him on. Uncle Gerhard just looked per-
turbed by the whole affair. Russell, Allingham, and
Warner were flat-out worried.

Margaret and Sarah Allingham watched intently.
Excitement shone in the eyes of both women.

Preacher didn't really notice any of that at the
moment. He was too busy defending himself as
Stahlmaske came at him again.

Preacher was getting the hang of fighting a left-
handed man. The next time he parried one of the
count's strokes, he slid his blade along Stahlmaske's
until the hilts clashed with each other. Preacher
knew this might be his only chance, so he relied on
sheer strength again and twisted his sword as hard
as he could against Stahlmaske's.

The move wrenched the saber out of the count's
hand. It clattered on the deck at their feet. Preacher
jerked his own saber back and let the tip rest against
the hollow of Stahlmaske's throat, not quite hard
enough to draw blood.

The count's eyes widened. It was obvious he expected to die in the next second or two.

Preacher didn't press on the blade. He held it where it was for a couple of heartbeats, then stepped back and lowered the saber.

"We're done," he said. "Fight's over."

In a voice that trembled slightly with emotion, Stahlmaske said again, "This was to be a fight to the death."

"Well, let's say I just killed you, then, and let it go at that. I don't need to see you bleedin' to death on some riverboat deck. We both got better things to do than that."

"My honor—" the count began.

"You fought a good fight. You risked your life without flinchin'. *That's* the sort of thing that demonstrates a man's honor, not how the fight comes out."

Silence reigned over the riverboat as everyone waited to see what the count's reaction would be. After several moments that seemed even longer than they really were, Stahlmaske nodded.

"What you say is acceptable. But in turn you will have to accept my word that I did not fire that shot at you last night."

"Fine by me," the mountain man said. "I believe you."

He tossed the saber to the deck and held out his hand to his former opponent.

Stahlmaske hesitated, but only for a second. He stepped forward and took Preacher's hand in a firm grip. Since he was using his wounded arm, that must have hurt. He grimaced slightly.

"You're fortunate that I'm not quite as good with my left arm as I am with my right," he said.

Preacher chuckled.

"I know it. And I ain't one to complain about havin' a little luck on my side, neither."

Since the duel was over, people began talking again. Heinrich and Hobart were still excited about the battle they had just witnessed, and they babbled to each other in German about it. Gretchen just looked relieved, as did Russell, Allingham, and Warner. The three men gathered around Preacher but had the good sense not to congratulate him on his victory. There was no point in rubbing salt into the count's wounds.

"You'll need that cut on your side tended to," Russell said.

"It's just a scratch," Preacher said. "I'll dab a little whiskey on it. It'll be fine."

"How about some breakfast, then?"

"Now, that sounds pretty good," Preacher admitted. "Nothin' like fightin' a duel to work up a little appetite first thing in the mornin'."

"And I'll tell the crew to start getting some steam up," Warner said. "I want to be headed upriver before the sun's much higher in the sky!"

Half a mile away, two men were bellied down at the top of a slight rise. One of them, a lean man with a clean-shaven face heavily pockmarked by childhood disease, had a spyglass pressed to his right eye. He squinted through the lens as smoke began to rise into the morning sky from the river-boat's stacks.

"They're getting steam up," he told his companion without lowering the spyglass. "Reckon they'll be on their way pretty soon."

"We gonna hit 'em today, Claude?" the second man asked. He was about the same height as the first man but twice as wide, with a head like a stone block topped by curly brown hair. He sported a beard of the same shade. Both men wore buckskins.

"No, we'll wait a few more days," Claude said. "Let the boat get farther upriver. Maybe take 'em at Cougar Bluffs."

"And there'll be a bunch of fur company money onboard, right?"

"That's right, Wedge. The trader will have plenty of cash to buy pelts when the boat gets where it's going."

The *Sentinel* had something else on board be-sides money, Claude Binnion realized. Looking through the spyglass, he made out several figures on deck that he recognized as female. He couldn't tell any details from this distance other than that, but it didn't matter. A woman—any woman—was a rare and valuable thing on the frontier. He didn't know who those gals were or what they were doing headed upriver, and he didn't care.

The important thing was that when he and his men raided the *Sentinel,* the women would be part of the loot they carried away with them.

CHAPTER 14

Later that day as the *Sentinel* steamed upriver, Simon Russell approached Preacher while the mountain man stood at the bow on the passenger deck with Dog.

"Have you recovered from that fracas this morning?" Russell asked.

"That so-called duel?" Preacher snorted. "I ain't sure that little dustup was serious enough to call it a fracas."

"I don't know," Russell said as he leaned on the railing beside Preacher and looked out at the wide, muddy, slow-moving river in front of them. "It looked to me like the count came pretty damned close to sticking that saber in you a few times."

"If I worried about every time I've come close to dyin', I wouldn't have time to do anything else. And I figure I'll get in plenty more scrapes before my time's up."

"I wouldn't be a bit surprised." Russell paused for

a moment, then went on, "You know, we still didn't figure out who took that shot at you last night."

"I been ponderin' on it," Preacher said as his eyes narrowed in thought.

"Do you believe the count when he says he didn't do it?"

"As a matter of fact, I do. I don't like him, but I got a hunch he ain't a liar. As for ol' Gunther, what Stahlmaske says about him is probably right, too. He's the sort who'd rather rely on his fists than on a gun."

"So where does that leave you? Who else on this riverboat has any reason to be carrying a grudge against you?"

"That's a mighty good question," Preacher said. "I can't think of a soul. Hell, most of these folks, I barely know 'em."

That was true. Sarah Allingham might be a little angry with him for chasing her back to the boat the night before instead of succumbing to her feminine wiles, but that had happened *after* the shooting.

Anyway, Sarah didn't seem the type to resort to gunplay, either. Not as long as she thought she could get her way by pouting and being seductive.

"You have a reputation as being a bad man to cross," Russell mused. "Maybe if somebody was planning to cause trouble somewhere along the way, they might want to get rid of you before the time came."

"Like if somebody on board was workin' with a

bunch of those river pirates who've hit these boats before?"

"The thought crossed my mind," Russell said.

"Mine, too," Preacher admitted. "Right now that seems like the most likely explanation. Might be somethin' goin' on that we don't know anything about, though. Seems like we may have to just wait until whoever it was tries again."

"Paint a big target on your back and wait for somebody to shoot at it, in other words."

"Wouldn't be the first time," Preacher drawled.

"I'll keep my eyes open and see if I spot anybody acting suspicious."

Preacher nodded and said, "I'll do the same." He nodded toward the terrain on both sides of the river. "And I'll be watchin' out yonder, too, in case any trouble comes at us from that direction."

Later, after Russell had gone back into the salon, Preacher heard footsteps behind him again and looked over his shoulder to see Gretchen Ritter approaching him. That was a surprise. He didn't think the redhead had said more than a dozen words to him so far on this journey.

She wore her dark green traveling outfit, but her head was bare. Her thick auburn hair was even more beautiful with the sun shining on it. Now that Preacher got a closer look at her, he saw that her eyes were green, a shade lighter than her dress.

He nodded politely to her and said, "Good afternoon, Fraulein Ritter."

She cocked her head a little to the side.

"You speak German, Herr Preacher?"

"Not much," Preacher said with a smile. "I've known some German trappers and traders over the years. That's how I was able to pick up a few words. But you'll be better off stickin' to English, if that's all right with you."

"Of course. I made sure that I was reasonably fluent in your language before I ever came to this country."

He couldn't figure out what she wanted with him, so he asked, "How's the count doin'?"

"Albert is fine. One of the maids cleaned and dressed his wound. He insists that in a few days it will be completely healed." She smiled. "Albert does not like being less than perfect. He is very stubborn about such things."

"I got that feelin'," Preacher said dryly. He had a hunch Count Stahlmaske was very stubborn about everything.

"At any rate, I saw you standing out here and knew that I should speak to you."

"What about?" Preacher asked.

"I want to thank you."

He frowned.

"For what?"

"For not killing the man I am engaged to wed."

Not *The man I'm in love with* or *The man I'm going to marry,* Preacher thought. Gretchen made it sound more like a business arrangement, and he wondered if that was the case. Those nobles over in Europe were all the time marrying each other for financial or political reasons. Sometimes the easiest way to avoid going to war was to marry off some royal daughter to some other inbred, crown-wearing galoot.

"I never wanted to kill the count," he said. "Shoot, I never even wanted to fight that duel in the first place."

"Yet you struck Albert and provoked him."

"Only after he slapped me."

"Albert isn't accustomed to anyone defying his will."

"And I ain't used to folks slappin' me," Preacher said. "I don't care for it."

To his surprise, Gretchen laughed quietly.

"You two are like unstoppable forces of nature, bound on opposite paths," she said. "It was inevitable that you would clash, since the two of you are so much alike."

Preacher stiffened and said, "Now hold on there." He didn't cotton to anybody saying he was like an arrogant, stiff-necked Prussian nobleman. The way he saw it, he and Albert Stahlmaske were about as unlike as any two fellows could get.

"It's true," Gretchen insisted. "Both of you have a strict code of honor, and you'll allow no one to besmirch it. You stride through the world like giants, better than any of those around you."

"I never said that," Preacher insisted. "I've never tried to be high an' mighty in my life."

"That's just it." She smiled at him. "You don't have to try. You just *are*. So *danke,* Herr Preacher. Thank you for the life of my betrothed."

"Yes'm," Preacher replied. "You're welcome, I reckon." He didn't know what else to say.

"If you will excuse me . . ."

"Sure." Preacher nodded and tugged on his hat brim. Gretchen turned away and went back to her cabin.

That was mighty strange, Preacher thought. He felt an instinctive liking for Gretchen Ritter. She seemed a little more down to earth than the rest of her party.

He sensed that something wasn't right between her and the count, though, and he hoped whatever it was wouldn't lead to even more trouble before this ill-fated journey was over.

The count wasn't exactly friendly toward Preacher at dinner that evening, but he was civil enough. The two of them would never be friends, Preacher knew, but if they could make it to the mouth of the Yellowstone without trying to kill each other again, he'd consider that a successful trip.

There were no trees along the stretch of river where the *Sentinel* had tied up tonight, so Preacher decided to stay on board. He spread his bedroll among the crates of supplies on the cargo deck and turned in, with Dog and his weapons beside him as usual.

By staying on the boat, Preacher thought he might be making it easier for whoever had tried to kill him. The sooner he drew the varmint out of hiding, the better. He even stayed awake for a while after the riverboat had gotten dark and quiet, just in case anybody tried to sneak up on him, but no one came near him on the deck.

One of the crew always stood watch in the pilot house during the night to raise the alarm if Indians or river pirates attacked. Preacher thought that was a good idea, but he suspected the sentries sometimes dozed off at their post. Standing watch was boring, especially out here in the middle of nowhere.

Luckily, Dog was a light sleeper and had the keenest senses Preacher had ever encountered, so the big cur was like a second and even more effective guard.

All Dog had to do was lift his head from his paws where it had been resting, and Preacher was awake. He hoped like blazes that Sarah Allingham wasn't skulking around again, hoping to convince him to take a tumble with her. That wasn't going to happen, no matter how tempting she thought she was.

And to tell the truth, she was pretty damned tempting, Preacher thought as he pushed himself up on an elbow to take a look around the cargo deck.

He didn't see anyone moving, but a soft sound made him look up toward the passenger deck. Someone who seemed to be wearing slippers cat-footed along up there, sneaking along the line of cabin doors. Preacher spotted the skulker, but the shadows were too thick for him to identify him or her.

He lifted one of his pistols and pointed it toward the stealthy figure. He was in fairly deep shadow himself and didn't know if the lurker was aware of his presence. His muscles were tense as he waited for the explosion of a shot.

Instead, he heard a faint knock. Whoever was skulking around up there had stopped at one of the cabins and knocked on the door.

The door opened, allowing a faint glow to spill out. The way the light flickered, Preacher knew it came from a candle. A stray beam touched something bright and shiny as the mysterious figure entered the cabin.

That was blond hair that had flashed for a split-second in the light, Preacher realized. Only two people on the *Sentinel* had hair that fair: Sarah Allingham and her mother.

He could see well enough to count the cabin doors. As he did, he recalled which of the passengers went with that particular cabin.

Count Albert Stahlmaske.

"Oh, Lord," Preacher said. One of the senator's ladies had just slipped into the count's cabin in the middle of the night, and there wasn't much doubt about the reason for this nocturnal visit. There was some scandalous behavior going on, and that could only increase the chances of all hell breaking loose before the riverboat reached its destination.

But Preacher was damned if he was going to go up there and pound on the count's door like some outraged father or cuckolded husband. As long as the people involved didn't try to kill each other, their private goings-on weren't any of his business.

He had promised his old friend he would do his best to help get the passengers where they were going safely. He hadn't said anything about making sure they behaved themselves.

With a disgusted grunt, Preacher set his pistol down, rolled onto his side, and went back to sleep.

CHAPTER 15

The next couple of days passed peacefully enough. After everything that had happened the first day and a half on the river, that was a relief, Preacher thought. No one tried to kill him, and the countryside through which the riverboat passed seemed empty and tranquil.

Preacher knew there were Indians out there, but they avoided the river when the *Sentinel* steamed by. No doubt they heard the rumbling engine and the noisy splashing that the paddle wheel made and wanted nothing to do with the white man's great smoking river beast.

He still didn't know whether it was Margaret or Sarah Allingham who was carrying on with the count. Neither woman showed any signs of conducting an affair. It didn't really matter, of course. Either possibility likely would cause trouble if the senator ever found out.

In the middle of the third day after the duel, the boat's engine started making a racket that even

Preacher could tell wasn't right. Up in the pilot house, Captain Warner spun the wheel and angled the *Sentinel* toward the shore.

Simon Russell came along the deck and told Preacher, "Something's wrong. I'm going to find out what it is."

He started up the stairs to the pilot house. Preacher followed, giving in to curiosity. He hadn't been up there yet, and he wanted to sample that view Warner had mentioned.

It was a good one, Preacher discovered as he and Russell entered the pilot house. With windows all around, the tall structure commanded a view of several miles on both sides of the river. He needed to spend more time up here, Preacher told himself.

Captain Warner glanced around at the two men with a disgusted expression on his beefy face.

"Just got a shout from the engine room, as if I needed one," he told them. "Those repairs we did back in St. Louis didn't hold. We're gonna have to put in to shore for a while."

"Do we need to turn back?" Russell asked. He looked and sounded as if that possibility didn't appeal to him at all.

"Not hardly," Warner replied with a wave of the hand he lifted from the wheel. "We can take care of the problem just as well here as we could back in St. Louis. Anyway, we'd have to fix it before we could turn around and go back, so there's no real point to that. Don't worry, Simon, this is just a minor setback. It sounds worse than it really is."

"I hope you're right about that," Russell said

dubiously. "I realize, problems with the boat are beyond my control, but it'll still reflect badly on me with the company if we have to abandon the trip."

"That's not going to happen," Warner promised. "This boat is going to be fine. Hell, she's practically new. Never been this far up the river before. There are always little problems with a new boat. It just takes time to work them all out."

"All right, do whatever you need to do."

"We will." As Warner maneuvered the *Sentinel* closer to the riverbank, he asked, "What do you think of it, Preacher?"

"Pretty interestin'," the mountain man said. "You were right about bein' able to see a long way from up here."

"You have to in order to pick out any problems up ahead in the river. Think you'd care to be a riverboat pilot? Once we're back in a wide, clear stretch of river, I could let you handle the wheel for a while if you'd like."

Preacher laughed and shook his head.

"You'd be temptin' fate if you let me do it," he told the captain. "No need for that."

"Well, if you change your mind, let me know. There's no other feeling like it."

Preacher didn't doubt that, but there was no feeling like waking up on a crisp, clear, high country morning, either, and he wasn't going to trade that permanently for anything.

The terrain through which the river passed had gotten a bit more rugged with limestone ledges cropping out here and there along the wooded banks. Away from the stream, the countryside was still mostly grassy flatlands. Warner steered the boat to a spot between two of those ledges. Crewmen leaped ashore to tie it up.

Warner went down to the engine room to supervise the repairs while Preacher and Russell stopped on the passenger deck. The other members of the party had emerged from their cabins when the boat began to put in to shore. Now they gathered around curiously.

As the nominal leader of the group, Senator Allingham asked, "Why have we stopped, Simon? I hope there's nothing seriously wrong."

"Captain Warner assures me that it's just a minor malfunction of the engine, like they had to deal with back in St. Louis," Russell explained.

"Will we be stopped here for long?" Stahlmaske asked.

"I don't really know. Would you like for me to find out?"

"Very much so," the count replied. "If we're going to be here for a while, I'd like to take our horses off the barge and go for a ride."

Preacher didn't think that was a very good idea. When Russell glanced at him, he frowned to show his disapproval.

On the other hand, he couldn't really blame Stahlmaske for feeling that way. He had been stuck on this riverboat for several days, too, and was getting a little restless himself. He knew Horse would relish the opportunity to stretch his legs a little.

The problem was that it would be more difficult

to protect the travelers if they were away from the riverboat.

"Well, I don't know if we'll be here long enough for that," Russell said. "I doubt it."

"Find out," the count snapped. "I came on this journey to see your country and report my impressions back to King Friedrich Wilhelm, not to be stuck in a cabin all day or stand at the railing watching an endless current of muddy water flow past."

He had a point, Preacher thought. And Russell knew that Stahlmaske was too stubborn to back down, so he nodded and said, "I'll go talk to the captain."

Preacher didn't want to pay a visit to the smoky, stinking engine room, so he stayed where he was instead of accompanying his old friend down to the lower deck. He approached the count and asked, "How's the arm?"

The two of them had been keeping a wary distance from each other since the duel. Stahlmaske flexed his arm, nodded, and said, "Fine, of course. It was a mere scratch, nothing more."

Preacher knew the wound had been more serious than that, judging by the amount of blood that had soaked into the count's shirtsleeve. But he didn't mention that, just nodded and said, "I'm glad to hear it."

"Perhaps if we leave the boat for the afternoon we can do a bit of hunting, *nicht wahr*? You American frontiersmen are all skilled hunters, eh, like your Daniel Boone?"

"Well, I never met ol' Dan'l, just heard stories

about him, but it's true that those of us who make our livin' by trappin' are pretty good hunters. We have to be, otherwise we'd be liable to starve to death."

"And is there game in abundance in this area where we find ourselves?"

"Plenty," Preacher replied with a nod. "Mostly deer and antelope."

"What about the bison?" Roderick asked with his usual eagerness. "We've heard that there are huge herds of the beasts covering half the continent."

Preacher chuckled.

"There are plenty of buffalo, but not quite that many. Most of 'em are farther west, but I reckon you might run across some in these parts. We're bound to see a few herds before we get to the Yellowstone."

"I would like to take part in a buffalo hunt," the count declared. "I think that would be very exciting."

"That depends. Get a stampede started and it can be pretty dangerous, too."

"Do you think danger frightens me, Preacher?"

"No," the mountain man said. "I don't reckon it does."

But maybe it ought to, Preacher added silently. A man who felt no fear was usually a fool and often wound up dead because of it.

Sarah Allingham spoke up, saying, "I'd like to go riding, too."

"Nonsense," her mother said immediately.

"I've ridden horses in Washington, Mother, and you know it."

"I thought that was a bad idea, too," Margaret said. "And this wilderness is certainly not Washington. It wouldn't be safe."

"It will be if Preacher comes along," Sarah insisted. "That's what he's here for, isn't it, to keep us all safe?"

Preacher's eyes narrowed. He'd thought he was coming along on this journey to fight Indians or river pirates, not to play nursemaid to a bunch of spoiled pilgrims. Obviously, though, that was how some of them regarded him. It was enough to make him want to take Dog and Horse and clear out right now.

But he couldn't do that without breaking his promise to Simon Russell. Being true to his word, though, didn't mean he had to go along with every crazy notion these folks came up with.

"I reckon the ladies better stay here on the boat," he said in a hard, flat tone that brooked no arguments. "If any of you gents want to ride out a ways and maybe hunt a little, I suppose we could use some fresh meat. We won't be gettin' very far from the river, though, and you'll all have to do like I tell you."

"I'm agreeable with that," Allingham said.

Stahlmaske nodded curtly and said, "I will defer to your experience in these matters, Preacher . . . within reason. But do not forget, I am a soldier and a hunter myself."

"I'll keep that in mind," Preacher said. "And all this depends on whether or not we're actually gonna be here long enough to go to the trouble."

"Perhaps Herr Russell will return soon and let us know."

It was a few more minutes before Russell returned from the engine room. During that time, Roderick, Heinrich, and Hobart talked excitedly about riding out away from the river and hunting. At least, that's what Preacher thought they were talking about, judging by the occasional English words they used. Most of the conversation was in German.

He went over to Gerhard and asked the count's uncle, "Are you comin' with us, Herr Stahlmaske?"

Gerhard gave him an acerbic look through the spectacles that perched on his nose.

"I most certainly am not. My days of galloping about the countryside and shooting at wild animals are long since over, thank God."

"I hope mine never are," Preacher said honestly. "The day I can't go lookin' for some sort of excitement is the day they can lower me in the ground."

Russell came up the stairs from the lower deck and rejoined the group.

"Captain Warner says we're going to be here for a couple of hours, at least, while his crew works on the engine," he told them. "So if you want to take a short ride away from the river, Count, I suppose that'll be all right."

"Excellent. I have hunting rifles and fowling pieces for everyone. I'll have my servants bring them out, then they can prepare the horses for riding."

Preacher planned to put his own saddle on Horse. He wouldn't ask any man to do a chore like that for him. That would have rubbed him the wrong way. Clearly the count had a different opinion of the matter.

"How many of us are going?" Stahlmaske went on. "You, Senator, and you, Herr Russell?"

Allingham nodded and said, "I wouldn't miss it."

"And I reckon I'd better come along, too," Russell said. Preacher figured he didn't want to let his charges out of his sight.

"Seven of us, then," Stahlmaske said with a nod as he looked around at his brother, the Ritter twins, and Preacher. "A large enough party to handle any sort of trouble we might run into, eh?"

Preacher hoped he was right about that.

CHAPTER 16

Horse was ready to get out and run. Preacher could tell that from the way the big stallion acted as he saddled up. Some of the *Sentinel*'s crew pulled the barge right up against the bank, and once the gate was lowered the horses had no trouble jumping to shore, where Gunther, Ludwig, and Egon were waiting to get them ready to ride.

Roderick emerged from his cabin wearing buckskin trousers, a fringed buckskin jacket, and a broad-brimmed gray felt hat that was too large for his head. Preacher looked away so the young man wouldn't see his grin. Somebody back in St. Louis had seen Roderick coming, that was for sure.

Heinrich and Hobart wore buckskins, too, although like Roderick's outfit they were too fancy to be the real thing. The twins' hats fit a little better, though.

Senator Allingham and the count wore sturdy clothes, nothing gaudy like the younger men. And Preacher and Russell just wore their usual garb.

When Ludwig and Egon brought out the rifles, Preacher wasn't surprised to see that they were on the fancy side, too, with lots of polished wood and gleaming brass fittings. What the weapons looked like didn't matter all that much as long as they shot straight and true. Preacher was willing to bet these rifles were pretty accurate. The count wouldn't settle for anything less.

Stahlmaske turned to Preacher and asked, "Would you like to try one of these?" He held out a rifle with an elaborate design carved into the stock and a brass butt plate.

"No, thanks, I'll just shoot my own if I see anything that needs shootin'," Preacher said. He hefted his long-barreled flintlock with its plain, unadorned stock that showed the signs of long use. Its barrel didn't shine much in the sun, either.

That rifle had saved Preacher's life more times than he could possibly remember.

"Suit yourself," Stahlmaske said with a shrug.

As the men swung up into their saddles, Captain Warner came out onto the deck from the engine room.

"I'll try to have this boat ready to go by the time you gentlemen get back," he told them. "Want me to blow the whistle when we're done, so you'll know?"

"That's a good idea," Russell said. "As soon as we hear it we'll head back, if we haven't already."

He and Preacher lifted hands in farewell, as did Senator Allingham. The count couldn't be bothered with that, and the three younger men were still chattering with excitement as they urged their mounts into motion.

Roderick and the twins bounced awkwardly in their saddles, Preacher noted with some wry amusement. It was obvious they weren't experienced riders. If they had to travel very far on horseback, they would be sore as hell the next day. Luckily for them, they probably wouldn't have to.

The count, on the other hand, seemed born to the saddle. Preacher figured he had done a considerable amount of riding as a military man. Allingham was comfortable on horseback, too, which surprised Preacher.

"You sit that saddle like you've done some ridin' before, Senator," Preacher commented as the group headed southwest away from the river.

"I was born and raised on a farm," Allingham replied. "I could ride our old horse almost before I could walk." He chuckled. "Although I was considerably older than that before I ever knew what a saddle was."

"I was a farm boy, too," Preacher said. "Never really took to it, though. I didn't mind the work, but there were just too many other places I wanted to go and things I wanted to see. I reckon that's why as soon as I got old enough, I headed for the tall and uncut."

"There were times I was tempted to do that as well."

"How in the world did a Vermont farm boy wind up bein' a senator?"

"Hard work, I suppose, but first and foremost was my mother's insistence that I have a proper education. Her father had been a schoolmaster, so she knew quite a bit. After she had taught me as much as she could, she made arrangements for me to attend school in the village near where we lived. My father didn't like that very much—he was a simple man and didn't see the need of a bunch of book learning, as he called it, plus he didn't want to lose my help on the farm—but he was willing to go along with it since that was what my mother wanted. I wound up working for one of the merchants in town and he took a liking to me and helped me go to Harvard and study law. That was where my political career really began, I suppose."

Preacher had a feeling that was a story Allingham had told many times before, probably in speeches, but it had the ring of truth to it anyway. Even though they had wound up in very different places in life, he and Allingham had started out sort of alike. Neither would have been happy following the other's path, but they had those origins in common, anyway.

The liking he felt for the senator made him regret that much more the secret he knew. Either the man's wife or daughter was carrying on with Count Stahlmaske, and Preacher knew Allingham would be upset no matter which one it was.

Gretchen Ritter probably wouldn't be happy about it, either, he thought . . . although given the coolness in her tone when she had spoken to him about the count, it might not bother her that much that her fiancé was seeing another woman. As long as the affair didn't interfere with their upcoming marriage, she might not really care.

All that was too murky for a straightforward man like Preacher to muddle through. He put it out of his mind and concentrated on their surroundings. The last thing they needed to do was to blunder into some Pawnee hunting party. The count might lose his head and try to bag himself an Indian. That would be a disaster.

When they had ridden about a mile from the river, Roderick suddenly stood up in his stirrups, pointed, and exclaimed, "Look! Over there!"

Preacher had already seen the little herd of antelope, about a dozen strong. And the animals had heard Roderick's shout, as was demonstrated by the way their heads popped up from their grazing. Before the riders could do anything except rein in and reach for their rifles, the antelope were off like a shot, running swiftly and gracefully across the prairie.

Roderick started to raise his rifle anyway, but his brother spoke sharply to him in German. Roderick lowered the weapon and looked sheepish.

"I'm sorry, Albert," he said. "I know I should not have alarmed them that way. I was just so excited."

"When you are hunting, excitement is your enemy," Stahlmaske told him. "You must remain in control of your emotions at all times. And never waste powder and shot, as you were about to. You stood no chance of hitting any of those animals."

"Yes, Albert, I know."

"See that you remember," the count said as he heeled his horse into motion again.

Everything Stahlmaske had said was right, mused Preacher, but he hadn't had to chew the youngster out that way. Somebody could be right and still be a pure-D jackass about it. Stahlmaske seemed to be good at that.

Preacher moved Horse over alongside Roderick's mount and said quietly, "I was about to point out those antelope. But don't worry about it, because there'll be some more along after a while. Or something else. There's no shortage of game out here. If nothin' else, we'll scare up some prairie chickens."

Stahlmaske had forged on ahead about twenty yards. Keeping his voice low, Roderick said, "I don't think Albert will be content to shoot chickens. He wants trophies."

"Trophies ain't good for anything except takin' up space on the wall. You can't eat 'em or do anything else with 'em. You just remember that, Roderick."

The young man smiled and nodded.

"I'll try to."

"I'd better not let your brother get too far ahead. Wouldn't want him to run into trouble."

Although it might serve him right, Preacher thought as he urged Horse to a faster pace so he could catch up to the count.

Just in the past few minutes as he was talking to Roderick, the mountain man had gotten a funny feeling, a little prickling on the back of his neck that served as a warning. Normally, Preacher would have thought that it meant they were being watched, but as he scanned the countryside around them, he didn't see a thing out of the ordinary.

Despite that, he wasn't going to disregard his instincts. The count might not like it, but Preacher decided they weren't going to get much farther away from the *Sentinel* before turning back.

Claude Binnion was hunkered next to a fire in the river pirates' camp next to the river, roasting a rabbit skewered on a stick, when the swift rataplan of approaching hoofbeats made him look up. Big Wedge was on the other side of the fire, watching hungrily as the rabbit's carcass sizzled and popped. A dozen other men were scattered around the camp, some playing cards, some sleeping, some cleaning weapons. The gang's six canoes were pulled up on the shore nearby.

The sound of the horse finally penetrated Wedge's hunger. He frowned and said in his dull-witted fashion, "Hey, Claude, somebody's comin'."

"I hear him," Binnion said. "That'll be Hackney, more than likely. Here, take this rabbit."

He handed the stick to Wedge and stood up. His hand went to one of the pistols tucked in the waistband of his trousers. Except for the clearing where they were, the trees and brush were thick along this stretch of river, which was the reason he had picked this spot for the gang's camp. He couldn't see the rider just yet. He didn't think the sound meant trouble, but he would be ready to pull that gun and shoot if he needed to.

The hoofbeats slowed down as the rider entered the trees and weaved through the growth. When he came out into the clearing at the river's edge, Binnion relaxed. Just as he had thought, the newcomer was Hackney, a member of the gang who stayed on shore most of the time and took care of their horses.

The pirates did most of their traveling by water, of course, plying the Big Muddy in their canoes. But they had half a dozen animals if they needed them for scouting or packing purposes. That was what Hackney had been doing today, ranging back downriver to check on the progress of the *Sentinel*.

"What did you find, Jed?" Binnion asked as Hackney dismounted. "Is that boat still headed in this direction?"

"Nope," Hackney replied. He was a small, rat-faced man who looked like he'd been born to be a petty criminal—and he hadn't failed in that destiny, either. "The boat's put in to shore."

Binnion frowned.

"It's a long time until dark. No reason for Warner to be stopping already."

"I think they must be havin' engine trouble. That's not why I got back here in such a hurry, though, Claude. A bunch of the passengers rode out on those horses they've been pullin' behind 'em on that barge."

Binnion felt his heart start to beat a little faster.

He asked, "When you say a bunch, how many do you mean, exactly?"

"I counted seven men, all of them armed. Looked like they were goin' huntin. Some of 'em were dressed pretty fancy."

"Did they see you?"

"No, I stayed well out of sight just like you told me to," Hackney said.

Wedge said, "That means seven men who ain't there to put up a fight and defend the boat." He might be simpleminded, but he had a way of cutting right to the heart of the matter at times.

"Yeah," Binnion mused as he rubbed his chin in thought.

Hackney said, "I thought this might be a good chance for us to jump the ones who are left."

"We don't have to wait until they get to Cougar Bluffs for us to take 'em, Claude," Wedge urged. In his excitement he waved the rabbit carcass on the stick. "And you said they had women with 'em!"

"Yeah, but they'll have guards for the fur company's money among the crew, too," Binnion said. "I don't know who those passengers are, but we don't know that they will put up much of a fight. I'd rather wait until we can get onboard before they know what's going on."

He saw the eagerness on the faces of the men who had gathered around the fire. They wanted that loot, and they wanted the women. But in his time as an outlaw, Binnion had learned not to act impulsively. He made a plan and stuck to it, and so far that had worked pretty well.

"We'll hit the boat at Cougar Bluffs, like we said," he told them, and his voice was flat and hard enough that they knew he didn't want any argument. He softened it a little to encourage them as he went on, "And when we do, boys, it'll be the biggest payoff yet. I can feel it in my bones."

CHAPTER 17

Count Stahlmaske was still in a bad mood because Roderick had ruined their chances of shooting some of the antelope. Preacher knew the nobleman was going to complain when he had to turn back to the river before much longer.

Luck was with them, however. They had only gone another quarter of a mile after spooking the antelope before they topped a small rise and saw a number of massive, shaggy animals spread out across a broad, shallow valley.

Preacher estimated there were about five hundred buffalo in the herd, which meant it was a small one indeed. Some of the vast herds farther west had a million or more of the creatures in them. In the past he had watched from hilltops while buffalo as far as the eye could see streamed past him like a brown river, the herd moving all day without ever coming to an end.

Stahlmaske jerked his horse to a halt and said, "Bison!"

"Yep," Preacher agreed. "I reckon that's their real name, at least accordin' to what my friend Audie tells me, but everybody I know calls 'em buffalo."

"Whatever they're called, they're magnificent."

The count was whispering, so Preacher told him, "You don't have to worry about them hearin' you. Buffalo don't hear all that well, and their eyesight is even worse. Mainly you have to worry about 'em catchin' your scent, but the wind's blowin' toward us right now. You could almost walk right up to 'em if you wanted to."

"I don't want to walk up to them." Stahlmaske lifted his rifle. "I want to shoot one of them."

"We're close enough. We'll get down from the horses and you can take good aim—"

"Shooting them from this distance doesn't seem very sporting. They won't even know who is killing them. How do the Indians do it? I'm told they're the greatest buffalo hunters of all."

Preacher shook his head.

"That's not the same thing. Indians hunt mostly with bows and arrows, so they have to get a lot closer. They'll start a herd runnin' and then get right in amongst 'em on their ponies—"

"Then that's what I want to do," the count interrupted. Without giving Preacher a chance to tell him what a damn fool notion that was, he kicked his horse in the flanks and sent the animal lunging forward at a gallop.

"Son of a—" Preacher grated before he bit back

the rest of the curse and turned in the saddle to shout at Russell, "Simon, keep the rest of 'em here!"

Then he and Horse raced after the count.

Stahlmaske began shouting and waving his rifle in the air as he rode. Buffalo might not have the keenest ears in the world, but even they could hear this lunatic charging toward them, Preacher thought. Sure enough, they began to move, first in an ungainly trot, then a run that still looked a little awkward but covered the ground amazingly fast.

They couldn't outrun Stahlmaske's horse, though. It was a fine, strong animal, and it quickly began to catch up with the buffalo in the rear of the herd. Dust boiled up from the hooves churning across the prairie and obscured the figure on horseback.

As fast as the count's horse was, Preacher's stallion was faster. Horse stretched his legs and seemed to fly over the ground. Clouds of dust rolled around him, too. Preacher wanted to draw even with Stahlmaske's mount before they were among the running buffalo. He knew that if the count's horse stumbled and went down in the stampede, the buffalo would crush him into something that didn't even resemble a human being.

The rumble of hooves filled the air so that Preacher couldn't hear anything. Dust stung his eyes and clogged his mouth and nose. Stahlmaske was just ahead of him now. A few more strides and Preacher would be even with him.

The count lifted his rifle to his shoulder and fired into the charging brown mass beside him. It was a good shot, because the buffalo stumbled. Preacher knew the animal was hit. A second later the buffalo's front legs collapsed and it went down, rolling toward Stahlmaske's horse.

The horse screamed in fear as the dying buffalo tangled in its legs. Preacher was close enough now to reach over and grab the count's arm.

"Kick your feet loose!" he bellowed at Stahlmaske.

The Prussian must have realized how much danger he was in. He kicked out of the stirrups just as his horse tumbled out from under him. If not for the incredible strength of Preacher's grip, Stahlmaske would have fallen, too. Preacher jerked the man toward him, and Stahlmaske grabbed desperately at Horse's saddle.

He was able to hang on for the couple of heartbeats that Preacher needed to pull away from the stampeding buffalo. The mountain man let go as soon as they were clear, and Stahlmaske crashed to the ground to roll over twice. Then he lay there, evidently stunned, as the buffalo herd moved on up the valley. They would stop in a few minutes, Preacher knew, and return to grazing, their momentary panic quickly forgotten.

He heard horses coming and turned to see the whole group galloping toward him and the count. Roderick was in the lead, barely staying in the saddle as he called, "Albert! Albert, *mein Gott*! Are you all right?"

Coughing from the dust he had swallowed and

gasping for breath, Stahlmaske pushed himself into a sitting position and glared at Preacher, who sat nearby on Horse.

"You could have broken my neck, dropping me on the ground like that!"

"You'd have broken a lot more than your neck if you'd fallen in the middle of those buffs," Preacher shot back at him.

"My horse—" The count stopped with a sharply indrawn breath as he turned his head to look at the gruesome remains of his horse.

"Yeah, that's what you would've looked like," Preacher said grimly. "So maybe you better be grateful the only thing that happened is you got dropped on your rear end."

The others rode up and reined in. Roderick and the Ritter twins dismounted with awkward haste and hurried over to Stahlmaske. The count waved them away in irritation and snapped, "Get away from me. I'm all right."

"Let me help you up," Roderick offered, but his brother jerked his arm away.

Russell and Allingham moved their horses over beside Preacher. The senator said quietly, "That was the most amazing thing I've ever seen, Preacher. I thought beyond a shadow of a doubt that the count was doomed."

"He came mighty damn close," Preacher agreed. "Roderick, you and your brother will have to ride double. We're goin' back to the riverboat."

"Nonsense," Stahlmaske said as he got to his feet.

"Roderick, you give me your horse and ride with Heinrich or Hobart. What happened to my rifle?" He looked down at his clothes, stared at them in horror for a second, and then exploded in what had to be German curses. He sputtered, "I . . . I'm covered in . . . in . . ."

"You sure are," Preacher drawled, and he figured he probably enjoyed that a little more than he should have.

Stahlmaske was still fuming—and reeking of buffalo droppings—by the time they got back to the *Sentinel.* Gunther came out to meet them. The count dismounted and shoved the reins of Roderick's horse into Gunther's hand. He stalked past the servant and went across the board that had been laid from the deck to the shore.

Gretchen Ritter, Margaret Allingham, and Sarah were at the railing on the passenger deck with Captain Warner. The captain called to the group, "I was just about to blow the whistle to let you know we're ready to go again. Looks like you ran into some trouble."

Ludwig and Egon hurried to take charge of the horses as the others swung down. Preacher shook his head to tell them that he would take care of Horse himself. He told Warner, "The count's a mite shaken up but not really hurt."

Stahlmaske probably heard that as he climbed

the stairs to the second deck, but Preacher didn't care.

Gretchen started toward the stairs to meet Stahl-maske, but Margaret put a hand on her arm to stop her.

"You might want to leave him alone right now, my dear," the senator's wife said. "A man whose pride and dignity have been wounded doesn't want to be around the woman he's going to marry until he's had a chance to clean up a little."

Gretchen nodded and said, "*Danke.* I think you are right, Mrs. Allingham."

"I usually am when it comes to men," Margaret said.

Preacher overheard that conversation and wondered again if it had been Margaret he had seen sneaking to the count's cabin a few nights earlier. That late-night visit had not been repeated as far as he knew, but he couldn't be certain that Stahlmaske and his lover hadn't gotten together again.

Preacher unsaddled Horse and led the stallion back onto the barge. Horse's speed was as responsible as anything else for saving the count's life today.

As Preacher stepped ashore after tending to Horse, Allingham approached him and said, "Come up to the salon with me, Preacher. I'd like to buy you a drink."

Allingham wasn't actually buying anything—the American Fur Company was furnishing everything on this trip—but Preacher supposed it was the gesture that counted. He and the senator went aboard the riverboat, climbed to the second deck, and went into the salon where they joined Simon Russell and Captain Warner.

"Simon's been telling me about what happened, Preacher," Warner said. "Good Lord, I never heard of such a thing. Talk about snatching somebody from the jaws of death!"

"Hooves of death is more like it," Preacher said with a wry smile.

"It would have been an ugly way to die, that's for sure," Russell said.

"And quite possibly the ruination of my career," Allingham added. "The president is counting on me to see to it that Count Stahlmaske enjoys his visit to our country and returns to Washington safely. If anything were to happen to him . . ."

Allingham shook his head and didn't complete the sentence, but he didn't have to. His meaning was clear.

"Well, I think this deserves a drink," Warner said, "and then I need to get back up to the pilot house. We've got several hours of daylight left, so we can put some more miles behind us." He paused, then added, "I'd really like to get past Cougar Bluffs tomorrow."

CHAPTER 18

Preacher was familiar with the stretch of the river known as Cougar Bluffs. He had paddled through there many times in a canoe, bound up or down the Big Muddy. It was about half a mile long, although it seemed longer than that because the stream made several sharp bends as it narrowed down and ran between steep limestone bluffs that rose about fifty feet.

When they were within a few miles of the bluffs the next day after the ill-fated and almost disastrous buffalo hunt, Preacher climbed to the pilot house and said to Captain Warner, "You reckon you could put in to shore for a few minutes?"

The captain frowned in surprise.

"Why would we do that?" he asked. "The engine's running fine today."

"I know that," Preacher said, although in truth all he could go by was the way the engine sounded. The dials and gauges connected to the engine room and mounted on the wall of the pilot house didn't mean anything to him. "I'm gonna take Horse and Dog and do a little scoutin'."

"You think there might be trouble up ahead at the bluffs," Warner guessed.

Preacher shrugged.

"River pirates been known to hang around there before. It's a good place for an ambush."

"That's true. Because of the way the river winds around, you can't take it very fast, and there are plenty of places to hide, too." Warner gave a decisive nod and used the speaking tube to call down to the engine room and order a slowdown. He spun the wheel and turned the *Sentinel* toward the shore.

By the time Preacher reached the passenger deck, Simon Russell had come out of the salon where he'd been with the others in the party. With a worried frown on his face, he asked, "Is something wrong, Preacher?"

"I don't know," the mountain man replied. "I had a feelin' yesterday that somebody might be keepin' an eye on us, and this boat'll be a pretty temptin' target when we go past Cougar Bluffs. Thought it might be a good idea to take a look around on horseback before we get there."

Count Stahlmaske had followed Russell out of the salon and arrived in time to hear Preacher's answer. He nodded and said, "A reconnoitering expedition. An excellent idea. I'll join you."

"Don't recollect askin' for company," Preacher said flatly.

Stahlmaske returned the cool stare that the mountain man gave him. He said, "You forget that

I am a military man, Herr Preacher. I have tactical experience."

"You never fought river pirates."

"I've fought the French and the Austrians."

Preacher's grunt told plainly how unimpressed he was by that claim. The count flushed angrily.

"I will follow your orders," he said, although Preacher could tell it cost him an effort to make such a promise.

"You were supposed to do what I told you yesterday, and instead you chased off after those buffalo and almost got yourself killed."

"I realize you saved my life," Stahlmaske said stiffly. "I owe you a debt of gratitude. I will pay it by allowing you to be in command of this scouting foray."

"That's mighty generous of you," Preacher said dryly. He could tell the count was getting even angrier, so he went on, "All right, you can come with me, as long as you do what I tell you. If you get yourself in trouble, though, don't expect me to yank you out of it."

"Agreed," Stahlmaske said with a brusque nod.

Russell asked, "Do you want me to come along, too?"

Preacher thought about it for a second, then said, "No, you better stay on board, Simon. If there's trouble, I'd like to know there's a good fightin' man here to take charge."

"Thanks, Preacher. I can do that."

Preacher hoped his old friend was right and that

time and city living hadn't softened Russell too much.

Once the riverboat was tied up, it didn't take long to get Horse and one of the other mounts off the barge and saddled up. The count, wearing dark clothes and a black, flat-crowned hat, brought two pistols and a rifle with him. As the two men swung up into their saddles, crew members untied the lines and jumped back aboard. Warner waved from the pilot house and called, "We'll pick you up on the other side of the bluffs."

Preacher waved in agreement and turned Horse away from the river. He and Stahlmaske rode along the shore with Dog ranging ahead of them.

"Tell me about this place," the count said. "Why is it called Cougar Bluffs?"

Preacher described that stretch of the river, then said, "Years ago, when fur trappers were first goin' upriver to the mountains, there was a cougar that would stand out on one of the bluffs and yowl at the men as they paddled past in their canoes. It was like he was sayin' howdy to 'em, or maybe he was mad because they were out there in the river and he couldn't get to 'em. Either way, fellas got used to seein' him there, and they started callin' the place Cougar Bluffs."

"Is that a true story, or just a legend?"

"True story," Preacher said. "I saw the varmint myself, a time or two when I was young. Then he stopped showin' up. Everybody figured he got old and died, or else some other critter got him. Whatever happened to him, the name stuck."

"I'm surprised none of you rough and ready mountain men shot him."

Preacher shook his head.

"Nobody would've done that, because it got to where folks regarded him as sort of a good luck charm. Fellas who live up in the high lonesome for a while, mostly by themselves, tend to get a mite superstitious."

"Superstitions are for the ignorant peasants," Stahlmaske said with his customary arrogance. He couldn't seem to contain it for very long.

"Maybe so, but like I said, when you get up in that high country you'll see some things you can't really explain any other way."

The count let out a disdainful snort. Preacher let the subject drop. He knew arguing with Stahlmaske would be a waste of breath.

He led the count about half a mile away from the river before turning north so they were riding roughly parallel to the course of the stream. He saw the bluffs rising in the distance. From here they were just gray-green humps, mottled because of the thick brush that grew in places on them.

"Do you really think river pirates may be waiting there?" Stahlmaske asked. He didn't sound worried about the possibility. If anything, he was hopeful that the *Sentinel* might be attacked. He was ready for some excitement again.

"It's the best place along here to lay an ambush," Preacher replied.

"Surely they know that the riverboat captains are aware of the danger."

"Probably," Preacher agreed with a shrug. "But there's no other way for the boats to go. It ain't like they can avoid that stretch."

"But they can be prepared for trouble."

"Pirates don't care. If they didn't want to fight, they wouldn't be pirates in the first place. I reckon killin' just comes natural to most of 'em."

"They sound like the sort of men who make good soldiers, those who are eager to impose their will on others."

"I ain't so sure about that," Preacher said slowly. "I ain't been a soldier since the Battle of New Orleans, back in fourteen, but it seems to me a good soldier's got to be willin' to take orders, too."

"These pirates don't follow the commands of their leader?"

"I suppose they do, as long as he's strong enough that they're more scared of him than they are of the folks they're fightin'."

Stahlmaske nodded and said, "Exactly. You're agreeing with me whether you know it or not, Preacher."

The mountain man just grunted. He couldn't help but recall what Gretchen had said about him and Stahlmaske being too much alike. It gave him the fantods to think that she might be right in some ways.

After a few moments of silence, the count asked, "What are we looking for?"

"If there's an ambush, likely the pirates will have some riflemen on at least one of the bluffs, maybe both," Preacher explained. "They'll try to pick off the cap'n in the pilot house or at least make him dive for cover so he won't be able to handle the wheel. The rest of the gang will be waitin' in canoes just around one of the bends where they can't be seen until the boat's almost right on top of 'em. They'll paddle out and jump aboard and try to wipe out any of the crew that puts up a fight. In every bunch there's nearly always a fella who can steer a boat and another who can run the engine. They'll take over, bring the boat to shore, and loot whatever they want off of it."

"They sound like barbarians."

"That's a pretty good description of 'em," Preacher agreed.

"Sooner or later they'll be wiped out. Civilization always triumphs over barbarism."

Preacher knew better than that. He figured it was the other way around. But a man like Stahlmaske could never understand that.

That was one way they were different, anyway, the mountain man thought with some degree of satisfaction.

After a few more minutes, Stahlmaske asked with a note of worry creeping into his voice, "These pirates . . . what will they do if they take over the boat and find women aboard?"

"You're just now thinkin' about that?"

"Answer the question," Stahlmaske snapped.

"They'll do just what you'd think they'd do," Preacher said. His voice took on a grim edge, too. "Most of 'em are just as bad as what you'd expect, and they ain't gonna treat the ladies gentle-like."

The count muttered something in German, then said, "Then we must hurry and make sure the boat is not steaming into a trap!"

"That's what we're here for," Preacher said. He lifted his head a little as he heard the distant wail of a steam whistle. "That's Cap'n Warner lettin' us know the *Sentinel*'s almost at the bluffs. I told him to signal me so I could tell where the boat is."

He turned Horse and started up a slope that led to the limestone outcroppings over the river. Trees and brush covered the way ahead. Preacher took his rifle from the sling that held it and rode with the weapon across his saddle, ready for use. Stahlmaske followed suit as he fell in alongside the mountain man.

They hadn't reached the bluff when Preacher saw a sudden puff of smoke from the trees. A second later he heard a rifle ball hum past his head.

"It's an ambush, all right!" he called to Stahlmaske as he kicked Horse into a run. "Come on!"

CHAPTER 19

Claude Binnion waited in the middle of the lead canoe, his hands wrapped tightly around the flint-lock rifle he held. Behind him was Big Wedge, the most powerful paddler in the gang. In the front of the canoe sat a man named Hiram Bracknell, also a strong paddler and a good shot with both rifle and pistol.

The other canoes bobbed on the river just behind the spot where Binnion's canoe floated. A few yards away, the rocky bluff jutted out into the Missouri, forming one of the sharp bends that the stream took as it passed through Cougar Bluffs. Because of that bend, Binnion couldn't see the approaching riverboat but he could sure hear it, both the rumbling engine and the splashing paddle wheel at the back of the vessel.

Binnion looked around at his men and grinned in anticipation. Some of them had been a little surly since the day before when he had vetoed the idea of attacking the riverboat while some of the male passengers were gone. Binnion had stuck stubbornly to his plan, though, and now they were all going to see that he had made the right decision.

He looked up at the bluff on the near side of the river. Two riflemen were posted up there, good marksmen who would pepper the pilot house with shots. A third man was on the far bluff, charged with the same task. If any of them got a clear shot at whoever was handling the wheel, Binnion had told them to go ahead and kill him. At the very least their shots would make the pilot dive for cover.

That wouldn't make the engine quit, of course, but with no one at the wheel the *Sentinel* would have to come to a halt. The river was too narrow here—no more than fifty yards across—and had too many bends to risk steaming on blindly. The boat would crash into the bluff on one side or the other unless it stopped.

As soon as the boat began to slow, the men waiting in the canoes would spring into action. Wedge and the other paddlers could drive the sleek, lightweight craft across the river's surface at a fast rate of speed. They would pull alongside the *Sentinel* before the crew could mount a defense and leap aboard to wipe them out.

Then would come the best part: gathering up the loot.

Which in this case included women.

Binnion's heart slugged heavily in his chest at the thought. It had been a while since he'd had a woman. He intended to claim the best-looking one for himself, and none of the others would dare to argue with him.

Anyway, they all knew they could have her when he was done with her. They would just have to be careful not to kill her. She would be worth money when Binnion got around to selling her. Any white woman was, out here on the frontier.

The boat's engine was loud enough now that he knew it would be only a matter of minutes, maybe even seconds, before it rounded the bend. He could even see the black smoke from its stacks rising above the bluff.

Binnion glanced back at Wedge and asked, "Ready?"

The big man grinned and nodded.

The *Sentinel*'s bow came into view, followed by the passenger deck and pilot house and the twin stacks.

From atop the bluffs, shots boomed, echoing back from the limestone cliffs. Binnion saw the figure in the pilot house disappear. The man was either hit or had dropped to the floor to get out of the line of fire. The paddle wheel began to slow down.

"Go!" Binnion shouted to Wedge and Bracknell. "Get us out there!"

Powerful muscles drove paddles into the water, and the canoe sprang forward. The others were right behind.

Shots banged from the riverboat's cargo deck.

The crew was ready to do battle, Binnion realized. They hadn't been taken by surprise after all. Somebody on board had suspected that they might be steaming into an ambush.

But it didn't make any difference. Everything in life carried risks. As far as Binnion was concerned, a man had never really lived until he had put his own life on the line and seized whatever he wanted.

Rifle balls plunked into the muddy water not far from the canoes, raising little splashes. The lightweight bark craft were moving so fast, though, that it was difficult to draw a bead on them. Binnion always launched his attacks at an angle, too, so the man in the middle in each boat who wasn't paddling had an unobstructed line of fire at the defenders.

Binnion spotted a man kneeling behind one of the crates on the cargo deck. He lifted his rifle to his shoulder, smoothly earing back the hammer as he did so. He settled his sights on the little bit of the man's head he could see and pressed the trigger. The rifle boomed and kicked back against his shoulder.

When the smoke from the exploding powder cleared a second later, Binnion saw the man sprawled on the deck next to the crate, his head a gory mess where the heavy lead ball had blown away a good chunk of it. He started reloading as more shots came from the other canoes.

By the time Binnion had his rifle ready to fire again, Wedge and Bracknell expertly brought the canoe alongside the riverboat. With the ease of long experience, Binnion stood up and leaped from the canoe onto the *Sentinel*'s deck. Wedge was right behind him, wielding his favorite weapon, a double-bitted ax. The big man handled the ax as easily as anyone else would a tomahawk.

Blood and slaughter, Binnion thought as his lips drew back from his teeth in a grimace. Two of his favorite things in the world. The only things he liked better were money and women.

And soon he would have those prizes as well.

Preacher didn't know how many riflemen were hidden in the trees on top of the bluff. If there was just one, the varmint would have to reload before he could fire again.

Unless, of course, he had a second rifle. Or some pistols.

Preacher knew he'd just have to risk that. Besides, with Horse running at top speed, it wouldn't take long to cover the ground between Preacher and the enemy.

Count Stahlmaske pushed his mount into a hard gallop, too, but the valiant animal couldn't keep up with Horse. Neither could Dog. But all of them headed for the bluff overlooking the river as fast as they could.

Over the thundering hoofbeats, Preacher heard more shots. That meant the rest of the river pirates were attacking the *Sentinel*. He hoped the folks on the boat could hold out long enough for him to give them a hand.

As he reached the trees, a rifle roared again somewhere close by. This time the ball came close enough that he felt the heat of its breath on his cheek as it went by.

He had the ambusher spotted now, though, and as he dived from the saddle with his rifle in one hand he jerked the tomahawk from behind his belt with the other. He rolled over as he landed and came up throwing at the man who crouched next to a limestone boulder, feverishly trying to reload.

Preacher's aim was true. With a *thunk!*, the tomahawk's blade struck the pirate in the center of the forehead, splitting his skull like a melon and cleaving into his brain. He dropped his rifle and staggered backward, pretty much dead on his feet already, just a creature of spasming nerves and muscles.

He disappeared, plummeting off the edge of the bluff without even a scream.

Preacher ran toward the river with his rifle, his gaze darting among the trees and brush as he searched for more of the pirates. He didn't see any on this side of the river, but as he reached the edge of the bluff and looked across the stream, he spotted more powder smoke on the opposite side.

He wasn't surprised to see that the pirates had put marksmen on the other side of the river as well. He saw a rifle flash over there, then lifted his own weapon and fired at the spot.

The brush thrashed for a second, then a man appeared clutching his chest with his left hand. He had a pistol in his right hand, and as he stumbled forward he tried to raise the gun and fire. The range was really too far for a handgun, but the pirate must have realized that Preacher had mortally wounded him and was just trying for one last shot before he died.

He didn't make it. He went off the edge of the bluff, too, and as he fell the gun in his hand discharged harmlessly into the air. This man still had a scream left in him as he fell the fifty feet to the river's surface. The big splash when he hit the water swallowed his dying shriek.

Preacher glanced down at the river. He couldn't see Captain Warner in the pilot house, and the big paddle wheel had come to a stop with water dripping from the blades that weren't submerged in the river. Canoes full of pirates swarmed on the river on the far side of the boat. Men leaped from the smaller craft onto the cargo deck. Guns blasted and shouted curses filled the air.

A rifle went off to Preacher's left. When he looked in that direction he saw the count standing there with gray smoke curling from the barrel of his weapon. Across the river, another body rolled out of the brush. This man didn't fall off the bluff. He died before he could get there, lying on his back with his arms flung out to the side.

"He was drawing a bead on you," Stahlmaske said.

Preacher nodded and said, "I'm obliged to you. That was a good shot."

"It would appear that we are even now," Stahlmaske said coolly.

Preacher wasn't going to argue the point, but the situations weren't exactly the same, he thought. The count might well have saved his life, but they couldn't be completely certain of that. The pirate might have missed.

And Preacher hadn't been engaged in doing something incredibly stupid at the time, either.

He shoved that out of his mind and looked down at the riverboat as he reloaded. The battle continued on board the *Sentinel.* Several of the pirates had made it onto the riverboat, but a couple of them lay sprawled on the deck, cut down by pistol fire from the crew.

The crewmen were pinned down at the moment, though, by rifle fire coming from the pirates still in the canoes. Warner's men had to stay low behind the crates of supplies and couldn't put up much of a fight anymore.

Simon Russell fired two pistols from the passenger deck, then had to duck back as rifle and pistol balls swarmed around him.

"Mein Gott!" the count exclaimed. "Is that my brother?"

It was Roderick, all right. He had come out onto the passenger deck and had a pistol in his hand. He seemed to be struggling to load it.

"Does he know how to use a gun?" Preacher asked grimly.

"Not well," Stahlmaske said. "He should be somewhere safe."

"If those pirates take over the boat, there won't be nowhere safe down there." Something else caught

Preacher's eye, and he stiffened as he saw several of the pirates, led by a brown-bearded giant waving an ax around almost like it was a toy, charge toward the stairs leading up to the passenger deck.

If those murderous bastards reached the boat's second level, there was no telling how much bloody havoc they might wreak.

Preacher muttered, "Oh, hell," and shoved his empty rifle into the hands of the startled Count Stahlmaske. He took off his powder horn and handed it to the nobleman as well. "Hang on to these for me, would you?"

He pulled his pistols from his belt, dropped them on the ground, and turned toward the edge of the bluff. He leaped off, his hat flying into the air, and plunged toward the river straight as an arrow.

CHAPTER 20

The daring leap wasn't as foolhardy as it might have appeared. In a lot of places, jumping into the Missouri River from that height would mean a pair of broken legs, at the very least.

But since the river narrowed considerably as it passed through Cougar Bluffs, that meant it deepened as well. Preacher knew that and knew there was enough water for his dive. His feet hit the river and he went deep under the surface, all the way to the bottom, in fact. He kicked against it and shot back up.

He had grabbed a big breath as he fell, but as his head broke back out into the open he was glad to haul in some more air. He started swimming toward the *Sentinel* with strong strokes. The riverboat wasn't far away, and it didn't take Preacher long to reach it.

With water streaming from his buckskins he pulled himself onto the cargo deck and looked toward the stairs. Gunther had appeared from somewhere and met the charge of the pirates. Like two bulls, he and the huge cutthroat with the ax had locked horns, only in this case they were struggling over the blood-smeared weapon, straining and heaving like a couple of primitive titans. Their swaying forms blocked the narrow stairs halfway up to the passenger deck.

Preacher hit the pirates from behind, striking like a whirlwind. He drove his knife deep into the back of one man, ripped the blade free, and flung the corpse to the side. He kicked another man off the boat, slashed the knife across the throat of yet another so that hot blood fountained redly into the air.

The embattled crewmen, inspired by Preacher's leap from the bluff and his furious attack on the pirates, charged from their hiding places and joined in the fray. In close quarters like this, it was mostly knives and fists and clubs.

The knot of men fighting for their lives surged back and forth across the deck at the foot of the stairs. Above them, Gunther and the big pirate with the ax continued their desperate struggle as well.

Preacher broke free of the melee and started up the stairs just as the big pirate finally succeeded in wrenching his ax back away from Gunther. The blade flashed in the sun as the ax rose and fell twice.

Gunther sagged back on the stairs, a crimson flood springing from the hideous wounds the blows from the weapon had opened on the side of his neck. He pawed weakly at the pirate but couldn't stop him as the man bounded over him and headed for the passenger deck.

Preacher saw there was nothing he could do for Gunther. The big Prussian was going to bleed to death in a matter of moments. The stairs were already awash with gore around him.

Gunther looked up and met Preacher's eyes for a second, and the mountain man realized there was something he could do for him after all. He reached down and squeezed Gunther's shoulder as the light went out of the servant's eyes.

Then Preacher raced on up the stairs after the killer with the ax.

As he reached the passenger deck, he saw that the pirate had set his sights on Roderick Stahlmaske. Roaring, the man held the ax above his head and thundered toward Roderick, who was still fumbling with his pistol.

Preacher had lost his knife in the battle at the bottom of the stairs, and his tomahawk was still lodged in the skull of the man he had killed on top of the bluff. So he had only his bare hands as he went after the man with the ax.

Suddenly Roderick lifted the pistol with both hands and pulled back the hammer. He aimed it at the charging giant and pulled the trigger. The pistol roared as smoke and flame spouted from its muzzle.

Preacher didn't know if Roderick had tried to aim or had just fired blind, but either way luck was with him. The ball struck the pirate in the right thigh and knocked that leg out from under him.

He fell and hit the deck so hard that the impact jolted the ax out of his hands.

Preacher lunged after the ax as it slid across the deck. He scooped it up and whirled, figuring to use the weapon against its former owner.

The pirate was already back on his feet, though, hobbling toward the edge of the deck as fast as his wounded leg would take him. All the fight had gone out of him. He vaulted over the railing and dropped to the cargo deck.

The injured leg folded up underneath him again when he landed, but this time he just rolled off the boat and disappeared into the river. Preacher didn't know what was going to happen to the pirate—he hoped the son of a bitch either bled to death or drowned—but he didn't feel like going after him.

"Are you all right?" he asked Roderick, who was pale and shaking.

"J-ja, I think so," the young man answered. "That . . . that man . . . he was a behemoth!"

"I reckon," Preacher agreed.

Roderick stared at the bloody ax in Preacher's hand.

"He was going to chop me up into small pieces!"

"More than likely. You better reload that gun if you can."

Roderick swallowed and bobbed his head up and down.

"Yes, I . . . I think I'm getting the hang of it now!"

Preacher went over to the railing and looked down to see that the surviving pirates were fleeing.

They must have encountered a lot more resistance than they expected, and when Preacher and Count Stahlmaske had killed the bushwhackers posted on top of the bluffs, that had changed the odds. Those riflemen hadn't been able to pick off the defenders from above, as the pirates had probably been counting on.

Roderick followed the mountain man to the railing and pointed the pistol at the canoes.

"Should I try to shoot one of them?" he asked.

Preacher shook his head. That might just draw some return fire, and Roderick had already had one narrow escape today. No need for the youngster to push his luck.

"No, let 'em go," Preacher said. "We bloodied 'em pretty good. They'll probably be holed up somewhere lickin' their wounds for a long time."

A few final shots from the crew members hurried the pirates on their way. The canoes disappeared around the next bend, going as fast as their occupants could paddle them. Preacher didn't see the ax-wielding giant among them and hoped the bastard was at the bottom of the Missouri River by now.

Simon Russell hurried along the deck toward Preacher and Roderick. He called, "Preacher! Are you all right?"

"Better than I got any right to be, I reckon," Preacher replied with a nod.

"I saw that dive from the bluff. You're right, you ought to be dead after doing something that crazy!" Russell looked at the younger man and added, "How about you, Herr Stahlmaske?"

Roderick nodded.

"I'm fine, thanks to Preacher."

"No thanks to me," the mountain man said. "You winged that big varmint on your own."

"Pure luck, I assure you."

"We all need some on our side now and then." Preacher turned back to Russell. "Have you seen the captain?"

Before Russell could answer, the boat's whistle blew. Preacher looked up to see Warner standing in the pilot house, evidently unharmed. The captain waved down at them and called, "I'll put in to shore as soon as we're clear of the bluffs!"

"That's a good idea," Preacher said. "We'll need to see just how badly everybody's hurt."

Two members of the crew had been killed in the fighting. Gunther was the only servant to be killed or even wounded. All three men were laid to rest that evening in graves dug on a hillside overlooking the river.

The half-dozen dead pirates had been shoved over the side into the Big Muddy. The fish could dispose of them, and good riddance, thought Preacher. He had taken a tomahawk off one of the corpses to replace the one he'd lost in the river.

Leading Horse, Count Stahlmaske had ridden along the bluffs until he could get back down to the river and rendezvous with the *Sentinel*. If he was relieved that his brother, uncle, and fiancée had come through the attack all right, he didn't really show it. He was, however, upset that Gunther had been killed.

"True, he was a thick-headed brute with a bad temper," the count said as he talked with Preacher, Russell, Allingham, and Warner on the passenger deck that evening after the burials, "but he was quite useful at times."

"There's a good chance he saved your brother's life by slowin' down that fella with the ax," Preacher said. "That gave Roderick time to get his gun loaded. Then he was lucky enough to actually hit the varmint."

"Luck indeed. Roderick has never been a good shot."

Allingham said, "I'm told you made an incredible leap from the bluff, Preacher."

"Just figured I'd better get down to the boat as fast as I could," the mountain man said with a shrug. "I knew you folks could use my help."

"Now, now, no false modesty. Everyone came through with flying colors today. Those pirates were whipped so thoroughly I wager they'll think twice before attacking us or any other riverboat ever again."

Preacher hoped the senator was right about that. The *Sentinel* still had to get the rest of the way to the Yellowstone River—and back.

Claude Binnion listened to the curses of angry men and the moans of wounded ones. The only one who wasn't carrying on was Big Wedge, who maintained a stoic silence as Binnion cleaned the hole in his leg with corn liquor and then bandaged it tightly.

"You'll be able to get around a little, Wedge," Binnion said as he sat back from the chore. "You probably ought to stay off the leg as much as you can for a few days, though."

"All right, Claude. Thanks for helpin' me. I thought I was a goner."

"You damn near were. If we hadn't spotted you and pulled you out of the river, you might've drowned."

The remaining pirates were several miles upstream from Cougar Bluffs. They had pulled their canoes ashore, hidden them in some brush, and then made camp several hundred yards away from the river. They weren't in any shape to fight again so soon, so Binnion hoped the riverboat would just steam on past without anyone noticing them.

From where he hunkered near a small fire, glaring into the flames like a greenhorn, Hackney said bitterly, "We should've jumped the sons o' bitches yesterday. We could've taken over the boat then. They wouldn't have been able to stop us."

Binnion stood up and walked over to the fire. He said, "If you've got something to say to me, Jed, you better say it to my face. Otherwise I might not hear it."

"Sorry, Claude," Hackney muttered, still without looking up. "Forget it."

"No, I mean it," Binnion went on. "If you think

somebody besides me can do a better job of leading this bunch, I want to know about it. Maybe you?"

As he spoke, Binnion let his hand rest on the bone grips of the big knife sheathed at his waist. The camp had gone quiet. Even the wounded men had stopped moaning.

"Hell, no," Hackney replied hastily. "I never said I was any kind of leader."

"That's right, you didn't." Binnion looked around at the other men. "Anybody else here want to speak up?"

No one did.

"I know things didn't work out today like I planned," Binnion went on after a moment. "I've led you boys to plenty of good loot in the past, though, and I damn sure will again. Today was just bad luck all around."

Wedge said, "What happened today was that Preacher was there."

Binnion turned to stare at him and repeated, "Preacher?"

"He was there, Claude, I swear it. I seen him once in St. Louis. Somebody pointed him out to me that day, and I ain't never forgot. He was the fella who killed our men on the bluff and then jumped into the river from up there."

"Wedge is right, Claude," Bracknell said. "I saw him, too, and now that Wedge mentioned his name, I know why he looked familiar. That was Preacher, sure enough. He killed more of our men than the rest of that bunch put together."

"Well, that just means we've got a score to settle with this Preacher fella," Binnion said with soft menace. "Mark my words, there'll come a time when we see Preacher again, and it'll be sooner than he thinks. And this time . . . he'll be the one who dies."

CHAPTER 21

Cougar Bluffs was the most likely spot for an attack by river pirates, but just because the *Sentinel* was past that point, Preacher knew there was no guarantee they wouldn't be ambushed again. He didn't expect the same bunch to make another try so soon after losing so many men, but anything was possible. There might be other gangs of cutthroats lurking ahead of them, too.

Preacher suggested to Captain Warner that he double the guards at night, and the captain was quick to agree.

When trouble cropped up again a few nights later, though, it didn't come from the shore.

The boat was tied up along a nice stretch of river with a number of good places along the bank for Preacher to spread his bedroll, so he was enjoying spending an evening under the stars again. Dog lay beside him. The horses had been led off the barge and were picketed nearby, taking advantage of the opportunity to graze. If any Indians slipped up and tried to steal the animals, they would get a surprise. Dog and Horse both would raise a ruckus if that happened.

Preacher dozed but didn't fall fully asleep as the boat grew dark and quiet. He hadn't forgotten about what he had seen that night a week or so earlier, when one of the Allingham women had slipped into the count's cabin, but since the incident hadn't been repeated he had let it drift to the back of his mind.

A hint of movement dimly glimpsed on the passenger deck brought it back into the forefront of his thoughts. Silently, he sat up and watched an indistinct figure glide along behind the railing. It was almost like a ghost, Preacher thought.

The shape disappeared, and he knew it had vanished into one of the cabins. Preacher didn't have to think very hard to know which one. He would have bet a hat that the phantom figure had gone into Count Stahlmaske's cabin.

Somebody needed to have a good long talk with the count and tell him that it wasn't very smart to be carrying on with another man's wife or daughter. Maybe Stahlmaske's uncle should be the one to do that. Preacher knew good and well the count would never take any advice from him.

He lay back down and resolved to speak to Gerhard the next day, as soon as he got a chance to talk to the older man in private. Preacher didn't know if it would do any good or not, but at least he would make the attempt.

A couple of minutes later something crashed on board the *Sentinel,* and a woman screamed.

So much for good intentions.

Preacher bolted up, grabbed his pistols from the ground beside his bedroll, and dashed to the boat with Dog following close behind him. Both of them leaped easily to the cargo deck. From the pilot house, one of the crewmen on guard duty shouted, "Hey, what's going on down there?"

Another scream from the woman was the only answer. Preacher could tell that the shrill sound came from the passenger deck. He went up the narrow staircase in four bounds.

As he ran along the deck he heard men grunting, accompanied by the thud of fists against flesh and another crash as something was knocked over. The first crash, he reckoned, had been somebody kicking a cabin door open.

It didn't take a genius to figure out which cabin. He headed for the one belonging to Count Stahlmaske.

He got there just in time to hear the solid smack of another punch landing cleanly. A figure rocketed at him, and Preacher barely had time to set his feet and catch the man who collided with him. He still held the pistols, so he thrust his arms under the other man's arms and held him up.

The man had come through the open door backward, knocked through it by a powerful blow. The man who had thrown that punch charged out of the cabin, saw Preacher standing there with the first man, and roared, "Hang on to him, Preacher.

I'm going to teach that bastard a lesson he'll never forget!"

Just as the mountain man had thought, the battle was between Stahlmaske and Senator Josiah Allingham, and since the count was the one leaning against Preacher, half senseless and shaking his head groggily, it was clear that the politician was winning.

And possibly losing his career at the same time, Preacher thought, once word of this incident got back to Washington.

The only real question was which woman was going to emerge from Stahlmaske's cabin.

Preacher got the answer a second later when Margaret Allingham appeared and clutched frantically at her husband's arm.

"Josiah, stop!" she cried. "Please don't do this!"

Allingham wore a nightshirt. His wife was clad in some sort of flimsy wrapper. The count still had on his boots and trousers but was bare from the waist up. The sordid conclusions Preacher had reached were true. That was obvious now.

Allingham shook off his wife's hands and stepped toward Preacher and the count. His fists were up, ready to strike again.

Preacher swung Stahlmaske to the side and said, "Damn it, hold on there, Senator. You don't want to do this."

"You're wrong, Preacher. I want to do this more than I've ever wanted to do anything. I *need* to do this." Allingham pointed a trembling finger at the count. "Do you know what he was . . . what he and my wife were . . . My God, I would have rather been struck blind than to ever see such a thing!"

"If you didn't want to see it, why did you kick the door open?" Margaret screeched at him. "Why couldn't you have just left well enough alone, Josiah?"

"Well enough alone?" Allingham repeated in a shocked tone. "You think allowing my wife to commit adultery is leaving well enough alone?"

"As long as it doesn't interfere with your career in Washington, why not?" Margaret asked coldly. "Good Lord, if you'd stayed out of this it might have even helped your career."

His wife's callous words rocked Allingham more than any physical blow could have. Preacher could tell that by the way the senator gasped and took a step back.

"Let . . . let me go," Stahlmaske muttered thickly.

Preacher did. The count leaned against the railing and breathed heavily. He reached up with one hand and took hold of his chin to work his jaw back and forth, evidently trying to see if it was broken.

The commotion had attracted attention from other quarters. Several people approached along the deck in various forms of nightclothes. Preacher recognized Simon Russell, Roderick, Gerhard, and Heinrich and Hobart.

There was no sign of Gretchen, or of Sarah Allingham, for that matter.

"Albert, are you all right?" Roderick asked anxiously. "What happened here? What are you . . ."

The young man's voice trailed off as he looked

around. There was enough moonlight for him to
see the way Allingham stood between Margaret and
Stahlmaske. Something about that arrangement
must have struck Roderick as familiar.

"Again, Albert?" he said.

Stahlmaske shook off the effects of Allingham's
punches and stood straighter.

"How dare you judge me?" he snapped at his
brother. "It's not your right to do so."

"I'm sorry," Roderick said instantly.

"Don't be," Allingham told him. "He deserves all
the scorn you can give him. The only kind of nobleman your brother deserves to be called is a royal
bastard!"

Stahlmaske took a step toward the senator.
Preacher and Russell both got between them.

"When we get back to Washington and I speak to
your President Jackson, you are finished!" Stahlmaske said. "I will personally see to it that your
political career is over!"

"You think I care?" Allingham said. "After this,
do you think it really matters?"

"When you calm down it will," the count said
with a sneer. "But then it will be too late. You should
have learned to accept such things. They mean
nothing, after all."

"Nothing?" Margaret asked with a slight tremble
in her voice. "What we had between us meant nothing, Albert?"

Stahlmaske blew out an exasperated breath and
shrugged.

"A few moments of physical pleasure, that's all,"

he said. "Did you believe it to be something more than that?"

For a second Preacher thought Margaret was going to launch herself at Stahlmaske and try to claw his eyes out, but she controlled the furious impulse. With tears running down her cheeks, she turned and went hurriedly toward the cabin she had shared with her husband.

Preacher had a hunch that Allingham wouldn't be going back there tonight. Maybe not for the rest of the journey to the Yellowstone and back.

"Everybody needs to just settle down," Russell said, making patting motions in the air with his hands. "This is all over. Just go back to your cabins and cool off."

"You do not give me orders, Herr Russell," Stahlmaske said. His customary arrogance had returned in full force.

"I'm just saying that's the best thing to do right now. Any more arguing or fighting is just going to make things worse."

"You're wrong about that, Simon," Allingham said. "Beating that worthless scoundrel within an inch of his life is the best thing *I* can do right now."

"You think so, Senator? How's that going to change a damned thing, really?"

Allingham didn't have an answer for that question. He stood there with his hands hanging at his sides, no longer clenched into fists, and glared at Stahlmaske.

The count returned the glare for a second, then strode toward his cabin, obviously unapologetic.

Roderick looked like he wanted to say something to the senator, maybe offer an apology on behalf of his brother, but then he changed his mind. Allingham wouldn't have believed it or accepted it anyway, thought Preacher.

The group on deck broke up, the men drifting away until Preacher and Russell were left standing there by themselves. Russell sighed and said, "I'm wondering if it's too late to just say the hell with this job and head back to the mountains with you, Preacher."

"Sounds like a mighty fine idea," Preacher said, "except for one thing."

"What's that?"

"Without us around to take care of 'em, you really think this bunch can make it to the Yellowstone and back alive?"

Russell's gloomy silence was all the answer either of them needed.

CHAPTER 22

Preacher's diminutive friend Audie could recite much of Shakespeare's work, and Preacher had spent many an evening around a campfire listening to the former professor spout lines from the plays written by the man Audie called the Bard of Avon.

It seemed like all those plays were packed full of treachery and sneaking around and folks carrying on shamelessly with people they weren't married to, even the ones that were supposed to be comedies.

The whole situation on the *Sentinel* was starting to remind Preacher of one of those plays.

The atmosphere on board the riverboat was tense the next day. Allingham and the count stayed well clear of each other. Any time one of them was in the salon, the other wasn't.

Margaret Allingham stayed in her cabin all day, as did Gretchen Ritter. Gretchen must have heard about what had happened and was embarrassed to show her face after it had been revealed to every-

one on board that her fiancé was a philanderer.
And Margaret, Preacher thought, was just embarrassed, period. One of the female servants took
meals to both women.

Preacher, Russell, and Captain Warner were in
the pilot house late that afternoon when they heard
someone climbing the stairs. A moment later the
door opened and Josiah Allingham lumbered in, a
gloomy expression on his face.

Preacher wasn't too happy to see the senator. He
had come up here to get away from the drama and
trouble going on down on the passenger deck.

"Gentlemen, is it all right if I join you?" Allingham asked.

The pilot house wasn't very big, but having four
people in it wouldn't be too crowded. Without that
to use as an excuse, Preacher supposed the captain
couldn't deny Allingham entrance.

"Sure, come on in, Senator," Warner said gruffly.
"You haven't been up here yet, have you?"

"No, I haven't," Allingham replied as he stepped
inside and closed the door behind him. He looked
around through the open windows and went on,
"You really have a spectacular view from up here,
don't you?"

"Best on the river," Warner agreed. "You take
one of those bigger boats, the side-wheelers that go
up and down the Mississippi to New Orleans, and
they have an extra deck on 'em that puts the pilot
house up even higher. You can really see from one

of those. But I like this boat, myself." He chuckled. "She and I seem to understand each other."

"Like in a good marriage," Allingham said, and that cast an immediate pall on the conversation. He hurried on, "I'm sorry, I didn't mean to—"

Russell told him, "Don't worry about it, Senator. I reckon all of us have had our share of personal problems at one time or another."

"I just wish mine hadn't ruined this journey for everyone."

"The journey's not ruined," Warner said. "We're still going to the mouth of the Yellowstone, and when we get there we'll be trading with trappers who come from a hundred miles or more all around. I expect we'll take on a mighty fine load of pelts, just as planned. No offense, Senator, but that's all the American Fur Company really cares about."

"I don't suppose, then, that there's any chance we could turn around and go back now?"

The other three men in the pilot house stared at the senator. Preacher was as surprised as Russell and Warner, but he didn't figure this discussion was really any of his business, so he kept his mouth shut.

Warner finally answered the senator's question by saying, "I reckon I'd probably lose my job as the captain of this boat if I did that."

"And I'd be out of a job, too," Russell added. "The company's counting on me to deliver that load of pelts."

Allingham sighed and nodded.

"I shouldn't have even asked," he said. "I just

thought, if there was some way to put a stop to this misery . . ."

"We're all mighty sorry for your troubles, Senator," Russell told him, "but we have our own responsibilities."

"Of course you do. Please, just forget I said anything." Allingham turned to go, then paused. "If I could just . . . talk to someone about what happened . . ."

Preacher, Russell, and Warner glanced at each other like they all wished they were somewhere else right now. Just about anywhere else, in fact.

"You don't want to do that, Senator," Russell said after a few seconds. "It'll just make you feel worse."

"You're probably right. Are you married, Simon?"

"No, sir. Never have been."

"What about you, Captain?"

"Going on thirty years," Warner replied. "Six children and nine grandchildren so far."

Allingham smiled. "That's wonderful. I hope to have grandchildren some day."

Considering how hot-blooded the senator's daughter seemed to be, Preacher figured that was pretty well inevitable. He kept that thought to himself.

"Of course, it's going to be different now," Allingham went on. "Everything will be different when we get back to Washington. I'll probably have to resign my seat in the Senate and move back to Vermont. I suppose I can work in the store again. Margaret will hate that . . . will hate me . . . but given that she already does . . ." He sighed. "I should have just let her continue. Confronting her certainly hasn't helped matters between us. My suspicions just ate away at me until I had to do something—"

He grunted and stumbled, bumping into Preacher. The mountain man grabbed Allingham to steady him and saw the arrow protruding from the man's upper right arm.

Instinctively, Preacher took note of the markings and fletching on the arrow. It was Pawnee, a tribe that was peaceful for the most part—but their warriors were excellent fighters when they decided to go on the warpath, as they obviously were now.

"Good Lord!" Russell exclaimed as he realized that Allingham had been shot. "Better pour on the steam, Captain!"

Warner had already grabbed the speaking tube.

"Give me all you got!" he shouted into it. "We've got Indians up here!"

The question was how many, Preacher thought as he lowered Allingham to the floor of the pilot house. The senator sat with his back propped against the wall. He had gone pale from the pain radiating from the arrow in his arm.

Preacher knelt beside him and said, "You'll be all right, Senator. It probably hurts like blazes, but I can tell it ain't a bad wound. You just sit right there and we'll tend to it later."

"We're . . . we're under attack," Allingham said unnecessarily. He seemed to be having a hard time believing it.

"Yep." Preacher raised himself higher but remained in a crouch as he scanned the landscape on both sides of the Missouri.

So far no other arrows had struck the pilot house. He hoped the one that had hit Allingham had been fired by a lone brave who happened to be on shore when the riverboat passed by and thought it would be good medicine to shoot an arrow at the smoking, rumbling monster.

Russell was on the other side of the pilot house, looking out the window warily. "See anything?" he asked Preacher.

"Not yet."

"That's a Pawnee arrow."

"Yeah, I know. Last I heard the Pawnee were pretty peaceful."

"You never know when something'll get them stirred up," Russell said. "I— Look out!"

This time it was a veritable storm of arrows descending on the riverboat, not just one. Preacher tackled Warner and knocked him to the floor as the missiles began to thud against the pilot house. Some of them came through the open windows and landed on the floor. One even stuck in the wheel.

"It's like those damned pirates all over again!" Warner yelled.

Actually, it was worse than that, thought Preacher. Less than two dozen pirates had attacked the *Sentinel* back at Cougar Bluffs. There was no telling how many Pawnee warriors were out there.

Another difference worked in their favor, though. They were in a fairly wide, straight stretch of the river. They didn't have to worry about crashing into a bluff.

"Keep us in the middle of the stream," Preacher snapped at the captain.

Warner nodded as he reached up to steady the wheel. He said, "I should be able to do that."

Preacher had his rifle with him. The first volley of arrows seemed to be over, so he cautiously lifted his head above the window. He bit back a curse as he saw Pawnee pouring out of the trees on both sides of the river. There had to be fifty or sixty of the warriors on each bank, maybe more. They pulled canoes out of the brush, shoved the light-weight craft toward the riverboat, hopped in and started to paddle.

This was a full-fledged attack, Preacher realized, not some isolated incident. And that didn't make any sense. The Pawnee didn't have any reason to come after the riverboat like this.

Guns blasted down below as the crew began to mount a defense, but they had to dive for cover as more arrows slashed through the air at the boat. Preacher slid his rifle over the window sill and drew a bead on the warrior in the front of the canoe closest to the *Sentinel*. He fired and saw the lead ball drive the Pawnee backward into the man behind him.

The canoe didn't slow down, though. None of them did.

On the other side of the pilot house, Russell's pistol roared. He cursed and said, "Why are they doing this?"

"Don't know," Preacher said as he reloaded, "but I reckon we'd better get down there. They're gonna be swarmin' all over the boat in a minute."

As he stood up, a desperate tactic occurred to him. He grabbed the wheel, said, "Sorry, Cap'n," and spun it. The *Sentinel* veered sharply to the right.

"What the devil are you doing?" Warner demanded. "You'll wreck us!"

"I'm gonna wreck some of them canoes first," Preacher said.

It was true. As the paddle wheel dug in the muddy water and sent the boat surging ahead, now its prow was aimed at the closest canoes. The Pawnee paddlers tried to get out of the way, but they didn't have time. The boat struck them, overturning some and splintering others. Warriors had to dive frantically into the river or were dumped in the water and trapped as the riverboat passed over them if they were too slow. Preacher figured some of them wouldn't survive being caught in the paddlewheel.

He spun the wheel back the other way to try to straighten the boat. Earlier in the journey, Warner had offered to let him try his hand at steering, but Preacher figured the captain hadn't meant like this!

He let go of the wheel, grabbed the rifle he had leaned against the wall, and plunged out of the pilot house with Russell right behind him. Down below, some of the Pawnee warriors who'd been in the river were now clambering onto the cargo deck.

From here on out it would be a hand-to-hand fight, with no quarter asked or given.

CHAPTER 23

As Preacher reached the passenger deck, he saw a Pawnee warrior with a painted face leap from a canoe onto the cargo deck and brandish a tomahawk as he charged toward a crewman who had taken cover among the supplies. The crewman was trying to reload a pistol but would never make it in time.

Smoothly, Preacher brought the rifle to his shoulder and fired. The ball ripped through the Pawnee's torso and spun him over the side. He went into the water with a big splash.

Unfortunately, several more warriors were already there to take his place.

Preacher dropped his rifle and pulled his pistols from behind his belt. Each pistol was double-shotted, with as heavy a charge of powder as it would bear. The way the Indians were pouring onto the boat, he didn't really have to aim. He just cocked the pistols, pointed them in that general direction, and pulled the triggers.

The guns roared thunderously, and when the powder smoke cleared a couple of seconds later, Preacher saw the bodies of several Pawnee sprawled on the cargo deck. More were coming on board, though, and some of them fired arrows at the mountain man. Preacher ducked as the missiles whipped over his head.

He didn't have time to reload, but he could use the empty pistols as clubs, which is what he did as he launched himself at a trio of warriors who charged up the stairs. He waded into the enemy, blocking a tomahawk as it descended toward his head, feeling bone crunch under a pistol as he smashed it against the skull of another Pawnee. He kicked one man in the belly and sent him tumbling back down.

It was a brutal fight, and Preacher's speed, skill, and experience were the only things that kept him from dying several times over during the clash. He hammered the empty pistols into the heads of his enemies until the weapons were knocked out of his hands.

Bodies had piled up on the stairs below him, some dead, some knocked senseless, and they began to serve as a line of defense because they kept more of the Pawnee from getting at him as easily.

Unfortunately there were other ways onto the passenger deck, including stairs on the far side of the boat. Some of the Indians even leaped up, caught hold of the railing, and climbed onto the *Sentinel*'s second level. Preacher heard shots and screams and angry shouts as the fight spread from down below, but he couldn't turn his back on the attackers right in front of him to see what was going on.

One of the warriors took a swipe at his head with a tomahawk that Preacher barely avoided. He caught hold of the man's wrist and twisted until he heard bones crack. As the Indian dropped the tomahawk, Preacher snatched it out of midair with his other hand and crashed it in the middle of the Pawnee's face. The man fell backward, dead, as Preacher wrenched the tomahawk free.

He pulled the tomahawk he had taken from one of the dead pirates from behind his belt and with one of the weapons in each hand charged down the stairs, stepping on corpses, feet sliding in pools of blood, staying on his feet somehow as the 'hawks whipped back and forth, shattering bone and ripping open flesh. Blood flew around Preacher in a sticky crimson spray.

By the time this fight was over, he was going to look as gruesome as those corpses he was tromping on—assuming he wasn't one of them!

As he reached the bottom of the stairs, the Pawnee who had still been battling with him gave up the fight and turned to flee. Some ran along the deck while others jumped back in the river. Several of the canoes were headed back to shore.

Preacher's heart slugged hard as he spotted flashes of bright hair in one of those canoes. Margaret and Sarah Allingham were both in the craft, struggling with a Pawnee warrior who was trying to push them down into the bottom of the canoe. The

Indian lashed out with a fist that caught Margaret on the jaw and dropped her in a limp heap, apparently unconscious.

Seeing that happen to her mother caused Sarah to scream and redouble her efforts to escape, but the Pawnee backhanded her and flung her down on top of her mother.

Preacher drew back his arm, whipped it forward, and let fly with the tomahawk. The 'hawk revolved through the air, going so fast it was only a blur, and struck perfectly with the blade lodging in the back of the Pawnee's head. He pitched over the side, dead, and Preacher had the satisfaction of knowing that the varmint wouldn't be hitting any more women.

Unfortunately, that did nothing to rescue Margaret and Sarah. They were still prisoners of the raiders, and the two Pawnee still in the canoe paddled hard to put the craft out of reach. It reached the shore a moment later and the Indians dragged the stunned women out of the canoe.

All the Pawnee were abandoning the fight now, as if they had gotten what they came for. Still holding the two tomahawks, Preacher ran along the deck, weaving around bodies of crewmen and Indians. As he reached the bow he saw that the Pawnee had taken more captives. Gretchen Ritter and Roderick Stahlmaske were in one of the canoes, looking terrified, and the count was in another, slumped down with blood on his head where he had been knocked unconscious.

Men with horses were waiting on shore for the Pawnee. Some of them were warriors, but a shock went through Preacher as he realized that some of the men waiting to take charge of the prisoners were white. That just made the mystery behind this attack deeper. Were the Pawnee working with river pirates now? Preacher found that idea almost impossible to believe.

He started to run back up to the passenger deck to retrieve his rifle, then realized there was no point in it. The other canoes had reached the shore, and the prisoners were being hauled out already. They would be out of range before Preacher could reload.

He leaned over to look back at the barge behind the riverboat. Several of the horses were down, skewered with arrows, but it looked like most of the animals had survived the attack, including Horse. That gave Preacher hope.

Because there was nowhere out here those bastards could go with the captives where Preacher couldn't track them down.

Simon Russell stumbled up to him.

"Preacher! Good Lord, man, are you all right?"

"Believe it or not, none of this blood is mine," Preacher said. "How about you?"

Russell held up his left arm to display the torn, bloody sleeve of his coat.

"An arrow nicked me," he said, "but the wound doesn't amount to much. What the hell happened here? The Pawnee wouldn't have done this on their own. They're not at war with us!"

"Somebody prodded 'em into it." Quickly, Preacher told Russell about the white men he had spotted on the riverbank, waiting with horses for the fleeing

Indians. "Whoever those fellas are, they put the Pawnee up to jumpin' us. From the looks of it, they were after the count. They probably took Roderick and the women along to use as hostages when we come after 'em."

"So they know we'll come after them," Russell said.

"I reckon you can bet on that," Preacher said with a decisive nod.

The only Indians remaining on the boat were either dead or dying. Like most tribes, the Pawnee didn't like to leave any of their fallen comrades behind. The mission they'd been on must have been pretty important for them to have done so, Preacher thought.

He and Russell checked on the crewmen who had been wounded during the battle and did what they could for the men, tying rags around the worst of the wounds as makeshift bandages to slow the bleeding. Then they headed up to the passenger deck to find out what had happened there.

The first thing they saw was one of the Ritter twins kneeling over the body of the other one, who lay on his back with a pair of Pawnee arrows protruding from his chest. His eyes stared sightlessly at the sky.

Gerhard Stahlmaske stood close by, wringing his hands. He appeared to be upset but unharmed.

"Hobart!" the surviving twin said as tears rolled down his cheeks. That meant he had to be Heinrich. He went on in German, evidently pleading in a grief-wracked voice for his brother not to be dead. Unfortunately, it was too late for that.

Russell put his hand on the youngster's shoulder and said, "There's nothing you can do for him, Heinrich. I'm sorry."

Heinrich looked up and said something else in German. Preacher had no idea what it was. He moved on past to Gerhard and said, "What about you, Herr Stahlmaske? Are you hurt?"

"Nein," Gerhard replied as he shook his head. "No, I . . . I am unharmed. The savages did not come after me." He clutched at the sleeve of Preacher's buckskin shirt. "But they took Albert and Roderick! And *ach,* poor Gretchen . . . When Hobart tried to help his sister, they . . . they killed him."

"I'm sorry," Preacher said. "But we'll get your nephews back safe and sound, I promise you that."

"How can you promise?" Gerhard cried. He waved a hand at the prairie southwest of the river. "They are gone! The savages have taken them, and *Gott* only knows where!"

The old man was correct that the Pawnee and their prisoners were out of sight now. Only a faint haze of dust hung in the air to show where the horses carrying them had galloped away.

"I know this country. I'll take a search party and go after them."

"But you will be outnumbered."

"Won't be the first time," Preacher said.

"And they have those poor ladies." Gerhard's eyes were wide with horror. Preacher figured he was thinking about what might happen to the female prisoners. It was true that might complicate any rescue efforts.

But it wouldn't stop them. One way or another, Preacher was going to get those folks back and find out the reason behind what had happened.

Captain Warner came down from the pilot house with Allingham leaning on him. The senator still had the arrow stuck in his arm. His voice was panic-stricken as he said, "Preacher, they took Margaret and Sarah! I saw them! The Indians have them!"

Preacher nodded and said, "I know, Senator. I saw 'em, too. I reckon Simon and I will be goin' after 'em pretty soon."

"I'm coming, too," Allingham declared. "I can use both a pistol and a rifle." He moved his wounded arm and grimaced at the pain. "Just yank this damned arrow out of my arm and let's get started!"

"Hold on, Senator," Russell said. "I don't know if it's a good idea for you to—"

"Damn it, man, we're talking about my wife and daughter! Of course I'm coming along."

"*Und* I as well," Heinrich Ritter said as he wiped away his tears. He no longer looked so young and innocent and enthusiastic. "Those savages, they have taken *mein* sister. *Und* they . . . they *haff* killed *mein bruder. Er ist todt!*"

Preacher wasn't sure if taking along a politician and a German youngster—neither of whom knew much of anything about the frontier—was a good idea. On the other hand, if Allingham really could use a gun, it might not hurt to have him along. Preacher didn't know how many of the crewmen had survived, so he wasn't sure how much of a rescue party he could assemble.

"Cap'n, why don't you go see to your crew?" Preacher suggested to Warner. "I'll take a look at your arm, Senator."

When he bared Allingham's arm, he saw that the arrow was lodged in the fleshy outer part of the upper arm. It hadn't penetrated all the way through, so Preacher took hold of the shaft.

"This is gonna hurt like hell, Senator," he warned.

"Just do what you need to do," Allingham told him through clenched teeth.

Doing it as quickly as possible, Preacher rammed the arrow the rest of the way through Allingham's arm so that the bloody flint head emerged from the front. He snapped off the head, then withdrew the shaft from the wound.

Allingham was even more pale now, and he had let out a groan when Preacher pushed the arrow on through. But he nodded and said, "All right, now you can bind it up. It won't stop me from riding."

While Preacher was doing that, Ludwig and Egon, the count's servants, came up to him.

"*Herr* Preacher," Egon said, "we are told you are forming a party to go after the savages who abducted the count."

"That's right," Preacher said.

"We would like to volunteer," Ludwig said.

"You boys know anything about fightin' Indians?" Preacher asked.

"Well . . . no," Egon said. "But we are good at following orders."

"We have been doing it all our lives," Ludwig added.

Again, having them along might help with the odds, but they could also cause problems.

"If you come with me, you'll have to keep up," Preacher cautioned them. "And if you get in any trouble, chances are you'll have to get yourselves out of it 'cause the rest of us will be busy tryin' to stay alive."

"We understand," Egon said.

"We must help the count," Ludwig said. "It is our duty."

"All right, go see if you can rustle up some guns." Preacher finished tying a strip of cloth from Allingham's shirt around the politician's wounded arm. "Once that arm stiffens up, you ain't gonna be able to use it much, Senator."

"I know that. But I can fire a pistol one-handed. And all I want is the opportunity to do so at the men who stole my wife and daughter."

Margaret Allingham's infidelity seemed to have been forgotten. That wasn't surprising. When it was a matter of life and death, other things often didn't matter anymore.

"When will we be leaving?" Allingham went on.

"Just as soon as we can," Preacher said.

He was all too aware that with every minute that passed, those prisoners were getting farther away from the river.

CHAPTER 24

Some of the horses had been wounded but not killed, something Preacher hadn't realized earlier. There were eight animals either unharmed or in good enough shape to ride, including his own stallion. That limited the size of the rescue party even more, because they had to be mounted.

Not only that, but if they succeeded in freeing the captives, some of the party would have to ride double as they made their escape. That would slow them down.

So, Preacher mused, he was going after a hundred or more Pawnee warriors with a politician, a German youth barely out of his teens, and a couple of servants who had no experience fighting Indians or anybody else. At least the two crewmen who would be going along were both big and strong from their work, even if they weren't veteran Indian fighters. And of course he and Russell had been to see the elephant, many times.

Yeah, the odds against them were pretty overwhelming, he decided. But they had no choice in the matter. As long as those prisoners were out there and in danger, Preacher had to try to help them.

Captain Warner came up to him as he was saddling Horse and said, "I can come along with you, Preacher. I'm not wounded, and I can shoot."

"You can also handle that dang riverboat," the mountain man said. "You're gonna be in charge here, Cap'n. If anything else happens, you'll have to deal with it."

"You think that's possible?" Warner asked with a frown. "You mean those Indians might come back?"

"They acted like they got what they were after. But there's no tellin' what else might come along. You have enough crewmen to get up steam if you need to?"

Warner nodded.

"Yeah, some of them are hurt, of course, but we can get the boat moving. We can't go on upriver, though, because then you wouldn't know where to find us when you get back with those folks."

Preacher liked the way the captain just assumed he would succeed in freeing the prisoners. He hoped Warner was right about that.

"If you have to leave, you can always turn around and come back later. And if you're gone when we get back here, we'll just follow the river north until we catch up with you."

"All right. But I plan on being right here," Warner said with a determined nod.

A short time later, the horses were saddled. The

members of the rescue party, some with bloody
bandages tied here and there, came ashore with
rifles, pistols, and all the powder and shot they could
carry. Enough weapons and ammunition had been
left on the *Sentinel* so the crewmen who were staying
behind could put up a fight if they needed to.

"We'll take care of burying those who were
killed," Warner promised as the men mounted up.
"Good luck to you."

"We'll see you when we get back," Preacher said.
He lifted a hand and waved the rescue party into
motion.

Since the terrain was generally flat in this region,
it wasn't long before they could no longer see the
river behind them, just a low line of green that
marked the vegetation along the stream. The prairie
was covered with thick grass that waved slightly in
the breeze blowing across it.

Preacher had no trouble following the trail left
by the Indians and their white companions. Other
people might not see the signs, but they were clear
as a map to his experienced eyes. Broken stalks of
grass lying in a different direction than the others
around them, overturned rocks, the occasional partial print of the unshod hoof of an Indian pony . . .
and the tracks of some shod horses as well, further
proof that the mountain man's eyes hadn't de-
ceived him. There really had been white men working with the Indians.

The rescue party had Dog with them, too, and
no creature on the face of the earth was better at

following a scent than the big cur. He bounded ahead of the group, nose to the ground.

As they rode, Allingham asked Preacher, "Did I hear you say that the Indians who did this are normally peaceful?" He sounded like he couldn't believe that, and with plenty of justification for feeling that way, thought Preacher.

"More often than not they are. The Pawnee have fought many a war against other tribes, usually the Sioux, but mostly they get along with the whites. They farm as much as they hunt and they live in permanent villages they don't leave except to go on buffalo hunts every year. Then they come back to the same place. In a lot of ways they're like white folks, so I guess that's how come they get along." Preacher shook his head. "When they get their dander up about somethin', though, you don't want to cross 'em. I reckon you saw that today."

"You sound almost as though you admire them."

"I admire most of the tribes in one way or another," Preacher said. "They live their lives in the way that suits 'em, and they're happy about it. Now, there are a few bunches that are too ornery even for me to get along with, mind you. Me and the Blackfeet won't never see eye to eye about nothin', I don't expect. They've tried to kill me a heap of times, and I've returned the favor. Never lost any sleep over it, neither." He rubbed his bristly jaw and frowned. "Can't say the same about the Pawnee. I'm sorry for those warriors I had to kill today. I want to know what drove 'em to it."

"They're savages," Allingham said. "Isn't that a good enough reason?"

"No, sir, it's not." Preacher told the senator the same thing he had discussed with Russell. "There were white men among 'em. Somehow, they convinced the Pawnee to help them do their dirty work."

Allingham stared at Preacher.

"That's insane. Who would do such a thing?"

"They grabbed the count and his brother. That's got to have something to do with it. Can you think of any reason somebody would want to kidnap Stahlmaske? Maybe something to do with the negotiations he came over here to carry on with our government?"

Allingham looked baffled. He said, "All the count is doing is discussing a minor trade agreement between the United States and the Kingdom of Prussia. The agreement is important to a number of people in Washington because they've come out in favor of it, so they want everything to go smoothly. But in the big scheme of things, I can't see that it'll really make that much difference. As much as anything else, I think this whole trip and its diplomatic trappings were just an excuse for Count Stahlmaske to come over here to America and have an adventure. He's a great favorite of King Friedrich Wilhelm."

"I reckon he's probably havin' more of an adventure than he ever wanted," Preacher said.

* * *

Most of the Indians had peeled away from the group when they were several miles away from the river, leaving the prisoners in the custody of about a dozen warriors and the four white men who obviously had masterminded the attack on the *Sentinel*. Albert Stahlmaske had never seen any of those men before, but their accents when they spoke among themselves told him they were Englishmen.

Stahlmaske's head ached abominably from the blow that had struck him down. He had been in the salon when the attack began, but he had rushed out on deck when he heard gunshots, shouts from the crewmen, and war cries from the savages. He seldom went anywhere without being armed, so there was a pistol in the pocket of his coat. He had pulled it out, waited patiently at the railing even though arrows were flying through the air around him, and when one of the canoes had come within range of his weapon, he had shot down the Indian crouched in the front of the craft.

Then, still cool in the face of danger, he had reloaded twice and killed two more of the howling savages before they swarmed onto the passenger deck and overran him. One of them had carried a war club of some kind. Stahlmaske had tried to take the bludgeon away from him, but the Indian had struck him instead, knocking him out.

As consciousness slipped away from him, he had assumed the savages would kill him, probably by cutting his throat. He would never wake up.

A shame he hadn't had the chance—or hadn't taken the chances he'd had—to tell Gretchen that he really did feel some honest affection for her. As much as he could feel for anyone, he supposed. He had never been given to any emotions other than pride and an overwhelming sense of his own superiority.

He hadn't come to until he was on the back of this horse, tied to a saddle. Leaning forward over the animal's neck the way he was, he couldn't see much. To his right his brother Roderick rode another horse, lashed onto the beast's back in much the same way Stahlmaske was. Roderick was awake, his eyes so wide with terror it seemed they might pop right out of their sockets.

"Albert!" Roderick exclaimed in a high-pitched voice that reminded Stahlmaske of a mouse's frightened squeak. "Thank God you're alive!"

Stahlmaske didn't respond to that. He lifted his head and looked around as best he could. He could see that a white man on horseback was leading Roderick's mount. He assumed the same was true for his horse.

That was . . . interesting. What were such men doing riding with Indians?

Thinking that their captors were probably Americans, Stahlmaske called, "You there! Leading my brother's horse! Let us go and I'll see to it that you're handsomely paid."

The man turned his head and let out a harsh laugh, but that was his only response.

Being laughed at like that angered Stahlmaske,

but tied hand and foot the way he was, there was nothing he could do about it. Not now, anyway.

But somehow he would have his revenge on these men, if it was the last thing he ever did.

Since then some of the Indians had gone their separate ways, and the group had moved around enough for Stahlmaske to see that he and Roderick weren't the only prisoners. Gretchen had been captured as well, along with the two Allingham women.

Stahlmaske was sorry to see that. He didn't want Gretchen to come to any harm. He didn't care as much about Margaret and Sarah, although the senator's wife certainly had been pleasant enough in bed.

Stahlmaske had given some thought to seducing the younger Allingham as well before this journey was over. Sarah was quite attractive, just the sort who needed an older man with a firm hand to initiate her into womanhood.

Now it was unlikely that would ever happen. The ladies might not survive very long in the hands of these primitive savages. He included the white men in that description. They were Americans, after all.

Only they weren't, he discovered. When they spoke to each other, the count recognized their accents as British. That made them somewhat more civilized than their former colonists, he supposed . . . but not much.

After what seemed like ages, the group came to a stop in the late afternoon. Up ahead, still a good distance away, was a line of low hills. Stahlmaske wondered if that was their destination.

The Englishman who'd been leading Stahlmaske's horse dismounted and came back alongside the animal. He was a red-faced man with a sweeping, rust-colored mustache. He pulled a knife from a sheath at his belt.

Stahlmaske waited calmly. If all these men wanted to do was murder him, they would have done it before now.

"If I cut you loose, do you promise not to cause trouble?" the man demanded.

"I promise nothing except to kill you and all your associates as soon as I get the chance," Stahlmaske said, putting as much cold hatred into his reply as he could.

"That's what I figured. That's why we're not going to give you that chance."

The Indians had dismounted as well. Several of them nocked arrows to bowstrings and pulled them back, aiming the weapons at the count.

The Englishman cut him loose. Stahlmaske slid to the ground. His balance deserted him for a second when he landed, but he caught hold of the saddle and braced himself until his strength returned.

"You're not going to allow those savages to kill me," he told his captor. "If you wanted me dead, I would be already."

"Maybe so, Count," the man said, "but don't push your luck."

The other prisoners were freed as well. Roderick

stumbled over to his brother and threw his arms around him in a clumsy embrace.

"Thank God we're both still alive!"

Stahlmaske pushed him away, his only concession to fraternity being that he wasn't too rough about it.

"Are you injured, Roderick?" he asked.

"N-no, I'm all right."

Stahlmaske turned to Gretchen and took the beautiful auburn-haired woman in his arms.

"My dear," he said. "I regret that you were abducted along with the rest of us."

She swallowed hard and said, "The savages . . . they killed my maid, Albert. It was terrible."

"I'm sure it was."

Stahlmaske glanced at the Allingham women, who huddled together clutching each other in their fear. There was no comfort he could offer them.

So he turned to their captors instead and demanded, "What is it you want of us?"

"It's simple, really," the man with the rust-colored mustache replied. "You're going to make us all rich men."

CHAPTER 25

Preacher called a halt after the rescue party had traveled several miles from the Missouri River.

"Why are we stopping?" Allingham wanted to know. "We can't afford to let them get any farther ahead of us, can we?"

"I got to take a look at this," Preacher said. He swung down from the saddle and walked around on the prairie for a few minutes, hunkering on his heels now and then to study the ground more closely.

Simon Russell said, "I think I'm seeing the same thing you are, Preacher. They split up, didn't they?"

Preacher straightened and nodded.

"Yeah. The biggest bunch headed that way." He pointed south. "The rest of 'em kept goin' northwest."

"Why would they do that?" Allingham asked. "And how will we know which group the prisoners are with?" He groaned briefly in dismay. "For that matter, how will we know that the prisoners weren't separated, too?"

Preacher waved a hand toward the south and said, "The ones who went that way are all on Indian ponies. There's a Pawnee village ten, fifteen miles in that direction, I recollect. I visited it once and smoked a pipe with 'em. All the shod horses went the other way, along with about a dozen of the Pawnee. My guess is that those white men and all the captives are with that bunch."

"You can't know that for sure," Allingham said.

Preacher shook his head.

"No, sir, I can't. You're right. But I'm convinced of it."

"That's good enough for me," Russell said. "I'd trust my own life to Preacher's instincts, Senator."

"I may well be trusting the lives of my wife and daughter to you, Preacher," Allingham said. "They mean more to me than my own life."

"I understand," the mountain man said. "If they went to all the trouble to take those prisoners, though, it makes sense that the men behind the raid would want to keep them with 'em."

Allingham sighed and nodded.

"You're right. Besides, we have a much better chance of rescuing them from a smaller group, don't we?"

"Yep. We might still be able to get 'em out of a Pawnee town, if that's where they were, but I'm hopin' this'll be easier."

Preacher mounted up and heeled Horse into

motion again. Dog ran ahead of him through the tall grass. Russell and Allingham flanked the mountain man, while the other five men trailed out behind.

Preacher could tell that the group they were pursuing was moving pretty fast, not wasting any time in putting some distance between themselves and the Big Muddy. If they kept going in the same direction, eventually they would come to the river again after it took its big curve to the west.

Before that they would have to cross a range of low, sandy hills. Those hills weren't rugged enough to slow anybody down very much, but they provided lots of good places for an ambush. Preacher knew he would have to keep that in mind if they hadn't caught up to the kidnappers before then.

Kidnappers was how he had come to think of them. The attack on the boat wasn't just a raid to do as much damage to the white men as the Pawnee could. Preacher's instincts told him it had been aimed specifically at grabbing the count. They had probably taken Roderick along thinking that they could use him as leverage against Stahlmaske if necessary.

Obviously, they weren't aware of just how cold and arrogant Albert Stahlmaske really was. Preacher wasn't sure if threatening his brother would have any effect on the count.

The possibility that he was ignoring something nagged at him. He said, "Senator, earlier I asked you if there was any reason for somebody to kidnap Count Stahlmaske. What about your wife and daughter? Could somebody with a grudge against you be tryin' to get back at you through them?"

"Good Lord, I have political enemies, of course, but no one who would do such a thing as that!"

"Are you sure? There've been duels fought over what happened in Congress, and fistfights on the floor of the Capitol, too, I recollect."

"Well, it's true that things have gotten out of hand at times," Allingham admitted, "but I still say no one in Washington would have done this. Not over politics."

"Are you a rich man? Maybe somebody figures on makin' you pay a big ransom to get Mrs. Allingham and Sarah back."

"If they are, they're going to be disappointed." Allingham's voice choked a little on the words as he went on, "I could raise some money, I suppose, but not enough to make it worthwhile threatening my family."

"That brings us back to the count—and his lady."

"Fraulein Ritter," the senator mused. "Her father actually is quite wealthy. He has a number of shipping interests. Not to be cynical, but I think that was the main reason behind the count's impending marriage to her. He comes from an old family— Castle Stahlmaske goes back to the Middle Ages, you know—but I don't think they have as much money as they once did."

"Well, there you go. Something else to think about."

"I'm sure we'll find out the motivation behind

this atrocity . . . *after* we've recovered the prisoners and returned them to safety."

Preacher knew that, but one reason he'd voiced his speculations to Allingham was to take the senator's mind off the danger his wife and daughter might be in. Brooding about that wouldn't help anything in the long run.

After a while Preacher held up his hand to signal another halt. Once again he dismounted to take a closer look at the ground. Russell joined him, and after a few minutes he said, "They stopped here for a little while."

"Yep," Preacher agreed. He pointed to the footprints he had spotted. "Looks like several folks wearin' boots and shoes. And from the looks of those tracks, some of 'em were women."

"Thank God!" Allingham exclaimed. "That proves we're following the right group, doesn't it?"

"I reckon it does."

"Why do you think they stopped?" Russell asked. "Just to let the prisoners stretch their legs?"

"Or maybe to have a talk about somethin'. Hard to say." Preacher gazed off to the north. "But after a while they mounted up and headed on that way, so I reckon we will, too."

"At least we know we're on the right trail now," Allingham said. "That's a huge relief."

The senator was right about that, Preacher thought as he swung up into the saddle. But they still had a big chore facing them. They were outnumbered two to one and had to worry about the safety of the prisoners, to boot. They couldn't just charge in with all guns blazing.

The sun dropped lower and lower toward the horizon. Allingham got worried again and asked, "Can we keep on trailing them once it gets dark?"

Preacher shook his head.

"No, there's too big a risk of losin' the trail. Not only that, if they make camp we might ride right into the big middle of 'em without any warnin'."

"But what about the kidnappers? Will they push on through the night?"

"They might," Preacher answered honestly. "Especially if they know where they're goin'."

"That means they'll be even farther ahead of us by morning!"

"It can't be helped, Senator. We'll catch up to 'em, even if it takes several days."

The rescue party had brought along some meager supplies, in case the pursuit lasted for days, and Preacher knew he could always catch a rabbit or a prairie chicken with a snare if he needed to. They might get hungry, but they wouldn't starve.

The problem was that the longer those women were held prisoner, the greater the chance they might be molested. Preacher didn't know if that was what the kidnappers had in mind, but with women as attractive as Margaret, Sarah, and Gretchen, that idea had to be in their thoughts.

He put Allingham's mind at ease the best he could, telling him, "Anyway, Senator, when I say that we'll have to stop for the night, that doesn't mean *all* of us will stop."

"You mean . . . ?"

"Dog and me might go on the scout," Preacher said.

They would have a cold camp tonight, Preacher informed the others an hour later as they were unsaddling their horses and picketing the animals so they could graze. The men they were pursuing were bound to know they were back here, but there was no point in announcing their position to the varmints with a fire.

The campsite the mountain man had chosen was beside a tiny creek that flowed through a shallow wash. Once everybody was settled in, Preacher said, "You'll want to keep a guard posted all night. It ain't likely any of that bunch we're after would double back and try to ambush us, but somebody should stay awake all the time anyway."

"I'll take the first watch," one of the crewmen volunteered. He was a tall, broad-shouldered man named Warburton.

"And I'll take the second," Russell said. With three shifts, the middle was the most difficult and needed the most experienced man. Softened by town living or not, Russell could still handle it, Preacher was confident of that.

"Allow me to take the third watch," Egon said. "I am accustomed to rising early. There was always much to do for the count, *ja*, Ludwig?"

"*Jawohl*," Ludwig agreed emphatically, bringing a faint smile to Preacher's face. He figured working for Count Stahlmaske was pretty close to hell on earth.

"I'll leave it up to you fellas to work out the details," Preacher said. "As soon as it gets a little darker, Dog and me are gonna take a look at what's ahead of us. Keep your eyes open for us, and don't shoot us when we come back. Simon, I'll do a whippoorwill call so you'll know it's me."

"All right, Preacher," Russell acknowledged with a nod.

Preacher hunkered on his heels next to the creek, ate a biscuit he had brought along from the riverboat's kitchen, washed it down with a couple of handfuls of water he scooped from the stream. It wasn't much of a meal, but living on the frontier had taught him how to survive on short rations when he needed to.

By the time he was finished, the last glow of sundown had faded from the western sky. The stars were out but the moon wasn't up yet, so the night was pretty dark, just the way Preacher wanted it. He picked up his rifle, rose to his feet, and said quietly, "See you boys later."

He trotted off to the north with Dog padding along beside him, going on foot instead of taking Horse because it would be quieter and he didn't know how far ahead of them their quarry might be.

Like the Indians, Preacher could travel this way for hours without stopping to rest. He kept track of the time by glancing at the stars now and then. He didn't want to get so far ahead of the rest of his party that he couldn't rejoin them by morning.

After a couple of hours, he slowed and then came to a stop as a faint scent of smoke drifted to his nose. He dropped to one knee and put a hand on Dog, who had also halted. He felt as much as heard the big cur's growl, so he knew Dog had smelled something, too.

"That's a campfire not far away, I reckon," he said in a half whisper. "Guess they figured they're far enough ahead there was no need to push on all night."

Preacher's keen eyes scanned the darkness in front of them but didn't see any sign of a fire. That was no surprise. They were in the southern edge of the sandy, grass-covered hills that stretched on north toward the Missouri River, so there were plenty of little depressions where someone could build a campfire without it being seen very far away.

It didn't matter whether he could see the fire. He and Dog could follow their noses right to it.

"Come on," he breathed to the big cur, "but take it slow and easy."

As they stalked forward carefully, the smell of smoke grew stronger. Preacher went to hands and knees to climb up a rise, and as he did he saw a faint glow on the other side that had to be coming from the campfire.

He bellied down and took off his hat for the last couple of feet. When he reached the crest he lifted his head so he could look over it, down into the shallow valley before the next hill rose.

The fire was small, fueled by dried buffalo chips so it gave off almost no smoke—but almost wasn't the same as none, so Preacher had been able to smell the fire.

The flames didn't give off much light, either, but enough for the mountain man to see the figures huddled on the ground nearby. He recognized the count, Roderick, and the three women. From the way they were lying, he knew their hands were tied behind their backs. That had to be pretty uncomfortable, but at least they were all still alive.

One of the white men stood near the prisoners, a long-barreled rifle cradled in his left arm. He was watching over the captives to make sure none of them got loose or tried anything else. The other three whites were on the far side of the fire, talking quietly among themselves.

The Pawnee were off to the left, keeping to themselves. The horses were over there, too, moving around a little on picket ropes as they grazed.

Preacher knew that Dog could stampede the horses without much trouble. He could shoot down the guard next to the prisoners before the man knew what was happened, then kill at least two of the other white men with his pistols. At worst that would leave the fourth man to be disposed of with knife or tomahawk. Preacher was confident he could do that.

And then the Pawnee would kill him and probably slaughter the prisoners, since whatever plan the white men had would collapse with them dead. As strong as the urge was to bust in there and commence to killin', Preacher knew he couldn't do it without risking the lives of the people he had come to rescue. Like it or not, he had to bide his time.

Dog rumbled deep in his throat, so quietly that the sound couldn't have been heard more than a foot or two away. Preacher heard it, though, and recognized it as a warning. At the same time, he counted the Pawnee warriors he could see.

Eleven.

There was a dozen Indian ponies.

That meant one of the warriors was somewhere out here in the darkness with him, and Preacher had no doubt the man was searching for anyone who would be daring enough to sneak up on the camp.

Judging by Dog's reaction, the Pawnee was close by, too.

CHAPTER 26

Preacher didn't move. He listened intently instead, and after a moment he heard the soft whisper of someone moving through the grass. The mountain man turned his head maybe an inch and watched from the corner of his eye as an indistinct shape moved through the starlight about twenty yards away.

Dog was pressed close against him. Preacher felt the vibration in the big cur's torso as Dog tried not to growl. Not a sound came from the animal. Preacher knew it was a real struggle for Dog not to leap up with a snarl and launch himself at the enemy.

The Pawnee scout moved on up the hill and disappeared over it. Preacher dared to breathe again. He and Dog hadn't been seen where they lay in the tall grass.

A few minutes later the scout completed his circuit of the camp and rejoined the other Pawnee.

Preacher crawled backward from the hilltop and took Dog with him.

When he was far enough away, he stood up and put his hat on. The urge to go back and try to rescue the prisoners was strong inside him, but he controlled it and turned to head back to where he had left the others. At least he could report to them that the captives were alive and seemed to be unharmed.

Tirelessly, Preacher trotted across the prairie, and his unerring instincts led him straight to the rest of the search party a couple of hours later. The moon had risen by now, and its silvery illumination spilling over the plains revealed the dark line of brush that followed the course of the creek. Preacher paused and imitated the cry of the whippoorwill so Russell would know he was coming in.

A moment later Preacher heard the return cry signaling that everything was all right. He jogged on into the camp.

They were all awake and on their feet. Before Preacher could say anything, Senator Allingham asked anxiously, "Did you find them? Are they all right?"

"Yeah, I found 'em, and as far as I can tell they're all fine, Senator. They were tied up, so they'll probably be pretty stiff and sore in the mornin', but they'll get over that."

"Thank the Lord!" Allingham said. "Where are they?"

"About seven, eight miles ahead of us. I can lead the way, if you fellas are up for the march."

"Just try and stop us," Russell said. "I want to get those varmints in my sights more than I've wanted anything in a long time."

"*Ja*," Heinrich agreed. "For their crimes they must pay."

The others all nodded, obviously eager to catch up to the kidnappers. Egon asked, "We will be there by morning?"

"We should be," Preacher said, "and with any luck, that'll be the best time to hit 'em."

Roderick had complained until exhaustion finally overcame him and he fell asleep. His brother actually felt some relief at that development. Listening to Roderick had been tiresome.

At least Gretchen had been relatively calm about their whole ordeal. Stahlmaske admired her. He still hoped that eventually he would have the chance to show his admiration by marrying her—and also by putting himself in charge of the fortune she stood to inherit someday.

Margaret and Sarah had done nothing but snivel and weep, of course. Precisely what he would have expected of soft American women.

They were asleep now, too, claimed by exhaustion as Roderick had been. Stahlmaske was the only one of the captives still awake. He watched through slitted eyes as the three Englishmen on the other side of the fire rolled up in their blankets and went to sleep. The savages had bedded down for the night, too.

That left only one man on guard, a florid-faced individual with a sandy mustache. He stood about ten feet from Stahlmaske, holding a rifle and looking around at the darkness.

"Englishman!" Stahlmaske whispered. "Englishman, do you hear me?"

The guard ignored him for a minute, but Stahlmaske was persistent. Finally the man turned to him and asked in a quiet voice, "What do you want?"

"Earlier your companion said that I was going to make you all rich men. I can make one man even richer—you."

"What is it you're going to do? Bribe me to let you loose?"

"That's right. Free me, my brother, and my fiancée, and I'll see to it that you're paid whatever you want."

"What about those other two women?" the guard asked.

"I care nothing about them. They can remain here with you. Do with them as you will."

The man said nothing, which made Stahlmaske believe that he was considering the offer. But then he laughed quietly and shook his head.

"What are you going to pay me with?" the Englishman demanded. "We know you don't have any money of your own. That's why you were going to marry that good-looking redhead!"

Stahlmaske's eyes widened as he lay there trying

to conceal his astonishment. How had the man known about the perilous state of the family finances? Was such a thing common knowledge in England? He didn't see how that could be possible.

"Maybe you should just shut up and try to go to sleep," the guard went on. "It'll be a long day tomorrow. You'll need your rest."

Stahlmaske tried to reclaim some of his bravado by saying, "You and your fellows will regret this. I intend to see to it that you're all hanged. That is, if I don't take you back to Prussia with me." He smiled. "I have a castle, you know. And there's a dungeon in that castle where suitable punishment for the likes of you can be arranged."

"You just go on thinking that, Count," the man said, clearly not worried.

Stahlmaske's teeth ground together in anger. It was bad enough that he was miserably uncomfortable, lying on the ground with his hands and feet tied. Now he had a maddening conundrum to plague him as well.

Just what sort of game were these damned Englishmen playing?

Once Preacher had been over a piece of ground he never forgot it. That natural ability had saved his life and the lives of others countless times in the past. He could only hope that tonight it would again.

The rescue party rode on horseback part of the

way, but he knew how well sound could carry at night so after a while he called a halt and told the men to dismount.

"We'll go the rest of the way on foot," he explained. "We don't want them to hear us comin'. When we get close enough, we'll leave one man with the horses and the rest of us will crawl up to the edge of their camp."

"We're still outnumbered two to one," Russell pointed out. "How do you plan to hit them?"

"You and me will take care of the four white men, Simon. Everybody else pour as much lead as you can into those Pawnee while they're asleep."

Allingham sounded shocked as he said, "But . . . but that's murder! To shoot sleeping, defenseless men—"

"It's the best way of tryin' to get your wife and daughter out of there with whole skins," Preacher finished for him in a flat, grim voice. "I understand what you're sayin', Senator, but those varmints killed Heinrich's brother and several members of the crew. They did their damnedest to kill a bunch more of us. There's a good chance I know some of those warriors. I'm sorry to have to fight 'em. But the lines are drawn and we don't have any choice."

Heinrich said, "I can shoot them, Herr Preacher. For Hobart."

Preacher nodded and clapped a hand on the young man's shoulder. He didn't say anything. He didn't need to.

Allingham sighed and said, "I understand. I just wish there were some other way to do it. But of course I'll do whatever is necessary to save Margaret and Sarah."

The eastern sky was tinged faintly with gray as Preacher and the other men approached the kidnappers' campsite. The sun would be up in another hour. This was the time when men slept the soundest, when those who were standing guard had the most difficulty staying awake and alert.

When Preacher called a halt again, he considered the men he had with him, then said, "Ludwig, I got a special job for you."

"Anything you wish me to attempt, Herr Preacher, I will do my very best," the servant vowed.

"I know you will. That's why I'm givin' you the job of stayin' here with the horses."

Ludwig's face fell in the moonlight.

"You do not wish me to come with you to fight those men?"

"There's a good chance we're gonna be leavin' outta there in a hurry," Preacher explained. "That means we'll need these horses to be right here waitin' for us. If they ain't, I reckon that means we're all plumb out of luck. So if you ain't up to the job of handlin' the horses and havin' 'em ready, I'll give it to somebody else."

"No, no," Ludwig said hastily. "I can do it. I did not understand."

"Well, now you do."

"Yes, of course. I will let nothing happen to the horses."

Preacher turned to the others and went on, "The rest of you will be comin' with me. You know what to do. There's a little hill overlookin' their camp. When Simon and I start down it after those white men, the rest of you open up on the Pawnee."

He got grim nods all around in response.

"Check your guns, and then we'll get started."

Preacher knew he was asking a lot of these men. None of them had any real experience in matters like this except him and Simon Russell. Whether that would be enough to allow the rescue party to succeed, only time would tell.

A few minutes later they set off toward the hills, leaving a nervous Ludwig behind them holding the horses.

Stahlmaske finally dozed off sometime during the night, but his sleep was restless and did nothing to improve his mood. When he awoke, however, his thoughts were clearer than they had been at any time since he'd been knocked unconscious during the attack on the riverboat.

What was happening to him still made no sense, but at least he finally knew who was responsible for it.

A different Englishman was standing guard now, a short, stocky man with fuzzy whiskers on the sides of his face. He had a shotgun tucked under his arm.

"You there," Stahlmaske said to the sentry, not bothering to try to keep the contempt he felt out of his voice.

"What do you want, you damn Dutchman?" the guard asked harshly.

Stahlmaske suppressed the anger that threatened to boil over inside him and said, "I would like to talk to my brother."

"Well, there he is," the Englishman said as he waved a pudgy hand at Roderick.

"May I move over there beside him?"

The guard chuckled.

"You'll have to squirm on your belly like a snake if you do, but be my guest, guv'nor."

Grimacing, the count rolled onto his side and began working his way laboriously across the ground toward Roderick, who was still asleep.

When he was close enough, he twisted around so he could kick Roderick's leg with his feet, which were bound together at the ankles. That roused Roderick from his slumber. He started to try to sit up and exclaim.

"Quiet!" Stahlmaske told him in an urgent whisper. "I don't want to wake the ladies."

"What . . . what is it?" Roderick stammered. "Is there trouble?"

Stahlmaske didn't respond to that question, but his contemptuous silence spoke volumes.

Roderick sighed and said, "Yes, of course there's trouble, isn't there, Albert? We're still prisoners. We still don't know what these awful men are going to do to us."

He cast a nervous glance toward the nearby guard as he spoke.

"No, we don't know what they're going to do," Stahlmaske agreed. "But at least now I know who they're working for."

Roderick's eyes widened as he stared at his brother.

"What . . . what do you mean, Albert? Are you saying that someone else arranged for us to be abducted?"

"That's right, although I have no idea why this person would do such a thing."

"Who is it?" Roderick asked anxiously. "Who is behind this whole horrible business?"

"Why, you should know that better than anyone, brother," Stahlmaske said coldly. "These men and their primitive allies are working for you."

CHAPTER 27

Roderick stared at him in the dim light, wide-eyed in apparent astonishment. The young man struggled to speak for a moment before he managed to say, "Working for . . . for me! That's insane, Albert! Why in heaven's name would you think they're working for me?"

"Because they know that our family fortune is gone," Stahlmaske replied coldly. "We've concealed that from the servants, from our business and political associates, from everyone outside the family. That means either you or Uncle Gerhard had to tell them . . . and Gerhard would never work with *Englishmen*."

Scorn dripped from the word when Stahlmaske spoke it.

"What makes you think I would?"

"You went to university in England. You know those people. It has to be you. Look me in the eye and tell me I'm wrong." Stahlmaske scoffed. "You know you could never lie to me, Roderick. You wouldn't dare."

"I . . . I . . ." Roderick's voice trailed off. He drew in a deep breath, and a cold expression settled over his face. He looked almost like a completely different person as he said, "You're right, I could never lie to you, Albert. But I could hate you for all the things you've done to me. And I do." He lifted his head and called to the guard, "Come over here and get these damned ropes off of me. Now!"

The man stared at him, mouth opening and closing like a fish out of water. He said, "But Herr Stahlmaske, we were told—"

"I don't care what you were told. I'm doing the telling now. Unless you want me to report to Lord Rutherford how uncooperative you were."

The man swallowed and nodded. He turned to the other Englishmen and called, "Boys, get up. The masquerade's over. We're takin' Mr. Roderick's orders now."

Stahlmaske lay there filled with fury as the men climbed out of their blankets, rubbing their eyes and looking surprised by this turn of events. To be betrayed was bad enough, but to be betrayed by one's own brother—

One of the men came over to Roderick and cut him loose. Roderick lifted a hand and said, "Help me up." He seemed like a different person now, cool and assured as he issued commands, instead of the fumbling, diffident younger brother he had always been around the count.

Clearly, his brother was a consummate actor, Stahlmaske thought.

"Blasted feet and legs are numb," Roderick complained as he leaned on the man who had freed him. "Did you have to make those bonds so tight?"

"Lord Rutherford said we were to make it look good, sir. He said you didn't want anybody getting the idea you were working with us."

"You work *for* me," Roderick snapped. "This was my idea. I'm in charge of the plan."

"All right," the man with the rust-colored mustache said. "What is it you want us to do?"

"We'll carry on just as planned. When the senator catches up to us, we'll kill him, Albert, and the women. I'll be the only survivor to tell the tale of how Senator Allingham plotted to have my brother kidnapped and murdered, only to have his efforts backfire and leave him and his family dead as well."

Roderick could walk again, the feeling having returned to his lower limbs. He strode over to Stahlmaske and smiled smugly down at his brother.

"You don't know how much I appreciate your weakness of the flesh, Albert. You made our story just that much stronger by dallying with the senator's wife. Now he has even more motivation for wanting you dead. When our agents in Washington and Berlin are finished spreading rumors, everyone will believe exactly what we want them to believe, including the king."

"Good Lord," Stahlmaske breathed. "You really

are a British secret agent. I dared to believe I was wrong."

Roderick shook his head and said, "I've been working for the British government and the Hudson's Bay Company for months now. I was acquainted with Lord Rutherford from my days at Oxford. His son and I were friends. When it was decided that you would come over here to negotiate with the Americans, His Lordship contacted me and proposed an allegiance. I knew the family's finances were failing and that if the Stahlmaske legacy were to be preserved, I would have to do it."

"So you sold out our honor to the damned British," the count accused with a sneer.

"Oh, God, don't get so high and mighty with me, Albert! You've always gotten everything you wanted. It was all just handed to you." Roderick glanced over at Gretchen, who was asleep in the depths of exhaustion. "Everything . . . just handed to you."

"Gretchen," Stahlmaske said hollowly. "This treachery of yours is because of Gretchen?"

"She could never really see me, not while my dashing older brother was around," Roderick snapped.

Stahlmaske stared at him for a couple of seconds, then began to laugh. He said, "Do you really believe that she would ever be interested in you that way, whether I'm alive or not? You poor, pathetic, deluded fool. But then, that's what you've always been, isn't it?"

Roderick stepped closer and kicked his brother in the side. Stahlmaske gasped, but he continued to give Roderick the same mocking grin.

"Roderick! What are you doing?"

The shocked cry came from Gretchen, who hadn't been as sound asleep as he thought, Stahlmaske realized. She had roused enough to see that Roderick was not only free, but to witness that brutal kick, as well.

"What are you going to do now, brother?" Stahlmaske asked Roderick, and then he began to laugh again.

Preacher didn't rush the other members of the rescue party as they neared the kidnappers' camp. They couldn't afford to do anything that might warn the men they were after. So they took their time, especially during the final approach.

The sky was gray enough for them to see a little, so Preacher was able to use hand signals as he directed the other men to crawl up the hill overlooking the camp. It would still be a while before the sun was up . . . but they could see well enough to shoot.

Before they reached the top of the slope, Preacher heard voices on the other side. Several men were talking, and fairly loudly, at that. Preacher breathed a curse. He had hoped that everyone would still be asleep except perhaps for a single drowsy guard. Now it was going to be much more difficult to take the kidnappers and their Pawnee allies by surprise.

He paused when he heard the voices, and so did the others. Preacher looked at Russell to his right and Allingham to his left and motioned with his head for them to proceed. All they could do at this point was carry on with the plan and see what the situation was when they reached the top of the hill.

What they found was something Preacher wouldn't have guessed in a hundred years.

The prisoners were still in roughly the same positions they had been in when Preacher spied on the camp earlier, except that Count Stahlmaske had moved closer to where his brother had been lying.

Roderick wasn't there anymore. He was on his feet, freed from his bonds, walking around and talking to Stahlmaske and to the four white men who had been with the Pawnee.

"What the hell?" Russell breathed from beside Preacher.

The mountain man lifted a hand and motioned for everyone to remain quiet.

"Let's listen and see what's goin' on here," he whispered.

Preacher felt Allingham stiffen beside him as Roderick talked. When Roderick got to the part about murdering the senator's wife and daughter, Preacher thought Allingham might leap up and charge down there.

Preacher put a hand on Allingham's shoulder to steady him. The mountain man wanted to find out as much as he could before he and his companions made their move.

When Gretchen Ritter woke up and wanted to know what was going on, Roderick went over and knelt next to her.

"Gretchen, please listen to me," he said. "You must understand, Albert was just using you. He just wanted your father's fortune. He never loved you. Otherwise he never would have dallied with that American trollop."

Next to Preacher, Allingham growled in anger at hearing his wife described that way. There might be a little truth in what Roderick said, but that didn't mean Allingham wanted to hear it. Preacher tightened his grip on the senator's shoulder.

"It's different with me," Roderick went on to Gretchen. "I love you, darling. I always have, ever since I first laid eyes on you. I . . . I hoped you would see the way I feel about you. I dared to hope you might feel the same way." His voice took on a sharp, bitter edge. "But Albert swooped in like a hawk, the way he always does. He sees something he wants, even if it's just a passing fancy, and he has to have it, no matter who else he may hurt by taking it." He turned his head to glare at his brother. "He doesn't care about anyone else. But I do. I just want the best for you, my dear, the very best, and if you do as I say, you shall have it."

Gretchen's expression had been getting more and more horrified as she stared up at him during his plea. When he paused, she burst out, "You're insane, Roderick! You're totally mad!"

His face hardened with hurt and anger.

"Why?" he demanded. "Why am I mad? Because I dared to want a beautiful woman for myself? For thinking that I'm just as good as my brother?"

He got to his feet and began to pace around, waving his arms as his emotions boiled over.

"As good as my brother?" he repeated. "I'm better than my brother! Albert is a cold, arrogant, insufferable ass!"

The young fella had a point there, thought Preacher.

"He doesn't deserve his success," Roderick went on. "He doesn't deserve you, Gretchen. And you deserve better than him."

He took a step toward her and reached out with a hand. She flinched back, clearly repulsed by the idea of him touching her.

Roderick jerked like he had stuck his hand in fire. He stood there staring at her for a long moment, then said, "This is your last chance, Gretchen. You can be part of this with me. We'll be married, after a suitable interval following Albert's death, of course—"

"No!" the auburn-haired beauty cried. "No!"

Roderick's expression hardened. He gave a curt nod and said, "Very well, then. You can die with the others when we get to the trading post." He motioned to the Englishmen. "Get them all up. It's light enough for us to push on. I want to reach our destination today."

Up on the hill, Russell leaned close to Preacher and whispered, "If we're gonna jump them—"

The mountain man shook his head and said, "We're gonna wait."

Allingham didn't like that idea. He said, "You

mean to wait while my wife and daughter are in danger?"

Preacher motioned for them to back away from the hilltop so that it would be easier to talk without running the risk of being overheard by their quarry.

When they had put some distance between them and the kidnappers' camp, Preacher called a halt and said, "I know how you feel, Senator, but your ladies are safe for right now. You heard Roderick. Nothing's gonna happen until they get where they're going. That's where they're gonna lay a trap for you."

"And what are we going to do about that?" Allingham wanted to know.

Preacher smiled and said, "Why, you're gonna waltz right into it."

CHAPTER 28

The kidnappers broke camp before the sun was up. They had made a skimpy breakfast on some hideous "delicacy" provided by the Indians that consisted of dried meat and a sort of gelatinous substance that Stahlmaske found almost inedible. At least there was coffee to wash the unappetizing stuff down with, although it was a bitter, unpleasant brew.

The Allingham women refused to eat. When awakened, they cried and whimpered and carried on to the point that Stahlmaske couldn't believe he had actually slept with one of them and considered seducing the other. When it came time to leave, they clung to each other and had to be forcibly separated by the Englishmen, who threw them onto horses and tied them in place again.

Roderick strutted around like he was a king, trying futilely to impress Gretchen. Seeing the way she responded to his brother with haughty disdain, the count was a bit regretful that he hadn't taken her more seriously earlier. He had been concerned primarily with her family's money and had failed to see that she really was a suitable mate for him in other ways as well.

And quite beautiful, of course. She would have made an appealing bed companion.

As the men were mounting up, after Stahlmaske had been put on a horse like the other three prisoners, he said to his brother, "Give up this madness, Roderick. You know as well as I that it will only come to a bad end."

"*You* will come to a bad end, Albert," Roderick said. "I, on the other hand, will be wealthy, as well as a valuable adviser to King Friedrich Wilhelm during the coming international crisis with the Americans."

"A false crisis that you intend to create at the behest of your British masters."

Roderick climbed onto his horse with his usual awkwardness. His diffident attitude had vanished, but not his physical limitations. He looked at Stahlmaske and shrugged.

"My British masters, as you call them, are paying me very well and helping me get exactly what I want. So who is really the master here, eh?"

With that he dug his heels into the flanks of his horse and got the animal moving.

The group rode north through the sandy hills. A couple of the Pawnee were a good distance out in front, scouting the way. Stahlmaske knew that at least one of the Englishmen spoke the natives' barbaric tongue, because he had seen the man speaking to them, pointing and gesturing as he did so.

Roderick and one of the Englishmen came next, followed by the other three white men and the prisoners, and finally the rest of the Pawnee war party brought up the rear. Thankfully, Margaret and Sarah Allingham had stopped crying and wailing. They rode side by side in stunned silence, their expressions dull and numbed by the fear they felt.

The Englishmen weren't leading the horses today, and the prisoners weren't tied as tightly and uncomfortably as they had been the previous day. They were able to ride sitting up straight instead of leaning over the horse's neck.

Stahlmaske knew it would do no good to try to get away, though. If any of the prisoners tried to make a break for freedom, the Indians would just chase them down in a matter of moments.

The count moved his horse over closer to Gretchen's and said, "My dear, I'm sorry that my brother has involved you in his madness. Had I been aware of this insane scheme of his, I would have put a stop to it immediately."

"I know that, Albert," she said. "What I cannot understand is what he hopes to gain by this. Surely he would not have done such a thing simply because he was . . . attracted to me."

"Beautiful women have been prompting men to do foolish things all the way back to the dawn of time," mused the count. "But I think Roderick's true motivation is the hatred and resentment he feels for me. Perhaps I deserve that. The shadow I cast has always engulfed him."

False modesty was not Stahlmaske's way, and this was as close to introspection and self-examination as he was ever going to get. He didn't really care what had incited his brother's treachery. He just wanted to figure out what he was going to do about it.

"Where do you think they're taking us?" Gretchen asked.

"Roderick mentioned something about a trading post. I didn't know the British had any posts in American territory."

"Perhaps that's what this is about. With trouble between the Americans and our government, they might be less likely to pay attention to what's going on out here on the frontier."

Stahlmaske frowned in thought. Gretchen was an intelligent woman. She might be on to something with that idea.

"Whatever the reason, I plan to put a stop to it," he said. "One thing we can be sure of, if this is Roderick's plan there's bound to be a flaw in it, something that will cause it to fail. It's only a matter of time."

"If Preacher is alive, he'll be coming after us, too."

Stahlmaske's frown deepened.

"Preacher," he said, his disdain for the mountain man obvious in his voice. "People seem to think the man can work miracles, but as far as I can tell, he's only one step above a savage himself!"

"Sometimes that's exactly what's needed," Gretchen said.

Preacher sent Russell and the other men back to fetch the horses, all except for Allingham, who begged to stay behind with Preacher and Dog.

"I want to stay here, closer to Margaret and Sarah," he explained. His voice was determined but also ragged with fear for his wife and daughter's safety.

Preacher considered the request for a moment, then said, "If you think you can keep a cool head, you can stay. You got to do everything I tell you, though."

"Of course. I just want to get them back safely, Preacher. Nothing else really means anything to me. Following your orders is the best way I can do that."

The senator was showing some sense. He and Preacher went back to the hill overlooking the camp while the other men headed back the way they had come.

The two of them watched as the kidnappers got ready to break camp. Roderick Stahlmaske was still giving orders. The four Englishmen didn't seem to have much respect for him, but they did what he told them to do, Preacher noted. More than likely they had been ordered by their real boss to go along with whatever Roderick wanted.

Preacher knew it was difficult for Allingham when he had to watch Margaret and Sarah crying in fear and clutching each other. To watch a loved one in danger like that and not be able to do anything about it had to be pure hell.

Allingham bit his lip and stayed quiet, though, as the sky lightened even more and the sun finally came up. He and Preacher had taken their hats off, and they kept their heads down so they wouldn't be spotted in the tall grass.

After the group had eaten breakfast, they got ready to move out. Allingham whispered to Preacher, "When will our men be back with the horses?"

"It'll probably be another hour, anyway," the mountain man replied.

"And during that time, those men will build up another lead on us."

"It'll be all right," Preacher assured him. "We'll be able to follow them. From the sound of what they said earlier, they don't really want to lose us. That's why they ain't goin' to any trouble to cover their trail."

"Because they're luring us into that trap you mentioned."

"Yep."

Earlier, he and Allingham and Russell had discussed what they would do when they caught up with the kidnappers. Preacher intended for Allingham and the other men, except for him and Russell, to approach openly. While they were doing that, the two frontiersmen would circle around and get behind the kidnappers to search for a way to free the prisoners. Those were all the details that could be worked out until they had gotten a look at wherever the group was bound and seen the lay of the land.

Once the kidnappers and their captives were gone, Preacher and Allingham could talk more freely. Allingham asked, "What was that about a trading post Roderick mentioned? Wouldn't any trading posts out here belong to the American Fur Company?"

"All the ones I know about do," Preacher agreed, "but I've been thinkin' about those fellas who are workin' with Roderick. A while back I tangled with some British government agents who were tryin' to ruin the American fur trade so that the Hudson's Bay Company and other English fur tradin' companies could get a better foothold down here. As long as there's been fur trappin' in the Rockies, the British have wanted to come down here from Canada and take over. Could be this is just their latest attempt."

"Stir up trouble between the United States and Prussia, eh? Maybe even start a war to keep Washington distracted?"

"I don't see how we're supposed to fight them dang Prussians when they're all the way around on the other side of the world."

"Our marines fought the Barbary pirates," Allingham pointed out. "That's a long way from here, too, and it's on the other side of an ocean. I suppose the United States and Prussia could attack each other if they wanted to badly enough. We could certainly make war on each other's shipping."

"Would the count gettin' killed make the Prussians mad enough to start a ruckus like that?"

"If it was made to appear that a United States senator was to blame for his death? Quite likely." Allingham let out a disgusted groan. "God, we all really played right into Roderick's hands, didn't we? The count by seducing my wife, Margaret by going along with it, and me by attacking him on the riverboat. Now everyone will believe whatever story Roderick's friends want to spread."

"He ain't got away with it yet," Preacher pointed out. "He still has to kill you and the count, remember, and we don't aim to let that happen."

A few minutes of silence went by, then Allingham said, "I can almost sympathize with him, you know."

"The count?"

"Roderick."

Preacher squinted at Allingham and asked, "How in blazes do you figure that?"

"Well, if you had to spend your whole life with Albert Stahlmaske as your brother . . . wouldn't you feel like killing him, too?"

Preacher laughed and said, "Now that you mention it, I reckon I might've done it a long time before now!"

They were chuckling over that when Dog growled. Dog's instincts warned the mountain man at the same time. He and Allingham were lying at the top of the hill on their bellies, peering in the direction the kidnappers had gone. Preacher rolled over fast and snatched his rifle from the ground just as something whipped past his ear.

He glanced over and saw a Pawnee arrow sticking in the ground where he had been only a second earlier. As he sat up he saw one of the painted warriors standing several yards away, drawing back his bowstring for another shot.

CHAPTER 29

Preacher fired the rifle without bringing it to his shoulder to aim, but the shot was true anyway. The ball punched into the warrior's belly and doubled him over. When he loosed the arrow as he died, it flew into the ground just a few feet in front of him, well short of Preacher and the senator.

The Pawnee wasn't alone. Several more warriors had crawled through the grass and closed in on the two white men. Now that there was no longer any need for stealth, they leaped to their feet and charged toward Preacher with shrill war cries.

The mountain man barely had time to drop his empty rifle and snatch the two pistols from behind his belt. He cocked the weapons as he brought them up and then pressed the triggers.

Smoke and flame geysered from the muzzles as the pistols roared. The shots drove two more of the Pawnee off their feet as blood spouted from the holes the balls ripped in their torsos. They hit the ground and stayed down.

That left two of the warriors still alive and in the fight, however. Allingham fired his rifle at one of them, but in his inexperience he rushed his shot and missed.

Fortunately for him, neither of the Indians paid any attention to him. Their efforts were focused on killing Preacher. The one in the lead dived toward the mountain man with the tomahawk in his hand streaking toward Preacher's head.

Preacher blocked the tomahawk stroke with the empty pistol in his left hand and crashed the one in his right against the side of the Indian's head with bone-shattering force. The warrior collapsed on top of Preacher with his body spasming in its death throes.

That left one of the Pawnee still in the fight. He drew back his bowstring and aimed an arrow past his dying companion's head at Preacher.

Before the man could loose the missile, Allingham surged up off the ground and threw his empty rifle in the warrior's face. It struck the Indian with enough force to throw off his aim. The arrow sailed harmlessly over the hilltop.

Preacher rolled the dead warrior to the side and came up with his tomahawk in hand. He threw it with blinding speed. The head caught the last Pawnee between the eyes, splitting his skull and killing him instantly. The dead man dropped to the ground as if all his bones had suddenly turned to liquid.

"Good Lord!" Allingham exclaimed in a shaky voice. "You just killed five men in a matter of seconds, Preacher!"

"Seemed like the thing to do at the time," Preacher drawled. "Otherwise they were gonna kill me." He shot a speculative glance at Allingham and added, "But not you, Senator."

"What do you mean by that?"

Preacher prodded one of the corpses with the toe of his boot and said, "If they wanted you dead, they had their chances. That fella who fired the first arrow could've put it right in the middle of your back, instead of aimin' it at me. They figured on killin' me and takin' you prisoner, so they could deliver you to Roderick."

"So you think these men were part of the group working for him?"

"Nothin' else makes sense," Preacher said.

"I thought the rest of the Indians went back to their village."

Preacher ran a thumbnail along his grizzled jaw and frowned in thought for a moment before saying, "I reckon that's what they wanted us to think. These men headed south with the others, then split off and doubled back. It was their job to trail Roderick and the others at a distance and deal with any pursuers." The mountain man's bushy black eyebrows drew down as his frown deepened.

"Makes me wonder if Russell and the others didn't head right back into an ambush."

"You mean they may not be coming to join us after all." The words from the senator were a flat, worried statement, not a question.

"Could be," Preacher said. "Could be you and me are the only ones left to rescue those prisoners. That'll make it harder, sure enough. But I ain't in the habit of givin' up as long as I'm still breathin'."

"How long do we wait before starting after Roderick and the others on foot?"

Preacher glanced at the sky. The sun was still fairly low, meaning it was early in the morning.

"We'll give 'em another hour or so," he decided. "If they're not back by then . . . well, I reckon we'll have a long walk in front of us, Senator."

Stahlmaske had never been so exhausted, not even when he had been in combat for hours on end. Every time the party stopped to rest the horses, the count's legs were weak and wobbly when he dismounted. He had to hang on to the saddle for a moment until he regained some of his strength and equilibrium.

It was humiliating having Gretchen see him this way. Even worse was the smug expression that appeared on Roderick's face. His perfect older brother wasn't so perfect after all, and Roderick was taking great pleasure in that fact even though he was exhausted himself.

They all were. The four Englishmen had kept the

group moving at a grueling pace all day, showing consideration only for the horses and then only occasionally.

The man with the rust-colored mustache seemed to be the leader of the quartet. Stahlmaske had overheard enough conversation between the Englishmen to know that the man's name was Battersby. He was big and brawny, with knobby-knuckled fists that showed he was no stranger to trouble.

The short, stout man with the bushy side whiskers was called Trout. Stahlmaske hadn't heard the names of the other two mentioned. Not that it mattered what their names were.

They would all die, by Stahlmaske's own hand if possible.

Then he would deal with Roderick.

Difficult as it was to believe, the group didn't even stop when night fell but rather pressed on to the north as the sky began to darken from blue to black and stars appeared here and there.

"How much farther are we going?" Stahlmaske demanded wearily. "You can't expect these ladies to keep riding indefinitely."

Roderick laughed.

"You mean you can't keep going, Albert," he said.

Stahlmaske couldn't control his anger. He said, "Damn you, look at them!"

It was true. Margaret and Sarah Allingham both looked like they were about to pass out. They would have fallen off their mounts if they hadn't been tied on. Gretchen was holding up somewhat better, but it was obvious she was nearing the end of her strength, too.

Roderick turned to Battersby and asked, "How much farther is it?"

"We'll be there in less than an hour," the Englishman replied.

"Danke." Roderick looked at Stahlmaske and said, "You and the ladies will just have to hold on for a short while longer, Albert."

"And then what?" Stahlmaske asked sharply. "You'll kill us?"

"Oh, no. We'll be waiting until the senator joins us. We have to make sure, you see, that everything is arranged precisely the way it should be. That's why we had to get all of you out here away from everyone else. I'm going to be the sole survivor of this debacle. After I've made my heroic trek through the wilderness, survived a myriad of hardships, and found the riverboat at last, no one will doubt the tale I tell."

"You're a real bastard," the count said. His voice was icy.

"I believe that would make you one as well," Roderick replied with a chuckle.

"I'm beginning to wonder about that. I don't see how I could have sprung from the same pair of loins as a treacherous cur such as yourself."

"Just shut up and ride," Roderick snapped. "We'll be there soon."

The journey seemed never-ending, but finally it did. Stahlmaske spotted a spot of light glowing far ahead of them. Slowly but surely, it grew brighter until he could discern that it was the glow of lamplight through a window. Under normal circumstances the warm yellow illumination would have seemed welcoming as it beckoned to them after a long, hard day in the saddle.

Instead, if Roderick had his way the light marked the place where the count and the three women would die, along with Senator Allingham.

Stahlmaske didn't care a whit about the boorish politician, but Allingham's death would mean that Roderick had succeeded, and Stahlmaske would do everything in his power to prevent that from happening.

The window was in a long, low building that sat on a low bluff next to a wide, slow-moving river. That was the Missouri, Stahlmaske realized. They had cut across country to intercept the stream again after it curved. He vaguely remembered the Missouri's serpentine course from a map he had studied back in Washington before embarking on this ill-fated expedition. As a military man, the count had always been interested in maps.

A couple of hounds heard them coming and ran out to bay at them. A door opened, spilling more light on the ground in front of the building. No one emerged, though, or even stepped into the doorway. The men inside were being careful.

"Is that you, Battersby?" someone called from inside. Stahlmaske suspected that rifles were already thrust through loopholes. If the answer wasn't to the liking of the defenders, they would open fire in a crashing volley that would sweep all the riders out of their saddles.

Well, except for the ones like him who were tied in place, Stahlmaske amended. They would die right where they were, on horseback.

"Of course it's me, Rothfuss, you bloody scoundrel. Who'd you think it would be?"

"Do you know where you are?"

"I know I'm bloody well not in Trafalgar Square!"

Stahlmaske recognized the exchange as a signal to let the men inside the cabin know that everything was all right. If Battersby hadn't mentioned Trafalgar Square, chances were the defenders would have opened fire.

As it was, one of them finally stepped into the doorway and waved an arm beckoningly.

"Come on in," he called. "Everything's fine here."

"Let's go," Roderick said. "I hope you enjoy the accommodations, Albert. The place isn't nearly as luxurious as you're accustomed to, I'm afraid. But it'll do to die in."

CHAPTER 30

Allingham's anxiety grew worse as the minutes dragged by that morning. Preacher could understand why. If more warriors from the Pawnee band had massacred Simon Russell and the other members of the rescue party and taken the horses, it would take days for Preacher and Allingham to catch up to their quarry on foot. Preacher didn't know if the senator was even up to such a trek, although he was sure Allingham would insist on going forward.

With the lives of his wife and daughter at stake, he couldn't really do anything else.

So it was with great relief that Preacher spotted the riders approaching in the distance. Allingham didn't seem to notice them, and Preacher didn't say anything until the men on horseback were close enough for him to recognize Simon Russell in the lead. Everything appeared to be fine.

"Here they come, Senator," the mountain man said.

Allingham had been sitting on the ground, looking depressed. Animated by Preacher's comment, he leaped to his feet and peered to the south, exclaiming, "Where— Oh, thank God! That's Russell, isn't it?"

"Yep," Preacher agreed. He took off his broadbrimmed hat and waved it over his head. He knew Russell was almost as keen-eyed as he was and would see the signal letting him know it was all right to come on in.

"We have a chance to save them now," Allingham said.

"We always had a chance. But we've got a better one with the horses, that's for sure."

Dog ran to meet the newcomers and then led them in, wagging his bushy tail as he did so because he was happy to be reunited with Horse. The two animals had been trail partners and genuine friends for a long time.

As they rode up with the rest of the rescue party, Heinrich Ritter and the two servants, Ludwig and Egon, stared at the Pawnee corpses. Russell didn't look particularly shocked to see the dead Indians.

"Looks like you had a little trouble here," he commented to Preacher as he dismounted.

"Not much to speak of," Preacher said. "Just a few varmints coverin' the rear. I was worried that you might run into more of 'em, though."

Russell shook his head and said, "We didn't see hide nor hair of any Pawnee."

"That's good. Roderick and the rest of that bunch pulled out a little after sunup. We'll let the horses rest a while and then get started after them."

Preacher could tell that Allingham wanted to mount up and gallop after the kidnappers right away. He would just have to figure out a way to be patient, though. A lot depended on those horses, and they had to be taken care of.

After a half-hour that probably seemed a lot longer to Allingham, the men swung up into their saddles and Preacher led the party northward on the trail of the kidnappers. They were several hours behind their quarry and likely wouldn't catch up before the sun went down.

Roderick had said that he wanted to reach their destination by that night, however, and when they did they would stop. Preacher and his men would push on. A showdown was coming, and the sooner the better as far as Preacher was concerned.

The inside of the British post was as primitive and crudely furnished as Stahlmaske would have expected here in this American wilderness. The floor was made of tree trunks split in half and roughly fitted together. The tables and benches were equally rough-hewn. Shelves loaded with trade goods—rifles, pistols, knives, axes, powder horns, shot pouches, food staples—lined the walls of the main room. In the back was a counter where trappers could barter with the man running the post, and to one side was a rough-and-ready bar made of splintery planks laid across whiskey barrels.

At gunpoint, the prisoners were herded in on legs shaky from fatigue. Rothfuss, the man who seemed to be in charge here at the post, was tall and almost painfully thin, with a pair of pince-nez perched on his nose.

"This is the lot you were after, then, eh?" he said as he looked at the captives.

"That's right," Battersby replied.

Rothfuss counted, pointing to each of the prisoners in turn, and then said, "There are only four of them. There were supposed to be five."

Roderick stepped forward and said, "There's no longer any need for the masquerade, my friend. My own role in this is now common knowledge."

"You're him, then," Rothfuss said. "The Prussian turncoat."

Roderick's face flushed angrily at the description. Stahlmaske let out a scornful laugh.

"I see that this man is well acquainted with you, brother," he said.

Roderick snapped, "I'm simply doing what's best for everyone concerned."

"Except those of us who are going to be murdered. Face it, Roderick. You're doing this to further your own cause, and no other reason. You're going to be responsible for the deaths of three women and your own brother because you're nothing more than a spiteful, greedy little swine."

Roderick's face twisted. He stepped closer to Stahlmaske and swung a vicious backhand that cracked across the count's face. It was an awkwardly thrown blow, but it landed with enough power to snap Stahlmaske's head to the side.

"I don't have to take your arrogant abuse anymore," Roderick said, panting a little from the rage that possessed him. "I'm in charge now, Albert, not you. You'll never run roughshod over me or anyone else, ever again."

Stahlmaske held up his bound hands and said, "It would be very, very different if I were free, eh? Then you wouldn't be so brave. You'd be a mouse again, instead of a bear."

"You think so, do you? I should—" Roderick stopped short, frowned at his brother for a second, and then shook his head. "No, you won't trick me into setting you free, even for a moment. You're going to remain helpless for the rest of your life . . . however long that may be."

"Speaking of which," Rothfuss said, "how do we know that senator fellow will actually show up the way we're counting on?"

"We have his wife and daughter. He'll come after us."

"Plus we made arrangements to have some of the Indians watch our back trail as well," Battersby added. "If they see a good opportunity, they'll capture Senator Allingham, kill whoever is with him, and bring him straight to us."

Gretchen spoke for the first time in hours, saying, "You're forgetting something, all of you."

"What would that be, my dear?" Roderick asked her.

"If he's alive, Preacher will be with the senator."

"A minister?" Rothfuss said as he frowned in confusion. "Why should we be worried about a minister?"

"He's not that sort of preacher," Roderick said, and now he was frowning, too.

Not in confusion, though, thought Stahlmaske. His brother was worried.

And as much as Stahlmaske might despise Preacher personally, he found himself hoping that Gretchen was right.

That uncivilized, unwashed mountain man might be their only real hope for survival.

Preacher pushed the party as fast as he dared without wearing out the horses. He could tell from the sign left behind by the men they were trailing that the kidnappers weren't hurrying. Preacher knew that his group had cut into their lead.

He didn't want to catch up to them in broad daylight, though, so he called a halt from time to time even though those delays chafed at Allingham.

He would probably feel the same way if a couple of women he loved were in the hands of that bunch.

As the sun began to go down and Preacher stopped again, Allingham finally burst out, "We have to keep going! We should have caught them by now!"

"We don't want them to see us comin', Senator," Preacher explained. "The darkness is our only chance of takin' 'em by surprise."

"We can't surprise them. You heard Roderick. They *want* us to find them. They'll be expecting us no matter when we attack them."

"The surprise will be in the *way* we attack 'em."

Allingham took off his hat and ran his hand over his head before he sighed in exasperation.

"I know. You've gone over the plan. And I hope it works. This waiting is just dreadfully hard. I wish we'd never left Washington. Margaret and Sarah would be safe now if we were still there."

Preacher had seen more bad things happen in cities than he had out here on the frontier, but he didn't figure the senator wanted to hear anything like that right now. So he just ambled over to the three Prussians and asked, "Are you boys doin' all right?"

Ludwig grimaced and said, "I did not know that riding horses would cause one to hurt so much." He reached down and rubbed the insides of his thighs.

Preacher chuckled. He said, "Yeah, it'll get to you after a while if you ain't used to it. You fellas will be good riders by the time this is over."

"If we survive," Egon said.

Heinrich Ritter said, "Nothing will stop me from freeing my sister and avenging poor Hobart's death. I would pursue those men all the way to the very gates of hell."

"Well, we shouldn't have to go quite that far,"

Preacher told him. "But it's good that you feel that way, Heinrich. Just keep your head and do what you're told when the time comes, and you'll be all right."

"I do not care about myself," Heinrich said with a shake of his head. "Only Gretchen and Hobart."

Preacher clapped a hand on his shoulder for a second and then moved on to Simon Russell. The former trapper had taken his hat off and hunkered on his heels, peering northward over the prairie in the fading light.

Preacher knelt beside him and said quietly, "They ain't far ahead of us now."

"I know. I can still read signs, even after spending too much time in town the past couple of years." Russell looked back over his shoulder at the others. "Still plan on using the senator as a distraction while you and I get in amongst the enemy?"

"Unless you have a better idea."

Russell shook his head.

"No, that stands more of a chance of working than anything else. But the odds are still going to be stacked pretty high against us, Preacher."

"I know."

Russell narrowed his eyes and asked, "If it comes down to it, do we save the women or the count?"

"I reckon you know the answer to that."

"If anything happens to the count, it could mean war between the United States and Prussia."

"We'll just have to risk it," Preacher said. "But we're gettin' those women out safe and sound, no matter what else happens."

Russell nodded and said, "All right, then. For what it's worth, I see things the same way."

"Never doubted it," Preacher said.

The other man chuckled, then said, "You know, I started to say that I was sorry I asked you to come along and got you mixed up in this mess. But I'm not sorry, Preacher. Hell, if it wasn't for you, we never would've stood a chance in the first place. So it's a good thing I decided to ask you for a favor. For old time's sake, you know."

Preacher nodded and told him, "Believe it or not, I'm glad I'm here, too, Simon." He grinned and added, "Shoot, if I hadn't come along, I probably never would've had the chance to have a swordfight with a Prussian count!"

CHAPTER 31

Lamplight glowed in the windows of the log and sod building on the bluff overlooking the river. The silvery moonlight revealed that the Pawnee warriors were camped about fifty yards to the left of the so-called trading post. A peeled-pole corral to the right held the horses.

"How many men do you reckon are in there?" Russell asked in a whisper as he and Preacher lay on their bellies about two hundred yards away, studying the place.

"Judgin' by the number of horses in that corral, probably about a dozen," Preacher replied.

"And there are a dozen of those Pawnee. That means we're outnumbered three to one."

"Hell, the odds are practically even, then," Preacher said with a grin.

Russell snorted and said, "I should've known you'd see it that way. You've always liked a good scrap better than anything else, haven't you?"

"Me?" Preacher said dryly. "I'm a peaceable man."

He grew more serious as Russell asked, "How are we gonna get in there? They're bound to have sentries posted."

"And some of those Pawnee could be out scoutin' around, too," Preacher said. "But I've got a hunch they won't be watchin' the river all that much."

Russell didn't respond for a moment as he was clearly lost in thought. Then he asked, "How do you figure to do it? We don't have any canoes."

"We'll head upstream, find some cottonwoods, and build us a raft so we can float back down behind them. It won't have to be anything fancy, just something that'll float and be big enough to carry you, me, and Dog."

Russell nodded slowly.

"How will we time it so we make our move at the same time as the others?" he asked.

"We ought to be able to get back here by dawn," Preacher said. "Allingham can wait until then."

"If we're not ready, they'll be serving themselves up on a platter," Russell cautioned.

"Maybe, maybe not. Those fellas may not have any experience, but I've got a hunch they'll fight hard."

"Whether they fight hard or not, they'll all get killed in the end," Russell said sourly.

"That just means we'd best hold up our end of the bargain." Preacher motioned with a jerk of his head for the two of them to withdraw.

They crawled backward on their bellies until they were out of sight of the British post, then stood up and trotted toward the spot where they had left the others. Dark shapes up ahead became men and horses.

Allingham greeted them with an anxious question, asking, "What did you find?"

Quickly, Preacher describe the layout, then added, "Simon and I are gonna see if we can't get into the place from the back. That way we can protect the prisoners and maybe even get them out of there before all hell breaks loose."

"In order to do that, you'll need something to distract Roderick and the others," Allingham said grimly.

"That's where you come in, Senator. Their whole plan falls apart if you're still alive to tell what really happened. So it's gonna be mighty important for them to get their hands on you."

"I'm going to dangle myself like bait, you mean."

"Hate to say it, but that's our best chance. It'll be pretty dangerous."

"With the lives of my wife and daughter at stake, I don't care how dangerous it is," Allingham declared. "I'll give up my own life for them if I have to."

Preacher didn't doubt it for a second. If they all got out of this alive, he didn't figure Josiah Allingham had much chance of ever being president or vice president. In fact, his career in Washington probably wouldn't last too long. The fella was just too decent and honorable to be much good as a politician.

They spent a few minutes going over the details of the plan, then Preacher and Russell departed on foot, leaving Horse and Russell's mount with the others. Dog bounded ahead of them as they trotted northwest, following a course that would bring them to the Missouri River a couple of miles upstream from the British post.

They traveled in silence now. The time for talking was over, unless one of them had something to say that was vital.

Preacher figured the time was after midnight when he and Russell reached the Big Muddy. They scouted along the river until they found a grove of cottonwood saplings. Hatchets and knives made short work of chopping down enough of the slender trees to build a raft. They trimmed the branches and then lashed the poles together with rawhide, carrying out the task with the smooth, practiced efficiency of men accustomed to surviving in the wilderness.

As they worked, Preacher said, "You should come back to the mountains and stay, Simon. Forget about livin' in town. You're still as good a man as you ever were."

"I don't know about that," Russell said. "I've gotten too used to having a feather bed under me and a roof over my head at night. Once a man turns his back on the mountains, I don't know if he can ever go back for good."

"Why'd you ever leave in the first place?" Preacher asked bluntly. He knew it was none of his business, but if Russell felt like that, he could say so.

Russell shrugged and said, "The company offered me good money to help run their operation out

here. I was just foolish enough to think that it might
be nice to have some more comfortable surroundings for a while. The ground gets mighty cold and
hard at night as you get older."

"You ain't that much older than I am," Preacher
pointed out. "We're practically the same age."

"Yeah, but you were born for this life. You'll still
be going off to see the elephant when you're eighty
years old, if you live that long!"

Preacher chuckled and said, "You're probably
right about that. I hope so, anyway."

He finished tying the last bit of rawhide in place.
When they put the raft in the river, the water would
shrink the rawhide even more and make the bonds
tight and unbreakable. Preacher nodded in satisfaction.

They carried the raft into the Missouri. It floated
without any signs of a problem. Preacher wouldn't
have wanted to travel for hundreds of miles on it—
it was barely big enough for him, Russell, and Dog
to sit—but it would do fine for floating a couple of
miles back downstream.

Preacher held the raft in place while Russell
fetched their rifles and the rest of their gear they
had left on the shore. When Russell was on board,
Preacher said, "All right, Dog, it's your turn."

The big cur looked skeptically at the raft and
whined. He was a strong swimmer, but evidently he
wasn't sure about climbing onto the floating platform.

"It'll be all right," Preacher assured him. "Go
ahead. Get your mangy carcass up here."

Stubbornly, Dog barked at him.

"All right, you can follow us along the shore, I reckon," Preacher said. "Just don't get lost."

Dog turned and ran off along the bank.

Russell said in an amazed tone, "It's like he understands every word you say to him."

"Well, why wouldn't he? We been together for a long time. Horse is the same way."

"You know, Preacher," Russell mused, "sometimes I think you don't realize just how special you really are."

Preacher snorted and pulled himself onto the raft. He picked up one of the long, slender poles they had cut to help them steer and avoid any obstacles in the river and used it to push the raft into deeper water. Preacher felt the current catch the makeshift craft and tug it along.

The raft began to go faster. Except in a few places, the Missouri had a reputation for flowing leisurely, but even that current felt fairly rapid when you were sitting on a tiny raft in the middle of the broad expanse of river. The raft tried to switch ends a few times, but Preacher and Russell stuck the cottonwood poles in the water and righted it.

In some places the terrain was almost flat where the land came down and joined the river. In others, sandstone bluffs twenty to thirty feet tall loomed over the water.

The British outpost sat on just such a bluff, Preacher recalled. He hoped he and Russell would be able to see it from the river so they would know they were in the right place.

That minor worry was unfounded. Preacher spotted the lights in the trading post's windows while the raft was still several hundred yards upstream. He pointed them out to Russell, and the two men began poling the raft closer to that shore.

Preacher looked at the eastern sky. The gray tinge he saw there told him that dawn was an hour, maybe a little more, away. He and Russell had plenty of time to get in position.

The face of the bluff looked dark, smooth, and sheer. Preacher knew that in reality it was rougher than it appeared and likely would have enough cracks, knobs, and projections to provide handholds and footholds as he and Russell climbed it.

As they angled toward shore, the bluff rose and cut off their view of the lights from the trading post. That didn't matter. Preacher knew they were in the right place.

They had already rigged slings for their rifles, so their hands would be free for climbing. They wouldn't be able to tie up the raft and keep it from drifting away, but that didn't really matter. One way or another, after what happened in the next couple of hours they wouldn't need it anymore.

Russell planted his cottonwood pole against the muddy river bottom and held the raft in place against the bluff while Preacher stood and reached up to search for a handhold. He found a knob of sandstone, wrapped his fingers around it, and then wedged the toe of his boot in a little crack. He pulled himself up a couple of feet and then reached back down.

Russell clasped Preacher's wrist while he found a hold with his other hand and a place for his feet. Then he let go and started to climb, too.

Underneath them, the raft drifted slowly back toward the middle of the river. Somebody would probably find it, maybe a hundred miles or more downstream, and wonder who had built it and why.

Side by side, the two men worked their way up the bluff. It was slow going. They had to pause every foot or so to shift their hands and feet to new locations. The strength of their grip was really all that supported them.

Even as superbly conditioned as Preacher was, his fingers began to ache after a while. That throbbing strain crawled through his hands and up his arms, finally settling deeply into his shoulders and back.

His muscles were strong enough to withstand the pain, and so was his iron will. He shoved the discomfort out of his mind and kept climbing.

Finally, they neared the top. Preacher reached over and tapped Russell on the shoulder, then signaled for him to stay put for a moment. Preacher intended to take a look around first and make sure no trouble waited on top of the bluff. Russell nodded in understanding.

Preacher pulled himself up so he could see over the edge. The log trading post sat there, dark and hulking, about twenty yards away. Preacher's keen eyes studied it in the light from moon and stars.

He was sorry to see that there was no door back here, and the two windows were shuttered. He had hoped to be able to get into the building from this direction, but that might not be possible, at least not without breaking through those shutters, which would cause too much racket.

But maybe there was something he hadn't seen yet, some other way inside. They would just have to take a closer look. He turned his head to glance down at Russell and tell him to come on up, but at that moment he caught a hint of movement from the corner of his eye.

Jerking his head around, Preacher saw a dark shape rise from the grass where it had been lurking. The shape of the figure and the feathers sticking up from the man's hair told him this was a Pawnee guard.

And the warrior was pointing a rifle at him, ready to blow him right off the face of the bluff.

CHAPTER 32

Before the Pawnee could pull the trigger, another shape streaked in from the side and crashed against him. The unexpected impact knocked the Indian off his feet, and when he hit the ground he found himself with more than a hundred pounds of fanged fury on top of him.

Those fangs made quick work of the warrior's throat, ripping it out in a gush of hot blood. The Pawnee's heels drummed against the ground as he died.

By the time Dog finished with his grisly work, Preacher had scrambled onto the bluff and unslung his rifle from his back. He didn't want to fire a shot because that would alert the kidnappers and their British cohorts that something was wrong, but the mountain man would shoot if he had to.

Luckily, he didn't see any more Pawnee as he scanned the area behind the trading post. Dog wasn't acting like there were any other threats, either. He stood over the warrior's corpse, shaking blood off his muzzle.

Preacher leaned over the rim and waved Russell up. When the man reached the top, he put his head close to Preacher's ear and whispered, "What happened?"

"Pawnee sentry," Preacher replied, so quietly that his answer couldn't have been heard more than a foot away. "Dog took care of him."

Russell nodded in understanding as he looked at the dark shape sprawled on the ground. He and Preacher got to their feet and stalked warily toward the building.

Preacher wasn't surprised that Dog had turned up just when he was needed most. The big cur had a way of doing that. Russell had said that Preacher wasn't aware of how unusual he and his trail partners were, but that wasn't really true. Preacher knew that the link between himself and Dog and Horse seemed almost supernatural at times.

Preacher had learned not to question such things. Instead he was just grateful for them. Both of his four-legged friends had saved his life many times in the past.

Preacher and Russell split up as they approached the trading post, Preacher going right and Russell going left. Preacher paused at the rear corner of the building and took his hat off, holding it in his left hand as he edged his head past the corner for a look.

There were a couple of lighted windows on this

end of the building. Preacher slid along the log wall toward the closest one. When he reached it he was even more careful about looking inside.

He was looking at the area behind a long counter where the proprietor of the place would dicker with trappers who brought in pelts to trade. It was empty at the moment, but he heard men moving around elsewhere in the building and smelled coffee brewing.

"I thought they would be here by now," a man said in a British accent. "We didn't make it hard for them to follow us."

"You must be patient, Battersby," another man replied. Preacher's jaw tightened as he recognized the smug voice.

It belonged to Roderick Stahlmaske.

"I've spent quite a bit of time with Senator Allingham over the past few weeks," Roderick went on. "He loves his wife, and I don't think even the fact that she was unfaithful to him will change that. Even if it does, we have his daughter, too, and he is nothing if not a devoted parent. He'll do anything in his power to save Sarah . . . even surrender himself to us."

"But that won't save her," the Englishman said.

"He doesn't know that," Roderick said with a chuckle. "He may suspect it, but he has no choice except to hope otherwise."

As Preacher eavesdropped on the conversation, his hands tightened on the rifle. Anger welled up inside him.

Not all of it was directed toward Roderick and his British allies, either. Preacher was mad at himself for letting the diabolical young man fool him. He had believed Roderick's eager-to-please, bumbling act as much as anyone else had.

Water under the bridge, Preacher told himself. All that mattered now was saving the prisoners and putting a stop to Roderick's plan to start a war between the United States and Prussia.

Preacher withdrew from the window and returned to the rear of the trading post. He found Simon Russell waiting there for him.

"Open windows on the other end of the building," Russell reported. "I couldn't actually see anybody, but I heard them talking clear enough."

"Same on this side," Preacher said. "I was hopin' they might have the prisoners locked up in a storeroom or something, and that maybe we could sneak in and get 'em out before the shootin' started. Looks like that's not the way it's gonna be."

"When they make their try for the senator, we can get in then through the windows and hit them from behind."

Preacher nodded and said, "That's the plan. Just keep your eyes open when you go in. We won't know exactly where the prisoners are until we get in there."

"If I get a shot at that son of a bitch Roderick, I'm taking it," Russell commented grimly.

"You're not the only one," Preacher said.

* * *

Stahlmaske woke up and realized he was lying on the floor on his side. Immediately, he was angry with himself because his mouth was open and he'd been drooling in his sleep. Such an undignified thing was beneath him. He struggled to sit up and acted like nothing had happened.

A few feet away, Gretchen still slept, leaning against a sack of flour. A few feet in the other direction, the Allingham women continued to huddle together as they slept, as if that would protect them.

For much of the night, Stahlmaske had worked with his bonds, trying to loosen them, before finally dozing off involuntarily. His efforts had not been successful. The men who had tied him were too good at their job.

Panic tried to take root inside him. He was running out of time to turn the tables on his treacherous younger brother. If something didn't happen soon, nothing was going to prevent Roderick from getting away with his scheme.

Maybe . . . just maybe . . . he should be like Gretchen and hope that Preacher would help them somehow, the count thought. That might be the only chance he and his fellow captives had left.

Seeing that Stahlmaske was awake, Roderick came over and stood there looming above him, clearly enjoying the superiority he imagined that position gave him.

"It'll be dawn soon," he said. "I'll see to it that you're all given breakfast."

"Why waste food on those you intend to murder?" Stahlmaske asked with a sneer.

"I don't think of it as murder. I'm merely helping my British friends get a foothold in the western half of the continent. Once they have everything under their control from the Canadian border down to the Spanish lands, the upstart Americans will find themselves surrounded. They'll have no choice but to eventually give up their foolish notion of being an independent country and beg the English to take them in as colonists once again."

"You're insane," Stahlmaske snapped. "Surely you've seen enough of the Americans in these past weeks to know that such a thing will never happen. They're too stubborn to allow it."

"They may not like it, but they'll be squeezed into British rule again. You'll see." Roderick smiled. "Or rather, you won't. But it will happen anyway, I assure you."

The tall, brawny Englishman called Battersby said from the front of the trading post, "Someone's coming, Herr Stahlmaske."

Roderick turned eagerly in that direction.

"Can you tell who it is?"

"I don't recognize him, but you might. Big bloke, rather distinguished looking."

"It must be the senator," Roderick said as he hurried toward the window where Battersby stood. He looked out into the gray light of dawn and went on excitedly, "That's him, all right. That's Senator Allingham."

"Better step back away from that window," Battersby cautioned. "Somebody might take a potshot at you."

Roderick quickly followed that advice. He said, "I didn't see anyone out there except Allingham."

"That doesn't mean they're not there."

"That's true," Roderick admitted. "It's hard to believe the senator could have followed us all this way by himself."

The mentions of her husband's name must have penetrated Margaret's restless slumber. She opened her eyes and pushed herself up as much as she could from the floor.

"Josiah is here?" she said. "He came after me?"

Roderick turned to her and nodded.

"That's right, Frau Allingham. It's difficult to believe that he would care enough about a trollop such as yourself to risk his own life, isn't it?"

"You don't know anything about life," Margaret told him coldly. "You're just a dreadful little boy, out to smash all the toys you're not allowed to play with."

Stahlmaske laughed out loud. His opinion of Margaret Allingham had just gone up a bit because of that cutting—and accurate—remark.

Roderick's face flushed. He blustered, "You'll be sorry you said that."

"I couldn't possibly regret that more than I regret everything else that's happened the past few weeks."

She glanced at Stahlmaske as she said that, and he knew she was talking about their affair. She certainly hadn't seemed to regret it while she was in his bed, but it didn't really matter now, he told himself.

If she wanted to repent of her so-called sins before she died, that was understandable.

"Hello in the trading post!"

They all heard Allingham's shout, including Sarah, who struggled into a sitting position and exclaimed, "Father!"

"Can you hear me in there?" Allingham went on.

Roderick approached the window cautiously, staying to the side so he wouldn't present a target for any marksmen outside, and replied, "We hear you, Senator."

"Are my wife and daughter all right?" Allingham's voice trembled a bit as he posed the question.

"They're fine, and they'll stay that way as long as you cooperate with us," Roderick replied.

"Send them out. Send them out to me and I'll do whatever you want, I swear."

"Ah, but it doesn't work that way, Senator," Roderick said, obviously immensely pleased with himself. "You see, I have the upper hand here. You'll do as I say. Lay down your guns and come on in."

"What's he doing?" Battersby asked suddenly. "He's taking cover in the trees, blast it! We should've shot him while we had the chance."

"Don't worry," Roderick said, although he sounded like he was having a hard time taking his own advice. "This is just a momentary setback."

From outside, Allingham called, "I'm not going to surrender until Margaret and Sarah are free. You don't have a choice, Herr Stahlmaske. You have to trade their lives for mine. Bring them out and I'll put myself in your hands."

Roderick cursed in Prussian for a moment before he said to Battersby and the others, "All right. Gag the others so they can't call out a warning, then we'll take them outside. Allingham wants a trade, so we'll give him one. And as soon as it's complete . . . kill the whole lot of them."

CHAPTER 33

Preacher crouched next to the rear wall of the trading post. He had found a gap between the logs that hadn't been chinked, and he had his ear pressed to it, listening to everything that was going on inside.

So he heard Roderick callously sentence the prisoners to death, along with Senator Allingham. With that massacre about to take place, everyone's attention would be focused on the tense situation in front of the building.

He motioned Simon Russell closer and whispered the details to him, then said, "You go in the window and try to protect the count and Miss Ritter. I'll go around front and deal with their plan to kill the senator and his ladies."

Russell nodded and whispered, "Good luck, Preacher."

"We'll all need it, I reckon," the mountain man agreed.

He cat-footed along the wall to the corner, then

turned it and stole forward. He stopped when he could see the line of cottonwoods about fifty yards away where Allingham had taken cover. The rest of the rescue party would be well hidden in there, too, Preacher thought, ready to open fire if they needed to.

He heard the front door open, then a British-accented voice called, "Hold your fire, Senator. I'm bringing your ladies out, just like you wanted." Quietly, the man added, "All right, you two, get moving. But don't forget we've got guns to your heads."

Preacher heard a muffled, unintelligible response. The kidnappers had gagged Margaret and Sarah so they couldn't warn Allingham about the double-cross, Preacher recalled. He had heard Roderick give the order earlier.

Preacher risked a look around the corner as the little group started out from the building. Margaret and Sarah were in the lead, their legs free now but their hands still tied together in front of them. Wads of cloth had been stuffed into their mouths and fastened in place with rawhide strips.

Right behind the two women came a pair of Englishmen, each with a cocked pistol pressed to the back of a prisoner's head. Four more British agents with rifles held ready emerged and formed a half-circle around the captives. Preacher didn't see Roderick and knew the plotter was still inside the trading post.

Sarah stumbled as she moved forward uncertainly. Margaret reached over with her bound hands and steadied her daughter. She stood straight and seemed calm. She had found a new reserve of strength somewhere, Preacher thought. She had to know she was going to her death—at least that was the plan—but she didn't show it. The mountain man actually admired her at that moment.

"Here they are, Allingham," the man holding the gun on Margaret called. "Come on out now. This is over."

From the trees, Allingham said, "Stop where you are and let them come ahead on their own. When they're safe, I'll surrender."

The Englishman jerked his head at his companions, indicating they should stop. He said, "That's not the way it's going to work. You come out where we can see you. We'll stay here, and you can meet the women as they come toward the trees."

For a moment, Allingham didn't respond, then he said, "All right. As long as nothing happens to my wife and daughter."

"That's up to you, mate." The man prodded his pistol against the back of Margaret's head and added, "Get goin', mum."

Slowly, Margaret and Sarah walked toward the trees. Margaret still had to brace up the obviously terrified and half-hysterical Sarah.

Under his breath, the leader of the British agents said to his companions, "As soon as they're all standing together, wipe them out."

Senator Allingham appeared next to one of the trees. His rifle was a little shaky as he came forward, but he didn't hesitate to stride straight into deadly danger. The gap between him and the two women steadily decreased.

"Easy, boys," the Englishman breathed. "Just half a moment longer . . ."

Margaret and Sarah couldn't control themselves anymore. Only a few yards separated them from Allingham. Suddenly they ran toward him.

They were trying to shield him from the kidnappers' guns, Preacher realized. He stepped around the corner, lifted his rifle, and yelled, "Get the ladies on the ground, Senator!"

Allingham reacted instantly, dropping his rifle, spreading his arms, and lunging forward to tackle his wife and daughter. His arms went around them as he crashed into them and bore them both to the ground, where Preacher hoped they would be out of the line of fire.

The kidnappers' response to Preacher's shout was swift as well. They pivoted toward him, and pistols and rifles roared. A veritable storm of lead whipped around the mountain man, who stood there coolly and pressed the trigger of his rifle.

The tall man who had been doing the talking for the Englishmen jerked back as the ball from Preacher's flintlock smashed into the center of his forehead and bored deep into his brain. He fell, dead before he hit the ground.

More shots blasted from the rest of the rescue party hidden in the trees. One of the British agents howled in pain and collapsed as a rifle ball broke his right thigh bone and knocked the leg out from under him, but the others managed to scramble back inside to what they considered safety.

But Simon Russell was already in there, and he was about to have help. Preacher didn't bother reloading his rifle. He dropped the empty weapon, whirled toward the nearest window, and called, "Now, Dog!"

The big cur had been waiting for the order. He leaped through the open window and disappeared inside.

While the kidnappers were forcing Margaret and Sarah Allingham outside, Count Stahlmaske scooted over closer to Gretchen, who looked calm but frightened.

"I can only tell you again how sorry I am that you became involved in this ridiculous situation, my dear," he said.

"I really thought Preacher would be here by now," Gretchen said. "If the senator is out there by himself, he's not going to be any match for these men."

"If only I were free—"

"Turn a little," Gretchen suggested. "They're not watching us very closely. Maybe I can untie your wrists."

Stahlmaske was about to tell her he had already tried that, but then he decided it couldn't hurt anything. Gretchen's fingers were slender and more supple than his, plus she had longer nails with which to work. He twisted his body so she could reach his hands bound behind his back, and she went to work.

He heard her mutter under her breath as she strained to free him. To his great surprise, it seemed to him that after only a few minutes the ropes around his wrists were a bit looser. She continued her efforts as shouting came from outside. Allingham was trying to talk the kidnappers into turning his wife and daughter loose.

Gretchen's breath suddenly hissed between her teeth in alarm. Stahlmaske turned his head and saw Roderick coming toward them.

"Don't the two of you look cozy, all huddled together that way?" he jeered. "Have you been thinking, Gretchen dear? Have you relented in your decision? I might be willing to allow you to live if you made it worth my while."

Gretchen pressed herself against Stahlmaske as if searching for sanctuary, but in reality she had increased her efforts to untie him. She said, "I would never have anything to do with you, Roderick, you know that. And if I did, it would only be so I could get close enough to cut your throat some night while you slept."

Roderick sighed and said, "Yes, I suppose that's exactly what you would do. Such a pity. I always thought that you and I—" He leaned forward suddenly and frowned. "What are you doing there? Are you trying to—"

Before he could finish the question, someone shouted outside and a great volley of gunfire crashed. At the same time, Stahlmaske felt the ropes around his wrists fall away. His hands and arms were free, but they were numb and useless from being pulled back into such an awkward position for so long.

He did the only thing he could. He jerked his legs up and then lashed out with them, driving his bound feet into Roderick's stomach with so much force it sent the younger man flying backward.

Stahlmaske waved his arms and flexed his fingers, trying to force feeling back into the limbs. He reached up, grabbed hold of the top of the counter against which they had been leaning, and pulled himself up. From the corner of his eye he saw a roughly clad man climbing in through a window and recognized Simon Russell from the riverboat.

Awkwardly because his ankles were still bound and he didn't have full use of his arms yet, Stahlmaske hopped around the counter and lunged toward several hatchets that lay on a shelf. He grabbed one, bent over, and chopped at the ropes around his ankles, heedless of any injury he might do to himself in his haste. The thick leather of his high boots turned aside the blade when his strokes missed.

Half a dozen British agents were still inside the trading post. When the shooting started outside, they had rushed toward the door, but one of the men spotted Russell and shouted a warning. As some of them whirled to meet this new threat, Russell fired his rifle, the report echoing deafeningly from the low ceiling. One of the Englishmen went down with a smashed shoulder.

Russell flung his empty rifle at the others and pulled the pistol from behind his belt. He raced forward to put himself in front of Gretchen as he raised the pistol and cocked it. A rifle ball ripped across his side as the British agents opened fire. The impact twisted him halfway around, but he stayed on his feet and squeezed the pistol's trigger. It boomed and sent a ball into the chest of another Englishman.

Stahlmaske's feet were free now, the severed ropes having dropped away from them. He snatched another hatchet from the shelf and rolled across the counter. A rifle ball chewed splinters from the planks as he did so. As he landed on his feet in front of the counter next to Russell, his arms whipped forward and the two hatchets flew through the air. Each of them struck one of the British agents. One went down with blood spouting from his throat where the hatchet had lodged, but the other man received only a minor injury.

That changed a second later when a gray, furry form slammed into him and knocked him off his feet. The man didn't even have time to scream before Dog's powerful jaws locked on his throat and ripped it out.

More of the kidnappers dashed back through the open door, fleeing from whatever was happening outside. Stahlmaske heard a lot of shooting and knew that a full-fledged rescue party must have arrived.

Preacher was probably out there somewhere, too, he thought.

* * *

The rifle fire from the rescue party hidden in the trees had driven the kidnappers back inside the trading post, but those left outside still had other problems. As Preacher ran toward the Allingham family, he glanced at the Pawnee camp and saw the warriors scrambling this way to get in on the fight.

He reached the Allinghams and bent down to take hold of the senator's arm.

"Head for the trading post, now!" he barked.

"But . . . but the rest of the kidnappers are in there," Allingham said as he pushed himself up on hands and knees, still hovering over his wife and daughter.

"Yeah, but the Pawnee are out here. Now move!"

Allingham scrambled to his feet and helped Margaret and Sarah up. As they broke into a run toward the trading post, Preacher pulled his other pistol from behind his belt and used it to wave the others out of the woods.

"Come on!" he shouted. "Into the trading post!"

Heinrich Ritter, Egon, Ludwig, Warburton, and the other crewman from the *Sentinel* burst out of the trees and dashed toward the building. Arrows began to fly through the air around them as Roderick's Pawnee allies opened fire.

Preacher had one loaded pistol, a tomahawk, and a knife to hold off a dozen bloodthirsty warriors.

Shouldn't be that hard, he thought with a grim smile on his face.

Probably all it would cost him was his life.

CHAPTER 34

Inside the trading post, Stahlmaske looked around for something else he could grab and use as a weapon. Russell had dropped to one knee, bleeding from the wound in his side, as he tried to reload his pistol. He knelt in front of Gretchen and shielded her with his own body.

Dog attacked like a whirlwind, dashing among the British agents, ripping and tearing with his fangs. Some of the men shot at him or tried to strike him with their rifles, but they were always a little too slow. The big cur kept them stalemated for a moment, and that was long enough for the situation to change again.

Allingham appeared in the doorway, herding his wife and daughter along with him. He steered them to cover behind some barrels and then thrust a pistol at the Englishmen. When the gun roared and smoke spouted from the muzzle, Rothfuss spun around from the impact of the ball and collapsed.

Heinrich Ritter burst through the doorway,

shrieking incoherently in vengeful rage. He lunged at the kidnappers and swung his empty rifle like a club.

Egon and Ludwig were right behind Heinrich. They had loaded pistols that they fired into the mass of Englishmen. Two brawny crewmen from the riverboat lunged into the trading post as well and instantly were locked in hand-to-hand combat with the enemy. Rock-hard fists thudded against flesh and bone.

Chaos reigned inside the trading post as the melee surged back and forth. All the guns were empty now, but they could still be used as bludgeons. Stahlmaske jerked one of the hatchets he had thrown from the throat of a dead man and waded in swinging with it.

With all this going on, no one spared a glance for Roderick, who had fallen in a corner after Stahlmaske kicked him. Curled in a ball around the pain in his belly, he crawled behind some kegs to take shelter from the battle.

Outside, Preacher fired his remaining loaded pistol toward the Pawnee warriors charging toward him. The weapon was double-shotted, as usual, and the distance was far enough for the balls to spread out a little as they flew through the air.

One of them struck a warrior in the jaw, ripping away a large chuck of it. The man stumbled forward with blood sheeting down his chest from the gruesome wound but collapsed after a few steps and pitched forward onto his ruined face.

The other ball punched into a warrior's chest and ripped through his right lung. He hit the ground, too, unable to go on as he began to drown in his own blood.

Preacher shoved the empty pistol behind his belt and jerked out his tomahawk and knife. The Pawnee probably could have riddled him with arrows as he stood there, but the defiance that showed in every tense line of his body was too much of a challenge to them. Several of the warriors yipped war cries and charged forward to take him on hand to hand.

Preacher had counted on them reacting like that. He met the attack with blinding speed, whirling, twisting, striking out faster than the eye could follow. His tomahawk crushed the skull of one warrior. His knife slashed deeply into the throat of another. He kicked a Pawnee in the belly, spun and shattered another's jaw with a swing of the tomahawk. Bodies littered the ground around him as more of the Indians closed in around him.

With blood dripping from the hatchet in his hand, Stahlmaske realized that none of the British agents were on their feet anymore. Caught up in the fever of battle like he was, for a second it was hard not to continue lashing out. He dragged in a deep breath, controlled his rampaging emotions, and took stock of himself.

He had several small wounds but nothing serious. Satisfied of that, he turned toward the counter to see if Gretchen was all right.

She was on her feet, having been freed by Simon Russell, who leaned on the counter and pressed a hand to his bloody side.

As Russell met the count's gaze, he said, "Preacher's still out there! Somebody needs to go help him!"

Stahlmaske nodded. He turned and started for the door, but as he did he bumped shoulders with Senator Allingham. The two men paused to glare at each other for a second, then Allingham said, "We should go give Preacher a hand."

Stahlmaske jerked his head in a nod and said, "*Ja.*"

They rushed out the door, Stahlmaske slightly in the lead.

At first he couldn't see Preacher, then he realized that the mountain man must be in the middle of the group of Pawnee warriors. He and Allingham charged the Indians and hit them from behind. Stahlmaske's hatchet rose and fell, chopping brutally, while Allingham wielded a broken rifle like a deadly club, smashing skulls and knocking warriors to the ground.

It took only a few seconds of bloody violence for Stahlmaske and Allingham to fight their way to Preacher's side. When they reached the mountain man, he didn't seem surprised to see them. The three of them stood back to back and continued battling the remaining warriors.

The combat didn't last long, however, and when it was over, Preacher, Stahlmaske, and Allingham were the only ones left on their feet. Blood smeared their hands and had splattered on their faces, but none of them were hurt seriously.

"Josiah!"

The cry made all three men turn quickly toward the trading post. Margaret and Sarah emerged from the building and ran toward them. They threw their arms around Allingham and hugged him tightly as they sobbed. He returned the embrace with a look of huge relief on his face.

"You're all right," he said as if he couldn't believe it. "You're both all right."

Gretchen was the next one out the door. She hurried to Stahlmaske and looked like she was going to hug him, too, but she stopped short and rested a hand on his arm instead.

"You're injured," she said.

He shrugged and told her, "Nothing to be concerned about. There is something I must tell you, though."

"What is it, Albert?"

"I was . . . wrong about you," Stahlmaske said, and clearly it cost him an effort to make that admission. "I thought you to be only a spoiled girl with a rich father. I see now that nothing could be farther from the truth."

Coolly, she said, "You think I didn't know you

were marrying me in hopes of one day controlling my father's fortune?"

"If you wish to end our betrothal—"

"I didn't say that." She moved closer to him. Now her arms went around his waist. "I didn't say that at all."

Stahlmaske lifted a hand, rested it lightly on her hair. It was an uncharacteristically tender gesture for him, but he thought he might grow to enjoy such things.

Heinrich Ritter came up to them to check on his sister. Stahlmaske kept his left arm around Gretchen's shoulders as he extended his right hand to the younger man.

"I saw you doing battle with the enemy," the count said. "You fought well, my friend."

Heinrich looked surprised but pleased by Stahlmaske's praise. He clasped his future brother-in-law's hand and said, "I fought to avenge poor Hobart. I could not let his memory down."

"You didn't," Stahlmaske told him. "I'm sure he is very proud of you."

Gretchen put her arms around her brother and hugged him.

"I know you would come after me, Heinrich," she told him. "I never lost faith in you."

Despite the grief over his twin's death that he obviously still felt, Heinrich beamed with pleasure at this reunion.

A few feet away, Simon Russell came up to Preacher with Egon and Ludwig on either side of him, helping hold him up. The mountain man said, "Blast it, Simon, you're hurt. Somebody needs to tend to that before you lose too much blood."

"I know, but I wanted to make sure you were all right first," Russell replied.

"Just banged up a mite," Preacher said with a smile. "I'll be fine. Now let's get you back inside and see if we can patch up that hole in your side."

They turned toward the trading post, and as they started in that direction, Egon frowned and asked, "What happened to Herr Roderick? I did not see him inside."

Preacher frowned and said, "I reckon he's got to be in there. There's no place he could've—"

He stopped short as a disheveled figure appeared in the doorway. Roderick stood there swaying a little, his eyes unnaturally wide and shining with an insane hatred. He held a keg in his hands and as he stumbled forward he raised it above his head.

"Albert!" he screamed hysterically. "Albert, you're not going to win again!"

Sparks sputtered from a length of fuse that disappeared into one end of the keg. Preacher realized there had to be black powder in there, and if Roderick succeeded in throwing it among them, the explosion might send them all flying into the air in pieces.

He reached over to Simon Russell and pulled the pistol from behind Russell's belt.

"Loaded?" he snapped.

Russell nodded.

Preacher pivoted smoothly, raised the pistol as

he pulled back the hammer, and fired. The ball tore through Roderick's right arm, shattering the elbow. Roderick howled in pain and dropped the keg, which fell to the ground behind him. He collapsed, clutching his wounded arm as he screamed in agony. He landed almost on top of the keg.

"Everybody down!" Preacher shouted as he dived to the ground.

The blast shook the earth underneath him. The thunder of the explosion was like a physical blow, stunning the mountain man for several seconds and making his ears ring. As that sensation faded, he lifted his head. Dirt and rocks pattered down around him. Some of the debris struck him in the back, but not hard enough to do any damage.

There was only a smoking crater in the ground where Roderick had been. Preacher looked but didn't see any of the young man left.

Gradually he became aware that he heard crying. He pushed himself up and looked around. All the others seemed to be all right as far as he could tell, but Margaret and Sarah were both sobbing, probably from the horror of what had happened. Allingham tried to comfort them.

Gretchen was pale and clearly shaken, too, although no tears ran down her face as she sat up from the ground. Stahlmaske was beside her, and his aristocratic features might as well have been carved from stone. Preacher didn't figure the count would grieve much for his brother.

As for Preacher, though, he was sorry for the fate that had overtaken Roderick Stahlmaske. He'd had to stop the crazed young man from killing all of them, so he didn't regret what he'd done, but it was a damned shame Roderick's jealousy and resentment had brought them all to this point and caused not only his own death but so many others. If things had been different, Roderick might have really been the likable young man he had pretended to be.

But there was no changing what was done. Preacher helped Russell to his feet and with assistance from Ludwig and Egon took his old friend inside the trading post so Russell could get the medical attention he needed.

They went around the hole in the ground, all that was left of Roderick Stahlmaske.

CHAPTER 35

The wound in Russell's side was a deep, bloody furrow. Preacher was sure it hurt like blazes, but once he had cleaned it out and packed it with a mixture of gunpowder and herbs, then bandaged it tightly, he felt confident that it would heal. They would need to keep an eye on Russell to make sure blood poisoning didn't develop, but other than that Preacher knew his old friend ought to recover just fine.

There was an assortment of other injuries among the former prisoners and the rescue party, but nothing serious. Preacher thought it best that Russell not try to ride for a few days, so he decided they would stay here at the trading post.

"Somebody might as well get some use out of the place," he said when he announced his decision.

"Seems to me the American Fur Company ought to take it over," Russell suggested. "That would be fitting, don't you think, since those Englishmen were trying to put the company out of business?"

"I think your bosses could send that Lord Rutherford, whoever he is, a letter explainin' what we found out about his plans, and I don't reckon he'd kick up too much of a ruckus about you takin' over the place. He probably wouldn't want it known that he was responsible for tryin' to start a war."

"He's a finance minister in the British government," Russell explained. "He'll want to cover his tracks, all right. But from what I've heard about him, he won't take kindly to losing."

"Are you sayin' he'll try to get even?"

"He might," Russell said.

Preacher shrugged and shook his head.

"I ain't plannin' to ever go to England, and if he wants to come after me out here on the frontier, I ain't particular worried about that. I sort of know my way around."

Russell grinned and said, "That's putting it mildly."

It took most of a day to drag off the bodies of the British agents and their Pawnee allies. Ludwig and Egon suggested digging graves for them. Preacher told them to go ahead if they wanted to, but he convinced them to make it a mass grave.

If they had been in the mountains he would have just dropped the corpses in a ravine, but out here on the prairie they didn't have that option. Preacher supposed that burying them was better than having a lot of scavengers around feasting on the remains.

During the days that passed, Stahlmaske and Gretchen Ritter spent most of their time together. They seemed to genuinely care for each other now, instead of just having a business arrangement between them.

She was a good influence on the count, Preacher thought. He and Stahlmaske would never be friends, but at least the Prussian wasn't as obnoxious as he had been. Now and then he still said something arrogant and insulting, but it seemed almost a matter of habit rather than anything he was actually feeling.

Once Preacher came upon Allingham and Margaret standing on the bluff overlooking the river, talking quietly and earnestly with each other. They seemed a little uncomfortable about being interrupted, so Preacher excused himself and left them alone.

Allingham sought him out later and said, "I suppose you're wondering what Mrs. Allingham and I were talking about out there earlier."

"That's none of my business," Preacher said with a shake of his head.

"I'm not sure I'd go so far as to say that. There's a good chance neither of us would be alive if it weren't for you, Preacher. We have you to thank for giving us a chance to continue our marriage."

"The two of you are gonna stay married, then." That came as no real surprise. Preacher had heard of people getting divorced, but it was extremely rare.

"Yes, of course. Margaret has . . . apologized . . . for her impulsive behavior. She realizes it was reckless and foolish, and I realize that it was not . . . entirely . . . her fault. She never really wanted to go to Washington. She would have been happier staying in Vermont."

"Maybe the two of you should go back there, then."

"I've been thinking the same thing," Allingham said with a nod. "My term in the Senate is over in less than two years. I think the time will have come to step down. I'm more suited to a life as a small-town merchant. And it'll be better for Sarah, too."

Preacher figured it was unlikely the senator's hot-blooded daughter would agree with that. But it was something Allingham would have to deal with, so Preacher didn't say anything other than to wish him and his family well.

There was a chance that the rest of the Pawnee who had attacked the riverboat would come looking for their fellow warriors when the group that had accompanied the kidnappers didn't return. Because of that, Preacher thought it was a good idea to post guards around the clock.

He was outside near the corral one evening when a figure came out of the shadows and approached him. Whoever it was didn't act threatening, but he shifted his rifle a little anyway so it would be ready if he needed it.

"Preacher, is that you?" a familiar voice asked.

He tried not to let the annoyance he felt show in his voice as he said, "What are you doin' out here in the dark, Miss Sarah?"

"Looking for you, of course," Sarah replied. "We

haven't really had a chance to talk in private since . . . since all those terrible things happened."

"Didn't know we had anything to say to each other that couldn't be said in front of all the other folks."

She came closer to him and said, "You know better than that, Preacher. There's always been something between us, whether you want to admit it or not."

"I reckon you're wrong about that."

"If you'd kiss me, you'd know I was right."

She was close enough now that Preacher was starting to feel uneasy. He said, "Girl, you're barely marryin' age, and I ain't in the market for a wife to start with."

"I haven't said anything about the two of us getting married," she pointed out.

"No, but I don't intend to get mixed up with a gal young enough to be my daughter. Now, you go on back inside. You might run into trouble out here."

"You mean Indians? I'm not scared of them as long as you're around."

"Well, you ought to be. For one thing, I'm supposed to be standin' guard, and you're distractin' me from my job."

Sarah laughed softly and said, "It's gratifying to know that I'm distracting you, anyway."

Preacher sighed. He ought to turn this little hellcat over his knee and give her a sound spanking, he thought, but that would probably do more harm than good. She didn't need anything to heat her blood up any more than it already was.

Instead he took hold of her arm and turned her toward the building.

"Back inside, now," he told her firmly.

"You're wasting your time arguing with me, Preacher. I always get what I want. And what I want is to stay out here with you."

That surprised him enough to make him stop steering her toward the door. He asked, "What did you say?"

"I said I want to stay out here with you. I don't want to go back to Washington when this trip is over. I don't even want to go back to St. Louis. When we get to the mouth of the Yellowstone, you're going on to the mountains, aren't you?"

"That's what I'm plannin'," Preacher admitted warily.

"I want to see them!" Sarah said, and he could hear the honest excitement in her voice. "I want to see something I've never seen before."

"There are mountains in Vermont. You said so yourself."

"Not like the Rockies. And *you* said *that*."

He frowned as he considered what she'd told him, then said, "So this is all about explorin'?"

"Well . . . not completely. I do find you very attractive in a gruff sort of way. I think we could have a wonderful time together. There's so much out here on the frontier you could show me."

"And most of it's dangerous," Preacher pointed out. "You just went through a mighty bad ordeal.

You don't want anything like that to happen again, do you?"

"It wouldn't with you around to take care of me."

Preacher wasn't so sure about that. Trouble generally seemed to find him, one way or another.

But to his own surprise he found himself thinking seriously about what she had said. He wasn't going to take her to the mountains now, that was for damned sure, but . . .

"Tell you what," he said. "Five years from now, if you still feel the same way, you get word to me through Simon and we'll talk about it."

"Five years is forever!" she objected.

"Not when you're my age. And the older you get, the faster it'll go for you, too. But you'll be grown then, and I wouldn't feel quite as much like I was stealin' you away from your folks."

"You'll still be twice as old as me."

"Yeah, just about it. But it'll be some different."

He was confident that in five years she would have completely forgotten about him. And if she hadn't . . .

Well, he would deal with that when the time came, he decided.

"All right," she said, "but I know what you're thinking. You're thinking that if I go back to Washington you'll never see me again. You're wrong, Preacher. I promise I'll show up when you least expect it."

He wasn't totally sure if that was a promise . . . or a threat.

* * *

With the Indian ponies they were able to round up, there were enough horses for everyone to ride and even some spare mounts. When they started back to where they had left the *Sentinel,* Russell's wound was healing well enough that it wouldn't hurt him to ride. They would keep the pace fairly slow, however, and follow the river instead of cutting back across the sandy, mostly barren hills. That route would be longer, but there would be plenty of water and game along the way.

Preacher and Russell took the lead, along with Dog. Preacher kept an eye on his old friend and called a halt whenever he thought Russell looked like he was getting too tired. Russell complained about being coddled, but Preacher thought he was glad they weren't pushing too hard.

Sarah kept her word and stayed away from Preacher when they camped at night. Her parents seemed to still be getting along well, as were Stahlmaske and Gretchen. This journey up the Big Muddy had been filled with more danger and adventure, more tragedy and treachery, than any of them had expected, but they seemed to have come through it all right.

That didn't explain why Preacher began to get an odd feeling as the days passed. It wasn't the sort of tingling he experienced when he was being watched by an enemy, but rather more of a vague apprehension as if something bad was up ahead of them.

Dog seemed to feel it, too, stopping now and then to gaze down the river and whine softly. Preacher trusted the big cur's instincts as much as he did his own.

But nothing seemed out of place when they finally spotted the riverboat tied up at the shore in the same place where they had left it. Captain Warner had said he would wait right here, and so he had. Preacher wouldn't have been surprised if the captain had gotten too anxious to wait and had started upstream. That was another reason to follow the river, so they would meet the *Sentinel* if it was steaming toward them.

"There it is," Heinrich said excitedly. "Soon we will be on our way again."

He waved for Egon and Ludwig to follow them and galloped toward the boat. Preacher thought Warner might see them coming and blow a blast on the whistle in greeting, but the *Sentinel* remained silent. No one was moving around on deck, and Preacher didn't see anybody in the pilot house, either.

He stiffened as he realized that and said to Russell, "Something's wrong, Simon. That damn boat looks abandoned."

"You think something happened to Captain Warner and the crew?" Russell asked with a worried frown.

"I don't know, but I reckon we'd better find out

before those young fools go chargin' right into trouble." Preacher turned in his saddle and said to Stahlmaske, "Count, best keep everybody here for a few minutes while Simon and I take a look around."

"You think something is wrong?" Stahlmaske asked.

"I don't know, but I sure as hell intend to find out."

Preacher heeled Horse into a run. Russell trailed a short distance behind them. Up ahead, Heinrich, Ludwig, and Egon had dismounted and jumped the short gap from the shore to the cargo deck. They went up the stairs to the passenger level, and Preacher couldn't see them anymore.

Preacher had his rifle in one hand as he swung down from the saddle and got ready to jump onto the riverboat. Before he could do that, a shot rang out and a splash leaped up from the water as the ball went into the stream almost at Preacher's feet.

He looked up and saw a dozen men lining the rail on the passenger deck, all of them except two aiming rifles at him and Russell. One of the men who didn't have a gun in his hands was slender, with a pockmarked face that wore an arrogant grin as he looked down at Preacher.

Beside that man loomed the massive river pirate who had killed Gunther Klostermann during the gang's first attack on the boat. He had both hands clamped around Heinrich Ritter's neck, and Preacher had no doubt the big, bear-like pirate could twist the youngster's head right off his shoulders if he wanted to.

"You and your friend better throw down those guns, Preacher," the leader of the gang drawled. "Otherwise we'll just go ahead and start the killin' right now."

CHAPTER 36

In that split-second, Preacher thought about how fast he could raise his rifle and put a ball through the brain of that hulking river pirate with his hands wrapped around Heinrich's neck.

Then the leader raised a hand and said, "Ah, ah, ah, I know what you're thinking, Preacher. You figure you can kill Wedge before he snaps this boy's neck like a stick. I don't think you can. And even if you do, I've got the cap'n of this boat and the members of the crew who weren't killed when we took it over stashed in the engine room with men pointing guns at them. If they hear any shooting out here, they'll open fire. It'll be a massacre in there. You think about that before you decide to do something foolish."

"Preacher . . . ?" Russell said.

Bleak trenches had appeared in the mountain man's rugged face. With a disgusted sigh, he lowered his rifle and said, "I reckon you've got the upper hand right now, mister."

"Damn right, I do. The name's Binnion, by the way. Claude Binnion."

"Don't figure I'll go to the trouble to carve it on the marker after I bury you. *If* I do even that much and don't just leave you for the wolves."

Binnion laughed and said, "Big talker. I like that. Now, you wave everybody on in here. Throw all your weapons onto the cargo deck. Rifles, pistols, knives . . . that tomahawk of yours. All of it goes onto the boat."

Preacher tossed his rifle onto the deck and followed it with his other weapons. He gestured for Russell to do likewise. Russell wasn't fond of the idea, that was obvious, but he went along with what Preacher wanted.

"That bastard's gonna just murder us all once we're disarmed," Russell warned.

"He thinks he is," Preacher said.

He turned and waved for the others to come ahead. Gretchen looked scared as she rode up alongside Stahlmaske. She could see her brother up there on the passenger deck, a prisoner of the pirates.

"You are surrendering to these men?" Stahlmaske demanded coldly.

"Don't have much choice if we don't want them to kill Heinrich and their other prisoners."

Stahlmaske looked like he was mad enough to chew nails, but he dismounted and tossed his pistol onto the deck.

Margaret Allingham said anxiously to her husband, "Josiah . . . this can't be happening again."

"It'll be all right, dear," he told her. He lowered his voice and added, "I'm sure Preacher has a plan."

As a matter of fact, he *did* have a plan, Preacher thought.

He just didn't know if it would work . . . or if it would get them all killed.

"Just what is it you're plannin' on doin' with us?" he asked Binnion. "You've already got the boat. You can loot everything on it and we can't stop you."

"What's on this boat doesn't amount to anything compared to what we can get for the senator there, and for those fancy foreigners. I figure the government will pay handsomely to get 'em back safe and sound."

"So it's ransom you're after."

"That's right." Binnion drew a pistol from his belt. "Now get onboard, all of you. You're goin' in the engine room with the rest of your bunch."

Preacher knew he couldn't allow them to be locked up. If that happened, they were doomed. Binnion had to keep Senator Allingham, Margaret, and Sarah alive, along with Stahlmaske and Gretchen and probably Heinrich, if he wanted to ransom them.

As for all the other prisoners, well, it would be a lot simpler and easier just to shoot them and drop them in the river.

Preacher wanted to get the door of the engine room open, though, before he made his move. While the gang was in the process of locking up their new prisoners, the guards inside the engine room might not be paying as much attention to their other captives. Slim as it was, that was the only chance they had.

Still covered by the rifles of the pirates up on the passenger deck, Preacher and his companions began stepping onto the riverboat. Binnion jerked his head and told the giant, "Come on, Wedge. Bring the boy."

They started down the stairs to the lower deck, Binnion in the lead with a jaunty step, convinced of his victory.

Carefully, Preacher glanced at the pile of weapons on the deck. The rifles and pistols were all loaded and needed only to have their hammers cocked before being ready to fire. As he stood next to Russell, Stahlmaske, and Allingham, he said so quietly only they could hear, "When I make my move, you fellas grab some of those guns and open up. Binnion's men know they need you alive, Senator, and you, Count, so maybe that'll make 'em hesitate just long enough before they start shootin'."

"What are you gonna do?" Russell asked under his breath.

"That big varmint's mine," Preacher said.

Binnion reached the bottom of the stairs and went over to the door into the engine room. He rapped on it with the butt of his pistol and called, "Open up, boys. We've got some new guests."

Wedge kept one hand on Heinrich's throat and clamped the other around his upper arm to shove him along the deck toward the door. Heinrich looked a little like he was choking and he probably was, because Wedge barely allowed his feet to touch the deck.

The door into the engine room swung open. Preacher looked past Binnion and saw several pirates in there, peering out to see what was happening instead of watching their prisoners.

This moment wouldn't come again, the mountain man thought.

In times of great danger, for Preacher to think was to act. He shouted, "Now!," lowered his shoulder, and rammed into Wedge with all the power and drive he could muster.

The pirates were taken by surprise, just as Preacher hoped they would be. That gave Russell, Allingham, and Stahlmaske time to snatch up two pistols apiece and raise them toward the passenger deck. Shots roared from the weapons.

At the same time, Preacher slammed into Wedge. It felt a little like running into a mountain. Wedge wasn't expecting it, though, and the collision drove him against the outer wall of the engine room. That impact jolted loose his grip on Heinrich's neck.

As Russell fired toward the pirates on the passenger deck, he shouted through the open door of the engine room, "Come on, Cap'n!" Bellowing angrily, Captain Warner and the surviving members of the *Sentinel*'s crew charged their guards. Guns boomed inside the engine room, but a second later the knot of struggling men spilled out onto the deck.

Preacher peppered Wedge's granite-like face with a series of jabs. Often with big men like that, they had a weak spot on their nose or chin.

Not Wedge, evidently. He didn't even seem to feel the punches. He still had hold of Heinrich's arm, so he swung the young man like a club and smashed him into Preacher.

That sent both Preacher and Heinrich sprawling on the deck. At least Heinrich was out of the giant's clutches now, Preacher thought as he rolled over and came up to meet Wedge's bullish charge.

Up on the passenger deck, half of the pirates had gone down under the thunderous volley from Russell, Stahlmaske, and Allingham. Unfortunately, that still left half of the gang to fight back, and under the circumstances none of them cared about keeping any of the prisoners alive. Lead balls rained down around the three men who tried to duck for cover.

One of the shots tore through Allingham's left arm and sent him toppling to the deck. Stahlmaske cried out in pain as a lead ball ripped through his thigh. Russell was luckier than he'd been at the trading post and was untouched this time. He scooped up another pair of pistols and blasted two more of the pirates to hell.

At that moment, Egon and Ludwig broke free of the men who had been holding them and tackled a couple of pirates at the railing from behind. They all went over and fell heavily to the cargo deck below.

Preacher ducked away as Wedge tried to envelop him in a bear hug. He knew that if Wedge got those tree-trunk arms around him, the massive pirate could crush every bone in his body. Preacher hooked a left and a right to Wedge's belly, but again the blows seemingly had no effect.

Wedge was pretty fast for a big man, although his movements had a certain lumbering quality about them due to his sheer size. Preacher had to dodge ham-like fists that might have torn his head right off his shoulders if they had connected.

He launched a kick at Wedge's groin, but the big man caught his foot before the blow could connect. Without much obvious effort, Wedge heaved Preacher over backward. Preacher slid on his shoulders across the deck and wound up next to the pile of weapons.

He grabbed his tomahawk and threw it. Wedge tried to bat it away but was too slow. The tomahawk struck his head a glancing blow, opening up a long gash that welled blood down the side of Wedge's face.

That infuriated him. He bellowed again and thundered toward Preacher. The mountain man rolled desperately to get out of the way of those trampling feet. He hooked a toe behind Wedge's left knee and kicked that leg with his other foot as hard as he could. He heard the sharp pop as the knee broke. Wedge screamed and toppled like a tree, falling off the boat into the river.

Preacher dived after him and landed on the big pirate's back before Wedge could rise from the muddy water along the shore. It wasn't deep here, but Preacher drove his knee into the small of Wedge's back and pinned him down. With both hands on the back of Wedge's head, Preacher forced his face into the bottom. Wedge bucked, but he wasn't as strong in the water and couldn't get the same sort of purchase. Preacher threw all his strength into the effort. He knew that Wedge's nose and mouth had to be clogged with mud by now. The man wouldn't be able to breathe at all.

It was a brutal, ugly thing, suffocating a man like this, but Preacher knew he had no choice. Gradually, Wedge's struggles became weaker. Preacher felt a shudder go through the giant frame. Then Wedge went limp.

Preacher didn't know how his friends were faring. This was the first chance he'd had to check. He raised his head and looked toward the boat.

Claude Binnion was backing away along the cargo deck, one arm looped around Sarah Allingham's neck so he could drag her with him as the other hand pressed a pistol barrel into her side. Facing him were Russell, Captain Warner, and several of the crewmen, all armed now.

"I'll kill her!" Binnion threatened. "She's coming with me, and you're gonna let me get away from here."

Binnion appeared to be the only one of the pirates still in the fight. The others were littered around the boat, either dead, unconscious, or badly wounded. He glanced toward where Preacher was rising out of the water and cried in alarm, "Wedge! Wedge! You've killed him, damn you!"

The sight of Wedge's body lying in the shallow water at the edge of the river had distracted Binnion enough that he didn't notice Heinrich Ritter coming up behind him. Heinrich must have circled the boat to get in that position. He moved quietly until he was close enough to rush Binnion.

The pirate heard Heinrich at the last second and tried to turn to meet his charge. Heinrich grabbed Binnion's wrist and thrust his arm up as Binnion pulled the trigger. The pistol barked, but the ball flew harmlessly into the air.

Preacher saw Stahlmaske lying on the deck near the weapons. The count's leg was bloody and useless, but he had pushed himself up so that he was leaning on his hands. Preacher called, "Count! Toss me a rifle!"

Stahlmaske did so, and Preacher caught the rifle deftly. As he brought it to his shoulder, he saw Heinrich grab Sarah and dive off the side of the boat with her, leaving Binnion standing there alone.

As the rifle boomed and kicked against Preacher's shoulder, Russell, Warner, and a couple of the crewmen fired as well. All five shots smashed into Binnion and lifted him off his feet with their force. He crashed down on his back, riddled through and through, and kicked a couple of times as he lay there dying. When those spasms stilled, Preacher knew it was finally over.

Heinrich and Sarah rose dripping from the water. She was crying, and he had his arms around her, trying to comfort her. She clutched at his shirt and buried her face against his chest.

Preacher smiled. It looked like ol' Heinrich might've solved his problem with Sarah, he thought.

She would remember how he had risked his life to save her.

Romance could wait for later. Right now there was still work to do, wounds to patch up, bodies to pitch in the river, blood to be swabbed off the decks.

The *Sentinel* and everyone on her had gone through a baptism of fire.

Except for Preacher. This sort of danger and sudden death was all too familiar to him.

Ten days later, the sternwheeler reached the mouth of the Yellowstone River. The rest of the journey to this point had been uneventful, thank goodness.

Warner's crew was a little shorthanded because of the men who had been killed in the various battles, so Heinrich, Egon, and Ludwig had pitched in to help. The captain told them they had the makings of good river men, if they wanted to stay once the boat got back to St. Louis. Preacher was pretty sure none of them would take him up on the offer.

As he'd hoped, Heinrich and Sarah had been spending a considerable amount of time together. Whether that would turn into something lasting, Preacher had no idea. Time had a way of taking care of things like that, one way or the other.

Allingham had been wearing a sling to support his wounded arm, but he seemed to be coming along well. He was more determined than ever to return to Vermont when his term in the Senate was finished, and Margaret was looking forward to that. They both were.

Count Stahlmaske had a devoted nurse in Gretchen. The rifle ball had missed the bone in his thigh, and the wound was healing. The count had already started walking a little with the help of a cane Preacher had made for him from the branch of a cottonwood. He hadn't offered his thanks for that gesture, nor had Preacher expected any.

Once the *Sentinel* was tied up, the crew began pitching camp on shore. The party would remain here for several weeks while fur trappers brought their pelts to sell to Simon Russell, representing the American Fur Company. Russell had asked Preacher again to stay on, to make the return trip downriver with them.

"We might run into more trouble," he pointed out as he and Preacher stood on the shore. Preacher was tightening the bindings on the supplies he had placed on the pack horse he'd brought along.

"You've got some good fightin' men along if you do," the mountain man replied. "I reckon they've proved that plenty of times over by now."

"Yeah, but that's not the same as having Preacher along," Russell argued.

"You'll be fine. Shoot, the way things usually go, you'll be *less* likely to run into trouble if I ain't anywhere around."

"You do seem to attract it," Russell said with a rueful chuckle.

"And I don't understand why. I'm—"

"A peaceable man," they both said together.

After Russell had said his goodbyes, Count Stahlmaske limped over to Preacher, using his cane to lean on. He gave the mountain man a brusque nod and said, "So, you are leaving."

"Yep. The other side of the mountain's callin' to me."

"You are a foolish American. You could be a rich man if you would work for the fur company. In ten years you might well be running the entire operation."

Preacher grunted and said, "No offense, Count, but what you just described sounds like pure dee hell to me."

"That is because you are a barbarian. A savage."

Preacher nodded gravely. "Yep."

Stahlmaske held out his hand and said, "But I wish you luck anyway. Even a barbarian can use some good fortune on occasion."

Preacher shook the count's hand. Neither man smiled. But Stahlmaske added quietly, "Once I might have been like you."

Preacher remembered how Gretchen had said that he and Stahlmaske didn't get along because they were too much alike. Maybe she was right. But each of them had taken his own path, and those trails led to far different places.

Preacher swung up into the saddle, hitched Horse into motion, said, "Come on, Dog," and rode west toward the mountains.

It felt good to be going home.

J. A. Johnstone on William W. Johnstone
"Print the Legend"

William W. Johnstone was born in southern Missouri, the youngest of four children. He was raised with strong moral and family values by his minister father, and tutored by his schoolteacher mother. Despite this, he quit school at age fifteen.

"I have the highest respect for education," he says, "but such is the folly of youth, and wanting to see the world beyond the four walls and the blackboard."

True to this vow, Bill attempted to enlist in the French Foreign Legion ("I saw Gary Cooper in *Beau Geste* when I was a kid and I thought the French Foreign Legion would be fun") but was rejected, thankfully, for being underage. Instead, he joined a traveling carnival and did all kinds of odd jobs. It was listening to the veteran carny folk, some of whom had been on the circuit since the late 1800s, telling amazing tales about their experiences, that planted the storytelling seed in Bill's imagination.

"They were mostly honest people, despite the bad reputation traveling carny shows had back then," Bill remembers. "Of course, there were exceptions. There was one guy named Picky, who got that name because he was a master pickpocket. He could steal a man's socks right off his feet without him knowing. Believe me, Picky got us chased out of more than a few towns."

After a few months of this grueling existence, Bill returned home and finished high school. Next came stints as a deputy sheriff in the Tallulah, Louisiana, Sheriff's Department, followed by a hitch in the U.S. Army. Then he began a career in radio broadcasting at KTLD in Tallulah, which would last sixteen years. It was there that he fine-tuned his storytelling skills. He turned to writing in 1970, but it wouldn't be until 1979 that his first novel, *The Devil's Kiss,* was published. Thus began the full-time writing career of William W. Johnstone. He wrote horror (*The Uninvited*), thrillers (*The Last of the Dog Team*), even a romance novel or two. Then, in February 1983, *Out of the Ashes* was published. Searching for his missing family in a postapocalyptic America, rebel mercenary and patriot Ben Raines is united with the civilians of the Resistance forces and moves to the forefront of a revolution for the nation's future.

Out of the Ashes was a smash. The series would continue for the next twenty years, winning Bill three generations of fans all over the world. The series was often imitated but never duplicated. "We all tried to copy the Ashes series," said one publishing executive, "but Bill's uncanny ability, both then and now, to predict in which direction the political winds were blowing brought a certain immediacy to the table no one else could capture." The Ashes series would end its run with more than thirty-four books and twenty million copies in print, making it one of the most successful men's action series in American book publishing. (The Ashes series also, Bill notes with a touch of pride, got him on the FBI's Watch List for its less than flattering portrayal of spineless politicians and the growing power of big government over our lives, among other things. In that respect, I often find myself saying, "Bill was years ahead of his time.")

Always steps ahead of the political curve, Bill's recent thrillers, written with myself, include *Vengeance Is Mine, Invasion USA, Border War, Jackknife, Remember the Alamo, Home Invasion, Phoenix Rising, The Blood of Patriots, The Bleeding Edge,* and the upcoming *Suicide Mission.*

It is with the western, though, that Bill found his greatest success. His westerns propelled him onto both the *USA Today* and the *New York Times* best-seller lists.

Bill's western series include *Matt Jensen, the Last Mountain Man, Preacher, the First Mountain Man, The Family Jensen, Luke Jensen, Bounty Hunter, Eagles, MacCallister* (an Eagles spin-off), *Sidewinders, The Brothers O'Brien, Sixkiller, Blood Bond, The Last Gunfighter,* and the new series *Flintlock* and *The Trail West.* May 2013 saw the hardcover western *Butch Cassidy: The Lost Years.*

"The Western," Bill says, "is one of the few true art forms that is one hundred percent American. I liken the Western as America's version of England's Arthurian legends, like the Knights of the Round Table, or Robin Hood and his Merry Men. Starting with the 1902 publication of *The Virginian* by Owen Wister, and followed by the greats like Zane Grey, Max Brand, Ernest Haycox, and of course Louis L'Amour, the Western has helped to shape the cultural landscape of America.

"I'm no goggle-eyed college academic, so when my fans ask me why the Western is as popular now as it was a century ago, I don't offer a 200-page thesis. Instead, I can only offer this: The Western is honest. In this great country, which is suffering under the yoke of political correctness, the Western harks back to an era when justice was sure and swift. Steal a man's horse, rustle his cattle, rob a bank, a stagecoach, or a train, you were hunted down and fitted with a hangman's noose. One size fit all.

"Sure, we westerners are prone to a little embellishment and exaggeration and, I admit it, occasionally play a little fast and loose with the facts. But we do so for a very good reason—to enhance the enjoyment of readers.

"It was Owen Wister, in *The Virginian*, who first coined the phrase *'When you call me that, smile.'* Legend has it that Wister actually heard those words spoken by a deputy sheriff in Medicine Bow, Wyoming, when another poker player called him a son of a bitch.

"Did it really happen, or is it one of those myths that have passed down from one generation to the next? I honestly don't know. But there's a line in one of my favorite Westerns of all time, *The Man Who Shot Liberty Valance*, where the newspaper editor tells the young reporter, 'When the truth becomes legend, print the legend.'

"These are the words I live by."

Turn the page for an exciting preview from
USA Today **Bestselling Authors**
William W. Johnstone and J. A. Johnstone

BUTCH CASSIDY: THE LOST YEARS

**"Johnstone is a masterful storyteller, creating
a tale that is fanciful and funny, exciting and
surprisingly convincing . . . great fun."**
—*Publishers Weekly*

**THE GREATEST WESTERN WRITER
OF THE 21ST CENTURY**

In a small Texas town in 1950, a Pinkerton detective
interrupts a game of dominoes to learn the truth about
Butch Cassidy—who is still very much alive.
He's the old-timer playing dominoes.

Seems that after the infamous shoot-out in Bolivia
that claimed the life of his partner, the Sundance Kid,
Butch returned to Texas to find a place to call home.
When he comes across a dying rancher who's been
shot by rustlers, Butch promises to avenge him—
and take over the ranch. As "Jim Strickland,"
Butch begins a new chapter in his life.
Yet trouble has a way of finding Butch.
A corrupt railroad baron pulls him into the most
dangerous train robbery he's ever attempted.
But if Butch Cassidy is to ride again,
he'll need a newer, and wilder, Wild Bunch . . .

On sale now, wherever Pinnacle Books are sold!

PROLOGUE

Zephyr, Texas, 1950

After the hot, bright sunlight outside, the grocery store was dim and pleasantly cool. Electric fans sitting here and there in open spaces on the shelves stirred the air around and blended the smells of pepper, vinegar, cinnamon, coffee, and a thousand other items into an aroma that intrigued the senses of Nathan Tuttle. The irregular slap of ivory against wood drew him toward the rear of the store. A bluish-gray haze of cigarette smoke hung in the air above the scarred wooden table back there, past the meat case and the counter where the cash register squatted.

Four men sat at the table playing dominoes. One of them, a stout man wearing a white apron, was probably the store's owner. Another wore jeans and a grease-stained mechanic's shirt with the name "Howard" stitched onto an oval patch sewn to it. The overalls and dirt-encrusted work shoes of the third man indicated that he was a farmer.

The fourth man, who had a brown, hand-rolled

cigarette dangling from his lips, was lean almost to the point of gauntness, his leathery face a study in planes and angles. He wore a straw cowboy hat tipped back on his head, revealing crisp white hair. His faded blue shirt had snaps on it instead of buttons. He sat with his back to the wall, facing the door, Nathan noted, so he would be able to see anyone who came in.

The man glanced up at the newcomer, and even though he had to be at least eighty years old, his eyes were those of a younger man, blue and piercing and intelligent. He had a small scar under the left one.

The old man looked down at the dominoes in front of him again, obviously dismissing Nathan from his thoughts. That came as no surprise. Tall, slender, and bespectacled, with a natural awkwardness about him, Nathan knew he wasn't a very impressive physical specimen. He liked to think he made up for that with his mind, but the jury was still out on that.

The storekeeper looked up at Nathan, too, and asked, "Something I can do for you, son?" In the middle of a hot afternoon like this, the store wasn't busy. In fact, Nathan was the only potential customer at the moment.

"I'm looking for Mr. Henry Parker," he said.

The glances the other three players shot toward the man in the cowboy hat told Nathan he had come to the right place.

"This here's Hank," the storekeeper said with a nod toward the old cowboy.

The man added a domino to the arrangement on the table and said, "Makes fifteen." A rectangular piece of board with holes drilled in it lay on the table near his left hand. The holes were arranged in five columns, with ten holes in each column. The cowboy took a small wooden peg and moved it up three holes. He didn't look at Nathan.

"Hello, Mr. Parker," Nathan said. "I was wondering if I could have a word with you."

Parker drew on the cigarette and let the smoke trickle out his nostrils.

"Go ahead."

"In private, if we could," Nathan said.

The farmer chuckled and said, "Sounds like you might be in trouble with the gov'ment, Hank. This boy looks like he might be a gov'ment man."

Parker finally looked up at Nathan again and asked, "You come from Washington, son?"

"No, sir. Dallas."

That brought more chuckles from the other three men, as if being from Dallas was almost as bad as being from Washington.

"We're right in the middle of a game here," Parker said. With a graceful motion, he gestured toward the dominoes on the table. "I'm ahead, and I only need thirty more points to go out."

The mechanic said, "The lousy dominoes I'm gettin' today, it might take me three hands to score that much count."

"Jim Strickland told me to look you up, Mr. Parker," Nathan said.

Parker's face looked like it might have been carved

from old wood. Without changing expression, he said, "Jim Strickland, eh? How is ol' Jim?"

"Very interesting," Nathan said.

The storekeeper asked, "Don't think I know a Jim Strickland. He any relation to the Stricklands up at Blanket? I recollect one named Mose, and another boy called Alvy, somethin' like that."

Parker shook his head and said, "Jim's no relation, as far as I know." He turned his dominoes face-down. "You fellas go on without me."

"You're quittin' in the middle of a game?" the farmer asked. "That ain't like you, Hank."

"Well, hell," Parker said as he got to his feet, "there'll always be another game, won't there?" He pointed to the store's entrance and went on to Nathan, "We'll go sit on one of the benches on the front porch and talk. You got to buy me a cold soda pop, though. It's hot out there today."

Nathan reached into his pocket for a coin and said, "Sure. How much?"

"Soda pop's a nickel," the storekeeper said.

Nathan handed him a dime.

"I'll get one for myself, too," he said as he went to the red metal drink box. He paused with his hand on the lid and looked back at Parker. "What would you like, sir?"

"Co'-Cola will be fine, son," Parker said as he stepped around the table and the other players.

Nathan took two bottles of Coca-Cola from the bed of half-melted ice on the bottom of the box, let them drip for a few seconds, and then popped the caps on the opener attached to the side of the box.

He handed one to Parker, and the two of them strolled outside together.

It was warmer out here, but at least the awning over the sidewalk put the wooden benches in the shade. The single block of businesses that constituted the community's downtown was all but deserted. No cars hummed past on the highway.

The two men sat down. Parker stretched his legs out in front of him and crossed them at the ankles. His plain brown boots showed signs of long wear.

"My name is Nathan Tuttle, sir."

"Am I going to be pleased to meet you, Nathan?" Parker asked with a faint smile on his face. "Or am I going to regret it?"

"I suppose that depends on our conversation."

"Ain't that always the way?" Parker lifted the bottle to his lips and let a long drink slide between them. When he lowered it, he went on, "What brings you to Zephyr besides a hankerin' to act all mysterious-like, Nathan?"

"I work for the Pinkerton Detective Agency." Nathan had intended to be very forthright and open, putting his cards on the table right away, so to speak. But something about Henry Parker was intimidating, despite his mild appearance and soft-spoken manner. After admitting that he was a Pinkerton, Nathan fell silent.

Parker took another drink of the soda and said, "Go on."

"My father was a Pinkerton agent," Nathan said. "So was his father before him."

"It's not a job that's usually handed down from father to son, from what I hear," Parker said.

"That's the way it worked in my family. My father and grandfather were both devoted to the idea of upholding the law."

"Most fellas who feel like that become cops, not strikebreakers and railroad goons."

Nathan bristled with anger, unable to suppress the reaction.

"That's not all the Pinkertons do. They pursue criminals all over the country."

"Is that what you're doin', Nathan?" Parker drawled. "Pursuin' a criminal?"

Nathan felt like the man was making fun of him. He knew that he ought to be used to that by now, but it still rankled him.

"As a matter of fact, I am," he said. Warming to his subject now, he continued, "A couple of years ago, not long after I went to work for the agency, I came into the possession of my grandfather's trunk. Inside it were a lot of his notebooks and papers concerning the cases he worked on. I found them to be fascinating reading, especially the ones about his search for one outlaw in particular: Butch Cassidy."

"When was this, when your grandpa was lookin' for Butch Cassidy?"

"Around the time of the First World War."

Parker shook his head slowly and said, "I hate to break it to you, Nathan, but he was wasting his time. Butch Cassidy was killed before that down in South America, in one of those countries that's even hotter than Texas. I remember hearin' all about it. Seems like it was . . . 1906, maybe. Somewhere around in there."

"1908," Nathan said. "In Bolivia, at a little town called San Vicente."

"See, there you go, you know a lot more about it than I do."

"That's where Robert LeRoy Parker and Harry Longabaugh, better known under their aliases Butch Cassidy and the Sundance Kid, supposedly were killed in a battle with the Bolivian army."

"Well, two men against an army . . . It don't sound very likely they would have come through that alive."

"The Pinkertons have never officially declared them dead."

"I don't reckon you have to be declared dead to *be* dead."

Nathan ignored that comment and went on, "My grandfather, Newton Tuttle, believed that while Longabaugh was indeed killed in Bolivia, Robert Parker survived the shooting, although he was wounded, and escaped from the Bolivians. A week after the battle at San Vicente, an American who appeared to be ill—or suffering from a gunshot wound—appeared in a coastal village in Chile and bought passage on a trading ship that took him to Lima, Peru. From there he was able to secure a berth on a liner bound for Liverpool. He traveled under the name Leroy Michaels."

"Now, I can see why you might think I'm related to Butch Cassidy, since my name's Parker and you say that was his real name, too . . . even though there are a whole heap of people with that last name. I don't recall that I've ever known anybody with the last name of Michaels, though."

"Robert Leroy Parker started calling himself Butch Cassidy after he met a rustler named Mike Cassidy," Nathan said. "The connection seems obvious to me."

"It's your story, Nathan," Parker said softly.

"Actually, it's my grandfather's story. He's the one who traced Leroy Michaels to England, where he recuperated from his wound and eventually traveled to France and Spain, only by then he was using the name Jameson Lowe. Jim Lowe was another name Butch used as an alias for a while."

Parker sipped from the soda bottle and said, "Go on."

"Eventually Jameson Lowe sailed to New York and disappeared. There's speculation that Etta Place, Harry Longabaugh's lover, was in New York about the same time, so it stands to reason that Cassidy wanted to see her and break the news of the Sundance Kid's death himself."

Nathan's eyes were keener than they looked behind his glasses. He didn't miss the way Henry Parker's hand tightened on the bottle when he mentioned Etta Place. Parker didn't say anything, though.

"Jameson Lowe dropped out of sight after his visit to New York. My grandfather actually hadn't been assigned to track down Butch Cassidy and determine once and for all if the outlaw was dead or alive. That was just a tangent off another investigation, but he became so interested in it that he continued to follow up on his own time after his superiors insisted that he drop the matter. He came to believe that Butch Cassidy was living in Texas under the name Jim Strickland and had become a successful rancher."

"What made him think that?" Parker asked.

Nathan hesitated, then said, "I don't really know. There are . . . gaps . . . in my grandfather's documentation of his investigation. I know at one point he planned to travel to Texas to meet this fellow Strickland and see if he was right. But I haven't been able to find any indication that he ever made the trip."

"And why do you think I'd know anything about Strickland?"

"Well . . . you agreed to talk to me after I mentioned the name, didn't you?"

That brought a slow chuckle from Parker. He said, "I just wanted to see what sort of burr you had under your saddle, son. I could tell as soon as you came in the store you were fit to bust about somethin'. You've spun an interestin' yarn, but what does it have to do with me?"

"I suppose I've talked around it for long enough, haven't I?" Nathan took a deep breath. "I've taken up the challenge where my grandfather left off, sir. I've been trying to find out what happened to Jim Strickland, and I've traced the man I believe was using that name through several more identities until I arrived at a conclusion. I believe that you are the man who was once known as Jim Strickland, Mr. Parker. Or should I say . . . Mr. Cassidy?"

For a long moment, Parker didn't say anything. Then he tipped his head back and let out an easy laugh.

"Son, you've been out in the sun too long," he said. "It's done somethin' to your brain. Do I really look like a famous owlhoot and train robber to you? I'm just a stove-up old cowboy."

"You seem rather spry for your age, sir . . . which, if I'm not mistaken, is just about the same age as Butch Cassidy would be if he survived that shootout in Bolivia. Mid-eighties, am I right?"

"Be eighty-five my next birthday," Parker said. "Just what the hell would you do, kid, if I said, yeah, I'm Butch Cassidy?"

Nathan was prepared for that question. He said, "In all likelihood, I wouldn't do anything. There are no charges still on the books against Butch Cassidy. I just want to know the truth. I want to know if my grandfather was right."

Parker still seemed amused. He took another drink and said, "Well . . . I'm not admitting anything of the sort, mind you, but folks around here seem to think I'm a pretty good storyteller. Tell you what I'll do. You've spun me a yarn, so I'll spin you a yarn of what it might have been like if I really was Butch Cassidy. How about that?"

"I'm more than willing to listen to anything you want to tell me, sir."

"All right, then." For a moment Parker squinted

as if in thought, then resumed, "If you're right about that wild idea you've got in your head—and I ain't sayin' you are, mind you—then the story you're lookin' for begins on a cold night in West Texas in 1914 . . ."

CHAPTER 1

When I saw the blue norther coming I would have found a place to hole up and wait it out, except there didn't seem to be any such a thing in these parts. It was a damn fool stunt to begin with, starting from San Antonio to El Paso on horseback in December. But I had never spent that much time in Texas, and I wanted to take a gander at some of the country. You hear Texans bragging about the place all the time, as they're in the habit of doing, and after a while you want to see it for yourself.

So I bought a couple of good horses and some supplies, figuring I'd use one of the animals as a packhorse and the other as a saddle mount and switch back and forth between 'em, and set off across country. I figured I'd probably run into some fences along the way, at least until I got farther west, but . . . well . . . fences have never bothered me all that much, if you know what I mean.

I could've bought a car and driven to El Paso, I

suppose—you could do that, even that far back— but while I could handle one of the contraptions if I had to, I'd never been comfortable doing so. The worry that the damned thing might blow up on me always lurked in the back of my mind.

So it was horseback for me, and that's how I came to be out in the middle of nowhere when the sky turned so blue it was almost black and the wind began to howl out of the north, bringing with it a bone-numbing chill. I lowered my head, hunkered deeper in my sheepskin coat, and kept going. Wasn't nothing behind me, so I knew it wouldn't do any good to turn around.

At least it wasn't raining or snowing, even though a thick overcast hung above me. I knew there had to be a ranch house somewhere ahead of me, and if I kept moving I'd find it. I knew that because if there wasn't, I stood a good chance of freezing to death before morning.

The light was starting to fade when I heard popping sounds. With the wind blowing so hard and making such a racket it was hard to be sure, but I thought they might be gunshots. It was hard to tell exactly where they came from, too, but I turned my horses in what I hoped was the right direction.

Now, you may think it was foolish of me, riding toward gunfire rather than away from it, but I looked at it like this: whoever was shooting that gun probably had a place to get in out of the weather, and that was what I needed more than anything else tonight.

The last of the gray light disappeared, and I was left to plod along in darkness. There had been only a handful of shots, and the shortness of the volley could mean almost anything, so I didn't see any real point in speculating about it. Keep going and I might find out, that's the way I looked at it.

My horse stopped short and shied back a step. I said, "Easy there, fella." I couldn't see what had spooked him.

I wasn't carrying a handgun, but I had a Winchester in a scabbard strapped to the saddle. I drew it out and worked the lever to throw a cartridge into the chamber. Then I swung a leg over the saddle and slid to the ground. The packhorse's reins were tied to the saddle horn. I hung on to the reins of the animal I'd been riding as I moved forward cautiously.

It only took a couple of steps to tell me why my horse had stopped. The ground fell away into a gully. I could barely make it out as it twisted across the plains like a snake.

If the gully wasn't too deep and the sides weren't too steep, the horses and I could climb down into it and get out of the wind, at least. I might find enough wood to build a small fire. It was a slender hope but better than nothing. Ever since night fell I'd been looking all around, searching for a yellow pinpoint of light that marked the window of a ranch house, but hadn't seen anything except endless darkness.

I put the rifle back in its sheath and hunkered on

my heels at the edge of the gully. I reached into my coat and fished a match from my shirt pocket. It lit when I snapped the head with my thumbnail, but the wind snatched the flame right out. Trying to get one burning up here was just going to be a waste of matches. I slid a foot over the edge and used it to explore the slope. It wasn't a sheer drop-off, so I had hopes of being able to get the horses down there.

The prairie was dotted with mesquite trees, their limbs skeleton-bare at this time of year. I tied the saddle horse's reins to one of them and went back to the edge of the gully. I was going to have to explore it by feel until I got down out of the wind.

I turned around so I was facing the slope and started climbing down. The gully wall was rough enough that there were plenty of places to brace myself. When I got down low enough that my head was out of the wind, the night was still plenty cold but not as breathtakingly raw.

My right foot came down on something soft that let out a loud groan.

I like to think my nerves are pretty steady, but I'd be lying if I said I didn't let out a holler and jump up in the air. When I came down I lost my balance and started rolling.

I was lucky that gully wasn't very deep. I only turned over a couple of times before I hit bottom. Even so, I landed hard enough to knock the wind out of me and send my hat flying.

"What the blue blazes!" I yelled when I got my

breath back. I probably said a few things that were worse than that, too, but I disremember.

Whoever or whatever I'd stepped on groaned again.

That pained sound, mixed in with the howl of the wind, gave me the fantods. I sat up and scuttled backward a little, well aware that I'd left my Winchester up on the flat with the horses and cussing myself for doing such a foolish thing. I hadn't expected to find anything in this gully, but I'd been around long enough to know that whatever you expect in life usually ain't what happens.

I didn't know if my companion could answer me or not, but I said, "Who's there?"

The answer came back in a weak voice.

"You have any . . . whiskey . . . *amigo*?"

Despite calling me *amigo*, he didn't sound like a Mexican, but I'd already discovered that in that part of Texas, most people, white and brown alike, spoke a mixture of the two lingos. And as a matter of fact, I did have a flask in my saddlebags. But before I fetched it, I wanted to find out more about what was going on here.

"Are you hurt, old son?" I asked.

The man tried to laugh, but it came out more like a pained grunt.

"You could . . . say that. Got a couple of . . . bullet holes . . . in my guts."

Well, that was bad, and a damned shame to boot. One bullet hole in the belly was enough to kill a man. Two and he was a goner for sure. But I said,

"Hold on, I'll see what I can do." I started to crawl toward the sound of his voice, then paused and asked, "You ain't fixin' to shoot me, are you?"

"No reason to," he said. "You ain't . . . one of the varmints who shot me. They've long since . . . took off for the tall . . . and uncut."

I found another match and lit it. This time I was able to keep it going by cupping my hand around the flame, although the wind caused it to dance around quite a bit. The feeble, flickering glow from it revealed a stocky man with a close-cropped white beard lying against the bank like he'd slid part of the way down it. His coat must have hung on something and stopped him. He had both arms crossed over his belly.

A glance over my shoulder told me that the gully was about a dozen feet wide, with a sandy, fairly level bottom. Clumps of brush grew here and there.

"Let me help you lay down, old-timer," I said, "and I'll take a look at those wounds."

"I told you . . . I want whiskey. Ain't nothin' you can do . . . about the other."

I figured he'd be more comfortable stretched out, though, so when the match burned down I shook it out and got hold of him, lifting him as gently as I could and easing him down so that his legs were in front of him on the gully floor and his back was leaned against the bank. He muttered some things I didn't understand, most likely complaints because I hadn't fetched that flask yet.

It took me only a few minutes to find my hat,

gather some dry branches from the brush, place them in a heap, and get a fire burning. Once the flames were going, they gave off enough light I could see a broken-down place in the bank where I thought I could get the horses down.

"I'll be back," I told the gut-shot old man.

"I ain't . . . goin' nowheres."

I brought the horses down one at a time and tied them to a sturdy-looking bush. They were close enough to the fire to draw a little warmth from it. Then I got the flask from my saddlebags and knelt next to the wounded man.

I uncapped the flask and held it to his mouth.

"Here you go."

He sucked at it greedily as I tipped it up. I didn't give him too much. The stuff was going to burn like fire when it hit the holes in his guts. He might pass out from it, and I wanted to know what happened to him.

Whoever shot him might still be roaming around, I thought, and I was curious just how trigger-happy they might be.

I set the flask aside and asked, "Who shot you, mister?"

"Abner . . ." he struggled to say.

"Somebody named Abner ventilated you?"

"No . . . damn it! That's . . . my name . . . Abner . . . Tillotson. Don't want to . . . cash out . . . without somebody knowin' who I am."

"All right, Mr. Tillotson. What happened?"

"Thought you was gonna . . . try to patch me up."

"I decided there wouldn't be a whole lot of point to it," I told him honestly. His coat was open enough for me to see how black with blood his shirt was underneath it.

He chuckled and said, "You're right . . . about that. I'll tell you . . . what happened . . . I was shot by three . . . no-account rustlers . . . that's what."

"You've got a spread hereabouts?"

"We're on it . . . the Fishhook."

"You have family there?"

"Naw . . . no family anywhere . . . just me. Three or four Mex hands . . . work for me part-time. None of 'em there now. I knew there was a norther comin' . . . so I rode out to . . . check on my critters. That's when I come across . . . them rustlers . . ."

"Who'd be out wide-looping cattle in weather like this?"

"Those no-good Daughtry boys . . . Stealin' comes as natural . . . as breathin' to them. They don't care . . . what the weather's like. They were pushin' . . . a dozen of my cows . . . toward their place. I yelled for 'em to stop . . . and they turned around and started . . . burnin' powder at me." Abner paused. "I could do with . . . another drink."

I gave him one. He winced, but he got it down.

"Where's your ranch house? I'll get you back there."

"Two miles . . . due west of here. It backs up . . . against a butte. You'll find it." He raised a blood-smeared hand and waved vaguely in the direction he'd mentioned. "But you'll have to . . . come back and get me later . . . if the coyotes ain't dragged me off. You got . . . somethin' else to do tonight."

"I wasn't planning on doin' anything except trying to keep from freezin' to death," I said.

"No . . . you're gonna go after . . . them Daughtrys . . . and settle accounts for me."

"Why the hell would I want to do that?"

The words came out of my mouth a mite harsher than I'd intended, but he had startled me with that flat pronouncement.

"Because I'm gonna . . . give you my ranch in return for . . . avengin' me."

I started to say something else, but he held up that bloody hand again to stop me.

"I've seen . . . a thousand drifters like you . . . in my time, son."

I doubted very seriously that he'd ever seen anybody exactly like me, but I wasn't going to argue with a dying man.

"I know what . . . you need," he went on. "You need a home. You ain't . . . as young as you used to be."

Well, he was right about that, I thought. I was pushing middle age, pushing it pretty hard, when you come right down to it.

"You're bound to be . . . gettin' a mite tired. You need a good place . . . to settle down . . . and the Fishhook's a fine spread. I'll sign it over to you . . . right here and now . . . if you give me your word you'll settle those rustlers' hash."

"You said there were three of 'em. Three against one ain't very good odds."

"Yeah, but I can tell by lookin' at you . . . You still got the bark on you, boy. I'm bettin' my ranch . . . you can do it." He laughed again. "Of course . . . I'm losin' one way or the other . . . ain't I?"

To this day, I don't know what made me do it. Maybe I just wanted to ease his way from this world into the next. But I said, "All right, Mr. Tillotson, I'll do it. I'll go after those rustlers. Can't promise you I'll kill all of them, but I'll do my damnedest."

"That's all . . . anybody can ask of a man. You got paper and . . . a pencil?"

"Yeah."

"Get it. Write out a bill of sale . . . I'll sign it. But gimme . . . another drink first."

I did that, then took out a book I'd bought in San Antonio. I'd picked it up because it was a story about a cowboy named Cassidy who had a bum leg, and that struck me as funny. The book had a blank page or two in the back, so I tore one of them out, flattened it on the cover, and after pausing to build up the fire a little and make it brighter, I used a stub of a pencil to scrawl a bill of sale transferring ownership of the Fishhook Ranch from Abner Tillotson to . . .

Until that moment I hadn't thought about what name I was going to put down. I had gone by several different names in my life. Sometimes it came in handy for a man in my line of work to be somebody else. I'd used the name Jim before, and to be honest I just plucked Strickland out of thin air. I didn't recall ever knowing anybody by that name.

So I wrote down "Jim Strickland," and then I read what I'd written to Abner. He managed a weak nod and said, "That'll be fine. You're a good man . . . Jim."

I don't know if he just ran out of breath before he said the name, or if he was telling me in his own way that he knew it wasn't real and didn't care.

He held out his hand and said, "Gimme the pencil. Afraid I'm gonna get blood on it."

"Don't worry about that," I told him.

He took the pencil. I held the book where he could sign his name on the page. His hand was shaking some, but I could read his signature. I didn't think anybody would dispute the bill of sale, since he didn't have any family, and anyway I wasn't sure I would ever use it. While the idea of settling down held some appeal, I didn't know if I could do it. I'd been on the drift for a long time.

When he was finished his hand fell back in his lap. He said, "You better . . . get after 'em now. They got a shack . . . couple miles north of here. Ain't much more than a lean-to . . . built against a little rise. Don't trust 'em . . . they're tricky bastards. I never should've . . . give' 'em any warnin' . . . Should've just started shootin' first myself. You might want to . . . bear that in mind."

"I sure will, Abner," I told him. "You better get some rest now, hear?"

"You think you could . . . see your way clear to

leavin' that flask with me . . . while you go after those skunks?"

"Sure, I can do that." I pressed the silver flask into the hand that had held the pencil. He had dropped it on the ground beside him.

"Much . . . obliged."

He seemed to be having trouble keeping his eyes open now. His head rested against the dirt wall behind him. His chest still rose and fell, but slow, slow.

I knew if I piddled around a little before riding out after the Daughtrys, Abner would be dead and I could forget the whole thing and go find the ranch house. His horse was long gone, doubtless having run off after the shooting, but I could pack his body in on my extra animal. I could even toss that bill of sale into the fire and watch it burn. A part of me wanted to. If I'd wanted to live the life of a rancher, I could've stayed in Utah when I was a kid.

Anyway, I couldn't rightfully condemn the Daughtry boys for rustling. My own past was not without blemish in that respect, and I never cared for the idea of being a hypocrite.

But shooting an old man in cold blood . . . well, I had to admit that rubbed me the wrong way. I didn't really know a blasted thing about Abner Tillotson, but I like to think I'm a pretty good judge of character, and my instincts told me he didn't deserve to go out like this.

I folded the page with Abner's signature on it

and stuck it in my hip pocket. Then I went over to my horse and put the book back in the saddlebags. I looked at Abner but couldn't tell if he was breathing or not.

"I'll be back, Abner," I told him anyway.

Then without thinking too much about what I was doing, I untied the reins, swung up into the saddle, and rode off into a dark, bone-chilling night in search of a trio of murdering rustlers.

CHAPTER 2

If you were to ask me about the coldest I've ever been, you probably wouldn't think that it would be when I was in Texas, what with me spending so much time in Utah, Wyoming, Idaho, and places like that. But all these years later, even on the hottest day of the summer, a shiver still goes through me when I think about that night ride across the Texas plains.

I left the packhorse in the gully with Abner. I left the fire burning, too, which went against the grain because of the danger of prairie fires. My hope, though, was that it would keep the scavengers away from him for a while. Maybe I would get back before the fire burned down completely.

He had said the Daughtry place was a couple miles north of the gully. It was too dark to be sure how much ground I was covering, but I was counting on spotting a lighted window to steer by. Until then I had to rely on instinct to keep me going in the right direction.

After a while, just when I started to worry that I was lost and wouldn't even be able to find my way back to the gully, a faint yellow glow appeared in the distance ahead of me. It was tiny at first but got bigger as I rode toward it. Eventually I was able to tell by its roughly rectangular shape that it was the window I'd been looking for.

From what Abner had told me, I felt confident that I was approaching the Daughtry place. He hadn't mentioned anybody else living around these parts.

With the wind blowing out of the north the way it was, I didn't think they would hear my horse's hoofbeats. Just to be sure, though, I reined in when we were about fifty yards away. I didn't see anything close by where I could tie the horse, so I let the reins dangle and left him ground-hitched. I pulled the Winchester from the scabbard and started toward the light on foot.

When I got closer I could make out more of the details, even on that dark night. The shack looked like a jumble of boards piled against the face of a little bluff. It had a tin and tar paper roof with the iron stovepipe sticking up through it. With the bluff to block the wind and a fire going in the stove, it might be halfway comfortable in there, I thought.

Off to the right was a shed that actually looked more sturdily built than the shack. I saw several bulky shapes huddled together in there. I guess the Daughtrys knew how important it was for a man to take care of his horse. Beyond the shed was a corral. The stolen cattle stood stolidly inside it with their back ends turned toward the wind.

It would have been easy enough to kick the door down and go in shooting. They wouldn't know I was anywhere around until it was too late for at least one of them, and probably two. Maybe, if I was really lucky, all three of them. I mulled it over for a minute or so and came mighty close to doing it that way.

But something stopped me. As I mentioned, I've had what you might call a checkered past, but for most of that time, even in my wildest years, I had managed not to kill anybody. There had come a point where that changed—sometimes there's just no other way out, and to be honest, there are some evil bastards in the world who just need killin'—but I still didn't want to ventilate anybody who didn't have it coming.

As I stared at that lighted window, I realized that I didn't know for an absolute certainty it was the Daughtrys in there. Even if it was, I didn't know who else might be in the shack with them. Wives, kids, maybe even an old dog or two. I didn't want any of them getting in the way of a stray bullet.

What I needed to do was draw them out some way, and I thought I saw a way to do it.

That stovepipe poked up through the tar paper fairly close to the bluff. I circled around and climbed the bluff well away from the shack. Even though I was only about eight feet higher than I had been, the wind felt even harder and colder up there. I tried to ignore it as I cat-footed toward the shack.

When I was behind that haphazard assemblage of lumber, I took off my coat. Under it I wore a thick flannel shirt and a pair of long underwear, but the wind cut through both garments like they weren't there. Shivering and trembling, I hung the jacket on the end of my rifle barrel and extended it toward the stovepipe. It almost reached. I gave the Winchester a flick of my wrist. The jacket jumped in the air and settled over the top of the pipe.

It wasn't blocked off as well as if I'd been able to get out on the roof and stuff something down the pipe. From the looks of that roof, though, if a pigeon landed on there it might fall through. Doing it this way, some of the smoke was going to escape, but I thought enough of it would back up into the shack to do the job.

I crouched there on the bluff waiting for something to happen. I didn't have to wait long. Somebody started yelling and cussing inside the shack. The door slammed open and three men stumbled out, coughing.

The Winchester held fifteen rounds, so I figured I could spare one. I put it into the ground near their feet, making them jump. They had made the mistake of all standing close together instead of spreading out, which told me they were pure amateurs when it came to being ambushed. I didn't want to give them a chance to realize that mistake, so I yelled, "Stand right where you are! I'll kill the first man who moves!"

Well, they moved, of course. They twisted around toward the sound of my voice. One of them even started to reach under his coat. He stopped when I worked the Winchester's lever and he heard that sinister, metallic *clack-clack*.

It was a dramatic touch and I shouldn't have done it. I should have already had a fresh round chambered. I have a liking for those little flourishes, though, and even though I've been told that they'll get me killed someday, a man's got to entertain himself from time to time.

Still coughing from the smoke that followed them out the door, one of the men shouted, "Who in blazes . . . are you?"

"Never mind about who I am," I yelled back at him. "Is your name Daughtry?"

"What the hell business is that of yours?"

I pointed the rifle at him and said, "Just answer the question." I tried to make my voice as cold and deadly as the wind.

"I'm Ned Daughtry," the man admitted. "These are my brothers Clete and Otto. You satisfied now, you son of a bitch?"

"Anybody else inside?"

A wracking cough bent the man forward. When it was over he said, "No, just the three of us."

"In that case," I told him, "Abner Tillotson says you should all go to hell."

That threw them. One of the others said, "Who's Tillotson to you?"

"A friend," I said. What else could you call somebody who was giving you a ranch?

That decided it. They knew they'd gunned Abner,

and they knew I'd come gunning for them in return. Wasn't nothin' left but to get to it.

So that's what they did.

I already had the Winchester pointed at one of them, so I went ahead and shot him as soon as they started to reach. The slug bored through him at a downward angle, bent him back, and dropped him to his knees. I worked the lever as I swung the rifle and fired two more rounds as fast as I could crank them off. Muzzle flashes lit up the night, but despite them I still couldn't see much. They returned fire. I went to one knee as a bullet whistled over my head.

For a couple of heartbeats the night was filled with fire and lead from both sides of the fight. A second Daughtry brother stumbled and fell. I tried to locate the third one so I could shoot at him some more, but he was gone.

I couldn't see him, but he might be able to see me. I flattened out on top of the bluff.

A part of my mind kept up with the shots even though I wasn't really thinking about it. So I knew I'd fired nine times and had six rounds left. That ought to be plenty, I thought, but first I had to have something to shoot at.

I couldn't see anything, couldn't hear anything except the wind. But I knew somewhere out there was a fella who wanted to kill me, and I didn't like the feeling. Not one bit.

He was a slick bastard. Got around behind me somehow. If he hadn't stumbled a little in the dark and made a tiny noise, he might've plugged me. As it was, I rolled over just in time to feel his shot whip past my ear and hit the ground instead of blowing off the back of my head.

A Winchester's not real good for close work. I got a shot off, but it must've gone wild because he was on me, kicking me in the side and screaming curses at me. I dropped the rifle, grabbed his leg, and heaved on it. He fell and landed on top of me, and we both went off the edge of the bluff and dropped two feet to crash onto the shack's roof.

It was just as flimsy as it looked. We broke through it and fell another few feet, landing on a table this time. He was still on top of me, and the impact was enough to knock the breath out of me for the second time tonight. I was half stunned and my muscles didn't want to work, but I forced them to anyway. I shoved him off the table onto the floor.

The smoke had cleared out some with the door open, but there was still enough of it in the air to sting my mouth and nose and eyes as I rolled off the table the other way. I put one hand on the table to steady myself as I looked around for a weapon of some sort. My rifle was still up on the bluff, and I didn't know if the last Daughtry had managed to hang on to his pistol when we fell through the roof.

He had. The damned thing blasted again as he rose up on the other side of the table. But he hurried his shot and it went into the wall behind me. I didn't give him a chance to get off another one. I grabbed the handiest thing I could and flung it at him.

That was a kerosene lantern sitting on a shelf

against the wall. It hit him and broke, and fire leaped up on his chest and set his beard on fire. He got so worked up about that, yelling and jumping around, that he forgot about trying to shoot me again. I leaped onto the table and pushed off of it into a diving tackle that took him off his feet. The back of his head hit the hard-packed dirt floor with a sound sort of like what you hear when you drop a watermelon. He didn't move after that, just lay there with the fire consuming his buffalo-hide coat, his beard, and his face.

I knew that was really going to stink, so I picked up the revolver he'd dropped, tucked it behind my belt, and grabbed his ankles so I could drag him outside.

I hadn't forgotten about the other two brothers, so as soon as I had the burning one out of the shack, I dropped his legs and drew the gun, even though I didn't know whether it still had any bullets in it. Turned out it didn't matter, because neither of the other Daughtrys were moving and never would again unless somebody picked them up and carried them. I didn't intend to waste that much effort.

From the corner of my eye I saw some other flames and looked up to see that the heat from the stovepipe had finally set my coat on fire. I let out a heartfelt, "Son of a *bitch*!" That coat was a good one, and without something to break the wind I might still freeze before morning.

Stay here tonight, I told myself. The shack was

pretty drafty, but there was a fire in the stove. I could make my way back to the gully in the morning.

But by then coyotes and maybe even wolves would've been at Abner's body for sure, and they might have gone after my packhorse and supplies, too. Sighing, I looked around the inside of the shack for something I could wear.

I found another buffalo-hide coat. It stunk to high heaven when I shrugged into it, but it was better than nothing. I found a box of cartridges, too, and reloaded the Colt I had picked up.

I stood by the stove for a few minutes to warm up as much as I could before venturing out into the night again. When I knew I couldn't postpone it any longer, I climbed up onto the ridge, got my rifle, and then went in search of my horse.

He had wandered off but hadn't gone far with his reins dangling like that. The whole affair had spooked him some. I hadn't had him long enough for him to be used to such violent ruckuses. Hell, *I* wasn't used to such ruckuses, and I'd been in the middle of plenty of them over the years. I had to whistle a little tune and talk soft to him for a few minutes before he settled down enough for me to catch him.

Maybe he just didn't want somebody wearing a coat that stunk that bad on his back.

Soon I was riding south again, hoping I could find the gully where I'd left Abner Tillotson and my other horse.

can alter the biology and chemistry of a disposal site. It places numerical limits on a dry weight basis on several pollution parameters (i.e., volatile solids, chemical oxygen demand, oil and grease, Kjeldahl nitrogen, mercury, lead, and zinc). If any one of these parameters exceeds the specified limits, the dredged spoils are considered to be polluted and unacceptable for open-water disposal. However, studies have shown that bulk sediment analysis does not predict short- or long-term release of contaminants. In addition, investigations have revealed that no relationship exists between bulk sediment concentration and bioaccumulation. Thus, bulk sediment analysis does not provide an adequate assessment of water quality effects nor any level of environmental protection.[143]

The elutriate test measures the quantity of a substance exhanged between the sediment and the aqueous phase during dredged material disposal and provides a basis for categorizing dredged spoils as polluted or nonpolluted. Bioassay tests yield an operational measure of the toxicity of dredged material on organisms. Selective chemical leaching, in turn, determines the chemical state of pollutants associated with dredged sediments.

Quantitative chemical analysis of the dredged sediments should also be conducted to accurately delineate the effects of suspended material on water quality. Examples of specific chemical analyses of the sediments include the determination of sediment sorption capacities, ionic and cationic sediment exchange capacities, and sediment elemental partitioning.[148] The partitioning of contaminants between solid and solution phases, the persistence of the pollutants sorbed to sediments in the estuarine environment, and the effects of contaminants on biota are all important in assessing the impact of dredged material.

While dredging and dredged material disposal cause a number of significant environmental impacts, they also produce some beneficial effects. For example, both activities can increase nutrient inputs, thereby enhancing primary productivity of a system. Dredging not only increases recreational and commercial usage of a waterbody, it also improves water circulation, which has important implications for physical, chemical, and biological processes, particularly in estuaries. Finally, dredging provides sediment for soil improvement, landfill, and beach restoration projects.

4. Oil Production and Marine Mining

Oil and gas are recovered from rigs stationed in the Gulf of Mexico, North Sea, and elsewhere. Accidents have occasionally occurred at some of these offshore sites, releasing hydrocarbons and other toxic chemicals into the sea. The environmental impacts of these events are usually less severe than those associated with large tanker spills and accidents at coastal installations that impact habitats and biotic communities in estuaries and along oceanic shorelines.

The mining of minerals on beaches and along the seabed on the continental shelf disrupts bottom habitats. Sand, gravel, tin, phosphorite, and salt have been mined from these areas for many years.[8] Sand, gravel, and tin are the most commercially important minerals mined in the sea. Various dredging methods are employed to recover them from the seabed. A number of beaches have been mined for their valuable placer deposits: magnetite (iron) in Japan, casserite (tin) in Malaysia and Indonesia, and rutite (titanium) sands in Sri Lanka and Brazil.[148] The recovery of these economic mineral deposits has locally altered bottom habitats and biotic communities.

5. Exploitation of Fisheries

One of the most profound and widespread impacts of human activity is the overexploitation of living resources, notably finfish and shellfish populations of recreational and commercial importance. This impact has been largely felt in neritic and estuarine waters, with deep-sea living resources being much less affected. Among the most exploited deep-sea fish are the roundnose grenadier (*Coryphaenoides rupestris*) and the roughhead grenadier (*Macrourus berglax*) taken mainly from waters in the Arctic and Northwest Atlantic, the blackcod (*Anoplopoma fimbria*) caught in the Pacific, and the orange roughy (*Hoplostethus atlanticus*) collected in large numbers around

New Zealand and Australia.[5] Since 1950, the global marine catch has increased approximately fourfold, to >80 million mt,[149] and during this 50-year period, landings from global fisheries have shifted from large piscivorous fishes toward smaller invertebrates and planktivorous forms.[150] The effect is most conspicuous in the Northern Hemisphere.

As larger and more commercially valuable species are overfished, the trend has been to move down to lower trophic levels to increase catch sizes. The shift has been away from long-lived, high-trophic-level species (e.g., cod and haddock) to low-trophic-level invertebrates and plankton-feeding fish (e.g., anchovies). This "fishing down" marine food webs, which has occurred at a rate of ~0.1 trophic level per decade over the past 50 years, appears to create impoverished and less valuable ecosystems.[150,151] In addition, such exploitation patterns are unsustainable.[150]

If trophic levels of fisheries landings continue to decline at the aforementioned rate, widespread collapse of marine fisheries is anticipated.[150] A strategy of fishing down the food web already appears to be having a global impact. For example, at least 120 of the world's 200 most commercially valuable species are overfished or fished to the limit. NOAA[152] provides examples. The exploitation of fisheries occurs in all the world's oceans and is evident at local and regional scales.[153,154] As exploitation of living resources in the sea has escalated, the total catch of world fisheries has shifted to one dominated by krill, cephalopods, and tunas.[155] To some degree, this change has spurred new aquaculture ventures to augment natural finfish and shellfish catches.

The overall effect of top-down fishing, therefore, is to shift a fishery to smaller species, and progressively to smaller individuals within these small species. Alterations in fisheries caused by overexploitation can impact the diversity of marine habitats.[149,156] As specified by Boehlert,[149]

> The changes in biomass associated with fisheries may alter trophic or energy flow pathways with consequences for ecosystem diversity and productivity.... Many of the effects of marine fisheries on diversity are distinct and obvious, but evidence is circumstantial or lacking for some of the potentially most devastating effects. On the time scale of decades, however, fisheries can change genetic, species, and ecosystem diversity from levels that have been achieved over millions of years through natural selection. There is little doubt that such changes in biodiversity will decrease the resiliency of species, communities, and ecosystems to respond to natural perturbations that occur on longer time scales. It is thus critical to understand the alterations that fisheries and other anthropogenic changes have wrought on marine diversity and to develop strategies that will ameliorate future ecological changes.

6. Boats and Marinas

Both boats and marinas are potentially significant sources of pollution in coastal waters. Marinas, in particular, are often hot spots for coliform bacteria and other pathogens, aliphatic and aromatic hydrocarbons, and heavy metals.[157–160] The use of antifouling paint, creosote, and other chemical preservatives are toxic to numerous organisms.[3,11] Benthic communities usually incur the most acute effects, with significant changes occurring in species composition, abundance, and diversity at marina sites. Wendt et al.,[161] for example, documented higher abundance of pollution-tolerant capitellid polychaete worms and lower species diversity in a benthic macrofaunal community at a marina location than at reference sites in South Carolina waters.

Tributyltin is one of the most acute toxins released to estuarine and marine systems. It bioaccumulates and can attain very high levels in marine mammals and other upper-trophic-level consumers.[162] However, tributyltin also causes significant impacts on benthic invertebrates, such as oysters and gastropods, being responsible for shell thickening, reduced growth rates, breakdown of sexual differentiation, and other undesirable effects.[3]

Operating boats are viewed by many as moving sources of pollution. Boats frequently lack onboard sanitation devices and hence commonly release raw sewage to coastal waters. Oil and fuel spills and leakages as well as engine exhausts are sources of PAHs.[163] Such pollution input degrades water quality, especially in shallow estuaries and coastal embayments with poor water circulation. In more recent years, the use of personal watercraft (i.e., jet skis) has physically disrupted many hectares of submerged aquatic vegetation and fringing wetlands habitat. Turbulence and wakes generated by personal watercraft and boats also have accelerated shoreline erosion. Waterbird nesting and staging areas are often impacted by the misuse of personal watercraft.[164]

Several recommendations have been advanced to mitigate impacts of marinas and boats on estuarine and marine environments. In regard to marinas, the U.S. Environmental Protection Agency[165] has proposed more effective siting of the installations to minimize habitat destruction. Other recommendations have included the application of improved methods and procedures to better control erosion, runoff, and spills. In addition, it has been suggested that dredging and other construction activities should be conducted at times when spawning, migration, and critical life stages of the biota will be least affected. Boating impacts, in turn, can be mitigated by having pumpout facilities readily available, and making slipside wastewater collection mandatory.[165]

7. Electric Generating Stations

Because of their demands for substantial quantities of condenser cooling water, large electric generating stations have often been sited in the coastal zone. However, a major by-product of power generation in the coastal zone is an array of environmental impacts. For example, significant calefaction of receiving waters occurs when waste heat is ejected at outfalls. In addition, biocidal and other chemical releases as well as impingement and entrainment of organisms at the plant sites can greatly increase mortality of many species, thereby adversely affecting biotic communities.[166–168]

Most effects of thermal discharges from power plants occur in near-field regions in relatively close proximity to the facilities. In these regions, it is common for the density, viscosity, surface tension, and nitrogen solubility of seawater to decrease as water temperature increases. In areas of high organic loading, anoxia or hypoxia may develop in summer as bacterial respiration accelerates. Large biochemical oxygen demands commonly arise in or near thermal discharge zones as a result of the proliferation of noxious phytoplankton blooms.

Physiological and behavioral responses of fauna exposed to heated effluent typically involve an alteration of metabolic rates leading to a diminution of growth, as well as behavioral adjustment manifested in avoidance or attraction reactions to the effluent. In the most severe cases, thermal death ensues because of the failure of smooth muscle peristalsis, denaturation of proteins in the cells, increased lactic acid in the blood, and oxygen deficit related to increased respiratory activity.[3,11] Sublethal effects that can be detrimental include a decrease in reproduction or hatching success of eggs and an inhibition in development of larvae. Changes in species composition, diversity, and population density of biotic communities in outfall canals and other near-field regions due to thermal discharges are not unusual. Excessively high or rapidly fluctuating water temperatures lead to heat- and cold-shock mortality in these areas, which occasionally causes shifts in community structure.

Most biocidal impacts at electric generating stations are related to the chlorination of condensers to control biofouling. Chlorine is typically injected at periodic intervals into cooling water systems to destroy bacterial slimes and macrofouling organisms (e.g., mussels) that adhere to heat exchanger surfaces. The buildup of fouling organisms in condenser tubes gradually lowers plant operating efficiencies. Chlorine has proved to be an effective method of biofouling control. However, the chlorination process is also detrimental to nontarget organisms, particularly phytoplankton and zooplankton. Mortality not only occurs in the facility itself, but also in outfall areas where residual chlorine may be extremely hazardous.

The most significant biotic impacts of power plant operation are associated with entrainment and impingement of organisms. Entrainment occurs when plankton, microinvertebrates, and small juvenile fish are drawn into condenser systems along with cooling water. These organisms are subjected to thermal stresses, hydraulic shocks, pressure changes, biocides, and mechanical damage during in-plant passage. Mortality is often extremely high. For example, the annual entrainment losses of eggs, larvae, and juveniles of some species commonly exceed a billion individuals at large power plants. In addition, some of the organisms that survive in-plant passage are killed by secondary entrainment in outfall waters. The absolute mortality depends in large part on the siting and cooling water system design of the plant, the volume and ambient conditions of the cooling water, as well as the density of entrainable organisms in intake waters, their size, life stages, and susceptibility to injury during in-plant passage.

Impingement impacts result when larger fish and invertebrates are impaled on intake screens. Annual impingement mortality of some species often exceeds a million individuals at larger facilities. The amount of mortality is largely a function of the behavior and physiology of the organisms, the configuration of the intake structure, the type of intake screens, and the intake flow velocity. Other factors that should be considered are the type of species impinged and their developmental stages, organismal migration periods, seasonal variations in species abundance, climatic changes, tides, and storms.

Although power plant impacts commonly result in the loss of large numbers of organisms, they have not been responsible for long-term, systemwide biological problems in estuaries or coastal embayments. Nevertheless, the high mortality associated with entrainment, impingement, and biocidal releases at these plants is a cause of concern, and new strategies should be pursued to mitigate it. This will likely entail retrofitting system components with the best available technology as well as modifying system operations.

8. Altered Natural Flows

As coastal populations continue to grow, increasing demands are being placed on freshwater supplies for domestic, agricultural, and other needs. In addition, waterways are being stabilized for protection of infrastructure. Channelization projects intended to control flooding facilitate downstream flow. Watershed development and urbanization increase the amount of impervious cover, thereby reducing infiltration and accelerating runoff. These effects are exacerbated by upland deforestation, wetlands degradation, and soil compaction, which contribute to greater stream flows and the loss of natural water storage capacity in river basins.

Some of the greatest changes in natural flow regimes are associated with the construction of water storage reservoirs and dams that reduce downstream flows and often lead to substantial streambed modification. The damming of major rivers for flood control and water supply development significantly alters freshwater inflow in impounded estuarine tributaries, such as the Tampa Bay system. Freshwater diversions for agricultural, municipal, and industrial purposes severely limit natural freshwater inflow to San Francisco Bay. In other areas (e.g., Sarasota Bay), excessive groundwater pumping and reduced freshwater inflow contribute to saltwater intrusion problems.[13]

Altered freshwater inflow to estuaries and the nearshore ocean is ecologically significant. Large increases or decreases of freshwater input as a result of human activities shift salinity gradients, which affect circulation patterns as well as various physical and chemical properties of a system. Such shifts in salinity can greatly influence the structure of biotic communities—particularly in estuaries—with the species composition, distribution, and abundance varying considerably with salinity changes along a gradient. Biotic productivity may also change dramatically in these impacted waters.[134]

9. Introduced Species

An emerging problem that is recognized in many U.S. and foreign estuaries is the proliferation of introduced species that threaten the ecological balance of these valuable systems. The intentional or accidental introduction of exotic species in coastal systems can drastically alter their food web structure. The invasive species are potentially an ecological danger because, in adopted habitats where natural controls are lacking, they often outcompete native forms and can rapidly dominate plant or animal communities. In extreme cases, biodiversity is greatly reduced and habitats are significantly altered. In addition, the trophic organization can be fundamentally altered through successful invasive predation and competition.

Problems with introduced species are well chronicled in U.S. estuaries. One of the most heavily impacted systems in this regard is San Francisco Bay, California, where nearly 250 species of plants and animals have been introduced.[169] Most macroinvertebrates along the inner shallows of the estuary are now introduced species, and more that half of the fishes in the delta region are exotic, non-native forms.[170,171] One introduced species, the Asian clam (*Potamocorbula amurensis*), has become extremely successful, altering planktonic and benthic communities in the process. It has outcompeted more favorable clam species (e.g., *Macoma balthica* and *Mya arenaria*) and decimated the phytoplankton community in Suisun Bay. The smooth cordgrass (*Spartina alterniflora*) has also successfully invaded the bay area and appears to be spreading quickly in fringing saltmarshes. There is concern that this invasion may shift sedimentation rates and alter natural habitat value. According to Cohen and Carlton,[169] San Francisco Bay may be the most heavily invaded estuary in the world.

In other estuaries the effects of introduced species are also serious. For example, the introduction of the brown mussel (*Perna perna*) in Corpus Christi Bay, Texas, has created significant fouling problems. Other potential problems of introduced species in the Gulf of Mexico are reported in Galveston Bay, Texas, and the Barataria–Terrebonne estuary in Louisiana. The introduction of the parasitic protozoan *Haplosporidium nelsoni* in the Delaware Estuary in the 1950s nearly destroyed the American oyster (*Crassostrea virginica*) fishery, which remains severely decimated to this day. Clearly, numerous impacts of introduced species are documented in estuaries nationwide. Measures must be taken to prevent the future careless introduction of nonindigenous species in U.S. coastal waters.

III. CONCLUSIONS

A multitude of anthropogenic impacts occur in estuarine and marine environments largely associated with pollution inputs, physical alteration and loss of habitats, and overexploitation of resources. Many of these impacts are most conspicuous at the land/sea margin where human activities are most intense. Rapid population growth and development in coastal watersheds are ultimately responsible for many of the persistent environmental problems. For example, deforestation and construction, landscape partitioning and paving, marsh filling and bulkheading, diking and lagoon formation, as well as dredging and dredged material disposal, not only degrade habitats, but also adversely affect biotic communities. Activities at ports, harbors, and coastal installations commonly produce hot spots of contamination. The release of agricultural, industrial, and municipal wastes can compromise the ecological integrity of receiving waters. The most acute environmental degradation is in urbanized and industrialized coastal systems.

The long-term viability of estuarine and marine environments depends on the formulation of sound management practices to control acute and insidious pollution problems as well as habitat loss and alteration. Several avenues must be followed. For example, Hoss and Engel[134] propose implementation of the following objectives: (1) enactment, coordination, and enforcement of municipal, county, and state land-use plans, so that development can be planned and orderly; (2) promotion and encouragement of local, state, and federal efforts to control and limit nonpoint-source runoff; (3) encouragement of contributors (homeowners, farmers, municipal governments, and managers of golf courses) of inputs of pesticides, herbicides, and fertilizers to use them in a prudent manner; (4) increased efforts by the scientific community to demonstrate in an understandable way the importance of coastal wetland habitat to fisheries; and (5) reinforcement of the fact that everyone contributes to the contamination problems affecting the environment and that each is environmentally responsible.

It is particularly important to formulate effective watershed plans that comprehensively address population growth and human activities in the coastal zone. Most anthropogenic impacts occur in coastal waters, and a significant number of these impacts are attributable to nonpoint-source pollution in nearby watersheds. Educational programs that focus on this issue must be developed for user groups.

In the case of habitats that have been adversely affected by anthropogenic activities, efforts should be made to restore, protect, and maintain them. The restoration of damaged coastal systems usually requires labor-intensive efforts such as hand-planting of seeds and seedlings, transplanting of plugs (i.e., sediment and the entire root–rhizome system), or transplanting of propagules and trees in wetland habitats.[172] Other habitat revitalization involves the movement of large volumes of sediment from one location to another. These projects typically require months or years to complete, but are necessary to achieve habitat recovery on a broad scale.

REFERENCES

1. Goldberg, E. D., Emerging problems in the coastal zone for the twenty-first century, *Mar. Pollut. Bull.,* 31, 152, 1995.
2. McIntyre, A. D., Human impact on the oceans: the 1990s and beyond, *Mar. Pollut. Bull.,* 31, 147, 1995.
3. Kennish, M. J., Ed., *Practical Handbook of Estuarine and Marine Pollution,* CRC Press, Boca Raton, FL, 1997.
4. Whitemarsh, D., Putting a price on the marine environment, *Mar. Pollut. Bull.,* 38, 65, 1999.
5. Gage, J. D. and Tyler, P. A., *Deep-Sea Biology: A Natural History of Organisms at the Deep-Sea Floor,* Cambridge University Press, Cambridge, 1991.
6. Côté, R. P., Marine environmental management: status and prospects, *Mar. Pollut. Bull.,* 25, 1, 1992.
7. GESAMP, Scientific Criteria for the Selection of Waste Disposal Sites at Sea, Reports and Studies No. 16, Inter-Governmental Maritime Consultative Organization, London, 1982.
8. Pinet, P. R., *Invitation to Oceanography,* Jones and Bartlett Publishers, Boston, 2000.
9. Clark, R. B., *Marine Pollution,* 3rd ed., Clarendon Press, Oxford, 1992.
10. McIntyre, A. D., The current state of the oceans, *Mar. Pollut. Bull.,* 25, 1, 1992.
11. Kennish, M. J., *Ecology of Estuaries: Anthropogenic Effects,* CRC Press, Boca Raton, FL, 1992.
12. Curtis, C. E., Protecting the oceans, *Oceanus,* 33, 19, 1990.
13. Kennish, M. J., Ed., *Estuary Restoration and Maintenance: The National Estuary Program,* CRC Press, Boca Raton, FL, 1999.
14. Kennish, M. J., *Pollution Impacts on Marine Biotic Communities,* CRC Press, Boca Raton, FL, 1998.
15. Nixon, S. W., Oviatt, C. A., Frithsen, J., and Sullivan, B., Nutrients and the productivity of estuarine and coastal marine ecosystems, *J. Limnol. Soc. S. Afr.,* 12, 43, 1986.
16. Valiela, I., Costa, J., Foreman, K., Teal, J. M., Howes, B., and Aubrey, D., Transport of groundwater-borne nutrients from watersheds and their effects on coastal waters, *Biogeochemistry,* 10, 177, 1990.
17. D'Avanzo, C. and Kremer, J. N., Diel oxygen dynamics and anoxic events in an eutrophic estuary of Waquiot Bay, Massachusetts, *Estuaries,* 17, 131, 1994.
18. Nixon, S. W., Coastal marine eutrophication: a definition, social causes, and future concerns, *Ophelia,* 41, 199, 1995.
19. Boynton, W. R., Hagy, J. D., Murray, L., Stokes, C., and Kemp, W. M., A comparative analysis of eutrophication patterns in a temperate coastal lagoon, *Estuaries,* 19, 409, 1996.
20. Lapointe, B. E. and Matzie, W. R., Effects of stormwater nutrient discharges on eutrophication processes in nearshore waters of the Florida Keys, *Estuaries,* 19, 422, 1996.
21. Valiela, I., McClelland, J., Hauxwell, J., Behr, P. J., Hersh, D., and Foreman, K., Macroalgal blooms in shallow estuaries: controls and ecophysiological and ecosystem consequences, *Limnol. Oceanogr.,* 45, 1105, 1997.
22. Parker, C. A. and O'Reilly, J. E., Oxygen depletion in Long Island Sound: a historical perspective, *Estuaries,* 14, 248, 1991.
23. Reyes, E. and Merino, M., Diel dissolved oxygen dynamics and eutrophication in a shallow, well-mixed tropical lagoon (Cancun, Mexico), *Estuaries,* 14, 372, 1991.

24. Taft, J. L., Taylor, W. R., Hartwig, E. O., and Loftus, R., Seasonal oxygen depletion in Chesapeake Bay, *Estuaries,* 3, 242, 1980.
25. Officer, C. B., Biggs, R. B., Taft, J. L., Cronin, L. E., Tyler, M. A., and Boynton, W. R., Chesapeake Bay anoxia: origin, development, and significance, *Science,* 223, 22, 1984.
26. Seliger, H. H., Boggs, J. A., and Biggley, J. A., Catastrophic anoxia in the Chesapeake Bay in 1984, *Science,* 228, 70, 1985.
27. Valiela, I., *Marine Ecological Processes,* 2nd ed., Springer-Verlag, New York, 1995.
28. Livingston, R. J., Eutrophication in estuaries and coastal systems: relationships of physical alterations, salinity stratification, and hypoxia, in *Sustainable Development in the Southeastern Coastal Zone,* Vernberg, F. J., Vernberg, W. B., Siewicki, T., Eds., University of South Carolina Press, Columbia, SC, 1996, 285.
29. Sindermann, C. J., *Ocean Pollution: Effects on Living Resources and Humans,* CRC Press, Boca Raton, FL, 1996.
30. Burkholder, J. M., Noga, E. J., Hobbs, C. H., Glasgow, H. B., Jr., and Smith, S. A., A new "phantom" dinoflagellate, causative agent of major estuarine fish kills, *Nature,* 358, 407, 1992.
31. Noga, E. J., Khoo, L., Stevens, J. B., Fan, Z., and Burkholder, J. M., Novel toxic dinoflagellate causes epidemic disease in estuarine fish, *Mar. Pollut. Bull.,* 32, 219, 1996.
32. Rawlins, B. G., Ferguson, A. J., Chilton, P. J., Arthurton, R. S., Rees, J. G., and Baldock, J. W., Review of agricultural pollution in the Caribbean with particular emphasis on small island developing states, *Mar. Pollut. Bull.,* 36, 658, 1998.
33. National Research Council, *Managing Wastewater in Coastal Urban Areas,* National Academy Press, Washington, D.C., 1993.
34. Williams, P. J. Le B., Biological and chemical dissolved organic material in seawater, in *Chemical Oceanography,* Vol. 2, 2nd ed., Riley, G. and Skirrow, O., Eds., Academic Press, London, 1975.
35. Ashton, P. H. and Richardson, B. J., Biological monitoring of the marine ocean outfall at Black Rock, Victoria, Australia, *Mar. Pollut. Bull.,* 31, 334, 1995.
36. Chapman, P. M., Paine, M. D., Arthur, A. D., and Taylor, L. A., A triad study of sediment quality associated with a major, relatively untreated marine sewage discharge, *Mar. Pollut. Bull.,* 32, 47, 1996.
37. Chisholm, J. R. M., Fernex, F. E., Mathieu, D., and Jaubert, J. M., Wastewater discharge, seagrass decline, and algal proliferation on the Côte d'Azur, *Mar. Pollut. Bull.,* 34, 78, 1997.
38. Adingra, A. A. and Arfi, R., Organic and bacterial pollution in the Ebrié Lagoon, Côte d'Ivoire, *Mar. Pollut. Bull.,* 36, 689, 1998.
39. Weston, D. P., Quantitative examination of macrobenthic community changes along an organic enrichment gradient, *Mar. Ecol. Prog. Ser.,* 61, 233, 1990.
40. Atlas, R. M., Petroleum biodegradation and oil spill bioremediation, *Mar. Pollut. Bull.,* 31, 178, 1995.
41. Abel, P. D., *Water Pollution Biology,* Ellis Horwood, Chichester, England, 1989.
42. National Academy of Sciences, *Oil in the Sea: Inputs, Fates, and Effects,* National Academy Press, Washington, D.C., 1985.
43. Carlberg, S. R., Oil pollution of the marine environment—with an emphasis on estuarine studies, in *Chemistry and Biogeochemistry of Estuaries,* Olausson, E. and Cato, I., Eds., John Wiley & Sons, Chichester, England, 1980, 367.
44. Cormack, D., *Response to Oil and Chemical Marine Pollution,* Applied Science, London, 1983.
45. Doerffer, J. W., *Oil Spill Response in the Marine Environment,* Pergamon Press, New York, 1992.
46. Pritchard, P. H., Bioremediation as a technology: experience with the *Exxon Valdez* oil spill, *J. Hazard. Mater.,* 28, 115, 1991.
47. Atlas, R. M., Petroleum biodegradation and oil spill bioremediation, *Mar. Pollut. Bull.,* 31, 178, 1995.
48. Simpson, R. D., Smith, S. D. A., and Pople, A. R., The effects of a spillage of diesel fuel on a rocky shore in the sub-Antarctic region (Macquarie Island), *Mar. Pollut. Bull.,* 31, 367, 1995.
49. Glegg, G. A. and Rowland, S. J., The *Braer* oil spill—hydrocarbon concentrations in intertidal organisms, *Mar. Pollut. Bull.,* 32, 486, 1996.
50. Lee, R. F. and Page, D. S., Petroleum hydrocarbons and their effects in subtidal regions after major oil spills, *Mar. Pollut. Bull.,* 34, 928, 1997.
51. Jones, D. A., Plaza, J., Watt, I., and Al Sanei, M., Long-term (1991–1995) monitoring of the intertidal biota of Saudi Arabia after the 1991 Gulf War oil spill, *Mar. Pollut. Bull.,* 36, 472, 1998.

52. Dauvin, J.-C., The fine sand *Abra alba* community of the Bay of Morlaix twenty years after the *Amoco Cadiz* oil spill, *Mar. Pollut. Bull.,* 36, 669, 1998.

53. Dean, T. A., Stekoll, M. S., Jewett, S. C., Smith, R. O., and Hose, J. E., Eelgrass (*Zostera marina L.*) in Prince William Sound, Alaska: effects of the *Exxon Valdez* oil spill, *Mar. Pollut. Bull.,* 36, 201, 1998.

54. Glegg, G. A., Hickman, L., and Rowland, S. J., Contamination of limpets (*Patella vulgata*) following the *Sea Empress* oil spill, *Mar. Pollut. Bull.,* 38, 119, 1999.

55. Hayes, M. O. and Michel, J., Factors determining the long-term persistence of *Exxon Valdez* oil spill, *Mar. Pollut. Bull.,* 38, 92, 1999.

56. Engelhardt, F. R., Effects of petroleum on marine mammals, in *Petroleum Effects in the Arctic Environment,* Englehardt, F. R., Ed., Elsevier Applied Science, New York, 1985, 217.

57. Waldichuk, M., Sea and oil pollution, *Mar. Pollut. Bull.,* 21, 10, 1990.

58. Ekker, M., Lorentsen, S.-H., and Rov, N., Chronic oil-fouling of grey seal pups at the Froan Breeding Ground, Norway, *Mar. Pollut. Bull.,* 24, 92, 1992.

59. Witt, G., Polycyclic aromatic hydrocarbons in water and sediment of the Baltic Sea, *Mar. Pollut. Bull.,* 31, 237, 1995.

60. Eisler, R., Polycyclic Aromatic Hydrocarbon Hazards to Fish, Wildlife, and Invertebrates: A Synoptic Review, Biological Report 85(1.11), U.S. Fish and Wildlife Service, Washington, D.C., 1987.

61. Albers, P. H., Petroleum and individual polycyclic aromatic hydrocarbons, in *Handbook of Ecotoxicology,* Hoffman, D. J., Rattner, B. A., Burton, G. A., Jr., and Cairns, J., Jr., Eds., Lewis Publishers, Boca Raton, FL, 1994, 330.

62. Fernandes, M. B., Sicre, M.-A., Boireau, A., and Tronczynski, J., Polycyclic hydrocarbon (PAH) distributions in the Seine River and its estuary, *Mar. Pollut. Bull.,* 34, 857, 1997.

63. Jackim, E. and Lake, C., Polynuclear aromatic hydrocarbons in estuarine and nearshore environments, in *Estuarine Interactions,* Wiley, M. L., Ed., Academic Press, New York, 1978, 415.

64. Guzzella, L. and De Paolis, A., Polycyclic aromatic hydrocarbons in sediments of the Adriatic Sea, *Mar. Pollut. Bull.,* 28, 159, 1994.

65. Bernard, D., Pascaline, H., and Jeremine, J.-J., Distribution and origin of hydrocarbons in sediments from lagoons, *Mar. Pollut. Bull.,* 32, 734, 1996.

66. Huggett, R. L., de Fur, P. O., and Bieri, R. H., Organic compounds in Chesapeake Bay sediments, *Mar. Pollut. Bull.,* 19, 454, 1988.

67. McLeese, D. W., Ray, S., and Burridge, L. E., Accumulation of polynuclear aromatic hydrocarbons by the clam *Mya arenaria,* in *Wastes in the Ocean,* Vol. 6, *Nearshore Waste Disposal,* Ketchum, B. H., Capuzzo, J. M., Burt, W. V., Duedall, I. W., Park, P. K., and Kester, D. R., John Wiley & Sons, New York, 1985, 81.

68. Windsor, J. G. and Hites, R. A., Polycyclic aromatic hydrocarbons in Gulf of Maine sediments and Nova Scotia soils, *Geochim. Cosmochim. Acta,* 43, 27, 1979.

69. Wade, T. L., Kennicutt, M. C., II, and Brooks, J. M., Gulf of Mexico hydrocarbon seep communities. Part III. Aromatic hydrocarbon concentrations in organisms, sediments, and water, *Mar. Environ. Res.,* 27, 19, 1989.

70. Lauenstein, G. G., Robertson, A., and O'Connor, T. P., Comparison of trace metal data in mussels and oysters from a mussel watch program of the 1970s with those from a 1980s program, *Mar. Pollut. Bull.,* 21, 440, 1990.

71. Shchekaturina, T. L., Khesina, A. L., Mironov, O. G., and Krivosheeva, L. G., Carcinogenic polycyclic aromatic hydrocarbons in mussels from the Black Sea, *Mar. Pollut. Bull.,* 30, 38, 1995.

72. Granby, K. and Spliid, N. H., Hydrocarbons and organochlorines in common mussels from the Kattegat and the belts and their relation to condition indices, *Mar. Pollut. Bull.,* 30, 74, 1995.

73. O'Connor, T. P., Trends in chemical concentrations in mussels and oysters collected along the U.S. coast from 1986 to 1993, *Mar. Environ. Res.,* 41, 183, 1996.

74. Baumard, P., Budzinski, H., Garrigues, P., Sorbe, J. C., Burgeot, T., and Bellocq, J., Concentrations of PAHs (polycyclic aromatic hydrocarbons) in various marine organisms in relation to those in sediments and to trophic level, *Mar. Pollut. Bull.,* 36, 951, 1998.

75. Farley, C. A., Plutschak, D. L., and Scott, R. F., Epizootiology and distribution of transmissible sarcoma in Maryland soft-shell clams, *Mya arenaria,* 1984–1988, *Environ. Health Perspect.,* 90, 35, 1991.

76. Connell, D. W., Prediction of bioconcentration and related lethal and sublethal effects with aquatic organisms, *Mar. Pollut. Bull.,* 31, 201, 1995.

77. Crews, D., Bergeron, J. M., and McLachlan, J. A., The role of estrogen in turtle sex determination and the effect of PCB, *Environ. Health Perspect.*, 103, 73, 1995.
78. Fry, D. M., Reproductive effects in birds exposed to pesticides and industrial chemicals, *Environ. Health Perspect.*, 103, 165, 1995.
79. Lahvis, G. P., Wells, R. S., Kuehl, D. W., Stewart, J. L., Rhinehart, H. L., and Via, C. S., Decreased lymphocyte responses in free-ranging bottlenose dolphins (*Tursiops truncatus*) are associated with increased concentrations of PCBs and DDT in peripheral blood, *Environ. Health Perspect.*, 103, 67, 1995.
80. Wolff, M. S. and Toniolo, P. G., Environmental organochlorine exposure as a potential etiologic factor in breast cancer, *Environ. Health Perspect.*, 103, 141, 1995.
81. Reddy, M., Echols, S., Finklea, B., Busbee, D., Reif, J., and Ridgway, S., PCBs and chlorinated pesticides in clinically healthy *Tursiops truncatus:* relationships between levels in blubber and blood, *Mar. Pollut. Bull.*, 36, 892, 1998.
82. Lee, J. S., Tanabe, S., Umino, H., Tatsukawa, R., Loughlin, T. R., and Calkins, D. C., Persistent organochlorines in Steller Sea Lion (*Eumetopias jubatus*) from the bulk of Alaska and the Bering Sea, 1976–1981, *Mar. Pollut. Bull.*, 32, 535, 1996.
83. Moore, M. J., Shea, D., Hillman, R. E., and Stegeman, J. J., Trends in hepatic tumors and hydropic vacuolation, fin erosion, organic chemicals, and stable isotope ratios in winter flounder from Massachusetts, USA, *Mar. Pollut. Bull.*, 32, 458, 1996.
84. Tanabe, S., Madhusree, B., Öztürk, A. A., Tatsukawa, R., Mujazake, N., Özdamar, E., Aral, O., Samsun, O., and Öztürk, B., Persistent organochlorine residues in harbour porpoise (*Phocoena phocoena*) from the Black Sea, *Mar. Pollut. Bull.*, 34, 338, 1997.
85. O'Shea, T. T. and Brownell, R. L., Jr., California Sea Lion (*Zalophus californianus*) populations and ΣDDT contamination, *Mar. Pollut. Bull.*, 36, 159, 1998.
86. Gutiérrez-Galindo, E. A., Rios Mendoza, L. M., Flores, Muñoz, G. F., and Villaescusa Celaya, J. A., Chlorinated hydrocarbons in marine sediments of the Baja California (Mexico)–California (USA) border zone, *Mar. Pollut. Bull.*, 36, 27, 1998.
87. Balls, P. W. and Campbell, D. C., Organochlorines in seawater and suspended particulates from Scottish coastal sites, *Mar. Pollut. Bull.*, 38, 142, 1999.
88. Pereira, W. E., Hostettler, F. D., Cashman, J. R., and Nishioka, R. S., Occurrence and distribution of organochlorine compounds in sediment and livers of striped bass (*Morone saxatilis*) from San Francisco Bay–delta estuary, *Mar. Pollut. Bull.*, 28, 434, 1994.
89. Fowler, S. W., Critical review of selected heavy metal and chlorinated hydrocarbon concentrations in the marine environment, *Mar. Environ. Res.*, 29, 1, 1990.
90. Mearns, A. J., Matta, M. B., Simececk-Beatty, D., Buchman, M. F., Shigenaka, G., and Wert, W. A., PCB and Chlorinated Pesticide Contamination in U.S. Fish and Shellfish: A Historical Assessment Report, NOAA Tech. Mem. NOS OMA 39, National Oceanic and Atmospheric Administration, Seattle, WA, 1988.
91. Vallette-Silver, N. J., The use of sediment cores to reconstruct historical trends in contamination of estuarine and coastal sediments, *Estuaries*, 16, 577, 1993.
92. O'Connor, T. P., Coastal Environmental Quality in the United States, Chemical Contamination in Sediments and Tissues, A Special NOAA 20th Anniversary Report, National Oceanic and Atmospheric Administration, Office of Ocean Resources Conservation and Assessment, Rockville, MD, 1990.
93. O'Connor, T. P., Recent Trends in Coastal Environmental Quality: Results from the First Five Years of NOAA Mussel Watch Project, National Oceanic and Atmospheric Administration, Office of Ocean Resources Conservation and Assessment, Rockville, MD, 1992.
94. O'Connor, T. P., Cantillo, A. Y., and Lauenstein, G. G., Monitoring of temporal trends in chemical contamination by the NOAA National Status and Trends Mussel Watch Project, in *Biomonitoring of Coastal Waters and Estuaries,* Kramer, K. J. M., Ed., CRC Press, Boca Raton, FL, 1994, 29.
95. Rainbow, P. S., The significance of trace metal concentrations in marine invertebrates, in *Ecotoxicology of Metals in Invertebrates,* Rainbow, P. S. and Dallinger, R., Eds., Lewis Publishers, Boca Raton, FL, 1993, 3.
96. Kennish, M. J., Trace metal-sediment dynamics in estuaries: pollution assessment, *Rev. Environ. Contam. Toxicol.*, 155, 69, 1998.
97. Kress, N., Hornung, H., and Herut, B., Concentrations of Hg, Cd, Zn, Fe, and Mn in deep-sea benthic fauna from the southeastern Mediterranean Sea: a comparison study between fauna collected at a pristine area and at two waste disposal sites, *Mar. Pollut. Bull.*, 36, 911, 1998.

98. Capuzzo, J. M., Burt, W. V., Duedall, I. W., Park, P. K., and Kester, D. R., The impact of waste disposal in nearshore environments, in *Wastes in the Ocean,* Vol. 6, *Nearshore Waste Disposal,* Ketchum, B. H., Capuzzo, J. M., Burt, W. V., Duedall, I. W., Park, P. K., and Kester, D. R., Eds., John Wiley & Sons, New York, 1985, 3.

99. Tselentis, B. S., Maroulakou, M., Lascourreges, J. F., Szpunar, J., Smith, V., and Donard, O. F. X., Organotins in sediments and biological tissues from Greek coastal areas: preliminary results, *Mar. Pollut. Bull.,* 38, 146, 1999.

100. Huggett, R. J., Unger, M. A., Seligman, P. F., and Valkirs, A. O., The marine biocide tributyltin: assessing and managing environmental risks, *Environ. Sci. Technol.,* 26, 232, 1992.

101. Larsen, P. F., Huggett, R. J., and Unger, M. A., Assessment of organotin in waters of selected Gulf of Maine estuaries, *Mar. Pollut. Bull.,* 34, 802, 1997.

102. Evans, S. M., Leksono, T., and McKinnell, P. D., Tributyltin pollution: a diminishing problem following legislation limiting the use of TBT-based antifouling paints, *Mar. Pollut. Bull.,* 30, 14, 1995.

103. Law, R. J., Blake, S. J., Jones, B. R., and Rogan, E., Organotin compounds in liver tissue of harbor porpoises (*Phocoena phocoena*) and grey seals (*Halichoerus grypus*) from the coastal waters of England and Wales, *Mar. Pollut. Bull.,* 36, 241, 1998.

104. Kennish, M. J., *Ecology of Estuaries,* Vol. 2, *Biological Aspects,* CRC Press, Boca Raton, FL, 1990.

105. van den Berg, C. M. G., Complex formation and the chemistry of selected trace elements in estuaries, *Estuaries,* 16, 512, 1993.

106. Cutter, G. A., Trace elements in estuarine and coastal waters, *Rev. Geophys.* (Suppl.), *Contrib. Oceanogr.,* 639, 1991.

107. Bryan, G. W. and Langston, W. J., Bioavailability, accumulation, and effects of heavy metals in sediments with special reference to United Kingdom estuaries: a review, *Environ. Pollut.,* 76, 89, 1992.

108. Bricker, S. B., The history of Cu, Pb, and Zn inputs to Narragansett Bay, Rhode Island, as recorded by salt-marsh sediments, *Estuaries,* 16, 589, 1993.

109. Rowlatt, S. M. and Lovell, D. R., Lead, zinc, and chromium in sediments around England and Wales, *Mar. Pollut. Bull.,* 28, 5, 1994.

110. Cortesäo, C. and Vale, C., Metals in sediments of the Sado Estuary, Portugal, *Mar. Pollut. Bull.,* 30, 34, 1995.

111. Everaarts, J. M. and Nieuwenhuize, J., Heavy metals in surface sediment and epibenthic macroinvertebrates from the coastal zone and continental slope of Kenya, *Mar. Pollut. Bull.,* 31, 281, 1995.

112. Jones, B. and Adnan, T., Distribution and speciation of heavy metals in surficial sediments from the Tees Estuary, northeast England, *Mar. Pollut. Bull.,* 34, 768, 1997.

113. Cheevaporn, V., Jacinto, G. S., and San-Diego-McGlone, M. L., Heavy metal fluxes in Bang Pakong River estuary, Thailand: sedimentary vs. diffusive fluxes, *Mar. Pollut. Bull.,* 31, 290, 1995.

114. Alexander, C. R., Smith, R. G., Calder, F. D., Schropp, S. J., and Windom, H. L., The historical record of metal enrichment in two Florida estuaries, *Estuaries,* 16, 627, 1993.

115. Viarengo, A., Heavy metals in marine invertebrates: mechanisms of regulation and toxicity at the cellular level, *Rev. Aquat. Sci.,* 1, 295, 1989.

116. Engel, D. W. and Brouwer, M., Crustaceans as models for metal metabolism. I. Effects of the molt cycle on blue crab metal metabolism and metallothionein, *Mar. Environ. Res.,* 35, 1, 1993.

117. Schlenk, D., Ringwood, A. H., Brouwer-Hoexum, T., and Brouwer, M., Crustaceans as models for metal metabolism. II. Induction and characterization of metallothionein isoforms from the blue crab (*Callinectes sapidus*), *Mar. Environ. Res.,* 35, 7, 1993.

118. Roesijadi, G., Behavior of metallothionein-bound metals in a natural population of an estuarine mollusc, *Mar. Environ. Res.,* 38, 147, 1994.

119. Astorga España, M. S., Peña Méndez, E. M., Lecaros Palma, O., and García Montelongo, F. J., Heavy metals in *Mytilus chilensis* from the Strait of Megallenes (Chile), *Mar. Pollut. Bull.,* 36, 542, 1998.

120. Haynes, D. and Toohey, D., The use of transplanted, cultured mussels (*Mytilus edulis*) to monitor pollutants along the Ninety Mile Beach, Victoria Australia. III. Heavy metals, *Mar. Pollut. Bull.,* 36, 396, 1998.

121. Cantillo, A. Y., Comparison of results of mussel watch programs of the United States and France with worldwide mussel watch studies, *Mar. Pollut. Bull.,* 36, 712, 1998.

122. Preller, R. H. and Cheng, A., Modeling and transport of radioactive contaminants in the Arctic, *Mar. Pollut. Bull.,* 38, 71, 1999.

123. Anonymous, Ban on sea dumping of radioactive wastes takes effect, *Mar. Pollut. Bull.*, 31, 194, 1995.

124. Boaden, P. J. S. and Seed, R., *An Introduction to Coastal Ecology*, Blackie and Son, London, 1985.

125. Kiefer, J., *Biological Radiation Effects*, Springer-Verlag, New York, 1990.

126. Fowler, S. W., Biological transfer and transport processes, in *Pollutant Transfer and Transport in the Sea*, Kullenberg, G., Ed., CRC Press, Boca Raton, FL, 1982, 1.

127. Valette-Silver, N. J. and Lauenstein, G. G., Radionuclide concentrations in bivalves collected along the coastal United States, *Mar. Pollut. Bull.*, 30, 320, 1995.

128. Anderson, S., Livens, F. R., and Singleton, D. L., Radionuclides in grey seals, *Mar. Pollut. Bull.*, 21, 343, 1990.

129. Calmet, D., Woodhead, D., and André, J. M., ^{210}Pb, ^{137}Cs, and ^{40}K in three species of porpoises caught in the eastern tropical Pacific, *J. Environ. Radioactivity*, 15, 153, 1992.

130. Berrow, S. D., Long, S. C., McGarry, A. T., Pollard, D., Rogan, E., and Lockyer, C., Radionuclides (^{137}Cs and ^{40}K) in harbor porpoises *Phocoena phocoena* from British and Irish coastal waters, *Mar. Pollut. Bull.*, 36, 569, 1998.

131. Beekman, R. L., Vernberg, F. J., and Vernberg, W. B., Sustainable development, in *Sustainable Development in the Southeastern Coastal Zone*, Vernberg, F. J., Vernberg, W. B., and Siewicki, T., Eds., University of South Carolina Press, Columbia, 1996, 1.

132. Nordstrom, K. L., Developed coasts, in *Coastal Evolution*, Carter, R. W. G. and Woodroffe, C. D., Eds., Cambridge University Press, Cambridge, 1994, 477.

133. Nordstrom, K. L., Beaches and dunes of human-altered coasts, *Prog. Phys. Geogr.*, 18, 497, 1994.

134. Hoss, D. E. and Engel, D. W., Sustainable development in the southeastern coastal zone: environmental impacts on fisheries, in *Sustainable Development in the Southeastern Coastal Zone*, Vernberg, F. J., Vernberg, W. B., and Siewicki, T., Eds., University of South Carolina Press, Columbia, 1996, 171.

135. Hall, C. A. S., Howarth, R., Moore, B., III, and Vorosmarty, C. J., Environmental impacts of industrial energy systems in the coastal zone, *Annu. Rev. Energy*, 3, 395, 1978.

136. Langford, T. E., *Electricity Generation and the Ecology of Natural Waters*, Liverpool University Press, Liverpool, England, 1983.

137. Shaw, D. G. and Day, R. H., Color- and form-dependent loss of plastic micro-debris from the North Pacific Ocean, *Mar. Pollut. Bull.*, 28, 39, 1994.

138. Robards, M. D., Piatt, J. F., and Wohl, K. D., Increasing frequency of plastic particles ingested by seabirds in the Subarctic North Pacific, *Mar. Pollut. Bull.*, 30, 151, 1995.

139. Lecke-Mitchell, K. M. and Mullin, K., Floating marine debris in the U.S. Gulf of Mexico, *Mar. Pollut. Bull.*, 34, 702, 1997.

140. Ribic, C. A., Use of indicator items to monitor marine debris on a New Jersey beach from 1991 to 1996, *Mar. Pollut. Bull.*, 36, 887, 1998.

141. Ribic, C. A., Johnson, S. W., and Cole, C. A., Distribution, type, accumulation, and source of marine debris in the United States, 1989–1993, in *Marine Debris*, Coe, J. M. and Rogers, D. B., Eds., Springer-Verlag, New York, 1997, 35.

142. De Grave, S. and Whitaker, A., Benthic community re-adjustment following dredging of a muddy-maerl matrix, *Mar. Pollut. Bull.*, 38, 102, 1999.

143. Engler, R. M. and Mathis, D. B., Dredged material disposal strategies, in *Oceanic Processes in Marine Pollution*, Vol. 3, *Marine Waste Management: Science and Policy*, Camp, M. A. and Park, P. K., Eds., Robert E. Krieger Publishing, Malabar, FL, 1989, 53.

144. Rhoads, D. C., McCall, P. L., and Yingst, J. Y., Disturbance and production on the estuarine seafloor, *Am. Sci.*, 66, 577, 1978.

145. Rhoads, D. C. and Boyer, L. F., The effects of marine benthos on physical properties of sediments: a successional perspective, in *Animal–Sediment Relations: The Biogenic Alteration of Sediments*, McCall, P. L. and Tevesz, M. J. S., Eds., Plenum Press, New York, 1982, 3.

146. Kenney, A. J. and Rees, H. L., The effects of marine gravel extraction on the macrobenthos: early post-dredging recolonization, *Mar. Pollut. Bull.*, 28, 442, 1994.

147. Kester, D. R., Ketchum, B. H., Duedall, I. W., and Park, P. K., Eds., The problem of dredged material disposal, in *Wastes in the Ocean*, Vol 2, *Dredged Material Disposal in the Ocean*, Kester, D. R., Ketchum, B. H., Duedall, I. W., and Park, P. K., Eds., John Wiley & Sons, New York, 1983, 3.

148. Meadows, P. S. and Campbell, J. I., *An Introduction to Marine Science*, 2nd ed., Blackie and Son, London, 1988.

149. Boehlert, G. W., Biodiversity and the sustainability of marine fisheries, *Oceanography,* 9, 28, 1996.
150. Pauly, D., Christensen, V., Dalsgaard, J., Froese, R., and Torres, F., Jr., Fishing down marine food webs, *Science,* 279, 860, 1998.
151. Williams, N., Overfishing disrupts entire ecosystems, *Science,* 279, 809, 1998.
152. NOAA, Our Living Oceans: Report on the Status of U.S. Living Marine Resources, 1993, NOAA Tech. Memo NMFS-F/SPO-15, *National Oceanic and Atmospheric Administration,* Washington, D.C., 1993.
153. Garcia, S. M. and Newton, C. H., Responsible fisheries: an overview of FAO policy developments (1945–1994), *Mar. Pollut. Bull.,* 29, 528, 1994.
154. Deimbling, E. A. and Liss, W. J., Fishery development in the eastern North Pacific: a natural-cultural system perspective, 1888–1976, *Fish. Oceanogr.,* 3, 60, 1994.
155. FAO Marine Resource Service, Review of the state of world marine fisheries resources, FAO Fisheries Tech. Pap. 335, 1993.
156. Gobert, B., Impact of the use of trammel nets on a tropical reef resource, *Fish. Res.,* 13, 353, 1992.
157. Voudrias, E., Evangelos, A., and Smith, C. L., Hydrocarbon pollution from marinas in estuarine sediments, *Estuarine Coastal Shelf Sci.,* 22, 271, 1986.
158. Nichols, J. A., Antifouling paints: use on boats in San Diego and a way to minimize adverse impacts, *Environ. Manage.,* 12, 243, 1988.
159. Milliken, A. and Lee, V., Pollution impacts from recreational boating: a bibliography and summary, Tech. Rept., Rhode Island Sea Grant College Program, Narragansett, RI, 1990.
160. Marcus, J. M., Swearingen, G. R., Williams, A. D., and Heizer, D. D., Polynuclear aromatic hydrocarbon and heavy metal concentrations in sediments at coastal South Carolina marinas, *Arch. Environ. Contam. Toxicol.,* 17, 103, 1988.
161. Wendt, P. H., Van Dolah, R. F., Bobo, M. Y., and Manzi, J. J., Effects of marine proximity on certain aspects of the biology of oysters and other benthic macrofauna in a South Carolina estuary, Tech. Rept. No. 74, South Carolina Wildlife and Marine Resources Department, Marine Resources Center, Charleston, SC, 1990.
162. Iwata, H., Tanabe, S., Miyazaki, N., and Tatsukawa, R., Detection of butyltin compound residues in the blubber of marine mammals, *Mar. Pollut. Bull.,* 28, 607, 1994.
163. Weinstein, J. E., Anthropogenic impacts on saltmarshes—a review, in *Sustainable Development in the Southeastern Coastal Zone,* Vernberg, F. J., Vernberg, W. B., and Siewicki, T., Eds., University of South Carolina Press, Columbia, SC, 1996, 135.
164. Kennish, M. J., The Barnegat Bay National Estuary Program: review of the 1995–1998 period, *Bull. N.J. Acad. Sci.,* 44, 1999.
165. USEPA, Coastal Marinas Assessment Handbook, U.S. Environmental Protection Agency, EPA 904/6-85-132, Atlanta, GA, 1985.
166. Van Winkle, W., Ed., *Proceedings of the Conference Assessing the Effects of Power-Plant Induced Mortality on Fish Populations,* Pergamon Press, New York, 1977.
167. Schubel, J. R. and Marcy, B. C., Eds., *Power Plant Entrainment: A Biological Assessment,* Academic Press, New York, 1978.
168. Hocutt, C. H., Stauffer, J. R., Jr., Edinger, J. E., Hall, L. W., Jr., and Morgan, R. P., II, Eds., *Power Plants: Effects on Fish and Shellfish Behavior,* Academic Press, New York, 1980.
169. Cohen, A. N. and Carlton, J. T., Accelerating invasion rate in a highly invaded estuary, *Science,* 279, 555, 1998.
170. Nichols, F. H. and Pamatmat, M. M., The Ecology of the Soft-Bottom Benthos of San Francisco Bay: A Community Profile, U.S. Fish and Wildlife Service, Biol. Rept. No. 85(719), Washington, D.C., 1988.
171. Herbold, B. and Moyle, P. B., The Ecology of the Sacramento–San Joaquin Delta: A Community Profile, U.S. Fish and Wildlife Service, Biol. Rept. No. 85 (7.22), 1989.
172. Alongi, D. M., *Coastal Ecosystem Processes,* CRC Press, Boca Raton, FL, 1998.

6.1 SOURCES OF MARINE POLLUTION

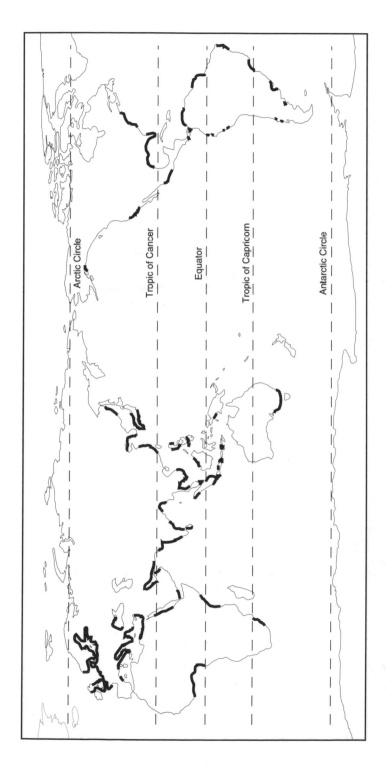

Figure 6.1–1 World chart highlighting coastal areas significantly impacted by humans (From Alongi, D. M., *Coastal Ecosystem Processes*, CRC Press, Boca Raton, FL, 1998, 327. With permission.)

Table 6.1–1   Major Problems in the World's Coastal Ocean

Eutrophication
Coastal development (including aquaculture)
Habitat modification/destruction/alteration
Disruption of coastal hydrological cycles (including river discharge)
Point- and nonpoint-source release of toxins and pathogens (including synthetic organic
  and petroleum-related chemicals)
Introduction of exotic species
Fouling by plastic litter
Buildup of chlorinated hydrocarbons
Shoreline erosion/siltation accelerated by deforestation, desertification, and other poor
  land-use practices
Unsustainable/uncontrolled exploitation of resources
Global climate change and variability
Noise pollution

Source: Alongi, D. M., *Coastal Ecosystem Processes,* CRC Press, Boca Raton, FL, 1998,
326. With permission.

Table 6.1–2   Major Uses of Coastal Resources by Humans

Fishing	Timber
Sand and gravel dredging	Harbors, marinas
Aquaculture	Housing and reclamation
Oil, gas, and mineral exploration	Tourism
Recreation	Waste disposal (including sewage)
Collecting and hunting (e.g., shells)	Canals and other diversions
Fuel	

Source: Alongi, D. M., *Coastal Ecosystem Processes*, CRC Press, Boca Raton, FL, 1998,
326. With permission.

Table 6.1–3   Sources of Pollutants in the Coastal Ocean Worldwide

Source	All Pollutants (% contribution)
Runoff and other land discharges	44
Atmosphere	33
Maritime transportation	12
Dumping	10
Offshore production sites	1

Source: From GESAMP, *The State of the Marine Environment,* Blackwell
Scientific, Oxford, 1990. Alongi, D. M., *Coastal Ecosystem Processes,*
CRC Press, Boca Raton, FL, 1998, 328. With permission.

Table 6.1–4   Major Sources of Coastal Marine Pollution in the United States[a,b]

Type of Pollutant	Source		
	Sewage Treatment	Industrial Facilities	Land Runoff
Nutrients (N and P)	41	7	52
Bacteria	16	<1	84
Oil	41	10	47
Toxic Metals	6	46	47

[a] Values in percents.
[b] Excludes dredged soils.
Source: Data from Natural Resources Defense Council, Washington, D.C.

Table 6.1–5   Point and Nonpoint Sources of Pollution in Marine Waters

Sources	Common Pollutant Categories
Point Sources	
Municipal sewage treatment plants	BOD, bacteria, nutrients, ammonia, toxic chemicals
Industrial facilities	Toxic chemicals, BOD
Combined sewer overflows	BOD, bacteria, nutrients, turbidity, total dissolved solids, ammonia, toxic chemicals
Nonpoint Sources	
Agricultural runoff	Nutrients, turbidity, total dissolved solids, toxic chemicals
Urban runoff	Turbidity, bacteria, nutrients, total dissolved solids, toxic chemicals
Construction runoff	Turbidity, nutrients, toxic chemicals
Mining runoff	Turbidity, acids, toxic chemicals, total dissolved solids
Septic systems	Bacteria, nutrients
Landfills/spills	Toxic chemicals, miscellaneous substances
Silvicultural runoff	Nutrients, turbidity, toxic chemicals

Source: U.S. Environmental Protection Agency, National Water Quality Inventory, Washington, D.C., 1986.

Table 6.1–6   Status of Pollutants from Land-Based Sources

Substance	Status of Science and Management	Known/Suspected Targets/Effects
Nutrients	Science limited	Eutrophication
	Conservative management possible	Harmful algal blooms
Sewage	Science adequate	Human health
	Management deficient	Pathogens
		Eutrophication
Oil/hydrocarbons	Science adequate	Animal health
	Management deficient	Decreased productivity
		Destruction of amenities
PAHs	Science limited	Human health
	Management deficient	Animal health
		Tainted food sources
Metals	Science adequate	Human health
	Management deficient	Animal health
Synthetic organics	Science limited	Human health
	Conservative management possible	Animal health
Radionuclides	Science adequate	Human health
	Management deficient	Animal health
Thermal	Science adequate	Animal health
	Conservative management possible	
Sediment	Science limited	Decreased productivity
	Conservative management possible	Destruction of amenities (habitats/organisms)
Litter	Science adequate	Animal life
	Management deficient	Destruction of amenities

Source: Modified from UNCED, Preparatory Committee for the United Nations Conference on Environment and Development, Options for Agenda 21: protection of oceans, all kinds of seas including enclosed and semi-enclosed seas, coastal areas and the protection, rational use, and development of their living resources, UNCED, UNEP, Geneva, 1991.

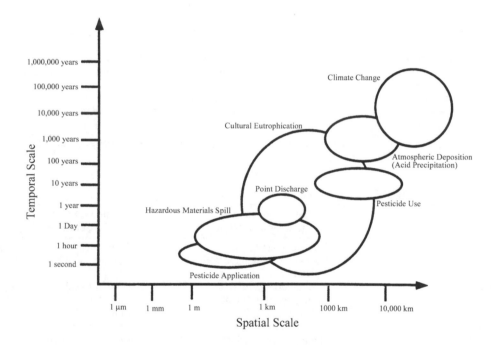

Figure 6.1–2 The overlap of spatial and temporal scales in chemical contamination. Just as there are
scales of ecological processes, contamination events also range in scale. Pesticide applications can range from small-scale household use to large-scale agricultural applications. The
addition of surplus nutrients and other materials due to agriculture or human habitation is
generally large scale and long lived. Acid precipitation generated by the tall stacks of the
midwestern United States is a fairly recent phenomenon, but the effects will likely be long
term. However, each of these events has molecular scale interactions. (From Landis, W. G.
and Yu, M.-H., *Introduction to Environmental Toxicology: Impacts of Chemicals upon Ecological Systems,* Lewis Publishers, Boca Raton, FL, 1995, 15. With permission.)

Table 6.1–7 List of Priority Pollutants Measured by the NOAA National Status and Trends Program in the Estuarine and Coastal Marine Waters of the United States

DDT and Its Metabolites	Polycyclic Aromatic Hydrocarbons
2,4'-DDD	
4,4'-DDD	2-Ring
2,4'-DDE	Biphenyl
4,4'-DDE	Naphthalene
2,4'-DDT	1-Methylnaphthalene
4,4'-DDT	2-Methylnaphthalene
	2,6-Dimethylnaphthalene
	1,6,7-Trimethylnaphthalene
Chlorinated Pesticides Other Than DDT	
Aldrin	3-Ring
cis-Chlordane	Fluorene
trans-Nonachlor	Phenanthrene
Dieldrin	1-Methylphenanthrene
Heptachlor	Anthracene
Heptachlor epoxide	Acenaphthene
Hexachlorobenzene	Acenaphthylene
Lindane (−HCH)	
Mirex	
	4-Ring
Polychlorinated Biphenyls	Fluoranthene
PCB congeners 8, 18, 28, 44, 56, 66,	Pyrene
101, 105, 118, 128, 138, 153, 179,	Benz[a]anthracene
180, 187, 195, 206, 209	Chrysene
Metals	5-Ring
	Benzo[a]pyrene
Major Elements	Benzo[e]pyrene
Aluminum	Perylene
Iron	Dibenz[a,h]anthracene
Manganese	Benzo[b]fluoranthene
	Benzo[k]fluoranthene
Trace Elements	
Arsenic	
Cadmium	6-Ring
Chromium	Benzo[ghi]perylene
Copper	Indeno[1.2,3-cd]pyrene
Lead	
Mercury	
Nickel	
Selenium	
Silver	
Tin	
Zinc	
Tri-, di-, and mono-butyltin	

Source: National Oceanic and Atmospheric Administration (NOAA), Ocean Assessments Division, Rockville, MD.

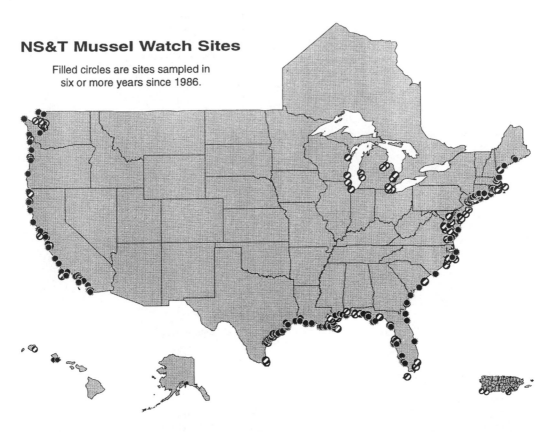

Figure 6.1–3 Map showing sampling sites of the National Status and Trends Mussels Watch Project. (From O'Connor, T. P. and Beliaeff, B., Recent Trends in Coastal Environmental Quality: Results from the Mussels Watch Project, NOAA Tech. Rep., Department of Commerce, Rockville, MD, 1995.)

Table 6.1–8   Summary of Pollutant Concentration Susceptibility in Estuaries

Most Susceptible Systems	Least Susceptible Systems
General population	General population
Brazos River**	Willapa Bay**
Ten Thousand Islands	St. Catherines/Sapelo Sound**
San Pedro Bay**	Penobscot Bay**
North/South Santee Rivers**	Humboldt Bay**
Galveston Bay**	Broad River**
Suisun Bay**	Hood Canal**
Sabine Lake**	Coos Bay**
St. Johns River*	Casco Bay**
Apalachicola Bay	Grays Harbor
San Antonio Bay**	Chincoteague Bay*
Connecticut River*	Bogue Sound**
Great South Bay*	St. Andrew/St. Simons Sound*
Merrimack River	Sheepscot Bay*
Atchafalaya/Vermillion Bays*	Apalachee Bay
Matagorda Bay*	Rappahannock River
Heavy industry	St. Helena Sound
Brazos River**	Puget Sound*
North/South Santee Rivers**	Heavy industry
Galveston Bay**	St. Catherines/Sapelo Sound**
Sabine Lake**	Hood Canal**
San Pedro Bay**	Penobscot Bay**
Connecticut River*	Casco Bay**
Calcasieu Lake	Humboldt Bay**
Hudson River/Raritan Bay	Buzzards Bay
Charleston Harbor	Boston Bay
Perdido Bay	Coos Bay**
Potomac River	Broad River**
San Antonio Bay**	Willapa Bay**
Mobile Bay	Bogue Sound**
Suisun Bay**	Puget Sound*
Great South Bay*	Narragansett Bay
Baffin Bay	Santa Monica Bay
Chesapeake Bay	Saco Bay
Agricultural activities	St. Andrew/St. Simons Sound*
Brazos River**	Agricultural activites
Suisun Bay**	Humboldt Bay**
North/South Santee Rivers**	Hood Canal**
St. Johns River*	Penobscot Bay**
Matagorda Bay*	Coos Bay**
Atchafalaya/Vermillion Bays*	St. Catherines/Sapelo Sound**
San Pedro Bay**	Chincoteague Bay*
Sabine Lake**	Bogue Sound**
Corpus Christi Bay	Long Island Sound
Galveston Bay**	Casco Bay**
San Antonio Bay**	Willapa Bay**
Winyah Bay	Broad River**
Albemarle Sound	Sheepscot Bay*
Neuse River	Klamath River
Laguna Madre	

**,* Systems that are present in all three categories are marked with two asterisks; systems present in two categories are marked with one asterisk.

Source: Biggs, R. B. et al., *Rev. Aquat. Sci.,* 1, 203, 1989. With permission.

6.2 WATERSHED EFFECTS

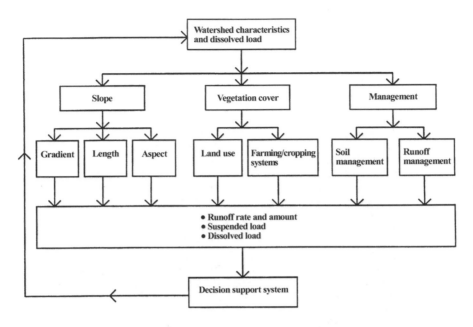

Figure 6.2–1 Watershed and management characteristics that affect the transport of suspended and dissolved loads. (From Lal, R., in *Integrated Watershed Management in the Global Ecosystem,* Lal, R., Ed., CRC Press, Boca Raton, FL, 2000, 96. With permission.)

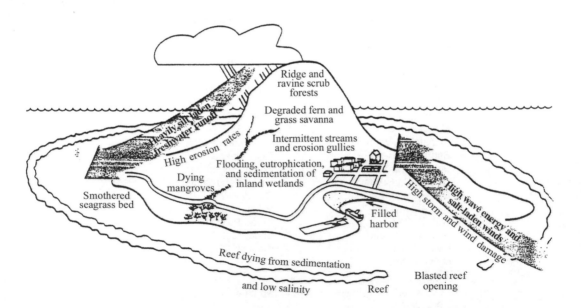

Figure 6.2–2 Excessive soil erosion is a severe problem in many coastal regions. (From Clark, J. R., *Coastal Management Handbook,* Lewis Publishers, Boca Raton, FL, 1996, 466. With permission.)

Table 6.2–1   Runoff and Sediment Load in Major Rivers of the World

River	Drainage Area (10^6 km²)	Runoff (km³/year)	Sediment Load (10^6 tons/year)
Amazon	6.2	6300	900
Danube	0.8	206	67
Ganges	1.5	971	1670
Irrawaddy	0.4	428	265
Magdalena	0.2	237	220
Mekong	0.8	470	160
Mississippi	3.3	580	210
Niger	1.2	192	40
Ob	2.5	385	16
Orinoco	1.0	1100	210
Yangtze	1.9	900	478
Yellow	0.8	49	1080
Yenisei	2.58	560	13
Zaire	3.8	1250	43

Data from Milliman and Meade, 1983; Van der Leeden et al., 1994. Full citations in original source.

Source: Lal, R., in Integrated Watershed Management in the Global Ecosystem, Lal, R., Ed., CRC Press, Boca Raton, FL, 2000, 8. With permission.

Table 6.2–2   Pollutants Associated with Urban Runoff, Monitoring Parameters, Pollutant Sources, and Potential Effects

Category	Parameters	Possible Sources	Effects
Suspended solids	Organic and inorganic TSS, turbidity, dissolved solids	Urban/agricultural runoff, combined sewer overflows (CSOs)	Turbidity, habitat alteration, recreational and aesthetic loss, contaminant transport
Nutrients	Nitrate, nitrite, ammonia, organic nitrogen, phosphorus	Urban/agricultural runoff, landfills, atmospheric degradation, erosion, septic systems	Surface waters, algal blooms, ammonia toxicity, groundwater, nitrate toxicity
Pathogens	Indicator bacteria (fecal coliforms and streptococci, enterococci), viruses	Urban/agricultural runoff septic systems, CSOs, boat discharges, domestic/wild animals	Ear/intestinal infections, shellfish bed closure, recreational/aesthetic loss
Organic enrichment	BOD, COD, TOC	Urban/agricultural runoff, CSOs, landfills, septic systems	DO depletion, odors, fishkills
Toxic pollutants	Trace metals, organics	Pesticides/herbicides, underground tanks, hazardous waste sites, landfills, illegal oil disposal, industrial discharges, urban runoff, CSOs	Lethal and sublethal to humans and other organisms
Salt	Sodium chloride	Road salting	Drinking water contamination, impact on non-salt-tolerant species

Note: TSS = total suspended solids; TOC = total organic carbon; CSO = combined sewer overflows; DO = dissolved oxygen; BOD = biochemical oxygen demand; COD = chemical oxygen demand.

Source: Bingham, D. R., in Applied Wetlands Science and Technology, Kent, D. M., Ed., Lewis Publishers, Boca Raton, FL, 1994, 248. With permission.

Table 6.2–3 Expected Effects of Stormwater Contaminants or Condition on Integrative Measures of Ecosystem Response

Input	Expected Environmental Consequence	Energy Dynamics	Food Web Structure and Complexity	Biodiversity	Critical Species	Genetic Diversity	Dispersal and Migration	Ecosystem Development
Suspended solids (organics)	DO depletion enrichment blanketing	1. Alter carbon flux 2. Reduce complexity of energy pathways and control functions	1. Reduce complexity in food web 2. Eliminate sensitive organisms 3. Favor species tolerant to low DO and high organic enrichment 4. Change connection between organisms and trophic levels	1. Minimal effect if source areas of colonizing species exist 2. Urbanization as a process reduces diversity so change must be viewed holistically	1. Direct effect on species intolerant of low DO and high organic enrichment 2. Indirect effects possible through food web alteration	1. Minimal short-term effect unless species permanently lost due to urbanization 2. Continuous discharges and highly variable discharges may lead to local loss of gene pool	1. Local effects on colonization in altered habitat 2. Potential interference with movement by blocking zones of passage	1. Alteration of successional processes may reset community to an earlier successional state 2. Enrichment leading to alternate stable state 3. Transient effects associated with frequency and magnitude 4. Continuous discharges block advanced successional states in zone of influence
Suspended solids (inorganics)	Blanketing morphological change	1. Reduce complexity of energy pathways and control functions	1. Favor species tolerant of high SS	1. Minimal effect if source areas of colonizing species exist	1. Direct effect on species intolerant of high SS	1. Minimal short-term effect unless species permanently lost due to urbanization	1. Local effects on colonization in altered habitat	1. High, continuous SS loading may retard succession of limit processes within a narrow range

Light reduction—1° productivity effect(s) Physical damage to organisms	2. Reduce primary production 3. Reduce access to buried carbon sources	2. Reduce complexity of food web 3. Eliminate sensitive organisms	2. Urbanization as a process reduces diversity so change must be viewed holistically	2. Indirect effects possible through food web alteration	2. Continued high variability may lead to local loss of gene pool	2. Potential interference with movement by blocking zones of passage	2. Low, transient SS loading may alter successional processes usually resetting to an earlier successional state
BOD/COD (oxygen demanding wastes) DO depletion enrichment	1. Alter carbon flux magnitude 2. Alter carbon flux pathways 3. Reduce complexity of energy pathways and control functions	1. Reduce complexity of food web 2. Eliminate sensitive organisms 3. Favor species tolerant to low DO	1. Continuous discharge can create zones of low diversity 2. Minimal effect of transient discharge if source areas of colonizing species exist 3. Urbanization as a process reduces diversity so change must be viewed holistically	1. Direct effect on species intolerant of low DO and high organic enrichment 2. Indirect effects possible through food web alteration	1. Minimal short-term effect unless species permanently lost due to urbanization 2. Continuous discharges and highly variable discharges may lead to local loss of gene pool	1. Local effects on colonization in altered habitat 2. Potential interference with movement by blocking zones of passage	1. Alteration of successional processes may reset community to an earlier successional state 2. Enrichment leading to alternate stable state 3. Transient effects associated with frequency and magnitude

(continued)

Table 6.2–3 Expected Effects of Stormwater Contaminants or Condition on Integrative Measures of Ecosystem Response (continued)

Input	Expected Environmental Consequence	Energy Dynamics	Food Web Structure and Complexity	Biodiversity	Critical Species	Genetic Diversity	Dispersal and Migration	Ecosystem Development
			4. Change connection between organisms and trophic levels					4. Continuous discharges block advanced successional states in zone of influence
Nutrients, N and P	1° productivity increase enrichment DO variability	1. Increased nutrient pool leads to higher 1° productivity and increased base of fixed carbon 2. Instability in energy processing possible as enrichment reduces functional redundancy 3. Effects of increased nutrients accumulate over space and time	1. Initial effects may be increased diversity with increased carbon-based food resources 2. Altered connectivity between organisms and trophic levels 3. Cumulative effect may be lower diversity	1. Expected increase or decrease through space or time dependent on loading 2. Effect location will not be adjacent discharge locations	1. Direct effect minimal 2. Indirect effects may alter role and capacity of keystone or resource species in ecosystem	1. Minimal short-term effect unless species permanently lost due to urbanization 2. Continuous loading may lead to local loss of gene pool	1. Minimal short-term effect 2. Continuous loading may lead to local change in habitat type or quality affecting dispersal success	1. Nutrient accumulation will establish new base for successional processes 2. Acceleration of processes possible

Metals	Toxicity (lethal effects, sublethal effects, bioaccumulation) Micronutrients— promote enrichment	1. Direct toxicity will reduce functional redundancy leading to greater variability in energy dynamics 2. Micro-nutrients may lead to system enrichment	1. Direct toxicity will simplify food web 2. Connection may be altered by elimination of sensitive species	2. Bioaccumulation or bioconcentration may produce effect through time or space that eliminate sensitive species and select for tolerant species producing permanent alteration of biodiversity	1. Direct toxic effect on sensitive species 2. Bioaccumulation and bioconcentration may raise contaminant levels to effect concentrations through time or space	1. Direct, short-term and indirect, long-term effects may limit genetic diversity to species capable of tempering toxic effect through transfer, chelation, or binding	1. Localized effects where exposure concentration exceeds tolerance of colonizing species, limiting dispersal 2. Shock loading may induce migration or movement	1. Shock loading may eliminate species, initiate successional processes, and lead to alternate stable state 2. Long-term maintenance of elevated concentration will select tolerant species and alter natural successional processes

(continued)

Table 6.2–3 Expected Effects of Stormwater Contaminants or Condition on Integrative Measures of Ecosystem Response (continued)

Input	Expected Environmental Consequence	Energy Dynamics	Food Web Structure and Complexity	Biodiversity	Critical Species	Genetic Diversity	Dispersal and Migration	Ecosystem Development
		3. Accumulation of toxic metals may reduce top-down control functions	3. Transient discharge effects limited to temporal alterations in web components and connections 4. Continuous discharges produce changes in components and connections through both time and space				3. Continuous discharges may create zones of contamination that affect dispersal	3. Accumulation or concentration in environment or organisms will limit diversity and alter ecosystem development
Toxic organics	Toxicity (sublethal effects, bioaccumulation)	1. Direct toxicity will reduce functional redundancy leading to greater variability in energy dynamics	1. Direct toxicity will simplify food web	1. Elimination of sensitive species, reducing biodiversity	1. Direct toxic effect on sensitive species	1. Direct, short-term and indirect, long-term effects may limit genetic diversity to species capable of tempering toxic effect through decomposition or transfer	1. Localized effects where exposure concentration exceeds tolerance of colonizing species	1. Shock loading may eliminate species, initiate successional processes, and lead to alternate stable state

| Transformation Product toxicity | 2. Accumulation of contaminats may reduce top-down control functions 3. Detoxication mechanisms have energetic cost to individuals that may affect energy dynamics | 2. Connection may be altered by elimination of sensitive species 3. Transient discharge effects limited to temporal alterations in web components and connections | 2. Bioaccumulation, bioconcentration, or sublethal effects may produce changes through time or space that eliminate sensitive species and select for tolerant species producing permanent alteration of biodiversity | 2. Bioaccumulation and bioconcentration may raise contaminant levels to concentrations that will affect critical species through time or space | 2. Shock loading may induce migration or movement 3. Continuous discharges may create zones of contamination that affect dispersal | 2. Long-term maintenance of elevated concentration will select tolerant species and alter natural successional processes 3. Accumulation or concentration in environment or organisms will limit diversity and alter ecosystem development |

(continued)

Table 6.2-3   Expected Effects of Stormwater Contaminants or Condition on Integrative Measures of Ecosystem Response (continued)

Input	Expected Environmental Consequence	Energy Dynamics	Food Web Structure and Complexity	Biodiversity	Critical Species	Genetic Diversity	Dispersal and Migration	Ecosystem Development
			4. Continuous discharges produce changes in components and connections through both time and space					
Ammonia	Environmental accumulation							
	Toxicity DO effect 1° productivity increase Enrichment	1. Toxic effects and DO depletion may reduce complexity and control functions 2. Increased nutrient pool leading to higher 1° productivity and increased base of fixed carbon	1. Reduce complexity of the food web 2. Eliminate sensitive organisms 3. Favor species tolerant of toxic effects or DO depletion changing components and connectance	1. Expected increase or decrease through space or time dependent on loading 2. Effect may be local or at some distance from discharge location	1. Direct effect on species intolerant to toxicant concentrations or DO depletion 2. Indirect effects possible through food web alteration	1. Minimal short-term effect unless species permanently lost due to urbanization 2. Continuous discharges and highly variable discharges may lead to local loss of gene pool	1. Shock loading may induce migration or movement 2. Continuous discharges may create zones of contamination that affect dispersal 3. Potential interference with movement by blocking zones of passage	1. Shock loading may eliminate species, initiate successional processes, and lead to alternate stable state 2. Long-term maintenance of elevated ammonia concentration or DO depletion will select tolerant species and alter natural successional processes

Hydrogen sulfide	Toxicity	1. Toxic effects may alter complexity of energy pathways and control functions	1. Reduce complexity of the food web 2. Eliminate sensitive organisms	1. Expected decrease through toxic effect	1. Direct effect on sensitive species	1. Minimal short-term effect unless species permanently lost due to urbanization 2. Continuous discharge of highly variable discharges may lead to local loss of gene pool	1. Local effects on colonization in altered habitat 2. Transient concentration may stimulate movement	1. Shock loading may eliminate species, initiate successional processes, and lead to alternate stable state
Bacteria	Public health risk Associated solids effects	1. Presence of bacteria often related to enrichment and corresponding change in energy dynamics	1. Direct effects through enrichment 2. Indirect effects may change components and connections	1. Minimal effect if source areas of colonizing species	1. Indirect effects possible through food web alteration 2. Disease induction possible	1. Minimal short-term effect unless species permanently lost due to urbanization 2. Long-term effects possible through alteration of environmental or biological conditions	1. Indirect effects possible	1. Alteration of successional processes possible

(continued)

Table 6.2–3   Expected Effects of Stormwater Contaminants or Condition on Integrative Measures of Ecosystem Response (continued)

Input	Expected Environmental Consequence	Energy Dynamics	Food Web Structure and Complexity	Biodiversity	Critical Species	Genetic Diversity	Dispersal and Migration	Ecosystem Development
Hydraulic dynamics	Washout of organisms Channel morphology and habitat change Erosion/ sedimentation	1. Removal or dislocation of organisms may alter control functions 2. Habitat alteration may exert control on energy dynamics	1. Organism removal or habitat change may alter both structure and connections	1. Minimal effect if source areas of colonizing species exist 2. Changed hydraulic dynamics may alter diversity— permanence of change dependent on permanence of habitat alteration	1. Direct effect on species affected by changed dynamics 2. Indirect effects possible through food web alteration	1. Minimal short-term effect unless species permanently lost due to urbanization 2. Altered dynamics may lead to local loss of gene pool	1. Altered dynamics may induce migration or movement 2. Scour and removal possible when hydrograph changed 3. Local effects on colonization in altered habitat	1. Alteration of successional processes usually resetting to an earlier successional state 2. Species dominance may change due to disturbance frequency and founder species effect
Temperature	Stress Environmental cues for biological activity Synergism with toxicity	1. Speed of energy transfer functions altered	1. Alteration of components and connections	1. Change in diversity may be due to direct or indirect causes by ecosystem properties, or processes affected by temperature	1. Temperature variability may alter species capacity to maintain viable populations	1. Gene pool may be altered by both direct and indirect effects	1. Variability may lead to increased migration	1. Successional process speed and duration may be altered by long-term temperature change

Synergism with metal toxicity Stress	2. Change in temperature may produce indirect alteration of carbon flux	2. Altered environmental state may affect toxicity leading to changes in components and connections 3. Changed cues may alter biological activity leading to changes in components and connections	2. Temperature cues may affect viability of populations		2. Altered cues may induce migration	2. Succession may be reset by temperature fluctuation
pH	1. Change in species composition may produce indirect effects that alter cabron flux	1. Alteration of components and connections 2. Altered environmental state may affect toxicity leading to changes in components and connections	1. Change in diversity may be due to direct or indirect causes by properties or processes affected by temperature	1. Direct effect on species intolerant of transient or permanent changes in pH 2. Indirect effects through alteration of toxic potential of contaminants to critical species	1. Gene pool may be altered by both direct and indirect effects	1. Variability may lead to increased migration 2. Transient changes may induce migration	1. Transient changes may reset successional processes 2. Permanent alteration may lead to blocked successional development

Note: SS = suspended solids; DO = dissolved oxygen; BOD = biochemical oxygen demand; COD = chemical oxygen demand.

Source: Herricks, E. E., in *Stormwater Runoff and Receiving Systems: Impact, Monitoring, and Assessment*, Herricks, E. E., Ed., Lewis Publishers, Boca Raton, FL, 1995, 27. With permission.

**Table 6.2–4   Options for Treatment of Pollution
                  from Stormwater**

Source Controls

Animal waste removal
Catch basin cleaning
Cross-connection identification and removal
Proper construction activities
Reduced fertilizer, pesticide, and herbicide use
Reduced roadway sanding and salting
Solid waste management
Street sweeping
Toxic and hazardous pollution prevention

Regulatory Controls

Land acquisition
Land-use regulations
Protection of natural resources

Structural Controls

Constructed wetlands
Detention facilities
Extended detention dry ponds
Wet ponds
Filtration practices
Filtration basins
Sand filters
Water quality inlets

Infiltration Facilities

Dry wells
Infiltration basins
Infiltration trenches
Porous pavement
Vegetative practices
Grassed swales
Filter strips

Source: Bingham, D. R., in *Applied Wetlands Science and
Technology,* Kent, D. M., Ed., Lewis Publishers, Boca
Raton, FL, 1994, 245. With permission.

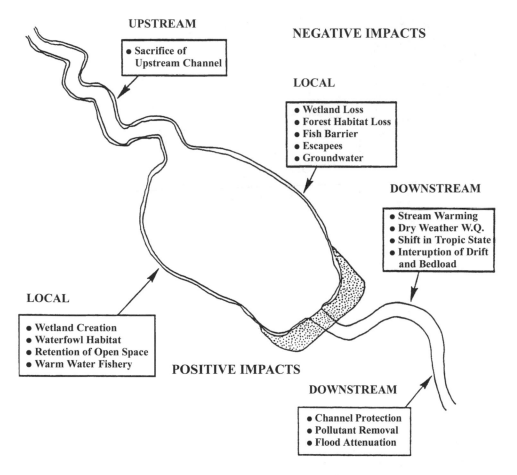

Figure 6.2–3 Schematic of the positive and negative impacts of ponds used in stormwater runoff control. (From Schueler, T. R. and Galli, J., in *Stormwater Runoff and Receiving Systems: Impacts, Monitoring, and Assessments,* Herricks, E. E., Ed., Lewis Publishers, Boca Raton, FL, 1995, 177. With permission.)

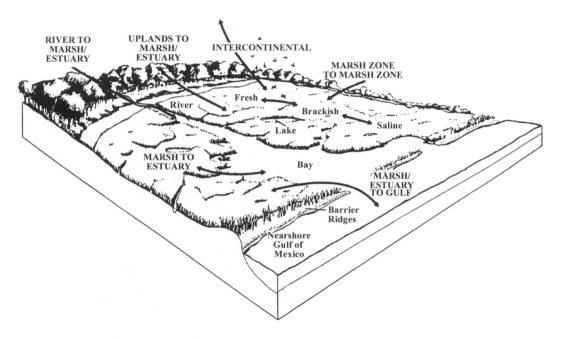

Figure 6.2–4 Wetlands, like this deltaic marsh, are closely linked to sea and upland ecosystems. (From Clark, J. R., *Coastal Management Handbook,* Lewis Publishers, Boca Raton, FL, 1996, 352. With permission.)

Table 6.2–5   Important Functions and Values of Natural Wetlands

Flood water storage	Nutrient removal/retention
Flooding reduction	Chemical and nutrient sorption
Erosion control	Food chain support
Sediment stabilization	Fish and wildlife habitat
Sediment/toxicant retention	Migratory waterfowl usage
Groundwater recharge/discharge	Recreation
Natural water purification	Uniqueness/heritage values

Source: Corbitt, R. A. and Bowen, R. T., in *Applied Wetlands Science and Technology,* Kent, D. M., Ed., Lewis Publishers, Boca Raton, FL, 1994, 222. With permission.

Table 6.2–6   Predicted Responses of Mangrove and Coral Reef Ecosystems to Global Climate Change

Rise in Mean Sea Level (Prediction: 6.0-cm rise per decade)

Mangroves
  Landward progression of mangroves; rate determined by rate of sea level rise
  Erosion at seaward front
  Altered zonation patterns
Coral reefs
  Will not threaten most coral reefs; advantageous for some, permitting vertical growth
  Will devastate habitability of low coral islands and corals of other low-lying areas

Increase in Atmospheric CO_2 Concentration (Prediction: 0.5% rise per year)

Mangroves
  Enhanced water
  May not increase canopy photosynthesis, growth, and litterfall
  Increased rate of vertical accretion
  Species responses will vary
Coral reefs
  Lower carbonate production due to surface water changes in alkalinity and ΣCO_2
  Increased algal growth and increased competition with corals
  Enhance the effect of nutrient pollution and overfishing

Increase in Atmospheric Temperature (Prediction: 0.3°C per decade)

Mangroves
  Expansion of mangroves into higher latitudes
  Increase in mangrove photosynthesis and respiration, litterfall
  Increase in rates of microbial decomposition
  Increase in plant and animal biodiversity
  Change in plant and animal densities, community composition, growth, and reproduction
  Reduced rate of vertical accretion
Coral reefs
  Will not threaten coral survival
  Decreased coral cover
  Increased bleaching of corals and other calcifiers
  Temperature extremes will endanger corals by increasing vulnerability to other stresses

Changes in Precipitation

Mangroves
  Decreased soil salinity and increased water content with increased rainfall will increase plant growth, and
    vice versa
  Changes in animal composition and zonation dependent on salinity tolerances
Coral reefs
  Decreased coral cover on coastal reefs
  Increased vulnerability to other stresses
  Increased rate of sedimentation, nutrients, and other contaminants onto reefs

Climate Change Impacts on Human Use and Exploitation

Mangroves
  Increased erosion
  Increased flooding in low-lying areas
  Increased salt intrusion
  Increased damage from storms
Coral reefs
  Increased localized damage
  Endangered species pressed to extinction (e.g., sea turtles)
  Shift in current patterns impeding reproduction and larval colonization
  Damaged ozone layer disrupting recruitment

Source: Alongi, D. M., *Coastal Ecosystem Processes,* CRC Press, Boca Raton, FL, 1998, 354. With permission.

Table 6.2–7 Description of Major Greenhouse Gases

Carbon dioxide (CO_2)	Currently responsible for approximately one half to two thirds of human contributions to global warming, the concentration of atmospheric CO_2 has risen 25% since the beginning of the Industrial Revolution. Combustion of fossil fuels and deforestation are the main sources of this increase. Because society's basic energy sources produce CO_2, its atmospheric concentration is projected to continue to increase unless strong measures are taken to encourage energy conservation, alternative energy sources, and forest preservation.
Methane (CH_4)	Although methane has a much lower atmospheric concentration than CO_2, it is a more potent greenhouse gas and its concentration is increasing at a rate of 1% per year. Sources include rice paddies, cows, termites, natural gas leakage, biomass burning, landfills, and wetlands. Of the major greenhouse gases, CH_4 concentrations may be the easiest to stabilize with modest cuts in emissions.
Nitrous oxide (N_2O)	The concentration of nitrous oxide in the atmosphere is increasing at a rate of 0.25% per year. Although nitrous oxide is a more potent greenhouse gas than CO_2, its contribution to global warming is lower because of its low concentration. Anthropogenic sources include fossil fuel and biomass combustion, agricultural fertilizers, and land disturbances. The relative contribution of natural and anthropogenic sources of N_2O is not well understood.
Chlorofluorocarbons (CFCs)	Invented in the 20th century, CFCs have been implicated not only in chemical destruction of the stratospheric zone, but also in greenhouse warming. Each CFC molecule has a direct warming effect several thousand times that of a CO_2 molecule. However, CFCs cause an indirect cooling effect by destroying ozone, another greenhouse gas. The extent to which the direct warming effect is offset by the indirect cooling effect has not yet been determined. CFCs are used in refrigerants, aerosol propellants, foam-blowing agents, and solvents. Their atmospheric concentration is increasing at a rate of 4% per year. Substitutes are being developed that are not as chemically stable and therefore will not accumulate as fast in the atmosphere. The Montreal Protocol, an international agreement, and recent U.S. measures currently limit production of these gases, but further limits may be necessary.

Source: EPA, Climate Change, EPA 230-F-95-002, U.S. Environmental Protection Agency, Washington, D.C., 1995.

6.3 CONTAMINANT EFFECTS ON ORGANISMS

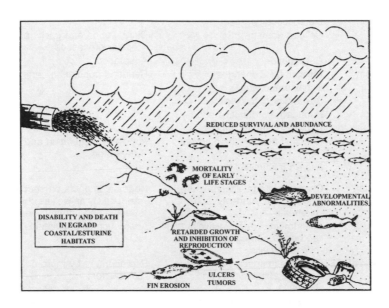

Figure 6.3–1 Some examples of the effects of contaminants on marine organisms. (From Sindermann, C. J., *Ocean Pollution: Effects on Living Resources and Humans,* CRC Press, Boca Raton, FL, 1996, 23. With permission.)

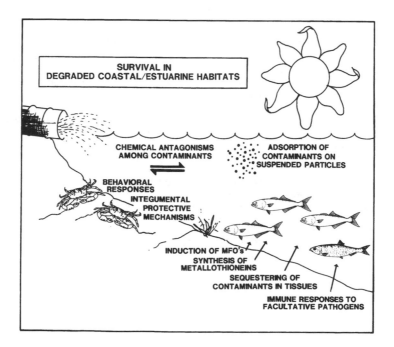

Figure 6.3–2 Some mechanisms that enhance the survival of marine organisms in degraded habitats. (From Sindermann, C. J., *Ocean Pollution: Effects on Living Resources and Humans,* CRC Press, Boca Raton, FL, 1996, 25. With permission.)

Table 6.3–1   Marine Organism Responses to Chemical Contaminants

Level	Responses	Effects at the Next Level
Cell	Toxication	Toxic metabolites available
	Metabolic impairment	
	Cellular damage	Disruption in energetics and cellular processes
	Detoxication	Adaptation
Organism	Physiological changes	Reduced population performance
	Behavioral changes	
	Susceptibility to disease	
	Reduced reproductive effort	
	Decreased larval viability	
	Readjustment in rate functions	Population regulation and adaptation
	Altered immunities	
Population	Changes in age/size structure, recruitment, mortality, and biomass	Negative impacts on species productivity as well as coexisting species and communities
	Adjustment of reproductive output and other demographic characteristics	Adaptation of population
Community	Changes in species abundance, species distribution, and biomass	Replacement by more-adaptive competitors
	Altered trophic interactions	Reduced secondary production
	Ecosystem adaptation	No change in community structure and function

Source: McDowell, J. E., *Oceanus*, 36, 56–61, 1993. With permission.

Table 6.3–2   Mechanisms of Resistance or Tolerance of Fish to Pollutants

External	Internal	Population
Environmental mitigation	Synthesis of metallothioneins	Selection by differential mortality for efficiency in coping with contaminants (for example, high antibody responders)
	Induction of mixed function oxygenases to metabolize organics	
Chemical antagonisms (for example, metals—reducing the additive effects on physiological processes)	Sequestering of fat-soluble toxic substances in fat	
	Shift to lactic acid metabolism in low-oxygen environment	
Adsorption of contaminants on suspended particles and removal from water column by sedimentation	Immune responses to facultative pathogens	
	Rate of uptake and release of heavy metal species may vary	
Microbial degradation of organics	Sequestering of contaminant in shell (Crustacea)	
Behavioral modification		
Retreat from toxic zones		
Altered migration patterns		
Integumental protective mechanisms		
Gill mucus		
Intestinal mucus		
Body surface mucus layer		
Antibodies in mucus		

Source: Sindermann, C. J., *Ocean Pollution: Effects on Living Resources and Humans,* CRC Press, Boca Raton, FL, 1996, 26. With permission.

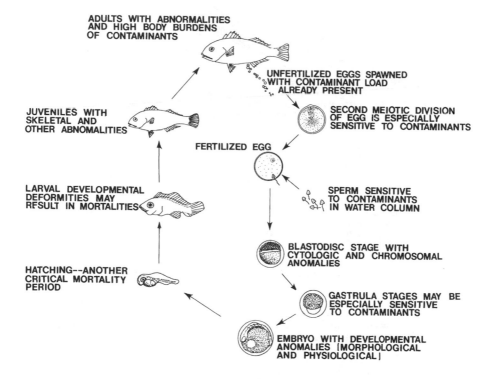

POLLUTION EFFECTS
ON LIFE HISTORY STAGES
OF FISH

ADULTS WITH ABNORMALITIES
AND HIGH BODY BURDENS
OF CONTAMINANTS

UNFERTILIZED EGGS SPAWNED
WITH CONTAMINANT LOAD
ALREADY PRESENT

JUVENILES WITH
SKELETAL AND
OTHER ABNORMALITIES

SECOND MEIOTIC DIVISION
OF EGG IS ESPECIALLY
SENSITIVE TO CONTAMINANTS

FERTILIZED EGG

LARVAL DEVELOPMENTAL
DEFORMITIES MAY
RESULT IN MORTALITIES

SPERM SENSITIVE
TO CONTAMINANTS
IN WATER COLUMN

HATCHING--ANOTHER
CRITICAL MORTALITY
PERIOD

BLASTODISC STAGE WITH
CYTOLOGIC AND CHROMOSOMAL
ANOMALIES

GASTRULA STAGES MAY BE
ESPECIALLY SENSITIVE
TO CONTAMINANTS

EMBRYO WITH DEVELOPMENTAL
ANOMALIES (MORPHOLOGICAL
AND PHYSIOLOGICAL)

Figure 6.3–3 Points in the life cycle when fish are especially sensitive to pollutants. (From Sindermann, C. J., *Ocean Pollution: Effects on Living Resources and Humans,* CRC Press, Boca Raton, FL, 1996, 133. With permission.)

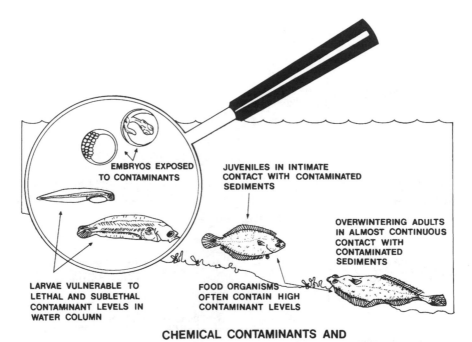

**CHEMICAL CONTAMINANTS AND
DEMERSAL FISH LIFE HISTORY STAGES**

Figure 6.3–4 Life history stages of demersal fish that are vulnerable to pollution. (From Sindermann, C. J., *Ocean Pollution: Effects on Living Resources and Humans,* CRC Press, Boca Raton, FL, 1996, 142. With permission.)

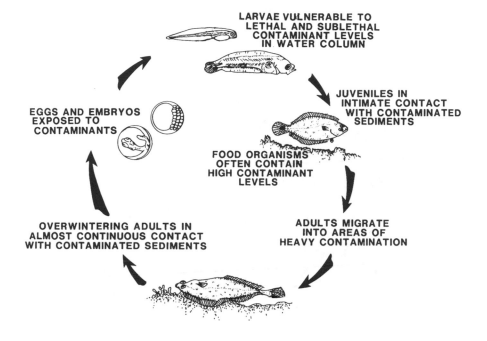

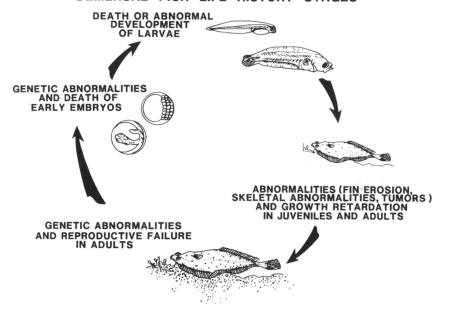

Figure 6.3–5 Life cycle of the winter flounder, *Pleuronectes americanus*, with potential pollutant impact points (above) and the effects of pollutants (below). (From Sindermann, C. J., *Ocean Pollution: Effects on Living Resources and Humans,* CRC Press, Boca Raton, FL, 1996, 22. With permission.)

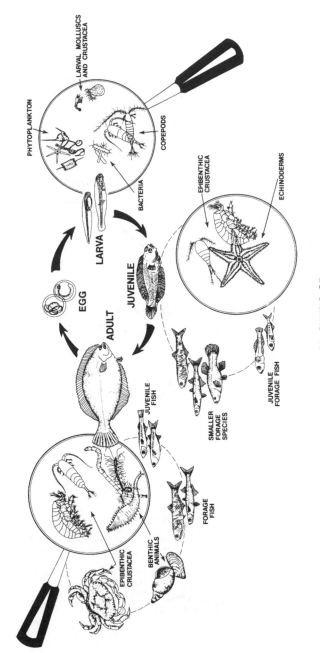

Figure 6.3–6   Effects of contaminants on food chains of winter flounder life history stages. (From Sindermann, C. J., *Ocean Pollution: Effects on Living Resources and Humans*, CRC Press, Boca Raton, FL, 1996, 146. With permission.)

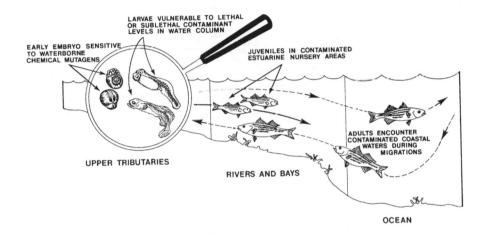

Figure 6.3–7 Life cycle of the striped bass, *Morone saxatilis,* with potential pollutant impact points. (From Sindermann, C. J., *Ocean Pollution: Effects on Living Resources and Humans,* CRC Press, Boca Raton, FL, 1996, 138. With permission.)

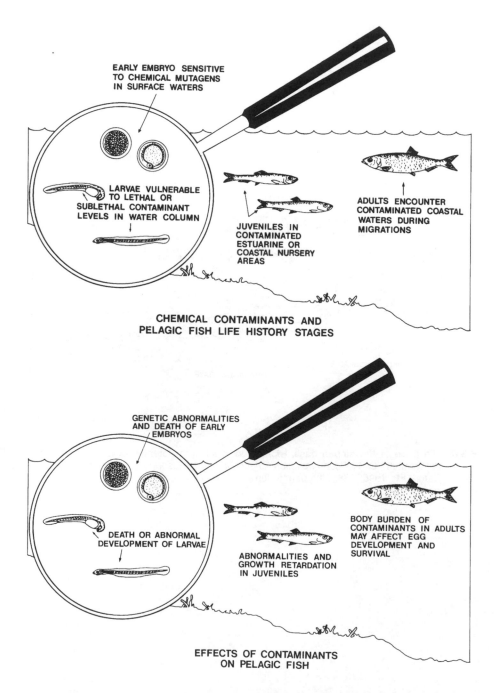

Figure 6.3–8 Vulnerable life cycle stages (top) and the effects of pollution (bottom) on Atlantic herring, *Clupea harengus*. (From Sindermann, C. J., *Ocean Pollution: Effects on Living Resources and Humans*, CRC Press, Boca Raton, FL, 1996, 121. With permission.)

Some pathways of pollution-induced effects on marine fish and shellfish

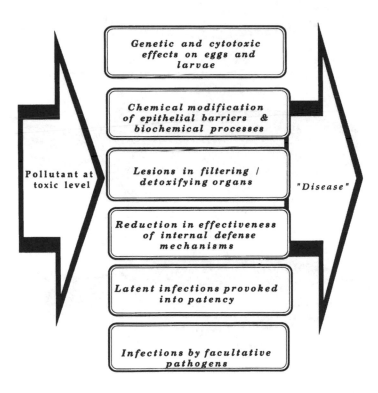

Figure 6.3–9 Some effects of pollutants on disease processes. (From Sindermann, C. J., *Ocean Pollution: Effects on Living Resources and Humans,* CRC Press, Boca Raton, FL, 1996, 55. With permission.)

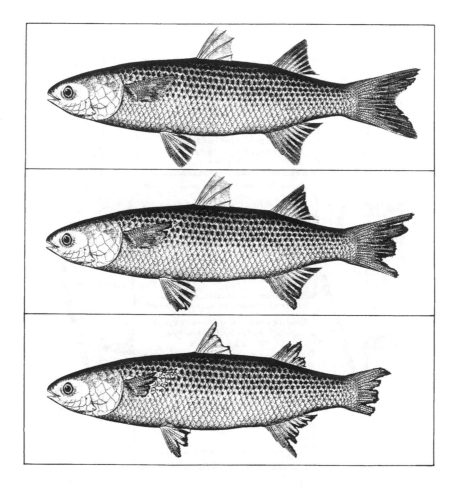

Figure 6.3–10 Fin erosion produced experimentally in mullet by exposure to oil. (Top) Initial fraying of caudal fin, (Middle) moderate erosion, and (Bottom) extensive erosion. (From Sindermann, C. J., *Ocean Pollution: Effects on Living Resources and Humans,* CRC Press, Boca Raton, FL, 1996, 54. With permission.)

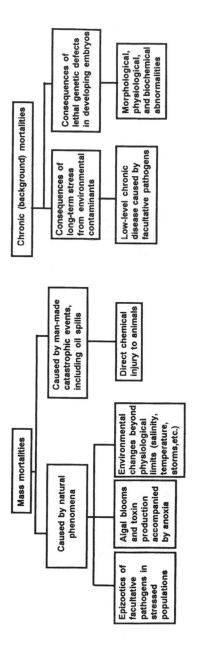

Figure 6.3–11 Causes of mortality in marine fish. (From Sindermann, C. J., *Ocean Pollution: Effects on Living Resources and Humans*, CRC Press, Boca Raton, FL, 1996, 134. With permission.)

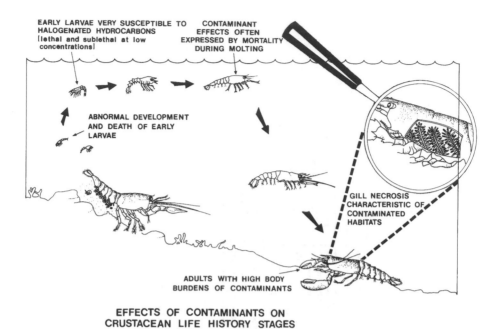

EFFECTS OF CONTAMINANTS ON
CRUSTACEAN LIFE HISTORY STAGES

Figure 6.3–12 Contaminant effects on crustacean life cycle stages. (From Sindermann, C.J., *Ocean Pollution: Effects on Living Resources and Humans,* CRC Press, Boca Raton, FL, 1996, 72. With permission.)

Table 6.3–3   Types of Shellfish Poisoning

Illness	Symptoms	Cause	Description
Paralytic shellfish poisoning	Numbness of lips, face, and extremities; visual disturbance; staggering gait; difficulty breathing; paralysis	Species of the dinoflagellate *Protogonyaulax* (formerly *Gonyaulax*)	About 12 forms purine-derived saxitoxins; water soluble; acts by blocking sodium channel needed to transmit nerve impulses
Neurotoxic shellfish poisoning	Nonfatal but unpleasant neurotoxic symptoms; strong action on cardiovascular system	*Ptychodiscus brevis* (formerly *Gymnodinium breve*)	Toxins have unusual polycyclic ether skeletons
Diarrhetic shellfish poisoning	Cramps; severe diarrhea; nausea; vomiting; chills; death rare	Species of dinoflagellates, *Dinophysis* and *Prorocentrum* in particular	*Dinophysis* toxin and okadaic acid; large, fat-soluble polyethers; can move across cell membranes and make them "leak"
Amnesic shellfish poisoning (domoic acid)	Nausea; vomiting; muscle weakness; disorientation; loss of short-term memory	Reported to be diatom *Nitzschia pungens*; toxin also found in species of the red alga, *Chondria*	Nonessential amino acid; mimics glutamic acid; affects brain and nervous system; found in digestive glands of contaminated shellfish

Source: Adapted from Pirquet, K. T., *Can. Aquacult.,* 4(2), 41, 1988. From Sindermann, C. J., *Ocean Pollution: Effects on Living Resources and Humans,* CRC Press, Boca Raton, FL, 1996, 103. With permission.

6.4 NUTRIENTS

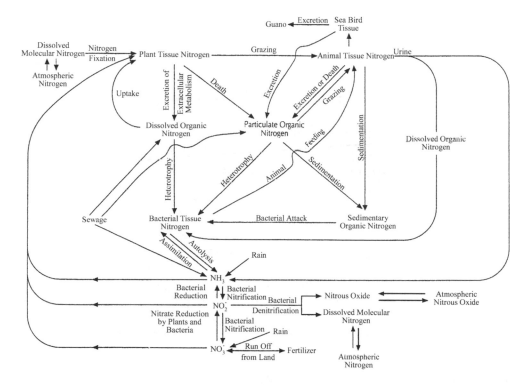

Figure 6.4–1 The nitrogen cycle in ocean waters. (From Millero, F. J. and Sohn, M. L., *Chemical Oceanography,* CRC Press, Boca Raton, FL, 1992, 336. With permission.)

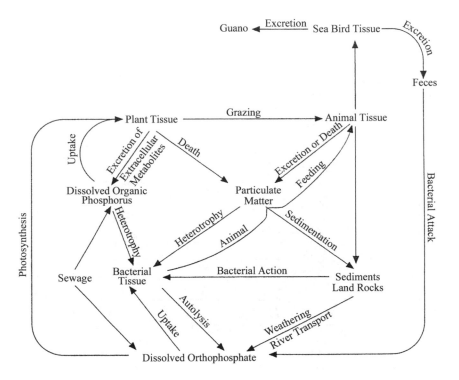

Figure 6.4–2 The phosphate cycle in ocean waters. (From Millero, F. J. and Sohn, M. L., *Chemical Oceanog-raphy,* CRC Press, Boca Raton, FL, 1992, 331. With permission.)

Table 6.4–1 Concentrations of Nitrogen and Phosphorus in 28 Estuarine Ecosystems[a]

Estuary	Nutrient Concentration	
	Nitrogen	Phosphorus
River dominated		
Pamlico River, North Carolina	1.5	8.0
Narrangansett Bay, Rhode Island	0.6	1.6
Western Wadden Sea, Netherlands	3.0	2.0
Eastern Wadden Sea, Netherlands	4.0	2.5
Mid-Patuxent River, Maryland	4.2	2.3
Upper Patuxent River, Maryland	10.0	2.0
Long Island Sound, New York	1.5	0.5
Lower San Francisco Bay, California	20.6	3.8
Upper San Francisco Bay, California	11.5'	2.0
Barataria Bay, Louisiana	4.6	0.8
Victoria Harbor, British Columbia	11.5	2.0
Mid-Chesapeake Bay, Maryland	4.5	0.6
Upper Chesapeake Bay, Maryland	5.0	6.0
Duwamish River, Washington	60.0	3.0
Hudson River, New York	5.0	0.16
Apalachicola Bay, Florida	10.0	0.1
Embayments		
Roskeeda Bay, Ireland	0.4	2.2
Bedford Basin, Nova Scotia	0.6	0.5
Central Kaneohe Bay, Hawaii	0.8	0.3
S.E. Kaneohe Bay, Hawaii	1.0	0.5
St. Margarets Bay, Nova Scotia	1.1	0.5
Vostok Bay, Russia	1.0	0.05
Lagoons		
Beaufort Sound, North Carolina	0.5	0.5
Chincoteague Bay, Maryland	3.2	2.5
Peconic Bay, New York	1.9	1.3
High Venice Lagoon, Italy	2.4	0.05
Fjords		
Baltic Sea	1.3	0.1
Loch Etive, Scotland	1.1	0.06

[a] Nutrient concentrations in μg-atom/l.

Source: Boynton, W. R., Kemp, W. M., and Keefe, C. W., in *Estuarine Comparison,* Kennedy, V. S., Ed., Academic Press, New York, 1982, 69. With permission.

Table 6.4-2 Dissolved and Particulate Nutrient Concentrations in Tropical Aquatic Ecosystems

	NH_4	NO_2–NO_3	DON	PON (µmol/l)	PO_4	DOP	POP	Si
Oceanic (near surface)								
Gulf of Mexico	0.0–0.7	0.0–0.1		0.1–0.6	0.0–0.5			0–3
Subtropical North Pacific		0.1–0.1		0.2–0.3	0.1–0.1			2–3
Equatorial Pacific			6.2–13.8					
Equatorial Atlantic	0.1–0.1	0.0–2.0					0.0–0.1	
South Pacific (Moorea)		–0.1		–0.3	–0.4			–2
Coastal (near surface)								
Campeche Bank	0.0–2.7	0.0–0.3		0.1–5.1	0.0–0.4		0.0–0.1	0–3
Gulf of Papua/Torres Strait	0.0–3.2	0.0–3.1	0.9–13.7		0.3–0.6	0.0–0.2		1–30
Central GBR (18–20S)	0.0–0.5	0.0–0.5	2.4–14.8	1.0–3.8	0.0–0.3	0.0–0.8	0.0–0.2	0–2
Barbados	0.5–2.7	0.4–5.1			0.1–0.2			
Upwelling								
Peru	0.0–3+	0.0–20+		3.0–14+	0.0–2.5+			0–25
Arabian Sea		0.0–20+			0.0–2.0+			0–16
Estuary (near surface)								
Cochin Backwater (India)		0.0–20.3		0.0–150.0				
Missionary Bay (Australia)	0.1–0.4	2.0–7.0		0.1–0.4	0.2–0.6			
Coral reefs, oceanic and atolls								
Canton Atoll	0.1–1.3	0.0–2.4			0.0–0.5			2–3
Enewetak Atoll	0.2–0.3	0.1–0.3	1.7–2.3		–0.2	–0.2		
Tonga Lagoon	0.1–0.7	0.1–1.0	1–23.0	3.0–10.0	0.1–0.9			17–91
Gilbert Islands	0.3–0.5	0.0–2.6	3.8–5.6		0.0–0.4			
Takapoto Atoll	–0.1	–0.2			–0.1			–0
Moorea		–0.1			–0.5			–2
Coral reefs, shelf and fringing								
Kaneohe Bay	0.4–2.4	0.1–2.6	3.4–7.5		0.2–1.0	–0.4		
Jamaica	0.1–3.8				0.0–0.7			
Lizard Island (GBR)	0.1–0.2	0.2–1.0	3–5.0		0.2–0.4			1–2
Davies and Old Reef lagoons (GBR)	–0.2	–0.4			–0.2			–1
Abrolhos Islands	0.1–11.0	0.8–5.2			0.2–2.9	0.0–4.9		1–7

Location							
Rivers							
Amazon	0.7–31.4	–8.5		–0.2			–128
Ganges		35.7–770.0		1.9–652.0			21–2869
Maroni (S. America)		5.0–9.0		–0.2			–191
Niger	–1.0	–7.6					–250
Bermejo (S. America)	0.8–35.7	5.5–52.1		0.8–3.3	0.1–0.8	1.5–230.0	
Orinoco				–0.2			–91
Zaire	–0.4	6.7–7.0		0.1–0.8			165–342
Streams							
Savannah Rivers (Uganda)	<0.4–3.9	0.0–61.0		1.1–30.3			87–603
Wet forest streams (Uganda)	<0.4–9.7	0.0–171.0		0.1–8.2			118–825
Lesser Antilles	<2.8–62.8	<8.1–179.0		0.1–1.5			42–533
Lakes							
Lake Waigani (PNG)	–4.4	–21.6	–723.0	–42.6	–22.0		
Lake Victoria (Uganda)	–28.6	–0.4		–0.3			
Lake Nabugado (Kenya)	–<7			–21.0			
Lake Kyoga (Kenya)	–14.0	14.0		–16.8			–326
Lake Chilwa (Malawi)		2180.0–5114.0		0.0–229.0			
Lagartijo Reservoir		4.3		–0.3			–478
Lakes Robertson/McIlwaine (Zimbabwe)	0.4–8.8	1.3–28.2		0.0–11.8			
Lake Calado (Brazil)	0.0–1.4	0.0–3.2		0.1–0.3			
Lake La Plata (Puerto Rico)	0.0–3.5	0.0–53.0	46.0	1.5–6.8			
Swamps and Wetlands							
Kawaga Swamp (Uganda)	–8.6	–0.3		–0.9			
North Swamp (Kenya)	–3.2	–4.6	–63.0	–871.0	–1.9		
Tasek Bara (Malaysia)	0.0–54.7	0.7–20.7	4–109.0	0.0–3.4	1.1–25.2	–30.6	–52
Papyrus swamps (Uganda)	–<0.4	0.0–30.3		0.2–1.3			34–558

Note: 0.0 = nondetectable; DON = dissolved organic nitrogen; PON = particulate organic nitrogen; DOP = dissolved organic phosphorus; POP = particulate organic phosphorus.

Source: Furnas, M. J., in *Pollution in Tropical Aquatic Systems*, Connell, D. W. and Hawker, D. W., Eds., CRC Press, Boca Raton, FL, 1992, 29. With permission.

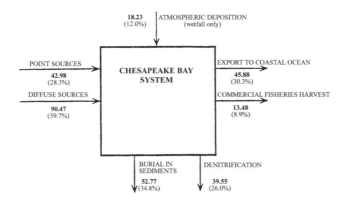

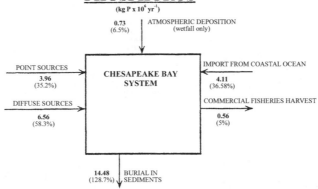

Figure 6.4–3 Simplified annual total nitrogen (TN) and total phosphorus (TP) budgets for the entire Chesapeake Bay system. (From Boynton, W.R., *Estuaries,* 18, 285, 1995. With permission.)

Table 6.4–3 **Summary of Average Annual Stocks (1985 and 1986) of Particulate and Dissolved Nitrogen and Phosphorus in the Water Column, Sediments, and Biota for Selected Areas of Chesapeake Bay**

	Nutrient Stocks	Maryland Mainstem Bay		Potomac River		Patuxent River		Choptank River	
		N	P	N	P	N	P	N	P
Water column[a]	Dissolved								
	Inorganic	9.11	0.333	2.76	0.159	0.13	0.018	0.26	0.028
	Organic	7.51	0.159	2.92	0.201	0.26	0.024	0.56	0.052
	Particulate	3.26	0.606	0.95	0.295	0.16	0.031	0.29	0.037
	Total	19.73	1.098	6.63	0.655	0.55	0.073	1.21	0.117
Sediment[b]	Dissolved	0.52	0.014	0.39	0.004	0.01	0.003	0.04	0.016
	Particulate	214.01	36.370	57.88	11.830	7.38	2.120	18.80	3.660
	Total	214.53	36.384	58.27	11.834	7.39	2.123	18.84	3.676
Biota	Macrozooplankton[c]	0.17	0.020	0.03	0.003	0.00	0.001	0.02	0.002
	Benthic	3.34	0.406	0.68	0.083	0.10	0.012	0.10	0.012
	Total macrofauna[d]	3.51	0.426	0.71	0.086	0.10	0.013	0.12	0.012

Note: All entries have units of kg $\times$ 10^6 N or P. See original source for specific references for these findings.

[a] Water-column data are from Magnien et al. (1990).
[b] Sediment data are from Boynton and Kemp (1985), Boynton et al. (1990), and J. Cornwell (personal communication).
[c] Macrozooplankton data are from Jacobs (1989).
[d] Benthic macrofauna data are from Holland et al. (1989).

Source: Boynton, W. R. et al., *Estuaries*, 18, 285, 1995. With permission.

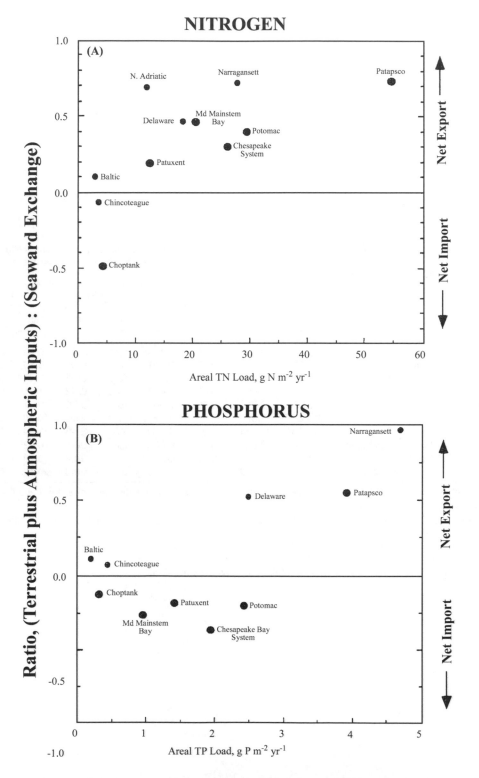

Figure 6.4–4 Scatter plots of annual areal loading rates of (A) nitrogen and (B) phosphorus vs. annual areal export:import ratio for Chesapeake Bay sites and several other locations where appropriate information is available. (From Boynton, W. R. et al., *Estuaries,* 18, 285, 1995. With permission.)

Table 6.4–4 Summary of Annual Loadings of TN and TP from Terrestrial and Atmospheric Sources for the Chesapeake Region[d]

Location	Point Sources TN[a]		Diffuse Sources TN[a]		Atmospheric Sources TN[c] (wet-fall)	Total Load (kg/year)	Areal Load (g/m²/year)
	AFL[b]	BFL[b]	AFL[b]	BFL[b]			
Nitrogen Inputs							
Maryland Mainstem Bay	9.48	9.67	50.72	4.49	6.24	80.60	20.54
Potomac River	2.64	9.30	19.76	1.87	1.92	35.49	29.33
Patuxent River	0.61	0.22	0.21	0.47	0.22	1.73	12.63
Choptank River	0.00	0.14	0.12	0.71	0.57	1.54	4.27
Phosphorus Inputs							
Maryland Mainstem Bay	ND	1.041	2.100	0.360	0.251	3.752	0.96
Potomac River	0.620	0.140	1.880	0.210	0.077	2.927	2.42
Patuxent River	0.070	0.046	0.010	0.060	0.090	0.195	1.42
Choptank River	0.000	0.052	0.010	0.030	0.023	0.115	0.32

Note: All entries have units of kg × 10⁶ TN or TP per year. TN = total nitrogen; TP = total phosphorus. See original source for specific references for these findings.

[a] Point and diffuse data are from Summers (1989) and were averaged for 1985 and 1986.
[b] Above fall-line (AFL) point and diffuse sources are measured as a composite at the fall-line. The relative contributions of point and diffuse sources were estimated by subtracting known above fall-line point sources from the total load measured at the fall-line. In one case the point source load slightly exceeded the combined load presumably because of TP losses during transport in the river. In all cases the sum of above fall-line point and diffuse sources is equal to the load measured at the fall-line. BFL refers to below the fall-line.
[c] Atmospheric deposition data are from Smullen et al. (1982) and were averaged for the period 1976 to 1981.
[d] Point and diffuse sources located above and below the fall-line are differentiated. The atmospheric source (wet-fall) includes deposition directly to surface waters.

Source: Boynton, W. R. et al., Estuaries, 18, 285, 1995. With permission.

Table 6.4–5 External Nitrogen (TN) and Phosphorus (TP) Loadings (10³ kg/year), Total Nitrogen to Phosphorus Loading Ratios (Atomic), Watershed and Estuarine Areas (km²), Watershed to Estuarine Area Ratios, and Watershed and Estuarine Area Normalized Loading (kg/km²/year) for the Upper Chesapeake Bay, Patuxent Estuary, and Potomac Estuary during 1985–1989

System	Total Load			Head of Estuary Load			Head of Estuary Load as a Percent of the Total Load		Watershed Area	Estuarine Area	Ratio of Watershed to Estuarine Area	Watershed Area Normalized Load		Estuarine Area Normalized Load	
	TN	TP	TN:TP	TN	TP	TN:TP	TN	TP				TN	TP	TN	TP
Mainstem	84,100	36.38	51	59,511	2167	61	71	60	86,979	3200	27	967	41.8	26,281	1137
Patuxent	1,981	152.6	29	1,182	88	30	60	58	2,358	141	17	840	64.7	14,050	1082
Potomac	37,357	2344	35	32,008	2007	35	86	86	36,563	1251	29	1022	64.1	29,862	1874

Source: Magnien, R. E. et al., Estuaries, 15, 497, 1992. With permission.

Table 6.4–6   Nitrogen (TN) and Phosphorus (TP) Loadings (10^3 kg/year) of Wastewater Treatment Plants (WWTPs) in the Patuxent River Watershed and the Estimated Total External Load Delivered to the Patuxent Estuary from 1963 to 1989

Year	WWTP Load			Total Load		
	TN	TP	TN:TP	TN	TP	TN:TP
1963	74	19	9	930	170	12
1967	300	78	9	—	—	—
1969–1971	—	—	—	1110	250	10
1973	624	169	8	—	—	—
1978	798	193	9	1500	420	8
1985	815	138	13	1771	187	21
1986	842	65	29	1745	140	27
1987	859	57	33	1972	143	30
1988	866	50	38	1987	116	37
1989	855	50	38	2441	166	32

Source: Magnien, R. E. et al., *Estuaries,* 15, 497, 1992. With permission.

Table 6.4–7   Nutrient Loading (kg × 10^6/year) of the Upper Potomac River Basin from 1983 to 1988

Year	River Flow[a]	Total		Oxidized Nitrogen	Total Nitrogen
		Suspended Solids	Total Phosphorus		
1983	413.6	1441.4	2.50	18.0	29.4
1984	463.1	1604.5	3.07	20.6	35.2
1985	324.5	2950.4	3.82	12.7	27.4
1986	228.6	769.1	1.25	9.8	16.2
1987	321.2	960.4	1.91	13.9	23.4
1988	245.1	977.2	1.79	9.2	16.9
Average	332.6	1450.5	2.39	14.0	24.8

[a] Flow = average daily discharge in m^3/s.

Source: Jaworski, N. A. et al., *Estuaries*, 15, 83, 1992. With permission.

Figure 6.4–5   Monthly river ammonia- and nitrate-nitrogen loading (kg × 10^6/month) for the Potomac River (1983 to 1986). (From Jaworski, N. A. et al., *Estuaries,* 15, 83, 1992. With permission.)

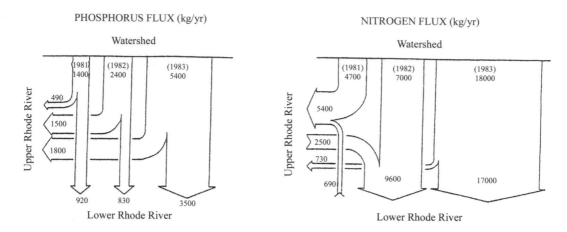

Figure 6.4–6   Variability of annual phosphorus and nitrogen fluxes into and out of the upper Rhode River estuary. (From Correll, D.L. et al., *Estuaries,* 15, 431, 1992. With permission.)

6.5 ORGANIC CARBON

Table 6.5–1   Concentrations of Organic Carbon in Natural Waters

Conc. of Organic Carbon (mg/l)	River	Estuary	Coastal Sea	Open Sea Surface	Deep	Sewage
Dissolved	10–20 (50)	1–5 (20)	1–5 (20)	1–1.5	0.5–0.8	100
Particulate	5–10	0.5–5	0.1–1.0	0.01–1.0	0.003–0.01	200
Total	15–30 (60)	1–10 (25)	1–6 (21)	1–2.5	0.5–0.8	300

Note: Numbers in parentheses represent extreme values.

Source: Head, P. C., in *Estuarine Chemistry,* Burton, J. D. and Liss, P. S., Eds., Academic Press, London, 1976, 53. Copyright 1976 Academic Press, Inc. (London) Ltd. With permission.

Table 6.5–2 Seasonal Maxima and Minima of Dissolved Organic Matter in Rivers

Location	Measurement	Maximum (Time, conc.)	Minimum (Time, conc.)	Remarks
Ganges River, Bangladesh	DOC	July 9.3 mg/l	June 1.3 mg/l	Max near crest
	Carbohydrate	June 1120 μg/l	October 141 μg/l	
	Amino acids	July 616 μg/l	March 150 μg/l	
Brahmaputra River	DOC	July 6.5 mg/l	Rest of year 1.3–2.6 mg/l	Rising water maximum
	Amino acids	August 262 μg/l	March 79 μg/l	
	Carbohydrate	July 985 μg/l	October 155 μg/l	
Indus River	DOC	Aug.–Sept. 22 mg/l	Low-flow period 1.2 mg/l min	Maximum range
Amazon River	DOC	May–June 6.5 mg/l	Feb.–March 4.2 mg/l	
Orinoco River, Venezuela	DOC	May and Dec. 5 and 4 mg/l	Jun.–Nov. 2–3 mg/l	
Gambia River, West Africa	DOC	September 3.7 mg/l	December 1.3 mg/l	
Columbia River	TOC	Spring-summer 3.2 mg/l	Late fall 1.8 mg/l	~89% dissolved
Tigris River, Iraq	DOM	April 13.7–21.5 mg O/l	October 0.3–1.6 mg O/l	As O_2 demand
Caroni River, Venezuela	DOC	Aug. and Jan. 8 mg/l	November 4 mg/l	Humic rich
Ems River, Netherlands	DOC	February 12 mg/l	Aug.–Sept. 4–5 mg/l	Increase in fall–winter
Guatemalan rivers	DOM	June–July 4–36 mg/l	June or Oct. 3–5 mg/l	Peak discharge July–August
Alaskan rivers	DOC	Variable 4–6 mg/l	Aug.–Sept. 1–2 mg/l	
Shetucket River, CT	DOC	May and Sept. 6.2–10 mg/l	Jan.–April 2–4 mg/l	Max. 26.4 mg/l in runoff
Ogeechee River, GA	DOC	Jan.–May 12–15 mg/l	Aug.–Dec. 6–8 mg/l	To 17 mg/l July storm
Westerwoldse Aa, Neth.	DOC	December 48 mg/l	July 13 mg/l	Winter pollution
Black Creek, GA	DOC	Jan.–May 31–38 mg/l	June–Dec. 14–28 mg/l	To 42 mg/l in storm
N. Carolina stream	DOC	July and Oct. 1.1 and 1.3 mg/l	April 0.4 mg/l	Undisturbed watershed
	DOC	July and Oct. 0.5 and 0.6 mg/l	April–May 0.3 mg/l	Clear-cut watershed
Little Miami River, OH	DOC	No pattern 12.5 mg/l	No pattern 2.5 mg/l	Pollution related
Loire River, France	DOC	Jan.–April, Dec. 5–6 mg/l	May 2.5 mg/l	
White Clay Cr., PA	DOC	Summer–fall 2–2.5 mg/l	Winter 1–1.5 mg/l	Higher DOC downstream
White Clay Cr., PA	DOC	Autumn 9–12 mg/l	Mid-winter 2–4 mg/l	To 18 mg/l fall peak
Hubbard Br., NH	DOC	No pattern 2 mg/l	No pattern <0.1 mg/l	Max. and min. in fall
Moorland Stream, U.K.	DOM	August up to 30 mg/l	February 0–3 mg/l	Peak flow in August

Note: DOC = dissolved organic carbon; DOM = dissolved organic matter; TOC = total organic carbon.

Source: Wotton, R. S., Ed., *The Biology of Particles in Aquatic Systems,* CRC Press, Boca Raton, FL, 1990, 85. With permission.

Table 6.5–3   Seasonal Maxima and Minima of Particulate Organic Matter in Rivers

Location	Measurement	Maximum (Time, conc.)	Minimum (Time, conc.)	Remarks
Ganges River, Bangladesh	Amino acids	July 2395 µg/l	March 24 µg/l	
	Carbohydrate	July 1672 µg/l	March 46 µg/l	
Indus River, Pakistan	POC	Aug. (1981–82) up to 16 mg/l	Feb. or April 0.3 mg/l	June and Sept. peaks (1983)
	Amino acids	Aug. or Sept. 659–2009 µg/l	Oct. or April 127–277 µg/l	Irregular sampling
	Carbohydrate	Aug. or Sept. 412–1105 µg/l	Feb., April, May 58–122 µg/l	Irregular sampling
Yangtze River, China	POC	July 17 mg/l	Jan.–Feb. 3 mg/l	Averages
Amazon River, near mouth	POC	Feb.–March 8.2 mg/l	May–June 1–2 mg/l	
Amazon River, upstream	POC	Feb.–March 15–20 mg/l	May–June 3.7 mg/l	
Guatemalan rivers	POC	June 7 mg/l	Nov.–April Undetected	Tributaries to 15 mg/l
Orinoco River, Venezuela	POC	No pattern 2.5 mg/l	No pattern 1 mg/l	
Gambia River, West Africa	POC	Early Sept. 2 mg/l	Oct.–Nov. 0.3 mg/l	No relation to discharge
Columbia River	POC	Summer 860 µg/l	Winter 2 µg/l	Highly variable
St. Lawrence River	POC (means)	May and Nov. 0.67 and 0.69 µg/l	February 0.24 mg/l	May, terrigenous; Nov., in situ
Erriff River, Ireland	POC	No pattern 4 mg/l	No pattern 0.25 mg/l	Runoff-related peaks
Bundorragha River, Ireland	POC	No pattern 0.9 mg/l	No pattern 0.3 mg/l	Steeper basin than Erriff
Loire River, France	POC	May–Aug. 6 mg/l	Nov. and March 2–3 mg/l	Increased at low water
Chalk Stream, England	POM	Fall–winter 10–12 mg/l	Summer 1–2 mg/l	Dry weight

Note: POC = particulate organic carbon; POM = particulate organic matter.

Source: Wotton, R. S., Ed., The Biology of Particles in Aquatic Systems, CRC Press, Boca Raton, FL, 1990, 88. With permission.

Table 6.5–4 Predominant Organic Compounds in Some Canadian Rivers

Sample Location	DOC (mg/l)	Rel. Color (col. units)	Humic Acid (mg/l)	Fulvic Acid (mg/l)	Tannins and Lignins (mg/l)	Phenols (mg/l)	Carbohydrate (mg/l)	Amino Acids (µg/l)	Total Pesticides (µg/l)
Thompson River at Savona (B.C.)	6	17	N.D.	2.1	0.4	N.D.	0.03	172	0.006
Saskatchewan River above Carrot River	13	10	1.7	8.0	1.3	N.D.	0.1	High	0.006
Yukon River at Dawson (Yukon)	5		N.D.	2.7	0.6	N.D.	0.2	676	0.002
Qu'Appelle River at Welby (Sask.)	12	20	0.8	12.0	1.4	N.D.	0.07	Low	0.004
Moose River at Mouth (Ont.)	18		7.1	11.3	4.0		N.D.	291	0.017
Richelieu River at St. Helaire (Que.)	8	10	N.D.	7.7	0.3	N.D.	0.09	189	0.006
St. Lawrence River at Levis (Que.)		10	0.3	6.8	0.7	0.003	0.08	Low	0.004
Annapolis River at Wilmot (NS)	7		0.6	5.2	1.2	N.D.		253	N.D.
St. John River at Woodstock (NB)	14	30	N.D.	12.6	4.0	N.D.	0.1	203	0.001
Exploits River at Millertown (Newf.)	7		0.6	5.5	1.4	N.D.	0.11	100	0.004

Note: DOC = dissolved organic carbon; N.D. = not detected.

Source: Afghan, B. K. and Chau, A. S. Y., Analysis of Trace Organics in the Aquatic Environment, CRC Press, Boca Raton, FL, 1989, 316. With permission.

Table 6.5–5   Seasonal Maxima and Minima of Dissolved Organic Matter in Estuaries and Coastal Marine Waters

Location	Measurement	Maximum (Time, conc.)	Minimum (Time, conc.)	Remarks
Estuary, Netherlands	DOC	Summer 4–5 mg/l	Fall 2 mg/l	Near mouth
	Amino acids	March 0.8 mg/l	Sept. 0.1 mg C/l	Near mouth
	DOC	No pattern 13 mg/l	No pattern 8 mg/l	
	DOC	June and July 2 mg/l	March and Nov. 0.3–0.5 mg/l	Autochthonous
	Amino acids	July 0.6–0.8 mg C/l	Feb.–March 0.1 mg C/l	Highest near mouth
Nile estuary	DOM (O$_2$ demand)	August 9.05 mg O/l	December 2.37 mg O/l	Temperature-dependent changes
Maine estuary	DOC	Summer 5–7 mg/l	Winter 1–2 mg/l	Up to 12.6 mg/l
	DFAA	No pattern 300 nM/l	No pattern 100 nM/l	Some summer low values
English Channel	DOC	March, July, Aug., Oct. 1.8–2.2 mg/l	March, April, June 0.8–1.2 mg/l	Lagged Chlorophyll *a*
	DON	Late summer 7 μmol N/1	Winter Undetectable	Summarized Station EI
	DFAA	Winter 3–4 μmol N/l	Summer 1 μmol N/l	
	DOC	June and Sept. 0.88 and 0.96 mg/l	March .56 mg/l	
	DON	April and Aug. 5–6 μg-atN/l	October 2.5 μg-atN/l	
Southern North Sea	DOC	Spring 1.7 mg/l	Winter 0.4 mg/l	Summer-up, autumn-down
Dutch Wadden Sea	DOC	May–June 4–5 mg/l	Winter 1–2 mg/l	Tidal inlet
Maine coast	DFAA	May 88 μg C/l	December 10 μg C/l	July & Oct. peaks
Louisiana coast	DOC	October 3 mg/l	January 1.5 mg/l	<Full year
Gulf of Naples	DOC	No pattern 31.4 mg/l	No pattern 0.4 mg/l	*Posidonia* seagrass bed
Strait of Georgia, B.C.	DOC	Summer 3 mg/l	November 1 mg/l	
Coastal pond, Cape Cod	Carbohydrate	April 2.9 mg/l	February 1.3 mg/l	Inverse to chlorophyll
Menai Strait, England	DOC	Autumn 3–4 mg/l	Winter 1 mg/l	Spring–fall increase
Irish Sea	DFAA	May and Sept. 31 and 25 μg/l	Feb. and Aug. 5–10 μg/1	Late bloom maximum
	Total AA	Jan. and July 120 and 111 μg/l	February 2 μg/l	Little pattern

Note: DOC = dissolved organic carbon; DOM = dissolved organic material; DFAA = dissolved free amino acid; DON = dissolved organic nitrogen; AA = amino acid.

Source: Wotton, R. S., Ed., *The Biology of Particles in Aquatic Systems,* CRC Press, Boca Raton, FL, 1990, 95. With permission.

Table 6.5–6 Concentration Ranges (μg/l) of the Major Identified Groups of Dissolved Organic Substances in Natural Waters

Dissolved Organic Substances	Rain	Groundwater	River	Lake	Sea
Volatile fatty acids	10	40	100	100	40
Nonvolatile fatty acids	5–17	5–50	50–500	50–200	5–50
Amino acids	—	20–350	50–1000	30–6000	20–250
Carbohydrates	—	65–125	100–2000	100–3000	100–1000
Aldehydes	—	—	~0.1	—	0.01–0.1

Source: Wotton, R. S., Ed., *The Biology of Particles in Aquatic Systems,* CRC Press, Boca Raton, FL, 1990, 119. With permission.

Table 6.5–7 Seasonal Maxima and Minima of Particulate Organic Matter in Estuarine and Coastal Marine Waters

Location	Measurement	Maximum (Time, conc.)	Minimum (Time, conc.)	Remarks
Estuary, Netherlands	Amino acids	May 1.5–1.6 mg C/l	February Near zero	Lower estuary
	Amino acids	July 4.2 mg C/l	February 0.1–0.2 mg C/l	Upper estuary
	POC	Summer 3 mg/l	Sept.–Feb. 1 mg/l	Lower estuary
	POC	No pattern 8–9 mg/l	No pattern Near zero	Upper estuary
	Amino acids	May 1.7 mg C/l	October <0.1 mg C/l	Lower estuary
	POC	Aug.–Oct. 10–20 mg/l	Nov.–July 2–8 mg/l	
Arabian Sea estuary	POC	June and Aug. 5.24 mg/l	Oct.–Jan. 0.28 mg/l	Max. during monsoons
Estuary, Brazil	TSM	Summer 78.2 mg/l	Winter 6.9 mg/l	TSM about 60% organic
	POC	Jan. and Nov. 2.1 mg/l	July and Oct. 0.6 and 0.3 mg/l	Near mouth
	POC	February 3.2 mg/l	July 0.5 mg/l	Upper estuary
Dutch Wadden Sea	POC	May 4–6 mg/l	Winter 0.5–1.0 mg/l	Tidal inlet
English Channel	POC	April and July 386 and 320 μg/l	Sept.–May 120–1.44 μg/l	
	PON	April and July 50 and 37 μg N/l	Sept.–March 8–17 μg N/l	
Galveston Bay, TX	Protein	May–June and Aug. 1.7 mg/l	January 0.2 mg/l	0.6 mg/l mid-August
	Carbohydrate	September 530 μg/l	Dec. and Aug. Near zero	Weak seasonal pattern
	Lipid	September 0.8 mg/l	February 0.1 mg/l	Similar to CHO pattern
Gulf of Naples	POM dry weight	No pattern 30 mg/l	No pattern 3.5 mg/l	*Posidonia* beds
Coastal Arabian Sea	POC	Nov. (30 m) 2.51 mg/l	May (surface) 0.52 mg/l	
Puget Sound	POC	July 40 μg/l	Sep.–March 50–100 μg/l	Surface

Table 6.5–7   Seasonal Maxima and Minima of Particulate Organic Matter in Estuarine and Coastal Marine Waters (continued)

Location	Measurement	Maximum (Time, conc.)	Minimum (Time, conc.)	Remarks
N. Dawes Inlet, AK	POC	July 1.22 mg/l	November 0.24 mg/l	
Funka Bay, Japan	POC	July 11.5 g C/m²	Early October 3.5 g C/m²	Integrated upper 50 m
	Protein	February 3 g C/m²	Early October 1.5 g C/m²	Integrated upper 50 m
Tripoli Harbor	POC	August 1.3 mg/l	Nov.–April 0.9–1.1 mg/l	Surface
Strait of Georgia, B. C.	POC	Summer 400 μg/l	November 170 μg/l	Seasonal means
Coastal S. California	POC	Feb. and March 351 and 235 μg/l	September 191 μg/l	Coastal stations

Note: POC = particulate organic carbon; TSM = total suspended material; PON = particulate organic nitrogen; POM = particulate organic matter.

Source: Wotton, R. S., Ed., *The Biology of Particles in Aquatic Systems,* CRC Press, Boca Raton, FL, 1990, 97. With permission.

Table 6.5–8   Seasonal Maxima and Minima of Dissolved Organic Matter in Saltmarsh Waters

Location	Measurement	Maximum (Time, conc.)	Minimum (Time, conc.)	Remarks
Texas marsh	DOC	July 37 mg/l	Winter 11–12 mg/l	
Louisiana bays	DOC	Early January 11.5 mg/l	Late Jan.–Nov. 5 mg/l	Minor changes after January
Estuary, SC	DOC	February 10.7 mg/l	July 3.2 mg/l	Flow-related variability
	DON	Jan. and Aug. 32–38 μg-atN/l	Sep., March, May 18–19 μg-atN/l	
	DOP	July 0.7 μg-atP/l	Nov.–Feb., Sept. Undetected	
Marsh, SC	DOC	Feb.–May 18.6 mg/l	December 3.1 mg/l	Runoff-related maximum
Marsh, VA	DON	Summer 1 mg/l	Winter 0.1 mg/l	
Tidal creek, SC	DOC	Fall 3.9 mg/l	Summer 2.8 mg/l	Seasonal means
Marsh, VA	DOP	July 0.25 mg/l	January <0.05 mg/l	
Duplin River, GA	DOC	Summer 9.6 and 9.2 mg/l	Winters 4.9 and 3.6 mg/l	Surface and bottom
Flax Pond, NY	DOC	July 2.5 mg/l	Jan.–March 1.5 mg/l	Extreme values

Note: DOC = dissolved organic carbon; DON = dissolved organic nitrogen; DOP = dissolved organic particles.

Source: Wotton, R. S., Ed., *The Biology of Particles in Aquatic Systems,* CRC Press, Boca Raton, FL, 1990, 92. With permission.

Table 6.5–9   Seasonal Maxima and Minima of Particulate Organic Matter in Saltmarsh Waters

Location	Measurement	Maximum (Time, conc.)	Minimum (Time, conc.)	Remarks
Texas marsh	POC	July 5–7 mg/l	Winter 3–4 mg/l	Usual values, not extremes
Louisiana bays	POC	Feb.–March 5–6 mg/l	Rest of year Negligible	
Marsh, SC	POC	Summer 4.6 mg/l	December 0.7 mg/l	
'	POC	Summer 2–3 mg/l	Winter ~1 mg/l	
	Particulate N	July 17 μg-atN/l	January 2 μg-atN/l	
	Particulate P	Sept. and Aug. 1.2–1.3 μg-atP/l	January 0.1 μg-atP/l	
Duplin River, GA	POC	Summer 5.9 and 4.3 mg/l	Winter 1.8 and 1.5 mg/l	Surface and bottom
Flax Pond, NY	POC	March and May 2.0 and 2.1 mg/l	Jan. and Dec. 0.2 mg/l	
Dill Creek, SC	POM	August 58.5 mg/l	Sept. and Dec. 0.4 and 0.5 mg/l	
Marsh, MA	POC	March and Sept. 1.0 and 1.6 mg/l	April–Aug., Nov. 0.03–0.6 mg/l	698

Note: POC = particulate organic carbon; POM = particulate organic matter.

Source: Wotton, R. S., Ed., *The Biology of Particles in Aquatic Systems,* CRC Press, Boca Raton, FL, 1990, 93. With permission.

Table 6.5–10   Accumulation of Organic Matter in Marine Sediments

	Percentage of Primary Production Accreting in Sediments	Sedimentation Rate (mm/year)
Oceanic sediments		
Abyssal plain, average of several sites	0.03–0.04	0.001
Central Pacific	<0.01	0.001–0.006
Off northwest Africa, Oregon, and Argentina	0.1–2	0.02–0.7
Peru upwelling, Baltic	11–18	1.4
Saltmarsh sediments		
Cape Cod, U.S.	5.3	1
Long Island, U.S.	37	2–6.3

Source: Valiela, I., *Marine Ecological Processes,* 2nd ed., Springer-Verlag, New York, 1995. With permission.

**Table 6.5–11   Accumulation of Organic Matter in *Spartina*
Marshes**

Area	TNPP Accumulating in Sediments (%)	Sedimentation Rate (mm/year)
Massachusetts	5.3	1
New York	37	2–6.3
	0	−9.5–37
North Carolina	75	>1.2
South Carolina	0	1.3

Source: Dame, R. F., *Rev. Aquat. Sci.,* 1, 639, 1989. With
permission.

**Table 6.5–12   Carbon Budget from the Major Organic
Decomposition Processes in the Sediments of a
New England Salt Marsh and Short Belowground
Spartina Production at the Same Site**

Process	Carbon Fluxes (g/m²/year)	BNPP (%)
Decomposition		
Aerobic respiration	361	31.7
Fermentation + sulfate reduction	432	37.9
Nitrate reduction	5	0.4
Methanogenesis	6	0.5
Burial	89	7.8
Export (as DOC)	36	3.2
Total losses	929	
Belowground production	1140	

Note: Decomposition was measured in terms of carbon dioxide.
DOC = dissolved organic carbon. BNPP = belowground net
primary production.

Source: Dame, R. F., *Rev. Aquat. Sci.,* 1, 639, 1989. With permission.

**Table 6.5–13   Yearly Carbon, Nitrogen, and Phosphorus Flux
in North Inlet on an Area of Marsh Basis**

	Carbon	Nitrogen	Phosphorus
POC	128		
DOC	328		
NH₄		6.3	
NO₂ + NO₃		0.9	
TN		42.7	
PO₄			1.7
TP			3.1
ATP	22	3.3	0.2
CHL-*a*	1.8	0.27	0.016
Zooplankton	−1.2	−0.26	−0.010
Macrodetritus	0.9	0.01	0.001
Birds	0.05	0.01	0.001

Note: C, N, and P fluxes in g/m²/year; drainage area = 2380 ha;
import = −; export = + (sign not shown).

Source: Dame, R. F., *Rev. Aquat. Sci.,* 1, 639, 1989. With permission.

Table 6.5–14 Flux Estimates from a Number of Marsh–Estuarine Systems Dominated by *Spartina alterniflora*

System	Type	POC	DOC	TOC	NH$_4$	NN	DON	PN	TN	PO$_4$	TP
Crommet Creek	I	68			2.1	0.3				0.6	3.2
Flax Pond	I		−8	53	−2.0	1.0				−1.4	−0.3
Canary Creek	I	−62	−38	−100	0.7	1.9	−0.9	−2.9	−1.2	−0.1	
Bly Creek	I	38	−260	−222	−0.8	0.3	−14.6	2.8	−12.5	−0.2	−0.7
Sippewissett	II	−76			−4.2	−3.9	−9.8	−6.7	−24.6	−0.6	
Gott's Marsh	II	−7			−0.4	−0.9	−2.1	−0.3	−3.7		−0.3
Rhode River	II					−3800			−8400		−2200
Ware Creek	II	−35	−80	−115	−2.9	2.2	−2.3		−2.8	−0.1	0.7
North Inlet	II	−128	−328	−456	−6.3	−0.9			−42.7		
Dill Creek	II	−303									−6.4
Sapelo Island	II	−208	−108	−316							
Carter Creek	III	−116	−25	−141	−0.3	0.3	−9.2	4.6	−4.0	−0.6	

Note: All values are in grams per square meter per year of marsh.

Source: Dame, R. F., *Rev. Aquat. Sci.,* 1, 639, 1989. With permission.

Table 6.5–15   Net Annual Fluxes of Particulate and Dissolved Carbon,
               Nitrogen, and Phosphorus from the Coral Creek System
               (Northeastern Australia) via Tidal Transport

Component	Net Annual Exchange (g/m²/year)	Proportion of Forest Primary Production Requirements (%)
Particulate Matter (mainly intact mangrove plant detritus)		
Particulate organic C	−327	−35.9
Particulate organic N	−3.7	−13.4
Particulate organic P	−0.25	−12.2
Dissolved Materials		
Dissolved organic C	7.3	0.8
Dissolved organic N	1.3	4.7
Dissolved organic P	0.37	17.9
NH_4	0.15	0.6
$NO_3 + NO_2$	−0.03	−0.1
PO_4	0.13	6.3
Total dissolved N	1.45	5.4
Total dissolved P	0.50	24.2

Note: The exchange rates are given in terms of forest area contained within
        the Coral Creek basin and in terms of net forest primary production
        requirements. A negative sign denotes net export.

Source: Connell, D. W. and Hawker, D. W., Eds., *Pollution in Tropical Aquatic
Systems,* CRC Press, Boca Raton, FL, 1992. 135. With permission.

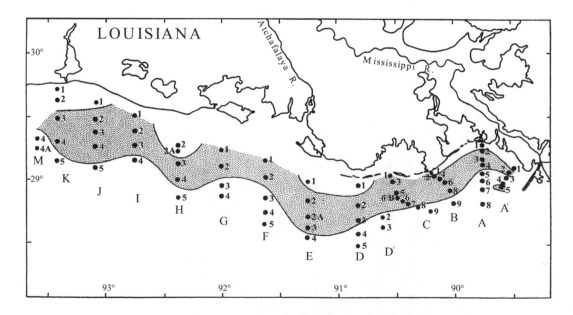

Figure 6.5–1 Distribution of hypoxic near-bottom waters off the Louisiana coastline in the Gulf of Mexico,
        July 16–20, 1991. (From Dortch, Z. et al., *Estuaries,* 17, 862, 1994. With permission.)

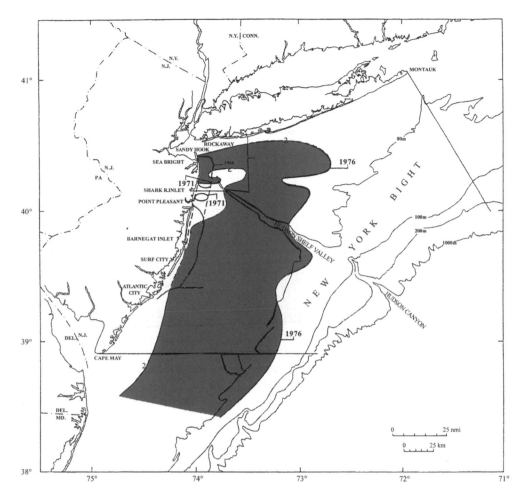

Figure 6.5–2 Approximate regions of oxygen-depleted (<2 ml/l) bottom waters in the New York Bight in 1968, 1971, 1974, 1976, and 1977. (From O'Connor, J. S., *A Perspective on Natural and Human Factors, MESA New York Bight*, State University of New York, Stony Brook, 1976. With permission.)

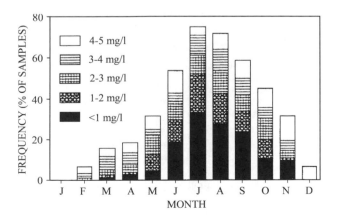

Figure 6.5–3 Frequency of five dissolved oxygen concentration ranges recorded at four monitoring stations in the Pamlico River estuary for the period 1975 to 1989. (From Stanley, D. W. and Nixon, S. W., *Estuaries,* 15, 270, 1992. With permission.)

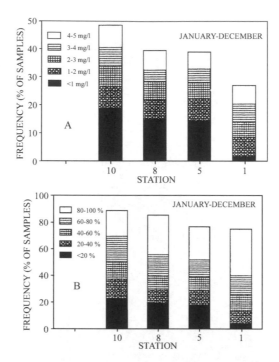

Figure 6.5–4 Frequency of five dissolved oxygen ranges (A) and percent saturation ranges (B) for each of four monitoring stations in the Pamlico River estuary for the period 1975 to 1989. (From Stanley, D. W. and Nixon, S.W., *Estuaries,* 15, 270, 1992. With permission.)

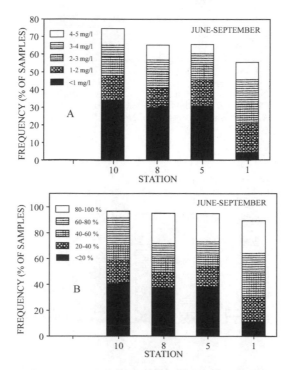

Figure 6.5–5 Frequency of five dissolved oxygen ranges (A) and percent saturation ranges (B) for each of four monitoring stations in the Pamlico River estuary for the period 1975 to 1989 (June to September data only). (From Stanley, D. W. and Nixon, S. W., *Estuaries,* 15, 270, 1992. With permission.)

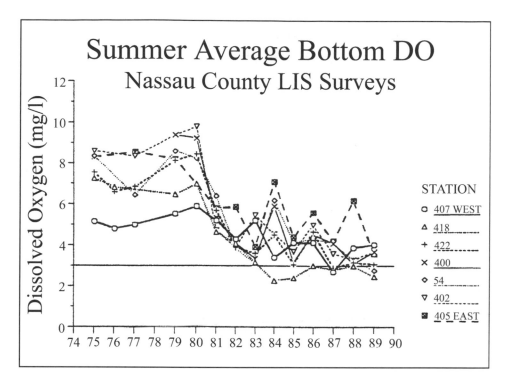

Figure 6.5–6 Summer average bottom dissolved oxygen values recorded at Nassau County Long Island Sound monitoring stations between 1975 and 1989. (From Parker, C. A. and O'Reilly, J. E., *Estuaries,* 14, 248, 1991. With permission.)

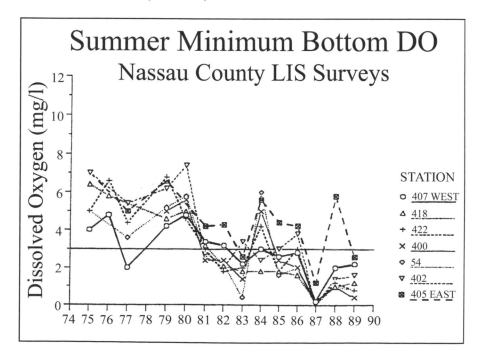

Figure 6.5–7 Summer minimum bottom dissolved oxygen values recorded at Nassau County Long Island Sound monitoring stations between 1975 and 1989. (From Parker, C. A. and O'Reilly, J. E., *Estuaries,* 14, 248, 1991. With permission.)

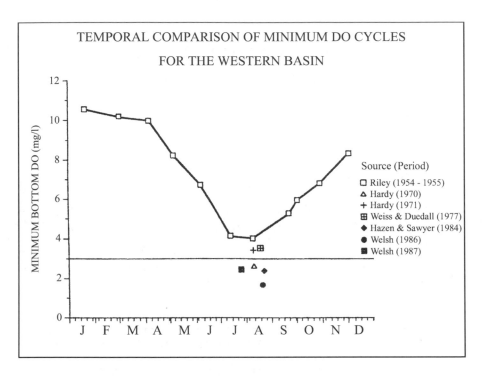

Figure 6.5–8 Temporal comparison of minimum bottom dissolved oxygen conditions for the western basin of Long Island Sound. (From Parker, C. A. and O'Reilly, J. E., *Estuaries,* 14, 248, 1991. With permission.)

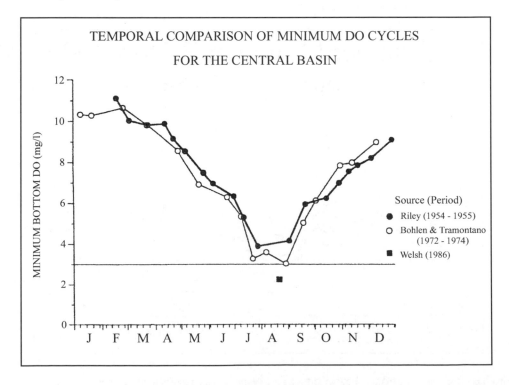

Figure 6.5–9 Temporal comparison of minimum bottom dissolved oxygen conditions for the central basin of Long Island Sound. (From Parker, C. A. and O'Reilly, J. E., *Estuaries,* 14, 248, 1991. With permission.)

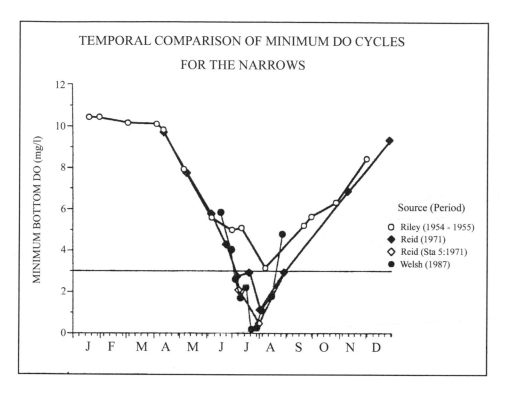

Figure 6.5–10 Temporal comparison of minimum bottom dissolved oxygen conditions for the Narrows of Long Island Sound. (From Parker, C. A. and O'Reilly, J. E., *Estuaries,* 14, 248, 1991. With permission.)

6.6 SEWAGE WASTE

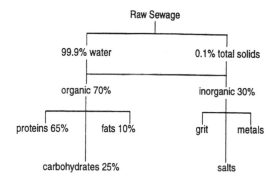

Figure 6.6–1 Composition of a typical raw sewage. (Adapted from Harrison, R. M., Ed., *Pollution: Causes, Effects, and Control,* 2nd ed., Royal Society of Chemistry, Cambridge, 1990. With permission.)

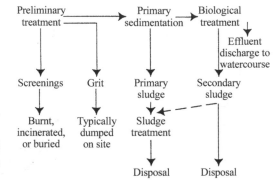

Figure 6.6–2 Flow diagram of a conventional sewage treatment works. (From Harrison, R. M., Ed., *Pollution: Causes, Effects, and Control,* 2nd ed., Royal Society of Chemistry, Cambridge, 1990. With permission.)

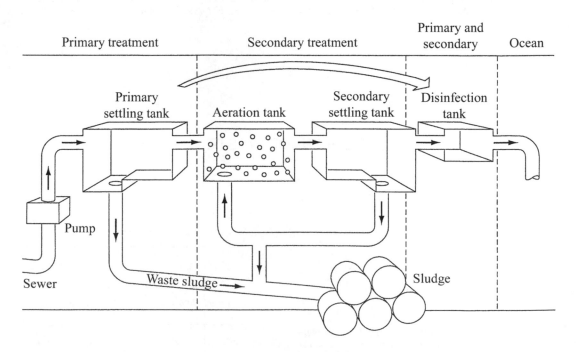

Figure 6.6–3 Scheme of primary and secondary treatment of sewage effluent and sludge. (From Duedall, I. W., *Oceanus*, 33, 29, 1990. With permission.)

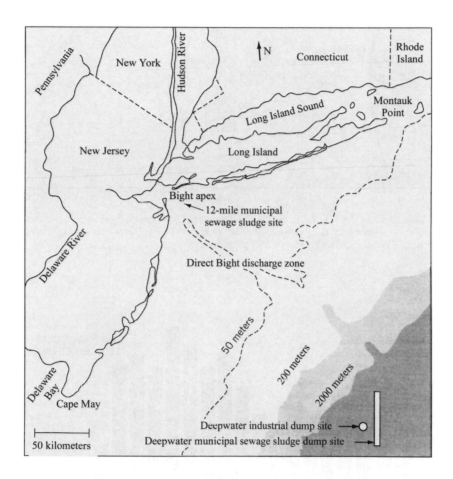

Figure 6.6–4 Map showing the locations of deep water dumpsites (lower right). (From Stegeman, J. J., *Oceanus*, 33, 54, 1990. With permission.)

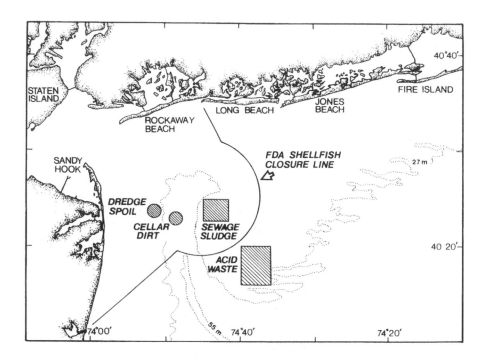

Figure 6.6–5 Map showing the location of the 12 Mile Dumpsite (Sewage Sludge) in the New York Bight Apex. (From Sindermann, C.J., *Ocean Pollution: Effects on Living Resources and Humans,* CRC Press, Boca Raton, FL, 1995, 275 pp. With permission.)

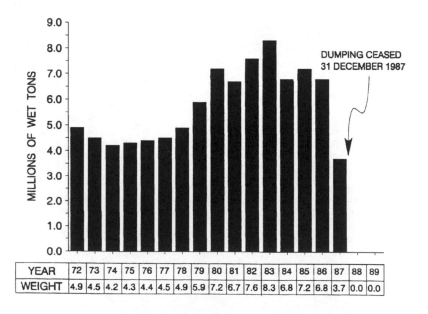

YEAR	72	73	74	75	76	77	78	79	80	81	82	83	84	85	86	87	88	89
WEIGHT	4.9	4.5	4.2	4.3	4.4	4.5	4.9	5.9	7.2	6.7	7.6	8.3	6.8	7.2	6.8	3.7	0.0	0.0

Figure 6.6–6 Estimated annual amounts of sewage sludge dumped in the New York Bight Apex from 1972–1989. (From Wilk, S. J. et al., in *Effects of the Cessation of Sewage Sludge Dumping at the 12-Mile Site,* Studholme, A. A. et al., Eds., NOAA Tech. Rept. NMFS 124, NOAA, Woods Hole, MA, 1995, 173.)

Table 6.6–1 Summary of Minimum Effective Toxic Concentrations (Mortality, Hatching, Feeding, Growth, Respiration, Filtration, Fertilization, Germination) and LC$_{50}$ Averages of Sewage Sludge on Marine Organisms

Organisms	Life Stage	Duration of Test[a]	Effect	Effective Concentration Range (%)
Pisces				
Agonus cataphractus	Adult	96 h	LC$_{50}$	0.28–>1.0
Clupea harengus	Larvae	24 h	Mortality	1.0
	Larvae	96 h	Mortality	0.1–1.0
	Embryo	6 d	Hatching	0.1–1.0
Cyprinodon variegatus	Larvae	96 h	LC$_{50}$	5.0–7.5
Gadus morhua	Larvae	24 h	Mortality	0.1–1.0
	Larvae	4 d	Feeding	0.1–1.0
	Embryo	6 and 9 d	Hatching	1.0
	Juvenile	79 d	Growth	0.01
Limanda limanda	Juvenile	85 d	Growth	0.03
Menidia menidia	Adult	96 h	LC$_{50}$	0.72–2.87
	Adult	96 h	LC$_{50}$	(0.56–3.95)
	Juvenile	96 h	LC$_{50}$	1.0–2.6
	Larvae	96 h	LC$_{50}$	3.9–6.5
	Juvenile?	96 h	LC$_{50}$	0.11–16.5
Menidia beryllina	Larvae	96 h	LC$_{50}$	2.3–8.1
Crustacea				
Anostraca				
Artemia salina	Larvae	24 h	LC$_{50}$	8.5–11.75
Copepoda				
Acartia clausii	Adult	48 h	LC$_{50}$	0.1–2.0
Eurytemora herdmani	Adult	96 h	LC$_{50}$	<0.02–0.36
Pseudocalanus minutus	Adult	96 h	LC$_{50}$	0.11–0.19
Temora longicornis	Adult	24 h	LC$_{50}$	0.1
Decapoda (Natania, Shrimps)				
Crangon crangon	Adult	96 h	LC$_{50}$	0.21–>1.0
		24 h	LC$_{50}$	0.16–>1.0
	Adult	96 h	LC$_{50}$	0.42–1.69
	Larvae	24 h	LC$_{50}$	0.0003–0.1
	Larvae	24 h	LC$_{50}$	0.36–>5.0
Palaemonetes pugio	Adult	96 h	LC$_{50}$	1.51–7.85
	Adult	96 h	LC$_{50}$	(1.87–8.40)
Mysidacea				
Mysidopsis bahia	Adult	96 h	LC$_{50}$	0.01–1.64
	Adult	96 h	LC$_{50}$	(0.36–2.80)
	Juvenile	96 h	LC$_{50}$	0.51–2.6
	Juvenile?	96 h	LC$_{50}$	0.005–4.2
Mollusca				
Cerastoderma edule	Adult	96 h	LC$_{50}$	0.54–>1.0
Littorina littorea	Adult	96 h	LC$_{50}$	>1.0
Mytilus edulis	Adult	96 h	LC$_{50}$	>1.0
	Adult	31 d	Respiration	0.021–0.42
			Clearance rate	0.021–0.42
			Condition	0.42
Echinodermata				
Arbacia punctatula	Sperm	1 h	Fertilization	0.15–1.63
Polychaeta				
Malacoceros fuliginosus	Adult	96 h	LC$_{50}$	>20.0
Scolelepis squamata	Adult	96 h	LC$_{50}$	19.8
Hydrozoa				
Laeomedea flexuosa	Adult	d?	Growth	1.0–2.0
Algae				*(continued)*

Table 6.6–1   Summary of Minimum Effective Toxic Concentrations (Mortality, Hatching, Feeding, Growth, Respiration, Filtration, Fertilization, Germination) and LC$_{50}$ Averages of Sewage Sludge on Marine Organisms (continued)

Organisms	Life Stage	Duration of Test[a]	Effect	Effective Concentration Range (%)
Isocrysis galbana	Adult	48 h	Loss from suspension	1.0
Skeletonema costatum	Adult	96 h	EC$_{50}$	0.77–42.0
Macrocystis pyrifera	Zoospore	48 h	Germination	0.56–1.0
Mesocosm				
Phytoplankton	Assemblage	4 mo	Depressed bloom	1.0–10.0

Note: Effective concentration is expressed as percentage sludge in the test sea water. Results of tests on the liquid fraction only are in parentheses.

[a] h = hours; d = days; mo = months.

Source: Costello, M. J. and Read, P., *Mar. Environ. Res.*, 37, 23, 1994. With permission.

Table 6.6–2   Distribution of Classified Estuarine Waters, 1985 to 1990

	Percent Classified							
	Approved		Prohibited		Conditional		Restricted	
Region	1985	1990	1985	1990	1985	1990	1985	1990
North Atlantic	87	69	10	29	1	1	2	1
Middle Atlantic	82	79	11	13	3	4	4	4
South Atlantic	75	71	22	21	3	4	<1	4
Gulf of Mexico	54	48	24	34	17	16	6	1
Pacific	42	53	40	31	18	11	1	5
Total	69	63	19	25	9	9	4	3

Source: NOAA, The 1990 National Shellfish Register of Classified Estuarine Waters, National Oceanic and Atmospheric Administration, Rockville, MD, 1991.

Table 6.6–3   Pollution Sources Affecting Harvest-Limited Acreage,1990[a]

Sources	North Atlantic		Middle Atlantic		South Atlantic		Gulf of Mexico		Pacific		Nationwide	
	Acres	%	Acres	%	Acres	%	Acres	%	Acres	%	Acres	%
Point Sources												
Sewage treat plants	238	67	641	57	374	44	973	27	75	25	2307	37
Combined sewers	21	6	224	20	0	0	211	6	0	0	457	7
Direct discharge	1	<1	84	7	5	1	920	25	6	2	1015	16
Industry	21	7	223	20	180	21	522	14	129	42	1077	17
Nonpoint Sources												
Septic systems	91	26	123	11	288	34	1763	48	57	19	2322	37
Urban runoff	75	23	655	58	290	34	1276	35	110	36	2412	38
Agricultural runoff	5	3	130	12	233	28	301	8	41	13	718	11
Wildlife	19	7	112	10	306	36	1115	30	39	13	1597	25
Boats	55	17	353	31	146	17	507	14	47	15	1113	18
Upstream Sources												
Sewage treat plants	2	1	104	9	9	1	1174	32	45	16	1334	21
Combined sewers	0	0	5	<1	0	0	134	4	0	0	0	2
Urban runoff	3	1	72	6	8	1	793	22	43	14	918	15
Agricultural runoff	0	0	1	<1	0	0	435	12	0	0	436	7
Wildlife	0	0	28	2	35	4	210	6	0	0	273	4

Note: Since the same percentage of a shellfish area can be affected by more than one source, the percentages shown cannot be added. They will not sum to 100.

[a] Acres are times 1000; % is percent of all harvest-limited acreage in region.

Source: NOAA, The 1990 National Shellfish Register of Classified Estuarine Waters. National Oceanic and Atmospheric Administration, Rockville, MD, 1991.

Table 6.6–4   North Atlantic Pollution Sources Affecting Harvest-Limited Acreage, 1990[a]

Sources	Maine		New Hampshire		Massachusetts	
	Acres	%	Acres	%	Acres	%
Point Sources						
Sewage treat plants	115	57	9	100	120	85
Combined sewers	0	0	1	11	21	15
Direct discharge	0	0	0	0	1	1
Industry	11	5	4	44	9	6
Nonpoint Sources						
Septic systems	82	40	2	22	7	5
Urban runoff	24	12	6	67	50	36
Agricultural runoff	0	0	6	67	5	4
Wildlife	0	0	6	67	19	14
Boats	17	8	5	56	38	22
Upstream Sources						
Sewage treat plants	0	0	0	0	2	1
Combined sewer	0	0	0	0	0	0
Urban runoff	0	0	0	0	3	2
Agricultural runoff	0	0	0	0	0	0
Wildlife	0	0	0	0	0	0

Note: Since the same percentage of a shellfish area can be affected by more than one source, the percentages shown cannot be added. They will not sum to 100.

[a] Acres are times 1000; % is percent of all harvest-limited acreage in state.

Source: NOAA, The 1990 National Shellfish Register of Classified Estuarine Waters, National Oceanic and Atmospheric Administration, Rockville, MD, 1991.

Table 6.6–5 Pollution Sources of Estuaries in the Northeastern United States—North Atlantic (acres ×1000)

Estuary	Point				Nonpoint					Upstream				
	STP	CSO	DD	IND	SEP	URO	ARO	WL	BTG	STP	CSO	URO	ARO	WL
Passamaquoddy Bay	4	—	—	—	2	—	—	<1	—	—	—	—	—	—
Englishman Bay	3	—	—	—	—	—	—	—	—	—	—	—	—	—
Narraguagas Bay	—	—	—	—	1	—	—	—	—	—	—	—	—	—
Blue Hill Bay	—	—	—	—	<1	—	—	—	—	—	—	—	—	—
Penobscot Bay	39	—	<1	2	39	7	—	—	—	—	—	—	—	—
Muscongus Bay	4	—	—	<1	3	2	—	—	—	—	—	—	—	—
Sheepscot Bay	15	—	—	6	12	1	—	—	<1	—	—	—	—	—
Casco Bay	23	—	—	—	10	2	—	—	17	—	—	—	—	—
Saco Bay	8	—	—	—	<1	4	—	—	—	—	—	—	—	—
Great Bay	2	—	—	1	2	1	—	—	—	—	—	—	—	—
Merrimack River	2	—	—	<1	<1	<1	—	<1	<1	2	—	2	—	—
Massachusetts Bay	89	9	—	2	1	12	—	<1	4	—	—	1	—	—
Boston Bay	*2*	*11*	*<1*	*6*	*<1*	*29*	—	*7*	*28*	—	—	—	—	—
Cape Cod Bay	<1	<1	<1	<1	2	3	1	6	2	—	—	—	—	—
Other	21	<1	—	3	19	14	4	12	4	—	—	3	—	—
North Atlantic total	238	20	—	21	91	75	5	19	55	2	—	3	—	—
% harvest-limited acreage	68	6	0	6	26	21	1	5	16	1	0	1	0	0
National total	2299	382	1011	1047	2325	2385	699	1552	1125	1337	142	1013	312	269
% harvest-limited acreage	36	6	16	16	36	37	11	24	18	21	2	16	5	4

Note: Subestuaries are in italics. STP, sewage treatment plant; CSO, combined sewer outfall; DD, direct discharge; IND, industry; SEP, septics; URO, urban runoff; ARO, agricultural runoff; WI, wildlife; BTG, boating; —, no acreage affected.

Source: NOAA, The 1990 National Shellfish Register of Classified Estuarine Waters, National Oceanic and Atmospheric Administration, Rockville, MD, 1991.

Table 6.6–6 Middle Atlantic Pollution Sources Affecting Harvest-Limited Acreage, 1990[a]

Sources	Massachusetts		Rhode Island		Connecticut		New York		New Jersey		Delaware		Maryland		Virginia	
	Acres	%	Acres	%	Acres	%	Acres	%	Acres	%	Acres	%	Acres	%	Acres	%
Point Sources																
Sewage treat plants	10	11	23	55	78	68	212	79	109	67	14	23	16	13	17	68
Combined sewers	4	5	7	17	26	23	135	50	52	32	0	0	0	0	0	0
Direct discharge	0	0	9	21	7	6	68	25	0	0	0	0	0	0	0	0
Industry	0	0	6	14	8	7	1	<1	32	20	3	5	6	5	167	63
Nonpoint Sources																
Septic systems	8	9	2	5	7	6	11	4	34	21	4	7	32	26	25	9
Urban runoff	11	13	7	17	61	54	250	93	121	74	5	8	38	31	162	61
Agricultural runoff	0	0	1	2	2	2	5	2	23	14	11	18	60	49	28	11
Wildlife	8	9	0	0	5	4	11	4	32	20	15	25	40	33	1	<1
Boats	7	8	16	38	48	42	32	12	62	38	0	0	15	12	173	66
Upstream Sources																
Sewage treat plants	11	13	11	26	51	45	0	0	5	3	0	0	0	0	26	10
Combined sewer	0	0	0	0	3	<1	0	0	2	<1	0	0	0	0	<1	<1
Urban runoff	10	11	17	40	9	8	0	0	5	3	0	0	5	4	26	10
Agricultural runoff	0	0	0	0	0	0	0	0	1	1	0	0	0	0	0	0
Wildlife	10	11	0	0	2	2	0	0	0	0	0	0	0	0	16	6

Note: Since the same percentage of a shellfish area can be affected by more than one source, the percentages shown cannot be added. They will not sum to 100.

[a] Acres are times 1000; % is percent of all harvest-limited acreage in state.

Source: NOAA, The 1990 National Shellfish Register of Classified Estuarine Waters, National Oceanic and Atmospheric Administration, Rockville, MD, 1991.

Table 6.6–7   South Atlantic Pollution Sources Affecting Harvest-Limited Acreage, 1990[a]

Sources	North Carolina		South Carolina		Georgia		Florida	
	Acres	%	Acres	%	Acres	%	Acres	%
Point Sources								
Sewage treat plants	167	35	47	54	38	31	122	73
Combined sewers	0	0	0	0	0	0	0	0
Direct discharge	0	0	0	0	5	4	0	0
Industry	83	17	46	53	43	36	8	5
Nonpoint Sources								
Septic systems	57	12	22	25	48	40	161	96
Urban runoff	77	16	39	45	34	28	140	84
Agricultural runoff	222	47	3	3	8	7	0	0
Wildlife	149	31	17	20	42	35	98	59
Boats	64	13	30	34	37	31	15	9
Upstream Sources								
Sewage treat plants	0	0	7	8	2	2	0	0
Combined sewer	0	0	0	0	0	0	0	0
Urban runoff	0	0	6	7	2	2	0	0
Agricultural runoff	0	0	0	0	0	0	0	0
Wildlife	0	0	19	22	16	13	0	0

Note: Since the same percentage of a shellfish area can be affected by more than one source, the percentages shown cannot be added. They will not sum to 100.

[a] Acres are times 1000; % is percent of all harvest-limited acreage in state.

Source: NOAA, The 1990 National Shellfish Register of Classified Estuarine Waters, National Oceanic and Atmospheric Administration, Rockville, MD, 1991.

Table 6.6–8   Gulf of Mexico Pollution Sources Affecting Harvest-Limited Acreage, 1990[a]

Sources	Florida		Alabama		Mississippi		Louisiana		Texas	
	Acres	%	Acres	%	Acres	%	Acres	%	Acres	%
Point Sources										
Sewage treat plants	394	45	86	27	27	17	265	18	201	24
Combined sewers	7	1	0	0	0	0	204	14	0	0
Direct discharge	2	<1	5	2	0	0	912	60	1	<1
Industry	205	24	0	0	39	25	218	14	60	7
Nonpoint Sources										
Septic systems	697	80	0	0	15	10	580	38	471	56
Urban runoff	466	54	0	0	32	20	643	43	135	16
Agricultural runoff	4	<1	18	6	0	0	59	4	220	26
Wildlife	528	61	41	13	8	5	415	28	123	15
Boats	64	7	1	<1	94	60	225	15	123	15

(*continued*)

Table 6.6–8 Gulf of Mexico Pollution Sources Affecting Harvest-Limited Acreage, 1990[a] (continued)

Sources	Florida Acres	%	Alabama Acres	%	Mississippi Acres	%	Louisiana Acres	%	Texas Acres	%
	\multicolumn{11}{c}{Upstream Sources}
Sewage treat plants	131	15	2	1	3	2	1038	69	0	0
Combined sewer	7	<1	3	<1	0	0	13	<1	114	3
Urban runoff	7	<1	211	67	3	2	562	37	10	1
Agricultural runoff	0	0	211	67	0	0	3	<1	221	26
Wildlife	141	16	0	0	0	0	3	<1	66	8

Note: Since the same percentage of a shellfish area can be affected by more than one source, the percentages shown cannot be added. They will not sum to 100.

[a] Acres are times 1000; % is percent of all harvest-limited acreage in state.

Source: NOAA, The 1990 National Shellfish Register of Classified Estuarine Waters, National Oceanic and Atmospheric Administration, Rockville, MD, 1991.

Table 6.6–9 Pacific Pollution Sources Affecting Harvest-Limited Acreage,1990[a]

Sources	California Acres	%	Oregon Acres	%	Washington Acres	%	Alaska Acres	%	Hawaii Acres	%
	\multicolumn{11}{c}{Point Sources}
Sewage treat plants	16	13	5	18	53	40	0	0	1	6
Combined sewers	0	0	0	0	0	0	0	0	0	0
Direct discharge	0	0	6	21	0	0	0	0	0	0
Industry	86	68	0	0	37	28	0	0	6	33
	\multicolumn{11}{c}{Nonpoint Sources}
Septic systems	11	9	9	32	37	28	0	0	0	0
Urban runoff	26	20	12	43	54	41	0	0	18	100
Agricultural runoff	18	14	8	29	15	11	0	0	0	0
Wildlife	18	14	0	0	4	3	0	0	17	94
Boats	25	20	6	21	10	8	0	0	6	33
	\multicolumn{11}{c}{Upstream Sources}
Sewage treat plants	0	0	2	7	43	33	0	0	0	0
Combined sewer	0	0	0	0	0	0	0	0	0	0
Urban runoff	0	0	0	0	43	33	0	0	0	0
Agricultural runoff	0	0	0	0	0	0	0	0	0	0
Wildlife	0	0	0	0	0	0	0	0	0	0

Note: Since the same percentage of a shellfish area can be affected by more than one source, the percentages shown cannot be added. They will not sum to 100.

[a] Acres are times 1000; % is percent of all harvest-limited acreage in state.

Source: NOAA, The 1990 National Shellfish Register of Classified Estuarine Waters. National Oceanic and Atmospheric Administration, Rockville, MD, 1991.

6.7 PATHOGENS

Table 6.7–1   Pathogens Likely To Be Associated with Sewage Sludge

Bacteria	Viruses	Protozoa	Helminths
Salmonella spp.	Poliovirus	*Entamoeba histolytica*	*Echinococcus granulosus*
Shigella spp.	Coxsackie A and B	*Acanthamoeba* spp.	*Hymenolepis nana*
Vibrio spp.	Echovirus	*Giardia* spp.	*Taenia saginata*
Mycobacterium spp.	Adenovirus		*Fasciola hepatica*
Bacillus anthracis	Reovirus		*Ascaris lumbricoides*
Clostridium perfringens	Parvovirus		*Enterobius vermicularis*
Yersinia spp.	Rotavirus		*Strongyloides* spp.
Campylobacter spp.	Hepatitis A		*Trichuris trichiura*
Pseudomonas spp.	Norwalk and related		*Toxocara canis*
Leptospira spp.	gastroenteric viruses		*Trichostrongylus* spp.
Listeria monocytogenes			
Escherichia coli			
Clostridium botulinum			

Source: Alderslade, R., in *Recent Experience in the United Kingdom: Characterization, Treatment. and Use of Sewage Sludge,* Hermite, P. L. and Ott, H., Eds., Reidel Publishing, Dordrecht, 1981, 372. With permission.

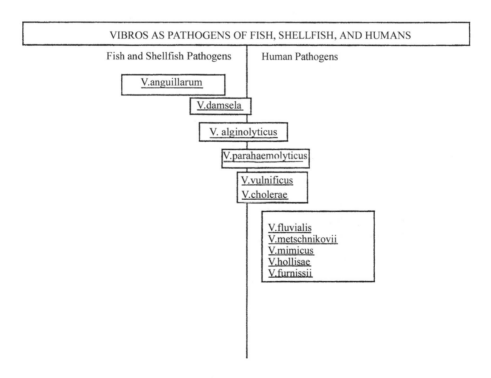

Figure 6.7–1 *Vibrios* as pathogens of fish, shellfish, and humans. (From Sindermann, C. J., *Ocean Pollution: Effects on Living Resources and Humans,* CRC Press, Boca Raton, FL, 1996, 87. With permission.)

Table 6.7–2 Bacterial Pathogens in Fish

Bacterium	Disease
Gram-Negative Pathogens	
Vibrio anguillarum[1,2]	Vibriosis
V. ordalii[1,2]	Vibriosis
V. salmonicida[1,2]	Vibriosis
V. alginolyticus	Vibriosis
V. damsela	Vibriosis
V. cholera (non-01)	Vibriosis
V. vulnificus (Biogroup 2)	Vibriosis
Aeromonas salmonicida[1,2]	Furunculosis
subsp. salmonicida	
subsp. achromogenes	
subsp. masoucida	
A. hydrophila[1,3]	Motile aeromonad septicemia
Pasteurella piscicida[1]	Pasteurellosis
Providencia rettgeri[3]	Bacterial hemorrhagic septicemia
Edwardsiella tarda[3]	Edwardsiellosis
E. ictaluri[1]	Enteric septicemia
Serratia plymuthica	Serratia septicemia
Yersinia ruckeri[1]	Enteric redmouth disease
Acinetobacter sp.	Acinetobacterosis
Pseudomonas anguilliseptica	Pseudomonas septicemia
P. chlororaphis	Pseudomonas septicemia
P. fluorescens[3]	Pseudomonas septicemia
Flexibacter psychrophilus[1]	Bacterial coldwater disease
F. columnaris[1]	Columnaris
F. maritimus	Flexibacterosis
Flavobacterium branchiophila	Bacterial gill disease
Sporocytophaga sp.	Saltwater columnaris
Rickettsiales[1,2]	Rickettsiosis
Renibacterium salmoninarum[1,2]	Bacterial kidney disease
Eubacterium tarantellus	Eubacterial meningitis
Carnobacterium piscicola	Pseudokidney disease
Vagococcus salmoninarum	Pseudokidney disease
Gram-Positive Pathogens	
Lactococcus piscium	Pseudokidney disease
Staphylococcus sp.	Staphylococcal septicemia
Streptococcus sp.	Streptococcal septicemia
Streptoverticillium	Streptomycosis
Clostridium botulinum	Botulism
Acid-Fast Pathogens	
Mycobacterium marinum[3]	Mycobacteriosis
M. fortuitum[3]	Mycobacteriosis
M. chelonei[3]	Mycobacteriosis
Nocardia asteriodes[3]	Nocardiosis
N. seriolae[1,2]	Nocardiosis

[1] Species of bacteria considered major or important pathogens of finfish.
[2] Species of bacteria considered obligate pathogens of finfish.
[3] Species of bacteria which are also associated with human disease.

Source: Couch, J. A. and Fournie, J. W., Eds., Pathobiology of Marine and Estuarine Organisms, CRC Press, Boca Raton, FL, 1993, 54. With permission.

Table 6.7–3   Viral Diseases of Marine Fish and Their Environments

Disease	Virus Classification	How known		Environment	
		Isolation	Em[a]	Marine	M & FW[b]
Infectious pancreatic necrosis (IPN)	Birnovirus	X	X	—	X
Viral hemorrhagic septicemia (VHS)	Rhabodovirus	X	X	—	X
Pacific salmon anemia virus (EIBS)	—	—	—	—	X
Viral erythrocytic necrosis (VEN)	Iridovirus	—	X	X	—
Chum salmon reovirus	Reovirus	X	X	X	—
Chinook salmon paramyxovirus	Paramyxovirus	X	X	X	X
Lymphocystis	Iridovirus	X	X	—	X
Atlantic menhaden spinning disease	?	X	X	X	X
Atlantic cod adenovirus	Adenovirus	—	X	X	—
Atlantic cod ulcus syndrome	Iridovirus	—	X	X	—
Atlantic salmon papillomatosis	?	—	X	—	—
Atlantic salmon swim bladder sarcoma virus	Reovirus	—	X	X	—
Pacific cod herpesvirus	Herpesvirus	—	X	X	X
Pleuronectid papilloma	?	—	—	X	—
Winter flounder papilloma	?	—	—	X	—

[a] EM = electron microscopy.
[b] M & FW = marine and fresh water.

Source: Couch, J. A. and Fournie, J. W., Eds., *Pathobiology of Marine and Estuarine Organisms,* CRC Press, Boca Raton, FL, 1993, 26. With permission.

Table 6.7–4   Bacterial Diseases of Mollusks

Name of Disease	Causative Agent	Host(s)	Ref.[a]
Gastropod acid-fast bacteremia	Unidentified acid-fast bacilli	Snails: *Biomphalaria glabrata* *B. pfeifferi* *Helisoma anceps*	Sparks, 1985; Michelson, 1961
American oyster vibrio cardiac endema or cardiac *vibriosis*	*Vibrio anguillarum*	Oyster: *Crassostrea virginica*	Sparks, 1985
	Achromobacter (?)	Oyster: *C. gigas*	Sindermann, 1970
Vibriosis of juvenile oysters	*Vibrio* sp.	Oysters: *C. virginica* *Ostrea edulis* Clam: *Mercenaria mercenaria*	Sindermann and Lightner, 1988; Elston et al., 1982
	Leucothrix mucor (?)	Clam: *Cardium edule*	Lauckner, 1983
Mycelial disease	Unidentified actinomycete (?)	Oysters: *C. virginica* *O. lurida*	Mackin, 1962; Lauckner, 1983
	Unidentified actinomycete (?)	Oyster: *C. virginica*	Meyers, 1981
Juvenile abalone vibriosis	*V. alginolyticus*	Abalone: *Haliotis rufescens*	Elston and Lockwood, 1983
	Opportunistic Gram-negative bacteria	Squid: *Loligo pealei* *L. plei* *Lolliguncula brevis* *Loligo opalesceni* *Ommastrephes pteropus*	Hulet et al., 1979; Leibovitz et al.,1977

[a] See original source for references.

Source: Couch, J. A. and Fournie, J. W., Eds., *Pathobiology of Marine and Estuarine Organisms,* CRC Press, Boca Raton, FL, 1993, 263. With permission.

TRANSMISSION OF *Haplosporidium nelsoni*

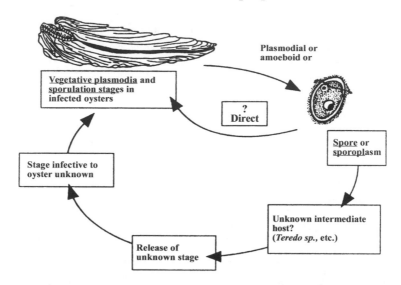

Figure 6.7–2 Diagram demonstrating incomplete knowledge of life cycle and mode of transmission of MSX (*Haplosporidium nelsoni*), one of the most devastating pathogens in oysters. (From Couch, J. A. and Fournie, J. W., Eds., *Pathobiology of Marine and Estuarine Organisms,* CRC Press, Boca Raton, FL, 1993, 54. With permission.)

6.8 OIL

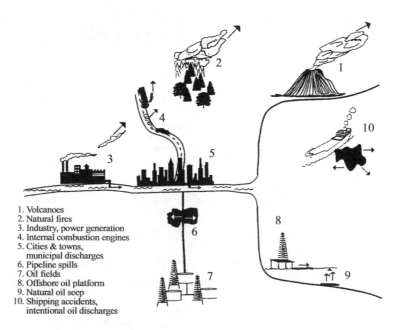

1. Volcanoes
2. Natural fires
3. Industry, power generation
4. Internal combustion engines
5. Cities & towns, municipal discharges
6. Pipeline spills
7. Oil fields
8. Offshore oil platform
9. Natural oil seep
10. Shipping accidents, intentional oil discharges

Figure 6.8–1 Sources of oil and polycyclic aromatic hydrocarbons in the marine environment. (From Albers, P. H., in *Handbook of Ecotoxicology,* Hoffman, D. J. et al., Eds., Lewis Publishers, Boca Raton, FL, 1994, 330. With permission.)

Table 6.8–1 Sources of Oil Pollution in Marine Environments[a]

Source	Oil Industry	Other	Total
Transportation			
Tanker operations	0.143		
Tanker accidents	0.110		
Dry docking	0.004		
Other shipping operations		0.229	
Other shipping accidents		0.018	
			0.504
Fixed installations			
Offshore oil production	0.045		
Coastal oil refineries	0.091		
Thermal loading	0.027		
			0.163
Other sources			
Industrial waste		0.181	
Municipal waste		0.635	
Urban runoff		0.109	
River runoff		0.036	
Atmospheric fallout		0.272	
Ocean dumping		0.018	1.251
Natural inputs		0.227	0.227
Biosynthesis			
Marine phytoplankton		23.582	
Atmospheric fallout		91–3.630	

[a] Values in million metric tons per year.

Modified from Clark, R. B., *Marine Pollution*, 3rd ed., Clarendon Press, Oxford, 1992, 172 pp.

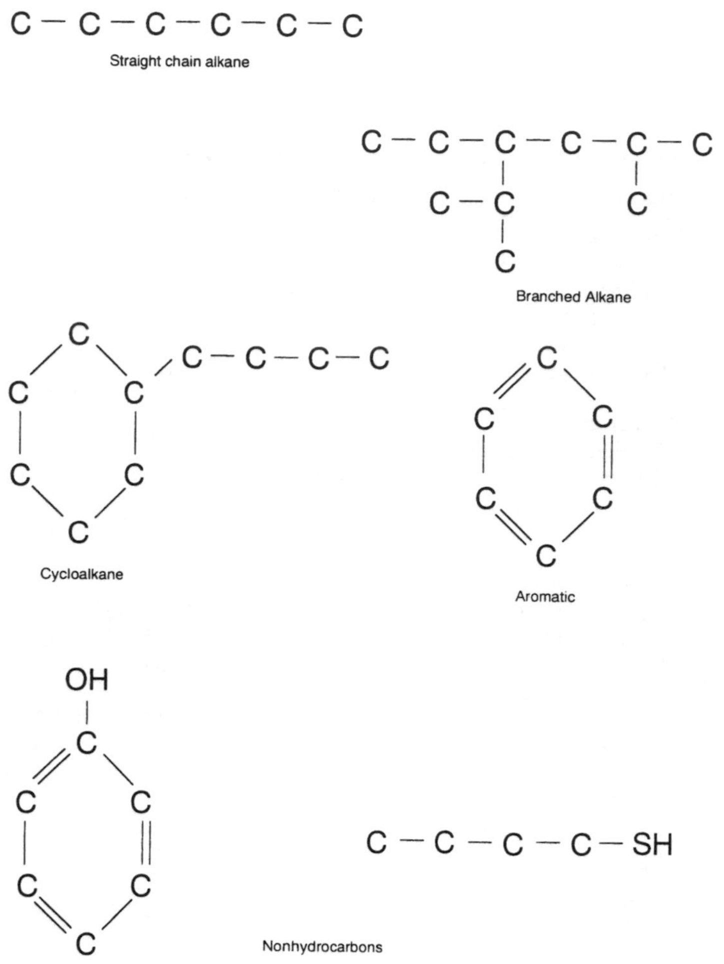

Figure 6.8–2 Types of molecular structures found in petroleum. Hydrogen atoms bonded to carbon atoms are omitted. (From Albers, P. H., in *Handbook of Ecotoxicology,* Hoffman, D. J. et al., Eds., Lewis Publishers, Boca Raton, FL, 1995, pp. 330–355. With permission.)

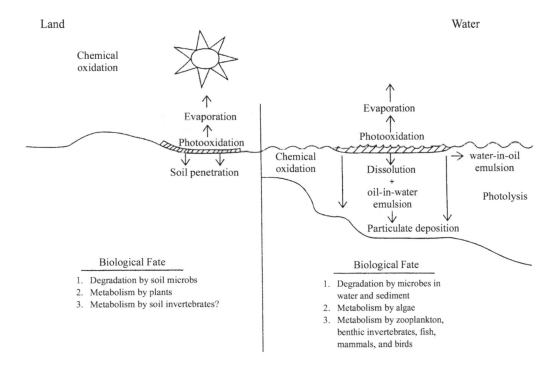

Figure 6.8–3 Chemical, physical, and biological fate of oil on land vs. in the sea. (From Albers, P. H., in *Handbook of Ecotoxicology,* Hoffman, D. J. et al., Eds., Lewis Publishers, Boca Raton, FL, 1994, 330. With permission.)

Table 6.8–2   Selected Large Oil Spills in Coastal Waters

Year	Polluter	Amount of Oil (tonnes)	Affected Area
1967	*Torrey Canyon*	117,000	U.K., France
1970	Texaco *Oklahoma*	31,500	U.S.
1976	*Urquiola*	100,000	Spain
1977	*Grand Zenith*	32,000	Canada (east coast)
1978	*Amoco Cadiz*	230,000	France
1979	*Ixtoc I* Platform	350,000	Mexican Gulf
1979	*Andros Patria*	60,000	Spain
1979	*Betelgeuse*	35,000	Ireland
1979	*Gino*	42,000	France
1979	*Aviles*	25,000	Arabian Sea
1979	*Atlantic Express*	276,000	Tobago
1979	*Burmah Agate*	40,000	U.S.
1979	*Independenta*	94,600	Turkey
1980	*Irenes Serenade*	102,000	Greece
1980	*Juan A. Lavalleja*	40,000	Algeria
1983	*Castello deBelver*	255,500	South Africa
1984	*Assimi*	51,400	Oman
1984	*Pericles GC*	46,600	Qatar
1985	*Neptunia*	60,000	Iran
1985	*Nova*	71,100	Iran
1989	*Exxon Valdez*	35,000	Alaska
1992	*Aegean Sea*	79,000	France, Spain
1993	*Brear*	84,000	Norway, Scotland

Source: Based on data in *The State of the Environment in OECD Member Countries.* Organization for Economic Cooperation and Development, Paris, 1979, and *OECD Environmental Data Compendium.* Organization for Economic Cooperation and Development, Paris, 1993. From Beer, T., *Environmental Oceanography,* 2nd ed., CRC Press, Boca Raton, FL, 1997, 219. With permission.

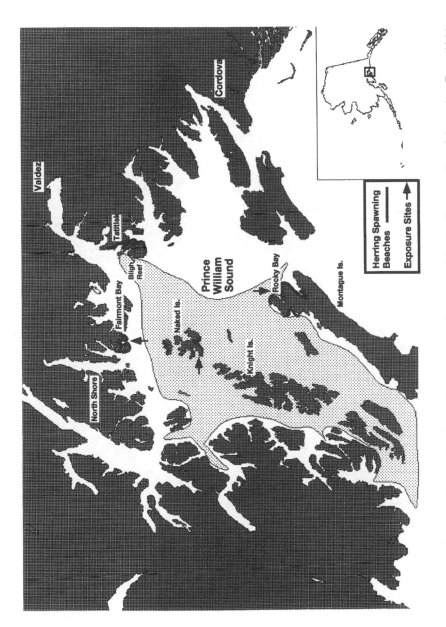

Figure 6.8–4 Map of Prince William Sound illustrating the oil trajectory following the grounding of the tanker *Exxon Valdez* on Bligh Reef in March 1989. (From Kocan, R. M., in *Techniques in Aquatic Toxicology*, Ostrander, G. K., Ed., Lewis Publishers, Boca Raton, FL, 1996, 87. With permission.)

Table 6.8–3 Some of the Commonly Reported Effects of Petroleum and Individual PAHs on Living Organisms[a]

Effects	Plant	Invertebrate	Fish	Reptile and Amphibian	Bird	Mammal
Individual Organisms						
Death	X	X	X	X	X	X
Impaired reproduction	X	X	X	X	X	
Reduced growth and development	X	X	X	X	X	
Impaired immune system						X
Altered endocrine function			X		X	
Altered rate of photosynthesis	X					
Malformations			X		X	
Tumors and lesions		X	X	X		X
Cancer			X	X		X
Altered behavior		X	X	X	X	X
Blood disorders		X	X	X	X	X
Liver and kidney disorders			X		X	X
Hypothermia					X	X
Inflammation of epithelial tissue					X	X
Altered respiration or heart rate		X	X	X		
Impaired salt gland function				X	X	
Gill hyperplasia			X			
Fin erosion			X			
Groups of Organisms[a,b]						
Local population changes	X	X			X	
Altered community structure	X	X			X	
Biomass change	X	X				

[a] Some effects have been observed in the wild and in the laboratory, whereas others have only been induced in laboratory experiments.

[b] Populations of chlorophyllous (microalgae) and nonchlorophyllous plants (bacteria, filamentous fungi, yeast) can increase or decrease in the presence of petroleum, whereas animal populations decrease.

Source: Albers, P. H., in *Handbook of Ecotoxicology,* Hoffman, D. J. et al., Eds., Lewis Publishers, Boca Raton, FL, 1994, 330. With permission.

Table 6.8–4 Summary of the Effects of Oil Spills on Marine Communities

Community	Effect	Period of Impact[a]
Plankton		
Phytoplankton biomass and primary production	Increase due to diminished grazing; depression of chlorophyll a	Days to weeks, during occurrence of slicks
Zooplankton	Population reduction: contamination	
Fish Eggs	Decreased hatching and survival	
Benthos		
Amphipods, isopods, ostracods	Initial mortality; population decrease	Weeks to years, depending on oil-retentive characteristics of habitat
Mollusks, especially bivalves	Initial mortality; contamination; histopathology	
Opportunistic polychaetes	Population increase	
Overall macrobenthic community	Decreased diversity	
Intertidal and littoral		
Meiofaunal crustaceans, crabs	Initial mortality; population decrease	Weeks to years, depending on oil-retentive characteristics of habitat
Mollusks	Initial mortality; contamination; histopathology	
Opportunistic polychaetes	Population increase	
Overall community	Decreased diversity	
Algae	Decreased biomass; species replacement	
Phanerogams	Initial die-back	
Fish		
Eggs and larvae	Decreased hatching and survival	Weeks to months
Adults	Initial mortality: contamination: histopathology	
Birds		
Adults	Mortality; population decrease	Years

[a] Period of impact depends on the scale and duration of the spill and on the oceanic characteristics of the specific system.

Source: Wolfe, D. A., in *Wastes in the Ocean*, Vol. 4, *Energy Wastes in the Ocean*, Duedall, I. W. et al., Eds., John Wiley & Sons, New York, 1985, 45. With permission.

Table 6.8–5   Sublethal Effects of Petroleum Exposure on Marine Organisms in the Laboratory[a]

Effect	Species	Exposure Regime and Effective Concentration[b]
Reduced avoidance response	Spotted seatrout larvae (*Cynoscion nebulosus*)	No. 2 fuel WSF for 48 h at 0.1–1.0 µg/g (nominal)
50% reduction in defense response to predator	Sea urchin (*Strongylocentrotus droebachiensis*)	Prudhoe Bay Crude WSF for 15 min at 50 ng/g (measured)
Oil detection, indicated by antennular flicking rate	Blue crabs (*Callinectes sapidus*)	Prudhoe Bay Crude WSF for 2 min at 2×10^{-6} µg/g (median threshold detection limit)
		Naphthalene for 3 min at 10^{-7} µg/g (median threshold detection limit)
Oil detection, indicated by antennular flicking rate	Dungeness crabs (*Cancer magister*)	Prudhoe Bay Crude WSF for 1 min at 0.1 µg/g (median threshold detection limit)
		Naphthalene for 1 min at 0.01 µg/g (median threshold detection limit)
Decreased burying or increased surfacing in sediment	Intertidal clams (*Macoma balthica*)	Prudhoe Bay Crude OWD for 180 d at 0.3 µg/g (response threshold)
Resurfacing within 3 to 5 days	Intertidal clams (*M. balthica*)	Prudhoe Bay Crude WSF for 6 d at ~0.3 µg/g (median response)
Failure to burrow	Intertidal clams (*M. balthica*)	Prudhoe Bay Crude WSF for 6 d at ~2.5 µg/g
38% depression of feeding rate	Copepods (*Eurytemora affinis*)	Aromatic heating oil WSF for 24 h at 0.52 µg/g
Depression of feeding rate	Copepods (*Acartia clausi* and *A. tonsa*)	No. 2 fuel oil WAF for 18 h at 250 ng/g
Depression of feeding rate	Amphipods (*Boeckosimus affinis*)	Prudhoe Bay Crude WSF for 16 weeks at ≤0.2 µg/g
Food detection and finding slowed by one half	Mud snails (*Ilyanassa obsoleta*)	No. 2 fuel oil OWD for 48 h at 0.015 µg/g
	Mud snails (*I. obsoleta*)	Kerosene WSF with a continuous exposure to 4 ng/g
Feeding rate and growth rate depressed	Rock-crab larvae (*Cancer irroratus*)	No. 2 fuel oil WAF for 27 d at 0.1 µg/g
Food detection (reduced antennular flicking in response to food extract)	Dungeness crab (*C. magister*)	Prudhoe Bay Crude WSF for 24 h at 0.25 µg/g
Inhibition of attraction to reproductive aggregation	Nudibranchs (*Onchidoris bilamellata*)	Toluene for 24 h at 32 ng/g
Reproduction (inhibited reproductive aggregation, delayed and reduced egg deposition)	Nudibranchs (*O. bilamellata*)	Prudhoe Bay Crude WSF for 14 d at 278 ng/g
Histopathology	Mummichogs (*Fundulus heteroclitus*)	Naphthalene for 15 d at 0.02 µg/g
Lateral line necrosis		Naphthalene for 15 d at 0.2 µg/g
Ischemia in brain, liver		
Inclusions in muscle columnar cells	Chinook salmon (*Oncorhynchus tshawytscha*)	Mixed aromatic compounds for 28 d at 5 µg/g in food
Delayed overall embryonic development	Pacific herring embryos (*Clupea harengus pallasi*)	Benzene for 24 h at 0.9 ng/g

[a] The effects documented here were selected based on the degree of realism of exposure conditions relative to chronic discharges and the potential significance of the measured effect to survival and reproduction of the organism. Many other sublethal effects have been documented at higher exposure concentrations.

[b] Exposure concentrations and compositional characteristics depend strongly on the techniques for preparing the oil–water mixtures. This table retains the designations used by the original authors for their preparations. WSF = water-soluble fraction, OWD = oil–water dispersion, and WAF = water-accommodated fraction.

Source: Wolfe, D. A., in *Wastes in the Ocean*, Vol. 4, *Energy Wastes in the Ocean,* Duedall, I. W. et al., Eds., John Wiley & Sons, New York, 1985, 45. With permission.

Table 6.8–6 Dispersed Oil and Oil Effects on Corals

Location	Type	Dispersant Used and Dilution	Conc. of Dispersant	Amount of Spill	Date	Resource Affected	Impact	Dispersant Effect
Bermuda	Field and lab	Corexit 9527 BP 1100 WD	1:20 1:10	Arabian light crude	1981–1986	Corals	6–24 h after, 1–50 ppm on *Diploria strigosa*	No effect to brief exposures; when oil dispersed 20 ppm polychaetes, bivalves, crustacea intolerant; unclear after 9 mo. whether dispersant had effect or not
Arabian Gulf	Field	Corexit 9527 (20:1)		Arabian light crude experiment	1980	Corals	No impact immediately, some death after 6 mo. during winter cold	
Panama	Field	Corexit 9527	50 ppm, 20:1	Prudhoe Bay crude experiment	1985	Corals, seagrasses, mangroves	No coral death at 24-h exposure	No death of corals with dispersant
Panama	Spill	Corexit 9527	20:1	50,000 medium weight crude	1986	Corals, seagrasses, mangroves	Coral death	Reports intertidal reefs, extensive mortality; subtidal to 2 m mortality
Jamaica	Lab	Ten dispersants	1:10	Venezuela light	1988–1989	Corals	Various	Three nontoxic, five highly toxic

Source: Connell, D. W. and Hawker, D. W., Eds., *Pollution in Tropical Aquatic Systems*, CRC Press, Boca Raton, FL, 1992. With permission.

Table 6.8-7   Tropical and Subtropical Seagrass Dispersant Oil and Oil Effects on Seagrasses

Location	Type	Dispersant Used (Dilution)	Type and Conc. of Dispersed Oil	Amount of Spill	Date	Resource Affected	Impact	Dispersant Effect
Miami, FL	Lab outdoors	Corexit 9527 (1:20)	50 ppm oil, 1:20, 24 h	50 ppm oil, lab	1984	Thalassia testudinum	LD_{50} 12- and 96-h bioassays, oil and dispersed oil	Oil with dispersant has lower toxicity than without dispersant
	Lab outdoors	Corexit 9527 (1:20)	LA crude, Murban	Lab	1983–1984	Thalassia	LD_{50} vs. time and conc. at 5 to 100 h	At medium conc.
						Halodule		High
						Syringodium		High
	Lab outdoors	Arco D-609 (1:10)	LA crude, Murban	Lab		Thalassia	LD_{50} 5 h 100 h	Low to medium
						Halodule		Low to medium
						Syringodium		Low to medium at 75 and 125 ml
	Lab outdoors	Conco K (K) (1:10)	LA crude, Murban	Lab		Thalassia	LD_{50} at 5 and 100 h	Medium to high
						Halodule		High
						Syringodium		High
Panama	Field	Corexit 9527	Prudhoe Bay crude, 50 ppm 24 h	Lab	1985	T. testudinum	None to Thalassia	No effect on Thalassia
Miami, FL	Lab outdoors	Corexit 9550 (1:20)	LA crude, 125 and 75 ml oil 1:20 disp. in 100,000 cc SW	Lab	1986	Thalassia	LD_{50} at 100 h	Low
						Halodule		Medium
						Syringodium		Low to medium
	Lab outdoors	OFC-D-607 (1:10)	LA crude, 75 and 125 ml	Lab	1986	Thalassia	LD_{50} at 100 h	Low
						Halodule		Low
						Syringodium		Medium
	Lab outdoors	Cold Clean 500 (1:10)	LA crude, 75 and 125 ml in 100,000 cc SW	Lab	1986	Thalassia	LD_{50} 100 h	Low
						Halodule		Low to medium
						Syringodium		Low
	Lab	Finsol OSP-7 (1:10)	LA crude, 75 and 125 ml in 100,000 cc SW	Lab	1986	Thalassia	LD_{50} 100 h	Medium
						Halodule		Low
						Syringodium		Low to medium low

Note: LA = Louisiana; SW = seawater.

Source: Thorhaug, A. et al., in Pollution in Tropical Aquatic Systems, Connell, D. W. and Hawker, D. W., Eds., CRC Press, Boca Raton, FL, 1992, 110. With permission.

Table 6.8–8 Dispersed Oil and Oil Effects on Mangroves

Location	Type	Dispersant Used and Dilution	Type of Oil	Amount of Spill	Date	Resource Affected	Impact	Dispersant Effect
Panama	Field	Corexit 9527, 24 h, 1:20	50 ppm Prudhoe Bay crude	Exp.	1984	Mangroves	Defoliation, death	Dispersed oil before it reached mangroves
Coast on Caribbean side of Panama	Accidental	Corexit 9527, 21,000 1, 1:20	Medium weight crude	55,000–60,000	April 27, 1986	*Rhizophora mangle*	Defoliation, death	
	Experimental	Corexit 9527, 1:20	Prudhoe Bay crude 50 ppm	Exp.	1985	*R. mangle*	28% trees defoliated	No defoliation at sites with dispersant
South Florida:Turkey Pt., Biscayne Bay	Field	Corexit 9527, 1:20	LA crude concentrated	Exp.	1982–1986	*R. mangle*		
Panama	Field spill	Corexit 9527, 1:20	Medium weight crude		Fall 1986	Mangroves *R. mangle*	Observed mangrove death	If dispersed before oil on mangroves, less mortality
Jamaica	Lab	11 dispersants	Venezuelan	Exp.	1988–1989	*Rhizophora* *Avicennia* *Laguncularia*	Defoliations, death of root	Various at 1250 ppm, not low

Note: Exp. = experimental; LA = Louisiana.
Source: Connell, D. W. and Hawker, D. W., Eds., *Pollution in Tropical Aquatic Systems*, CRC Press, Boca Raton, FL, 1992, 106. With permission.

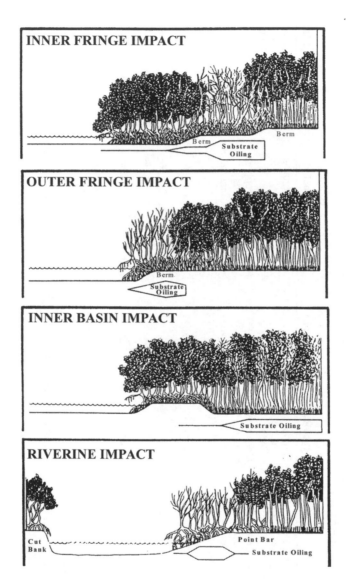

Figure 6.8–5 Potential effects of oil spills on various mangrove forest configurations. (From Clark, J. R., *Coastal Zone Management Handbook,* Lewis Publishers, Boca Raton, FL, 1996, 141. With permission.)

Table 6.8–9 Recovery of Various Ecosystems Subjected to Catastrophic Oil Spills

| Ecosystem Type | Time between Major Stresses (in years) | | | | |
	3	5	10	20	100
River					
Headwaters	50–70% of species recovered	Recovery less than 95% of species	Recovered	Recovered	Recovered
Middle reach	50–75% of species recovered	State of constant recovery less than 95% of species	Recovered	Recovered	Recovered
Slow	50–75% of species recovered	Recovery less than 95% of species	Recovered	Recovered	Recovered
Lakes	Most species would not be recovered	Biological integrity not maintained	State of constant recovery	Final state of recovery	Recovered
Estuaries	Principally clams and mollusks are recovered	Clam and mollusk populations still reduced	Recovered	Recovered	Recovered
Marine					
Beaches	Beaches are in state of final repopulation	Repopulated and probably recovered	Recovered	Recovered	Recovered
Rock shore	Colony communities not recovered	Colony communities generally recovered	Recovered	Recovered	Recovered
Tidal flat	Principally bivalves not recovered	Bivalves still reduced	Recovered	Recovered	Recovered
Marshes	Annual plants and short life span	Long-lived plants not reestablished; most organisms recovered	Final stages of recovery	Recovered except for very large systems	Recovery depends upon size of area affected
Open water	Very small area repopulated	Long life-span organisms in recovery	Most species present	Recovered except for very large systems	Recovery depends upon size of area affected

Source: Cairns, J., Jr., Ed., *Rehabilitating Damaged Ecosystems*, Vol. 2, CRC Press, Boca Raton, FL, 1988. With permission.

6.9 POLYCYCLIC AROMATIC HYDROCARBONS

Structure	1957 I.U.P.A.C. Name	Other Names	Mol. Weight	Relative Carcino-genicity[a]	Common Abbreviation (if any)
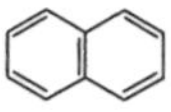	Naphthalene	–	128	–	–
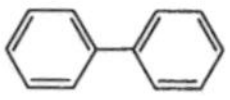	Biphenyl	–	154	–	–
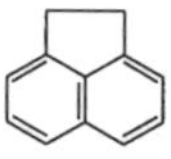	Acenaphthene	–	154	–	–
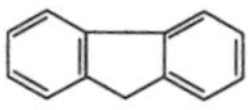	Fluorene	–	166	–	–
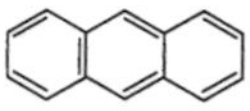	Anthracene	–	178	–	–
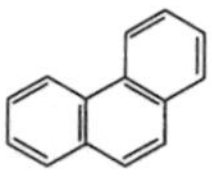	Phenanthrene	–	178	–	–
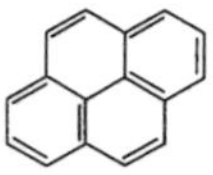	Pyrene	–	202	–	–
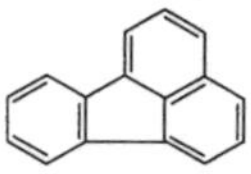	Fluoranthene	–	202	–	–
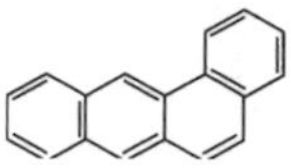	Benzo(a)anthracene	1,2 Benzanthracene	228	< +	B(a)A
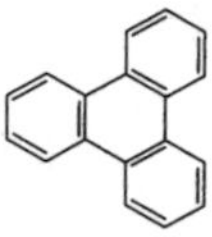	Triphenylene	–	228	–	–

Figure 6.9–1 Structures of PAH and other aromatic hydrocarbon compounds. (From Futoma, D. J. et al., *Polycyclic Aromatic Hydrocarbons in Water Systems,* CRC Press, Boca Raton, FL, 1991, 2. With permission.)

Structure	1957 I.U.P.A.C. Name	Other Names	Mol. Weight	Relative Carcino- genicity[a]	Common Abbreviation (if any)
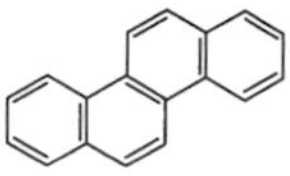	Chrysene	–	228	< +	–
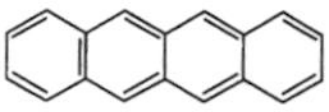	Naphthacene	Tetracene	228	–	–
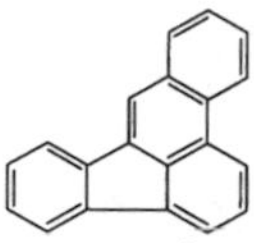	Benzo(b)fluoranthene	3,4 Benzfluoranthene	252	+ +	B(b)F
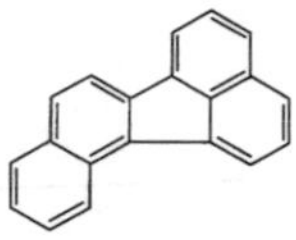	Benzo(j)fluoranthene	10,11 Benzfluoranthene	252	+ +	B(j)F
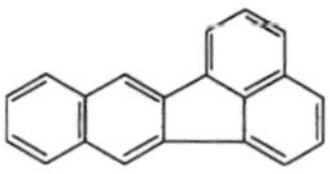	Benzo(k)fluoranthene	11,12 Benzfluoranthene	252	–	B(k)F
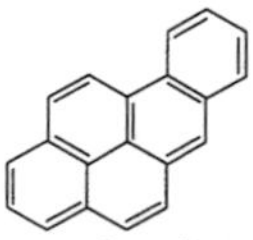	Benzo(a)pyrene	3,4 Benzopyrene	252	+ + + +	B(a)P
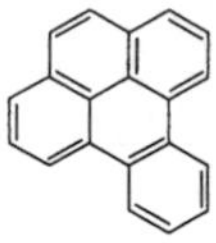	Benzo(e)pyrene	1,2 Benzopyrene	252	< +	B(e)P
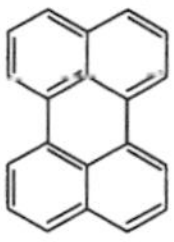	Perylene	–	252	–	–
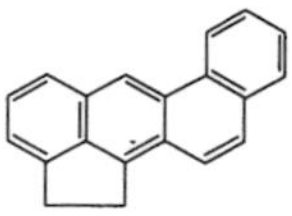	Cholanthrene	–	254	–	–
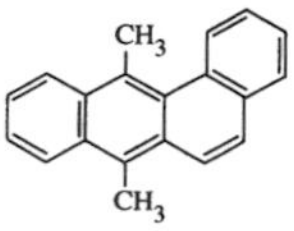	7,12 Dimethylbenz-(a)anthracene	7,12 Dimethyl-1,2-benzan-thracene	256	+ + + + +	–
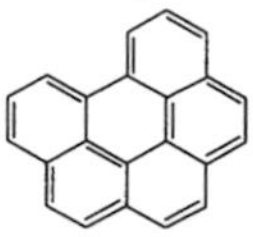	Benzo(ghi)perylene	1,12 Benzperylene	276	–	–

Figure 6.9–1 (continued)

Structure	1957 I.U.P.A.C. Name	Other Names	Mol. Weight	Relative Carcino- genicity[a]	Common Abbreviation (if any)
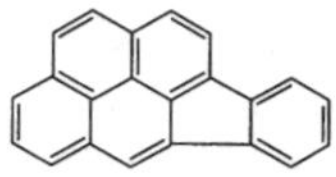	Indeno(1,2,3-cd)pyrene	o-Phenylenepyrene	276	+	IP
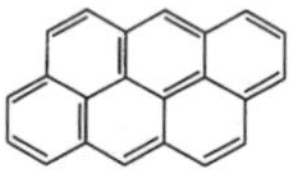	Anthanthrene	–	276	< +	–
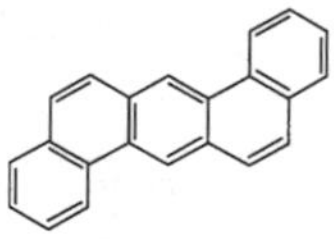	Dibenz(a,h)anthracene	1,2,5,6 Dibenzanthracene	278	+ + +	–
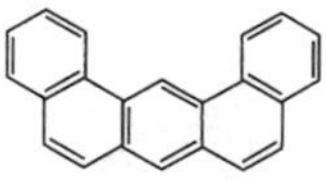	Dibenz(a,j)anthracene	1,2,7,8 Dibenzanthracene	278	–	–
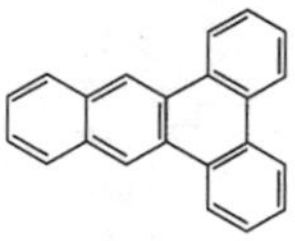	Dibenz(a,c)anthracene	1,2,3,4 Dibenzanthracene	278	–	–
	Coronene	–	300	–	–

[a] +++++ = extremely active; ++++ = very active; +++ = active; ++ = moderately active; + = weakly active; < = less than; — = inactive or unknown.

Figure 6.9–1 (continued)

Table 6.9–1 Major Sources of PAHs in Atmospheric and Aquatic Environments[a]

Ecosystem and Sources	Annual Input
Atmosphere	
Total PAHs	
Forest and prairie fires	19,513
Agricultural burning	13,009
Refuse burning	4769
Enclosed incineration	3902
Heating and power	2168
Benzo(a)pyrene	
Heating and power	
Worldwide	2604
United States only	475
Industrial processes	
Worldwide	1045
United States only	198
Refuse and open burning	
Worldwide	1350
United States only	588
Motor vehicles	
Worldwide	45
United States only	22
Aquatic environments	
Total PAHs	
Petroleum spills	170,000
Atmospheric deposition	50,000
Wastewaters	4400
Surface land runoff	2940
Biosynthesis	2700
Total benzo(a)pyrene	70

[a] Concentrations in metric tons.

Source: Eisler, R., Polycyclic Aromatic Hazards to Fish, Wildlife, and Invertebrates: A Synoptic Review, Biol. Rep. 85(1, 11), U.S. Fish and Wildlife Service, Washington, D.C., 1987.

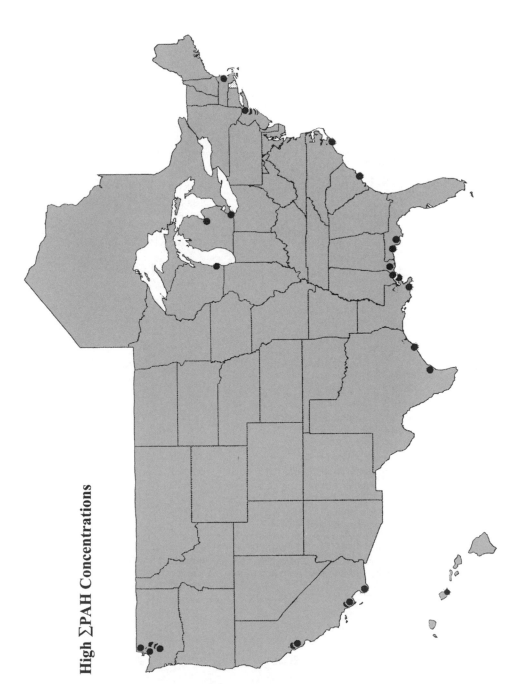

High ΣPAH Concentrations

Figure 6.9-2 Locations of high PAH concentrations recorded by the National Status and Trends Mussel Watch Project. (From O'Connor, T. P. and Beliaeff, B., *Recent Trends in Coastal Environmental Quality: Results from the Mussel Watch Project*, NOAA Tech. Rep., Department of Commerce, Rockville, MD, 1995.)

Table 6.9–2 Concentrations of PAHs in Sediments from Selected Estuaries in the United States

Estuary	Total PAHs
Casco Bay, ME	7320.00
Merrimack River, MA	1730.00
Salem Harbor, MA	10,220.00
Boston Harbor, MA	26,440.00
Buzzards Bay, MA	1710.00
Narragansett Bay, RI	2350.00
East Long Island Sound, NY	48,560.00
West Long Island Sound, NY	8430.00
Raritan Bay, NJ	5010.00
Delaware Bay, DE	330.00
Lower Chesapeake Bay, VA	410.00
Pamlico Sound, NC	219.25
Charleston Harbor, SC	802.98
Sapelo Sound, GA	22.28
St. Johns River, FL	1926.91
Charlotte Harbor, FL	26.51
Tampa Bay, FL	27.10
Apalachicola Bay, FL	200.25
Mobile Bay, AL	96.79
Round Islands, MS	52.36
Mississippi River Delta, LA	603.41
Barataria Bay, LA	106.08
Galveston Bay, TX	68.05
San Antonio Bay, TX	8.98
Corpus Christi Bay, TX	28.17
Lower Laguna Madre, TX	0.00
San Diego Harbor, CA	5000.00
San Diego Bay, CA	0.00
Dana Point, CA	22.87
Seal Beach, CA	257.96
San Pedro Canyon, CA	527.00
Santa Monica Bay, CA	68.25
San Francisco Bay, CA	5976.03
Bodega Bay, CA	11.00
Coos Bay, OR	234.67
Columbia River Mouth, OR/WA	145.03
Nisqually Reach, WA	0.00
Commencement Bay, WA	1200.00
Elliott Bay, WA	4700.00
Lutak Inlet, AK	0.00
Nahku Bay, AK	100.00

Note: Relatively high concentrations in San Francisco Bay, parts per billion.

Source: NOAA, National Status and Trends Program for Marine Environmental Quality; Progress Report and Preliminary Assessments of Findings of the Benthos Surveillance Project—1984, National Oceanic and Atmospheric Administration, Office of Ocean Resources Conservation and Assessment, Rockville, MD, 1987.

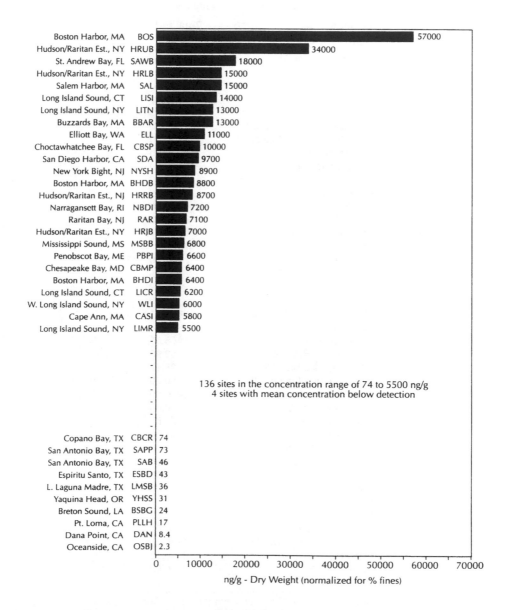

Figure 6.9–3 Total PAH concentrations in sediments of various estuarine and coastal systems of the United States. (From NOAA, A Summary of Data on Individual Organic Contaminants in Sediments Collected during 1984, 1985, 1986 and 1987, Tech. Mem. NOS OMA 47, National Oceanic and Atmospheric Administration, Rockville, MD, 1989.)

Table 6.9–3   PAH Concentrations (μg/kg) in Selected Shellfish and Finfish from Estuarine and Coastal Marine Waters

Taxonomic Group, Compound, and Other Variables	Concentration
Shellfish	
Rock crab, *Cancer irroratus,* edible portions, 1980	
New York Bight	
Total PAH	1600 FW
BaP	1 FW
Long Island Sound	
Total PAH	1290 FW
BaP	ND
American oyster, *Crassostrea virginica,* soft parts	
South Carolina, 1983, residential resorts	
Total PAH	
Spring months	
Palmetto Bay	520 FW
Outdoor resorts	247 FW
Fripp Island	55 FW
Summer months	
Palmetto Bay	269 FW
Outdoor resorts	134 FW
Fripp Island	21 FW
American lobster, *Homarus americanus,* edible portions, 1980	
New York Bight	
Total PAH	367 FW
BaP	15 FW
Long Island Sound	
Total PAH	328 FW
BaP	15 FW
Softshell clam, *Mya arenaria,* soft parts	
Coos Bay, Oregon, 1978–1979	
Contaminated site	
Total PAH	555 FW
Phenanthrene = PHEN	155 FW
FL	111 FW
Pyrene = PYR	62 FW
BaP	55 FW
Benz(*a*)anthracene = BaA	42 FW
Chrysene = CHRY	27 FW
Benzo(*b*)fluoranthene = BbFL	12 FW
Others	<10 FW
Uncontaminated site	
Total PAH	76 FW
PHEN	12 FW
FL	10 FW
Others	<10 FW
Bay mussel, *Mytilus edulis,* Oregon, 1979–1980, soft parts, total PAH	
Near industrialized area	106–986 FW
Remote site	27–274 FW
Sea scallop, *Placopecten magellanicus*	
Baltimore Canyon, east coast U.S.	
Muscle	
BaA	1 FW
BaP	<1 FW
PYR	4 FW

Table 6.9–3 PAH Concentrations (μg/kg) in Selected Shellfish and
Finfish from Estuarine and Coastal Marine Waters
(continued)

Taxonomic Group, Compound, and Other Variables	Concentration
New York Bight, 1980	
Edible portions	
Total PAH	127 FW
BaP	3 FW
Clam, *Tridacna maxima,* Australia, 1980–1982, Great Barrier Reef, soft parts, total PAH	
Pristine areas	<0.07 FW
Powerboat areas	Up to 5 FW
Mussel, *Mytilus* sp.	
Greenland	
Shell	60 FW
Soft parts	18 FW
Italy	
Shell	11 FW
Soft parts	130–540 FW
Bivalve mollusks, five spp., edible portions	6 (max. 36) FW
Decapod crustaceans, four spp., edible portions	2 (max. 8) FW
Softshell clam, *Mya arenaria,* soft parts, Coos Bay, Oregon	
1976–1978	
Near industrialized areas	6–20 FW
Remote areas	1–2 FW
1978–1979	
Near industralized areas	9 FW
Remote areas	4 FW
Finfish	
Fish, muscle	
Baltimore Canyon, east coast, U.S., five spp.	
BaA	Max. 0.3 FW
BaP	Max. <5 FW
PYR	Max. <5 FW
Smoked	
FL	3 FW
PYR	2 FW
Nonsmoked	
FL	Max. 1.8 FW
PYR	Max. 1.4 FW
Winter flounder, *Pseudopleuronectes americanus,* edible portions, 1980	
New York Bight	
Total PAH	315 FW
BaP	21 FW
Long Island Sound	
Total PAH	103 FW
BaP	ND
Windowpane, *Scopthalmus aquosus,* edible portions, 1980	
New York Bight	
Total PAH	536 FW
BaP	4 FW

Table 6.9–3 PAH Concentrations (µg/kg) in Selected Shellfish and Finfish from Estuarine and Coastal Marine Waters (continued)

Taxonomic Group, Compound, and Other Variables	Concentration
Long Island Sound	
Total PAH	86 FW
BaP	ND
Red hake, *Urophycus chuss*, edible portions, 1980	
New York Bight	
Total PAH	412 FW
BaP	22 FW
Long Island Sound	
Total PAH	124 FW
BaP	5 FW
Fish	
Marine, edible portions	Max. 3 FW
Nine spp.	15 FW
Greenland	65 FW
Italy	5–8 DW
Steak, charcoal broiled	11 DW

Note: ND, not detected; FW, fresh weight; DW, dry weight. See original source for specific references for these findings.

Source: Modified from Eisler, R., Polycyclic Aromatic Hazards to Fish, Wildlife, and Invertebrates: A Synoptic Review, Biol. Rep. 85 (1,11), U.S. Fish and Wildlife Service, Washington, D.C., 1987.

Table 6.9–4   National Status and Trends Sites Ranking among the Highest 20 in 1986, 1987, and 1988 and Overall for Total PAHs in Mussels (*Mytilus edulis, M. californianus*) and Oysters (*Crassostrea virginica, Ostrea sandivicensis*)

Code	Location	State	Species	Ranking				Significant Difference?	Trend
				1986	1987	1988	Overall		
SAWB	St. Andrew Bay	FL	cv	1	17t	√	3	no	no
EBFR	Elliott Bay	WA	me	2	13t	1	1	yes	no
HRUB	Hudson/Raritan Estuary	NY	me	3	2	√	4	yes	d
CBRP	Coos Bay	OR	me	4	√	√	9	yes	no
BHDB	Boston Harbor	MA	me	5	8	6	6	no	no
LITN	Long Island Sound	NY	me	6	10	15t	8	no	no
SGSG	Pt. St. George	OR	mc	7	√	√	16	yes	d
BHDI	Boston Harbor	MA	me	8t	4	3	5	yes	no
CBCH	Coos Bay	OR	mc	8t	√	√	13t	yes	no
BHHB	Boston Harbor	MA	me	10t	√	√	15	yes	no
PLLH	Pt. Loma	CA	mc	10t	—	√	√	yes	no
SIWP	Sinclair Inlet	WA	me	10t	√	√	19	yes	no
SCFP	Santa Cruz Island	CA	mc	13t	√	√	√	yes	no
SSSS	San Simeon Point	CA	mc	13t	√	√	√	yes	d
SCBR	S. Catalina Island	CA	mc	15	√	√	√	no	no
BPBP	Barber's Point	HI	os	16	√	√	√	no	no
HRJB	Hudson/Raritan Estuary	NY	me	17	3	4	7	no	no
NYSH	New York Bight	NJ	me	18	√	√	√	yes	no
NYLB	New York Bight	NJ	me	19t	15	√	√	yes	d
CFBI	Cape Fear	NC	cv	19t	√	√	√	no	no
CHSF	Charleston Harbor	SC	cv	19t	√	√	√	no	no
SDHI	San Diego Bay	CA	me	√	1	√	10	yes	no
MSBB	Mississippi Sound	MS	cv	√	5t	√	18	no	no
HHKL	Honolulu Harbor	HI	os	√	5t	√	√	yes	no
SFEM	San Francisco Bay	CA	me	—	7	13	11t	—	—
BBMB	Barataria Bay	LA	cv	√	9	√	√	no	no
CBSR	Choctawhatchee Bay	FL	cv	√	11	√	√	yes	no
BHBI	Boston Harbor	MA	me	√	12	5	13t	no	no
NYSR	New York Bight	NJ	me	√	13t	√	√	no	no

Code	Site	State	Species						
CBTP	Commencement Bay	WA	me	✓	16	9t	✓	no	no
BBPC	Biscayne Bay	FL	cv	—	17t	—	✓	no	no
BBAR	Buzzards Bay	MA	me	✓	19	17	✓	yes	i
RSJC	Roanoke Sound	VA	cv	✓	20	✓	✓	no	no
PCMP	Panama City	FL	cv	—	—	2	2	no	no
NMML	North Miami	FL	cv	—	—	7t	11t	no	no
APDB	Apalachicola Bay	FL	cv	✓	✓	7t	✓	no	no
CBCI	Chincoteague Bay	VA	cv	✓	✓	9t	✓	no	no
LICR	Long Island Sound	CT	me	✓	✓	9t	✓	no	no
BBSM	Bellingham Bay	WA	me	✓	✓	9t	✓	yes	i
DBAP	Delaware Bay	DE	cv	✓	✓	14	✓	no	no
IRSR	Indian River	FL	cv	—	—	15t	17	—	—
UISB	Unakwit Inlet	AK	me	✓	✓	18	✓	yes	i
LINH	Long Island Sound	CT	me	✓	✓	19	✓	yes	i
SSBI	South Puget Sound	WA	me	✓	✓	20	✓	yes	no
AIAC	Absecon Inlet	NJ	me	—	—	✓	20	—	—

Note: cv = Crassostrea virginica; me = Mytilus edulis; mc = Mytilus californianus; os = Ostrea sandvicensis; t = two or more concentrations were equal; d = decreasing trends; i = increasing trends. Note high ranking for San Francisco Bay relative to other systems.

Source: NOAA, A Summary of Data on Tissue Contamination from the First Three Years (1986–1988) of the Mussel Watch Project, NOAA Tech. Mem. NOS OMA 49, National Oceanic and Atmospheric Administration, Rockville, MD, 1989.

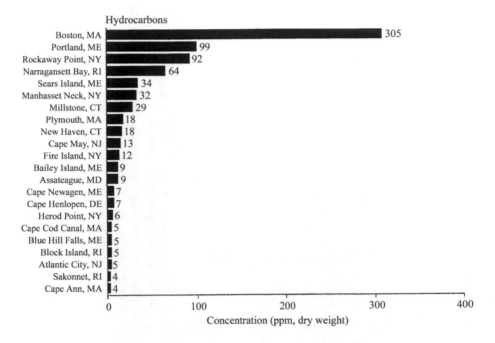

Figure 6.9–4 Concentrations of unresolved complex mixture hydrocarbons in mussels sampled in the north-eastern United States by the USEPA Mussel Watch Program. (From Larsen, P. F., *Rev. Aquat. Sci.*, 6, 67, 1992. With permission.)

Table 6.9–5   Toxicities of Selected PAHs to Marine Organisms

PAH Compound, Organism, and Other Variables	Concentration in Medium[a]	Effect
Benzo(*a*)pyrene		
Sandworm, *Neanthes arenceodentata*	>1000	LC_{50} (96 h)
Chrysene		
Sandwom	>1000	LC_{50} (96h)
Dibenz(*a,h*)anthracene		
Sandworm	>1000	LC_{50} (96 h)
Fluoranthene		
Sandworm	500	LC_{50} (96h)
Fluorene		
Grass shrimp, *Palaemonetes pugio*	320	LC_{50} (96 h)
Amphipod, *Gammarus pseudoliminaeus*	600	LC_{50} (96h)
Sandworm	1000	LC_{50} (96h)
Sheepshead minnow, *Cyprinodon variegatus*	1680	LC_{50} (96 h)
Naphthalene		
Copepod, *Eurytemora affinis*	50	LC_{50} (10 d)
Pink salmon, *Oncorhynchus gorbuscha*, fry	920	LC_{50} (24 h)
Dungeness crab, *Cancer magister*	2000	LC_{50} (96 h)
Grass shrimp	2400	LC_{50} (96 h)
Sheepshead minnow	2400	LC_{50} (24 h)
Brown shrimp, *Penaeus aztecus*	2500	LC_{50} (24 h)
Amphipod, *Elasmopus pectenicrus*	2680	LC_{50} (96 h)
Coho salmon, *Oncorhyncus kisutch*, fry	3200	LC_{50} (96 h)
Sandworm	3800	LC_{50} (96 h)
Mosquitofish, *Gambusia affinis*	150,000	LC_{50} (96 h)
1-Methylnaphthalene		
Dungeness crab, *Cancer magister*	1900	LC_{50} (96 h)
Sheepshead minnow	3400	LC_{50} (24 h)
2-Methylnaphthalene		
Grass shrimp	1100	LC_{50} (96 h)
Dungeness crab	1300	LC_{50} (96 h)
Sheepshead minnow	2000	LC_{50} (24 h)
Trimethylnaphthalenes		
Copepod, *Eurytemora affinis*	320	LC_{50} (24 h)
Sandworm	2000	LC_{50} (96 h)
Phenanthrene		
Grass shrimp	370	LC_{50} (24 h)
Sandworm	600	LC_{50} (96 h)
1-Methylphenanthrene		
Sandworm	300	LC_{50} (96 h)

[a] Concentrations in µg/l.

Source: Modified from Eisler, R., Polycyclic Aromatic Hazards to Fish, Wildlife, and Invertebrates: A Synoptic Review, Biol. Rep. 85(1, 11), U.S. Fish and Wildlife Service. Washington, D.C., 1987.

Table 6.9–6   Relative Carcinogenicity Index of
              Some PAHs

Compound	Carcinogenicity Index
Benzo(*a*)anthracene	+
7, 12-Dimethylbenz(*a*)anthracene	++++
Dibenz(*a,j*)anthracene	+
Dibenz(*a,h*)anthracene	+++
Dibenz(*a,c*)anthracene	+
Benzo(*c*)phenanthrene	+++
Dibenzo(*a,h*)fluorene	+
Dibenzo(*a,h*)fluorene	UC
Dibenzo(*a,c*)fluorene	+
Benzo(*b*)fluoranthene	++
Benzo(*j*)fluoranthene	++
Benzo(*j*)aceanthrylene	++
3-Methylcholanthrene	++++
Benzo(*a*)pyrene	+++
Dibenzo(*a,l*)pyrene	UC
Dibenzo(*a,h*)pyrene	+++
Dibenzo(*a,i*)pyrene	+++
Indeno(1,2,3-*cd*)pyrene	+
Chrysene	UC
Dibenzo(*b, def*)chrysene	++
Dibenzo(*def,p*)chrysene	+

Note: UC = unknown; + = low carcinogenicity; ++ =
          low to moderate carcinogenicity; +++ = mod-
          erate carcinogenicity; ++++ = high carcinoge-
          nicity.

Source: Afghan, B. K. and Chau. A. S. Y. Eds., *Analysis
of Trace Organics in the Aquatic Environment.* CRC
Press, Boca Raton, FL, 1989, 221. With permission.

Table 6.9–7 Commonly Reported Effects of PAHs on Living Organisms

Effects	Plant	Invertebrate	Fish	Reptile and Amphibian	Bird	Mammal
Individual Organisms						
Death	X	X	X	X	X	X
Impaired reproduction	X	X	X	X	X	
Reduced growth and development	X	X	X	X	X	
Impaired immune system						X
Altered endocrine function			X		X	
Altered rate of photosynthesis	X					
Malformations			X		X	
Tumors and lesions		X	X	X		X
Cancer			X	X		X
Altered behavior		X	X	X	X	X
Blood disorders		X	X	X	X	X
Liver and kidney disorders			X		X	X
Hypothermia					X	X
Inflammation of epithelial tissue					X	X
Altered respiration or heart rate		X	X	X		
Impaired salt gland function				X	X	
Gill hyperplasia			X			
Fin erosion			X			
Groups of Organisms[a,b]						
Local population changes	X	X			X	
Altered community structure	X	X			X	
Biomass change	X	X				

[a] Some effects have been observed in the wild and in the laboratory, whereas others have been induced only in laboratory experiments.

[b] Populations of chlorophyllous (microalgae) and nonchlorophyllous plants (bacteria, filamentous fungi, yeast) can increase or decrease in the presence of petroleum, whereas animal populations decrease.

Source: Albers, P. H., in *Handbook of Ecotoxicology.* Hoffman, D. J. et al., Eds., Lewis Publishers, Boca Raton, FL, 1994, 330. With permission.

6.10 HALOGENATED HYDROCARBONS

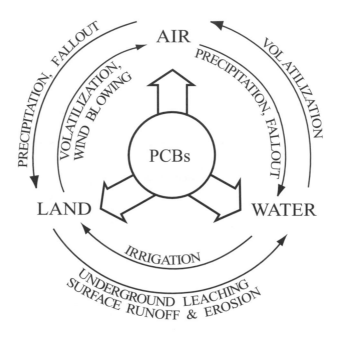

Figure 6.10–1 PCB environmental cycle. (From Lauber, J. D., in *PCBs and the Environment*, Vol. 3, Waid, J. S., Ed., CRC Press, Boca Raton, FL, 1986, 86. With permission.)

Table 6.10–1 **PCBs and Chlorinated Pesticides Listed in Terms of Status of Knowledge and Recommendations for Surveillance in Fish and Shellfish on a Nationwide Basis**

1. Contaminants of continuing concern; maintain surveillance
   PCBs
   DDT (mainly DDE)
   Dieldrin
   alpha (*cis*-)-Chlordane
   trans-Nonachlor
2. Contaminants of uncertain national concern
   Endosulfan
   Toxaphene
   PCP (pentachlorophenol)
   DCPA (dacthal)
   Endrin
   Kelthane
   Kepone
3. Contaminants apparently not of national concern; reduce surveillance frequency
   Aldrin
   Methoxychlor
   Heptachlor and heptachlor epoxide
   Mirex
   HCB (hexachlorobenzene)
   Lindane

Source: Mearns, A. J. et al., PCB and Chlorinated Pesticide Contamination in U.S. Fish and Shellfish: A Historical Assessment Report, NOAA Tech. Mem. NOS OMA 39, National Oceanic and Atmospheric Administration, Seattle, WA, 1988.

Table 6.10–2   Comparison of Atmospheric and Riverine Input Rates of Organochlorine Compounds to the World Oceans

Compound	Atmospheric	Estimated Riverine	% Atmospheric
ΣHCH	4754	40–80	99
HCB	77.1	4	95
Dieldrin	42.9	4	91
ΣDDT	165	4	98
Chlordane	22.1	4	85
ΣPCB	239	40–80	80

Note: Input rates are $\times 10^6$ g/a.

Source: GESAMP (IMCO/FAO/UNESCO/WMO/WHO/IAEA/UN/UNEP Joint Group of Experts on Scientific Aspects of Marine Pollution). Reports and Studies, Inter-Governmental Maritime Consultative Organization, London, 1989.

Table 6.10–3   Summary of the Total Deposition of Some Organochlorine Compounds to the Oceans

Compound	Atlantic North	Atlantic South	Pacific North	Pacific South	Indian	Mean Flux
ΣHCH	851	97	2640	471	698	4754
HCB	16.8	10	19.9	18.9	11.4	77.1
Dieldrin	16.6	2.0	8.9	9.5	6.0	42.9
ΣDDT	15.6	14.0	66.4	25.7	43.3	165
Chlordane	8.7	1.0	8.3	1.9	2.4	22.1
ΣPCB	99.7	13.8	35.5	29.1	52.1	239

Note: Deposition $\times 10^6$ g/a

Source: GESAMP (IMCO/FAO/UNESCO/WMO/WHO/IAEA/UN/UNEP Joint Group of Experts on Scientific Aspects of Marine Pollution). Reports and Studies, Inter-Governmental Maritime Consultative Organization, London, 1989.

Table 6.10–4   Flux of PCB to the Ocean Surface

	Flux (ng/m²/year)		
	Aroclor® 1242	Aroclor® 1254	Total
Particles			
Dry	16.0	41.0	57.0
Wet	250.0	650.0	900.0
Gas Phase			
Dry maximum	2100.0	1600.0	3700.0
Minimum	100.0	100.0	200.0[a]
Wet	9.0	9.5	19.0
Total	2375.0	2301.0	4676.0
Total flux to oceans ($\times 10^8$ g/year)	8.6	8.3	16.9

[a] Based on seawater composition $\simeq$ 0.5 Aroclors 1242 and 0.5 1254.

Source: Atlas, E. et al., in *PCBs and the Environment,* Vol. 1, Waid, J. S., Ed., CRC Press, Boca Raton, FL, 1986, 94. With permission.

Table 6.10–5   Ranges in PCB Concentrations (ng/l) Reported for Open Ocean, Coastal Waters, and Estuaries or Rivers

Area	Location	Range in PCB (ng/l)
Open oceans	North Atlantic	<1–150
		0.4–41.0
	Sargasso Sea	0.9–3.6
	North-South Atlantic	0.3–8.0
	Mediterranean Sea	0.2–8.6
Coastal waters	Southern California	2.3–36.0
	Northwest Mediterranean	1.5–38.0
	Atlantic Coast, United States	10–700
	Baltic coasts	0.3–139.0
		0.1–28.0
	Dutch coast	0.7–8.0
Estuaries/rivers	Wisconsin rivers, United States	<10–380
	Rhine–Meuse system, Holland	10–200
	Tiber estuary, Italy	9–1000[a]
	Brisbane River, Australia	ND–50
	Hudson River, United States	<100–2.8 × 10^6

Note: ND = not detectable (no limits quoted).

[a] As decachlorinated biphenyl equivalents.

Source: Phillips, D. J. H., in PCBs in the Environment, Vol. 1. Waid, J. S., Ed., CRC Press, Boca Raton, FL, 1986, 130. With permission.

Table 6.10–6   PCB Concentrations (ng/g dry weight) in Sediments of Chesapeake Bay Compared to Those of Other Major Estuarine and Coastal Marine Systems

Area	PCB Conc.
Mediterranean Sea	0.8–9.0
Gulf of Mexico	0.2–35.0
Chesapeake Bay	4–400
Tiber estuary	28–770
Rhine–Meuse estuary	50–1000
New York Bight	0.5–2200.0
Palos Verdes Peninsula	30–7900
Hudson River	tr–6700
Escambia Bay	190–61,000

Note: tr = trace. See original source for particular studies.

Source: Phillips, D. J. H., in PCBs and the Environment, Vol. 2, Waid, J. S., Ed., CRC Press, Boca Raton, FL, 1986, 132. With permission.

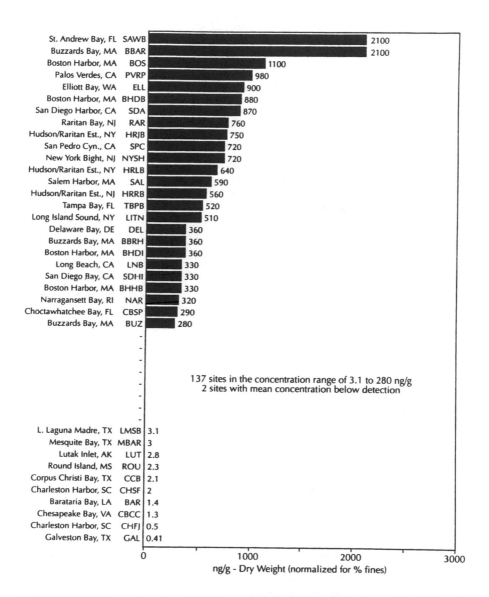

Figure 6.10–2 Total PCB concentrations in bottom sediments of various estuarine and coastal marine systems of the United States during the 1984–1987 survey period. Note elevated concentrations at Palos Verdes relative to the other systems. (From NOAA, A Summary of Data on Individual Organic Contaminants in Sediments Collected during 1984, 1985, 1986, and 1987, NOAA Tech. Mem. NOS OMA 47, National Oceanic and Atmospheric Administration, Rockville, MD, 1989.)

Table 6.10–7   PCB Concentrations in Open Ocean Plankton

Location	PCB conc. (ng/g wet wt)		
	N	Range	Mean
North Atlantic		300–450	380
Northeast Atlantic	22	10–110	
North and South Atlantic	53		200
South Atlantic	4	18–640	200
Western North Pacific	1		1.1
Bering Sea	3	1.0–1.6	1.3
Western South Pacific	3	1.2–2.3	1.7
Antarctic (Ross Sea)	1		<3
Antarctic (50–65°S, 124–126°E)	3	0.2–1.0	0.5

Source: Tanabe, S. and Tatsukawa, R., in *PCBs and the Environment,* Vol. 1, Waid, J. S., Ed., CRC Press, Boca Raton, FL, 1986, 151. With permission.

Table 6.10–8   Partitioning Values or Concentration Factors (PCBs in Lipids/PCBs in Water) for Zooplankton in Different Regions of Puget Sound

Region	Conc. Factor × 10^6			Dominant Fauna
	$N = 4$[a]	$N = 5$	$N = 6$	
Elliott Bay	1.06($\pm$0.81)[b]	1.42($\pm$1.06)	2.17($\pm$1.64)	Euphausiids
Main Basin	1.07($\pm$0.61)	1.90($\pm$1.25)	3.18($\pm$2.32)	Copepods
Whidbey Basin (Port Gardner)	0.80($\pm$0.38)	1.09($\pm$0.51)	1.47($\pm$0.75)	Copepods/euphausiids
Hood Canal	0.98($\pm$0.56)	0.74($\pm$0.52)	0.43($\pm$0.32)	Ctenophores
Sinclair Inlet	1.12($\pm$0.68)	3.61($\pm$2.02)	6.90($\pm$3.45)	Ctenophores
Admiralty Inlet and Straits of Juan de Fuca	0.34($\pm$0.21)	0.28($\pm$0.18)	0.29($\pm$0.18)	Copepods

[a] N = number of chlorines/biphenyls.
[b] Values in parentheses are standard deviations.

Source: Phillips, D. J. H., in *PCBs and the Environment,* Vol. 2, Waid, J. S., Ed., CRC Press, Boca Raton, FL, 1986, 142. With permission.

Table 6.10–9   Average Levels of PCBs (μg/kg wet) in Mussels
Measured during the MED-POL III Pollutant
Monitoring Program

| MED POL Region | No. of Samples | PCB | | |
		$\bar{X}$	σ	Range
Northwestern basin	17	307	266	22–1200
Tyrrhenian Sea	13	95	114	5–420
Adriatic Sea	159	84	221	5–2662
Aegean Sea	12	62	12	40–80

Source: Fowler, S. W., in PCBs and the Environment, Vol. 3, Waid, J. S.,
Ed., CRC Press, Boca Raton, FL, 1986, 222. With permission.

Table 6.10–10   Range of Tissue Contaminant Concentrations
Found in Mussel Species around the World[a]

Country	ΣPCBs	ΣPAHs	Cd
Netherlands	25–430	30–1300	0.3–2.5
Finland		440–1200[b]	
U.S.-east	low–930	low–3600	1.0–6.0
U.S.-west	low–4250		
Norway	76–276	2200–15,400	1.5–2.7
France[c]	250–1350	4000–20,000	1.0–4.0
Hong Kong	23–4480[b]		

Note: Tissue concentrations of contaminants were measured in
Mytilus edulis unless stated otherwise.

[a] Concentration of ΣPCBs and ΣPAHs in μg/kg dry weight; Cd in
mg/kg dry weight.
[b] Concentrations were transformed from wet weight to dry weight
assuming a ratio of 8.

Source: Eertman, R. H. M. and de Zwaan. A., in Biomonitoring of
Coastal Waters and Estuaries, Kramer, K. J. M., Ed., CRC Press,
Boca Raton, FL, 1994, 269. With permission.

Table 6.10–11   List of Target Chemical Residues Surveyed in U.S. Coastal Fish and Shellfish

Residue	Use and Occurrence
Polychlorinated biphenyls (PCB)	Dielectric fluid in capacitors: transformer fluid:
Total PCB	lubricants: hydraulic fluids; plasticizers; cutting oil
Aroclor® 1016	extenders; carbonless paper, banned in 1976; total
Aroclor 1242	is either sum of chlorination mixtures (Aroclors) or
Aroclor 1248	number
Aroclor 1254	
Aroclor 1260	
PCB by chlorination number (2–10)	
DDT and structurally related chemicals	
DDE (*o-p* and *p-p'*)	Insecticides; DDT metabolites
DDD (TDE: *o-p* and *p-p'*)	Insecticides; DDT metabolites
DDT (*o-p* and *p-p'*)	Insecticides; parents of DDD/DDE
Total DDT	Sum of parent and metabolites
Kelthane (Dicofol)	Acaricide; parent of DDE
Methoxychlor	Insecticide
Cyclodiene pesticides	
Technical chlordane	Insecticide; mix of constituents
Chlordane (*trans-* and *cis-*)	Insecticides; major constituents of technical chlordane
Nonachlor (*trans-* and *cis-*)	Insecticides; minor constituents of technical chlordane
Oxychlordane	Chlordane metabolite
Heptachlor	Insecticide; minor constituent of technical chlordane
Heptachlor epoxide	Metabolite of heptachlor
Endosulfan (I and II)	Insecticides; 7:3 mixture of stereoisomers
Endosulfan sulfonate	Metabolite of endosulfans
Aldrin	Insecticide
Dieldrin	Insecticide: Aldrin metabolite
Endrin	Insecticide
Hexachlorocyclohexane insecticides	
a-BHC	Constituent of BHC insecticide mix
Y-BHC (Lindane)	Insecticide; BHC constituent
Hexachlorocyclopentadiene pesticides	
Kepone	Acaricide, larvicide, fungicide, ant bait
Mirex	Insecticide (fire ant control)
Chlorinated camphenes	
Toxaphene	Insecticide (cotton)
Carboxylic acid derivatives	
2,4-D (2,4-DEP)	Weed herbicide (in cereals)
2,4,5-T	Wood plant herbicide
DCPA (dacthal)	Preemergence weed herbicide
Chlorinated benzenes and phenols	
HCB (hexachlorobenzene)	Fungicide
PCP (Pentachlorophenol)	Wood preservative

Source: Mearns, A. J. et al., PCB and Chlorinated Pesticide Contamination in U.S. Fish and Shellfish: A Historical Assessment Report, NOAA Tech. Mem. NOS OMA 39, National Oceanic and Atmospheric Administration, Seattle, WA, 1988.

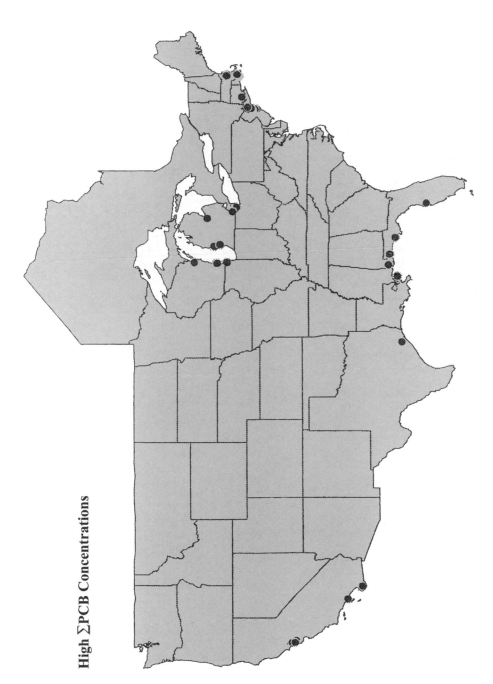

High ΣPCB Concentrations

Figure 6.10–3 Locations of high PCB concentrations recorded by the National Status and Trends Mussel Watch Project. (From O'Connor, T.P. and Beliaeff, B., *Recent Trends in Coastal Environmental Quality: Results from the Mussel Watch Project*, NOAA Tech. Rep., Department of Commerce, Rockville, MD, 1995.)

Table 6.10–12   National Status and Trends Sites Ranking among the Highest 20 in 1986, 1987, and 1988 and Overall for Total Polychlorinated Biphenyls (PCBs) in Mussels (*Mytilus edulis*) and Oysters (*Crassostrea virginica*)

Code	Location	State	Species	Ranking 1986	Ranking 1987	Ranking 1988	Ranking Overall	Significant Difference?	Trend
BBAR	Buzzards Bay	MA	me	1	1t	1	1	no	no
HRLB	Hudson/Raritan Estuary	NY	me	2	3	3t	2	yes	d
NYSR	New York Bight	NJ	me	3	17t	11	6	no	no
HRUB	Hudson/Raritan Estuary	NY	me	4	5t	2	3	no	no
SDHI	San Diego Bay	CA	me	5	4	5t	5	no	no
GBYC	Galveston Bay	TX	cv	6	8t	16	10t	no	no
NYSH	New York Bight	NJ	me	7	12	5t	7t	yes	no
BHDB	Boston Harbor	MA	me	8	5t	<	10t	no	no
BBGN	Buzzards Bay	MA	me	9	<	<	14	no	no
BBRH	Buzzards Bay	MA	me	10	1t	3t	4	no	no
BHDI	Boston Harbor	MA	me	11t	19	<	13	yes	d
LITN	Long Island Sound	NY	me	11t	8t	7t	9	no	no
EBFR	Elliott Bay	WA	me	13	<	<	19t	yes	d
BHHB	Boston Harbor	MA	me	14	13	<	18	no	no
HRJB	Hudson/Raritan Estuary	NY	me	15	<	10	15t	yes	no
LINH	Long Island Sound	CT	me	16	<	19t	<	no	no
LIMR	Long Island Sound	NY	me	17	<	14t	<	no	no
SAWB	St. Andrew Bay	FL	cv	18	<	17t	<	no	no
LISI	Long Island Sound	CT	me	19	<	<	<	no	no
NYLB	New York Bight	NJ	me	20	15	17t	19t	no	no
SFEM	San Francisco Bay	CA	me	—	5t	7t	7t	—	—
LIHH	Long Island Sound	NY	me	<	8t	<	17	yes	no
LIHR	Long Island Sound	CT	me	<	11	<	15t	yes	no
CBSP	Choctawhatchee Bay	FL	cv	<	14	<	<	no	no
MDSJ	Marina Del Rey	CA	me	<	16	<	<	yes	no
BHBI	Boston Harbor	MA	me	<	17t	<	<	yes	no
PBIB	Pensacola Bay	FL	cv	<	20	<	<	no	no
GBSC	Galveston Bay	TX	cv	—	—	9	12	—	—
APDB	Apalachicola Bay	FL	cv	<	<	12	<	yes	no
ABWJ	Anaheim Bay	CA	me	<	<	13	<	no	no
SFSM	San Francisco Bay	CA	me	<	<	19t	<	no	no
LICR	Long Island Sound	CT	me	<	<	19t	<	no	no

Note: me = *Mytilus edulis*; cv = *Crassostrea virginica*; t = two or more concentrations were equal; d = decreasing trends.

Source: NOAA, A Summary of Data on Tissue Contamination from the First Three Years (1986–1988) of the Mussel Watch Project, NOAA Tech. Memo NOS OMA 49, National Oceanic and Atmospheric Administration, Rockville, MD, 1989.

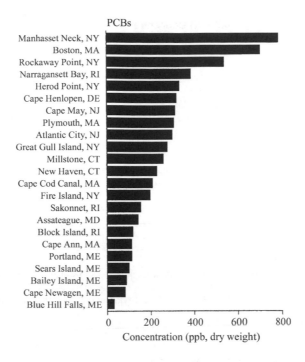

Figure 6.10–4   Concentrations of PCBs in mussels sampled at various sites from Maryland to Maine as part of the USEPA Mussel Watch Program. (From Larsen, P. F., *Rev. Aquat. Sci.,* 6, 67, 1992. With permission.)

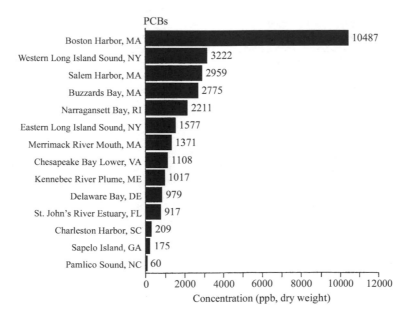

Figure 6.10–5   Concentrations of PCBs in Atlantic Coast fish liver tissue sampled by the NOAA Status and Trends Program. (From Larsen, P. F., *Rev. Aquat. Sci.,* 6, 67, 1992. With permission.)

Table 6.10–13   Total PCB Concentrations in Fish Livers from Nine
Estuarine and Coastal Marine Systems[a]

| Area | tPCB, ppm, ww | |
	1976–77	1984
Western Long Island Sound	0.62	0.81
Lower Chesapeake Bay, Virginia	0.62	0.28
Duwamish River/Elliot Bay, Washington	26.7	4.23
Nisqually Reach, Washington	0.31	0.49
Columbia River, Oregon	0.24	0.20
Coos Bay, Oregon	<0.20	<0.15
Southern San Francisco Bay, California	0.22	1.23–2.30
Palos Verdes/San Pedro Canyon, California	18.63	2.27
Dana Point, California	0.07	0.38
Median	0.31	0.49
Range: minimum	<0.20	0.15
maximum	26.7	4.23

[a] Values in ppm wet weight.

Source: Mearns, A. J. et al., PCB and Chlorinated Pesticide Contamination in U.S. Fish and Shellfish: A Historical Assessment Report, NOAA Tech. Memo NOS OMA 39, National Oceanic and Atmospheric Administration, Seattle, WA, 1988.

Table 6.10–14   PCB Concentrations in Open Ocean Fishes

| Location/Species | N | Analyzed Portion | PCB Conc. (ng/g fresh weight) | |
			Range	Mean
North Atlantic				
Flying fish		Whole		50
Flying fish (*Cypselurus exsilens*)		Muscle		1.4
Flying fish (*Prognichthys rondeletii*)		Muscle		4
Trigger fish (*Canthidermis maculatus*)		Muscle		1.9
Western North Pacific (off Japan)				
Emmelichthys struhsakeri	3	Whole	12–75	44
Tropidinis amoenus	3	Whole	17–71	35
Priacanthus boops	3	Whole	12–73	45
Bering Sea				
Herring (*Clupea pallasi*)	1	Muscle		80
Walleye pollock (*Theragra chalcogramma*)	2	Muscle	40–40	40
Flatfish (*Limanda aspera*)	7	Muscle	20–130	50
Chum salmon (*Oncorhynchus keta*)	1	Whole		5.0
Sockeye salmon (*O. nerka*)	1	Whole		15
Chum salmon (*O. keta*)	3	Whole	5.3–9.8	7.3
Walleye pollock (*T. chalcogramma*)	4	Whole	9.8–13	11
Eastern South Pacific (off Chile)				
Cheiloductylus sp.	5	Muscle	1.2–2.2	1.5
Merluccius australis	5	Muscle	0.3–0.6	0.4
Brama sp.	5	Muscle	0.6–1.6	0.9
Neophrynichthys marmoratus	4	Muscle	0.2–0.3	0.2
Coelorhyncus fasciatus	5	Muscle	0.1–0.2	0.2
Micromesistius australis	3	Whole	0.11–0.33	0.19
Coelorhynchus fasciatus	4	Whole	0.06–0.11	0.09
North Indian (Arabian Sea)				
Argyrops spinifer	2	Whole	0.74–1.4	1.1
Thryssa vitrirostris	3	Whole	0.93–2.0	1.6

Table 6.10–14   PCB Concentrations in Open Ocean Fishes (continued)

Location/Species	N	Analyzed Portion	PCB Conc. (ng/g fresh weight) Range	Mean
South Indian (off Australia)				
Coryphaena hippurus	5	Whole	0.02–0.05	0.03
Antarctic				
Two whole fish				2.0
Pagothenia borchgrevinki	21	Whole	0.18–0.77	0.31
Trematomus berenacchii	5	Whole	0.12–0.24	0.17
T. hansoni	4	Whole	0.28–0.59	0.48
T. newnesi	2	Whole	0.08–0.33	0.21

Source: Tanabe, S. and Tatsukawa, R., in *PCBs and the Environment,* Vol. 1, Waid, J. S., Ed., CRC Press, Boca Raton, FL, 1986, 152. With permission.

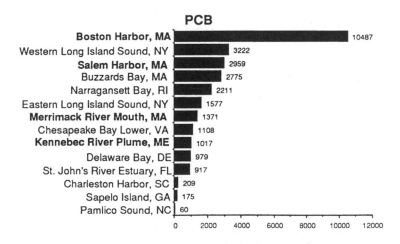

Figure 6.10–6 Concentrations (ng/g wet weight) of PCBs in Atlantic Coast fish liver tissue sampled in Chesapeake Bay and other estuarine systems by the NOAA Status and Trends Program. (From Larsen, P. F., *Rev. Aquat. Sci.,* 6, 67, 1992. With permission.)

Table 6.10–15   Summary of Action Limits and Proposed Criteria (in ppm wet weight) for PCBs and Pesticides in Fish or Shellfish

Chemical	FDA Action Limit	NSSP Shellfish	Predator Protection Levels NAS[a] Aquatic Wildlife	NAS[b] Marine Wildlife
Aldrin	0.30	0.20[c]	0.10[d]	[e]
Dieldrin	0.30	0.20[c]	0.10[d]	[e]
Endrin	0.30	0.20[c]	0.10[d]	[e]
DDT				
DDE (Sum)	5.0	1.5	1.0	0.05
DDD (TDE)				
Chlordane	0.3	0.03	0.10[d]	0.05
Heptachlor	0.3	0.20[c]	0.10[d]	0.05
Heptachlor epoxide		0.20[c]		
Lindane		0.20	0.10[d,e]	0.05
BHC (other than lindane)		0.20		
Methoxychlor		0.20		0.05
Endosulfan			0.10[d]	0.05
Mirex	0.1			0.05
Kepone	0.4 (crabs)			
	0.3 (fish, shellfish)			
Toxaphene	5.0		0.10[d]	0.05
HCB			0.1	0.05
2,4-D		0.50		
PCBs	2.0		0.5	0.5[f]
TCCD				

Note: FDA = U.S. Food and Drug Administration; NSSP = National Shellfish Sanitation Program; NAS = National Academy of Sciences.

[a] In whole fish.
[b] Homogenate of at least 25 fish of appropriate size and species.
[c] "Alert" level if combined value of the five pesticides exceeds 0.20 ppm wet weight: shellfish bed should be closed if combined values exceed 0.25 ppm wet weight.
[d] Singly or in combination with others listed.
[e] Sum of these four pesticides should not exceed 0.005 ppm wet weight.
[f] Add all Aroclors® for total.

Source: Mearns, A. J. et al., PCB and Chlorinated Pesticide Contamination in U.S. Fish and Shellfish: A Historical Assessment Report, NOAA Tech. Memo NOS OMA 39, National Oceanic and Atmospheric Administration, Seattle, WA, 1988.

Table 6.10–16   PCB Concentrations in the Blubber of Male Pinnipeds and Cetaceans

Location	Species	N	PCB Conc. (µg/g fresh weight) Range	Mean
Arctic				
Canada	Ringed seal	4	0.05–1.5	0.58
	Ringed seal	15	1–6	4.1
North Greenland	Atlantic walrus	8	0.16–1.1	0.36
North Atlantic				
Newfoundland	Harp seal	1		26
Gulf of St. Lawrence	Harp seal	7	6–22	13
Nova Scotia	Atlantic white-sided dolphin	1		37
Rhode Island	Striped dolphin	1		39
Caribbean	Long-snouted dolphin	1		5.0
South Atlantic				
Uruguay	Franciscana dolphin	5	3.2–18	6.8
North Pacific				
Bering Sea	Dalls porpoise	4	3.5–6.8	5.2
Japan	Striped dolphin	3	22–23	22
	Finless porpoise	2	64–96	80
	Pilot whale	1		2.0
California	Common dolphin	10	80–300	120
	Pilot whale	1		14
Hawaii	Rough-toothed dolphin	3	7.0–14	9.4
Eastern tropical	Striped dolphin	3	2.6–7.6	5.7
South Pacific				
Eastern tropical	Fraser's dolphin	1		5.2
	Striped dolphin	1		5.0
New Zealand	Dusky dolphin	1		1.4
Antarctic				
Syowa Station	Weddell seal	1		0.038

Source: Tanabe, S. and Tatsukawa, R., in *PCBs and the Environment,* Vol. 1, Waid, J. S., Ed., CRC Press, Boca Raton, FL, 1986, 153. With permission.

Table 6.10–17   Levels of PCBs (mg/kg) in Extractable Fat from Seal Blubber

Species	N	M	Range
Grey seal (*Halichoerus grypus*)			
Males and females			
Killed	60	110	47–330
Found dead	54	820	84–4500
Ringed seal (*Phoca hispida*)			
Males			
Killed	24	100	35–270
Found dead	12	240	38–640
Females			
Killed	61	93	27–190
Found dead	6	270	125–710
Common seal (*P. vitulina*)			
Pups			
Killed	30	43	18–100
Found dead	43	100	12–500

Note: The material is divided into actively killed animals and those found dead; N = number of specimens analyzed; M = mean value.

Source: Olsson, M., in *PCBs and the Environment,* Vol. 3, Waid. J. S., Ed., CRC Press, Boca Raton, FL, 1986, 181. With permission.

Table 6.10–18 PCBs (μg/g wet weight) in Eggs and Tissues of Mediterranean Seabirds

Species	Location	Tissue	No.	PCBs Range	$\bar{x}$
Cory's shear water (*Calonectris diomedea*)	Crete	Eggs	2	3.2–4.1	3.65
Manx shearwater (*Puffinus puffinus*)	Gibraltar	Muscle	2	0.99–1.1	1.02
Shag (*Phalacrocorax aristotelis*)	Gibraltar	Muscle	3	4.1–7.1	5.62
Lesser black-backed gull (*Larus fuscus*)	Gibraltar	Muscle	1		0.52
Herring gull (*L. argentatus*)	Madeira	Muscle	1		0.4
	Gibraltar	Muscle	3	0.82–3.8	2.12
	Balearic Iss.	Egg	1		11.0
	Rhone delta	Eggs	6	16–160	52
	Creta	Egg	1		5.32
	Cyprus	Eggs	2	1.2–4.2	2.7
	Tuscan Iss.	Eggs	25		~8.4
	Po delta	Eggs	4		4.0[a]
Audouin's gull (*L. augouini*)	Morocco	Eggs	3	3.1–4.2	3.82
	Balearic Iss.	Eggs	4	12.8–20.6	16.8
Black-headed gull (*L. ridibundus*)	Rhone delta	Eggs	4	1.6–7.8	5.45
	Po delta	Muscle	8	0.61–3.6	1.65
	N. Adriatic	Eggs	17		3.2[a]
Little gull (*L. minutus*)	Malta	Liver	1		3.6
Common tern (*Sterna hirundo*)	Po delta	Muscle	2	0.43–8.0	4.21
	Po delta	Eggs	22		3.2[a]
	N. Adriatic	Eggs	13		4.1[a]
Little tern (*S. albifrons*)	Sardinia	Eggs	12		~4.0
	N. Adriatic	Eggs	16		2.6[a]
	C. Sardinia	Eggs	6		2.8[a]
	S. Sardinia	Eggs	6		4.9[a]
Black tern (*Chlidonias nigra*)	Po delta	Muscle	1		<0.01
Coot (*Fulica atra*)	Po delta	Muscle	1		0.21
	Malta	Liver	1		0.1
	Po delta	Eggs	3		0.19[a]
Gull-billed tern (*Gelochelidon nilotica*)	S. Sardinia	Eggs	7		1.1[a]
	N. Adriatic	Eggs	15		1.7[a]
Slender-billed gull (*L. genei*)	S. Sardinia	Eggs	33		3.5[a]
Black-winged stilt (*Himantopus himantopus*)	N. Adriatic	Eggs	5		0.14[a]
Avocet (*Recurvirostra avocetta*)	N. Adriatic	Eggs	5		0.12[a]
Little egret (*Egretta garzetta*)	Po delta	Eggs	9		2.3[a]
Night heron (*Nycticorax nycticorax*)	Po delta	Eggs	8		2.3[a]

[a] Computed from dry weight values using wet/dry ratio of 3 for terns, 4.3 for gulls, and 3.5 for others.

Source: Fowler, S. W., in *PCBs and the Environment,* Vol. 3, Waid, J. S., Ed., CRC Press, Boca Raton, FL, 1986, 228. With permission.

Table 6.10–19   Accumulation of PCBs in Birds from Field Experiments

Avian Species	Residue Level in Prey	Residue Level (ppm, wet weight)				
		Whole Body	Muscle	Liver	Brain	Eggs
Great-crested grebe (*Podicep cristatus*)	0.17 (0.16–0.18)	—	—	11	—	—
	0.12 (0.04–0.35)	32	—	—	—	—
	0.8–1.3	—	—	—	—	13
Brown pelican (*Pelecanus occidentalis*)	0.19 (0.17–0.23)	—	—	—	—	2.2
White pelican	0.05–0.11	2.3	3.1	4.5	—	1.7
Double-crested cormorant (*Phalacrocoras auritus*)		3.6	2.3	2.0	—	5.7
White-crested cormorant (*P. carbo*)	1.6	6.2	—	—	4.4	2.9
White-tailed sea eagle (*Haliaetus albicilla*)	0.03–0.18	—	150–240	130	29–70	—
Common guillemot (*Uria aalge*)	0.27 (0.01–1.0)	—	—	—	—	7.9–21
	0.01–2.0	3.4	—	0.4	—	—
Herring gull (*Larus argentatus*)	2.2	—	—	—	—	124–157

Source: Peakall, D. B., in *PCBs and the Environment*, Vol. 2, Waid, J. S., Ed., CRC Press, Boca Raton, FL, 1986, 34. With permission.

Table 6.10–20   PCB Levels in Herring Gulls and Their Eggs

Location	Tissue	Residual Level (ppm, wet weight)
Norway (west coast)	Egg	3.1–12.6
Baltic (Gdansk Bay)	Muscle	23–150
Finland	Muscle	0.68–38
East Scotland	Muscle	0.2–1.2
Camargue, France	Egg	16–160
New Brunswick, Canada	Egg	3.1–8.2
Lake Ontario	Egg	74–261
Maine	Egg	(0–32.0)
		7.76 (30)
Virginia	Egg	(0.13–16.70)
		9.06 (28)
East Frisian Island, Germany	Egg	26.5
		5.5
Denmark (North Sea)	Egg	2.1 (1.3–2.6)
Baltic		92 (21–199)

Source: Adapted from Peakall, D. B., in *PCBs and the Environment*, Vol. 2, Waid, J. S., Ed., CRC Press, Boca Raton, FL, 1986, 43. With permission.

Table 6.10–21 PCBs in Miscellaneous Tissues and Fluids of Various Human
Populations

	Avg. Conc. (ng/m³) as Aroclor®		
	Total	1242	1254
Urban			
Denver, CO	2.25	1.80	0.45
Columbia, SC	4.70	3.20	1.50
Houston, TX	—	—	3.00
Minneapolis, MN	7.10	5.60	1.56
Chicago, IL	8.00	6.70	1.28
Madison, WI	7.50	6.50	1.05
Milwaukee, WI	2.25	1.64	0.61
Ontario, several cities			
	5.90	—	—
	0.21	—	—
Stockholm, Sweden	0.34	0.23	0.11
Jacksonville, FL	4.70	—	—
Gainesville, FL	20.00	—	—
Rural/suburban/coastal			
Pigeon Key, FL	—	—	0.41
North Inlet Estuary, SC	0.44	0.25	0.19
Texas Gulf Coast	—	—	0.52
	—	—	0.067
College Station, TX	—	—	0.29
White Sands, NM	—	—	0.11
Ontario Province			
	5.40	—	—
	0.19	—	—
Rural Sweden	0.07	0.04	0.03
Rural Norway	—	—	0.02[a]
Great Lakes			
Lake Michigan	0.87	0.65	0.22
Lake Superior	1.20	0.86	0.34
Marine			
Gulf of Mexico	—	—	0.16
Newfoundland	—	—	0.096
Barbados	—	—	0.065
Enewetak Atoll	0.11	0.061	0.049
American Samoa	—	—	0.012
Peruvian Coast	—	—	0.012
Bermuda	—	—	0.075
E. Indian Ocean	0.15	—	—
W. Pacific	0.34	—	—
Antarctic/Southern Ocean	0.11	—	—
Arctic Ocean	—	—	0.02[a]

Note: —, not measured or not reported.

[a] Pentachlorobiphenyls.

Source: Mes, J., in PCBs and the Environment, Vol. 3, Waid, J. S., Ed., CRC Press, Boca
Raton, FL, 1986, 51. With permission.

Table 6.10–22 Concentrations (ng/l) of DDT and Metabolites in Open Ocean Surface Waters

Region	N	p,p'-DDT	o,p'-DDT	p,p'-DDE	p,p'-DDD	ΣDDT
Mediterranean		(2–24)		(0.5–2.0)	0.7–2.0	
	3	1.2ᵃ		0.2 = ΣDDE + DDD		1.4
	16	0.4		0.2 = ΣDDE + DDD		0.6
	32	0.7		0.3 = ΣDDE + DDD		1.0
	35	0.5		0.5 = ΣDDE + DDD		1.0
Subarctic Atlantic	10	0.4		0.5 = ΣDDE + DDD		0.9
	73	0.2		0.4 = ΣDDE + DDD		0.6
	54	0.4		0.2 = ΣDDE + DDD		0.6
	49	0.2		0.1 = ΣDDE + DDD		0.3
Subtropical Atlantic	15	0.7		0.1 = ΣDDE + DDD		0.8
	30	0.3		0.2 = ΣDDE + DDD		0.5
	49	0.7		0.1 = ΣDDE + DDD		0.8
	39	0.5		0.2 = ΣDDE + DDD		0.7
Tropical Atlantic	11	0.3		0.4 = ΣDDE + DDD		0.7
	34	0.4		0.3 = ΣDDE + DDD		0.7
Northwest Atlantic Sargasso Sea	6	<8 ndᵇ		2.9 ± 2.7 (<0.35–7.5)	<0.8 nd	
	9	0.2 ± 0.1ᶜ (<0.15–0.5)	<0.05			
Northeast Atlantic						
Norway to Iceland		+ᵈ		+	+	500 ± 90
Norway to Ireland		2		+	+	500 ± 90
North Pacific (NC Pacific Gyre)	2	<0.002		<0.01		0.02 ± 0.01 (0.01–0.04)
Bering Sea	7	+		+	+	
Northwest Pacific	2	0.0016, 0.0007		0.0011, 0.0007		
	13	+		+	+	0.11 ± 0.05 (0.06–0.23)
	8	+		+	+	0.90 ± 0.26 (0.52–1.35)

(continued)

Table 6.10–22   Concentrations (ng/l) of DDT and Metabolites in Open Ocean Surface Waters (continued)

Region	N	p,p'-DDT	o,p'-DDT	p,p'-DDE	p,p'-DDD	ΣDDT
	6	+		+	+	0.25 ± 0.03 (0.22–0.27)
	8	+		+	+	0.38 ± 0.41 (0.02–1.17)
Northeast Pacific, Mexico	23	(<1–20)		(<1–<10)	(<1–<80)	
Indo-Pacific	15	0.03 ± 0.03 (0.005–0.091)	0.01 ± 0.01 (0.001–0.018)	0.004 ± 0.003 (0.001–0.013)		0.04 ± 0.04 (0.007–0.13)
Indian Ocean						
Arabian Sea and Bay of Bengal	6	+		+	+	0.10 ± 0.04
Antarctic (below Australia)	12	0.01 ± 0.01 (0.003 ± 0.053)	0.003 ± 0.002 (0.001–0.006)	0.002 ± 0.001 (0.001–0.005)		0.02 ± 0.01 (0.005–0.058)
China Sea	3	+		+	+	0.08 ± 0.02

Note: See original source for particular studies.

[a] Mean.
[b] Not detected.
[c] Mean ± SD (range).
[d] Present.

Source: Harding, G. C., *Mar. Ecol. Prog. Ser.*, 33, 167, 1986. With permission.

Table 6.10–23 Concentrations (ng/l) of DDT and Metabolites in Coastal and Nearshore Surface Waters

Region	N	p,p'DDT	p,p'DDE	p,p'DDD	ΣDDT
Baltic Sea					
Western Baltic Sea	21	0.2± 0.1 (0.1–0.3)		2.4 ± 0.6 (0.8–3.4)	
	18	0.2 ± 0.1 (nd–0.4)		0.1 ± 0.1 (nd–0.4)	
Mediterranean					
Marseilles		(70–180)	(30–120)		
Monaco	3				(0.04 ± 0.01[a] (0.04–0.05)
Northeast Atlantic					
British Isles	31	+[b]	+	+	0.05 ± 0.07 (<0.01–0.25)
Brest					1.5 ± 2.8
Northwest Atlantic					
North Carolina	4	nd[c] (<8.0)	7.9 ± 6.9 (3.5–18.1)	nd (<0.8)	
Texas (Corpus Christi Bay)	8				1.32 ± 1.04 (0.2–3.1)
Southwest Atlantic					
Brazil (Santos Estuary)	64				(nd–40)
Argentina[d] (Blanca Bay)	15	37.9 ± 87.2 (nd–346.0)		nd	
North Pacific					
Hawaii Canal	6	9.0 (0.4–41.0)	0.3 (0.1–0.6)	3.6 (0.1–10.0)	
Northeast Pacific					
San Francisco Bay	24	5 ± 5 (1–18)	2 ± 1 (1–4)	2 ± 2 (1–7)	8 ± 5 (3–23)
Monterey Bay to San Diego	4	+	+	+	2.4 ± 0.2 (2.4–2.7) (0.9–17.5)
California coast					
	7	0.5 ± 0.6 (<0.1–1.9)	1.0 ± 1.6 (<0.1–4.6)		
Southern California Bight	14	0.6 ± 0.3 (0.3–1.3)	0.10 ± 0.03 (0.06–0.13)		0.7 ± 0.3 (0.34–1.43)
Southern California	20	(<0.05–0.8)	(<0.05–5.9)	(<0.03–2.2)	
North Sea					
German Bight	24	0.3 ± 0.2 (0.1–0.6)		1.5 ± 0.6 (0.5–2.6)	
	17	0.33 ± 0.15 (0.11–0.63)	0.11 ± 0.06 (nd–0.21)	0.20 ± 0.15 (nd-0.57)	
Hanö Bight	8	0.04 ± 0.08 (nd–0.21)	1.7 ± 1.6 (0.8–5.2)		
Antarctic[e]					
Syowa Station	6	+	+		0.008 ± 0.008 (0.001–0.021)

Note: See original source for particular studies.

[a] Mean ± SD (range).
[b] Present.
[c] Not detected.
[d] *o,p'*-DDT, 13.4 ± 24.5, (nd–94.5).
[e] *o,p'*-DDT, +.

Source: Harding, G. C., *Mar. Ecol. Prog. Ser.,* 33, 167, 1986. With permission.

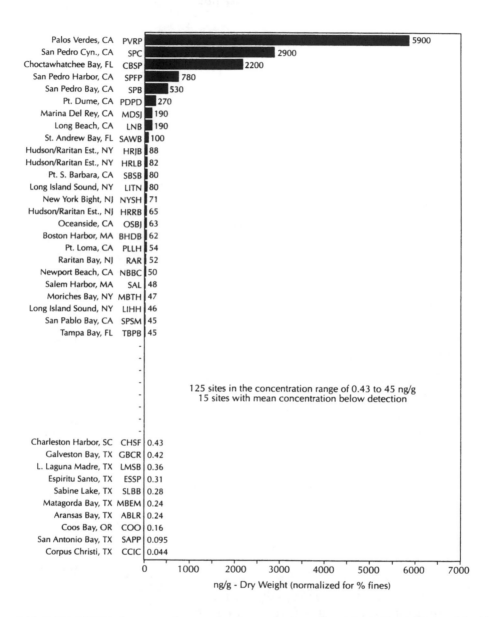

Figure 6.10–7   Total DDT in bottom sediments of various estuarine and coastal marine systems of the United States during the mid-1980s. Note elevated concentrations at Palos Verdes relative to the other systems. (From NOAA, A Summary of Data on Individual Organic Contaminants in Sediments Collected during 1984, 1985, 1986, and 1987, NOAA Tech. Memo NOS OMA 47, National Oceanic and Atmospheric Administration, Rockville, MD, 1989.)

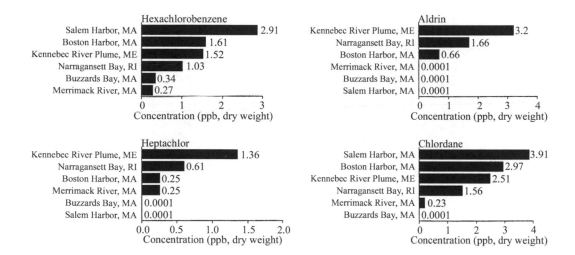

Figure 6.10–8 Concentrations of individual pesticides in New England marine sediments. (From Larsen, P. F., *Rev. Aquat. Sci.,* 6, 67, 1992. With permission.)

High ΣDDT Concentrations

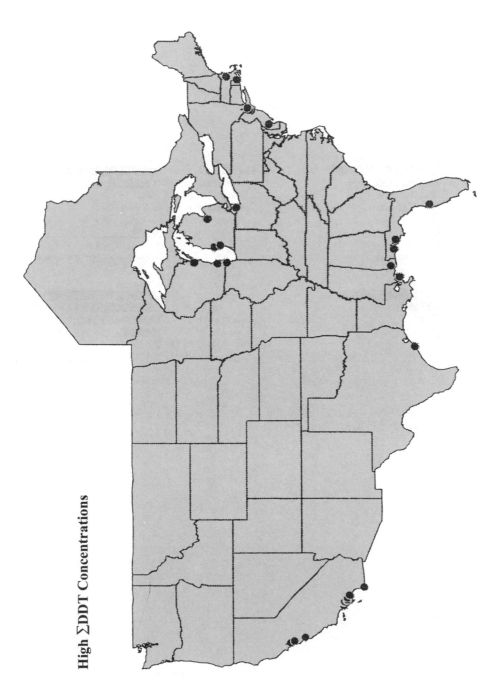

Figure 6.10–9 Locations of high DDT concentrations recorded by the National Status and Trends Mussel Watch Project. (From O'Connor, T.P. and Beliaeff, B., *Recent Trends in Coastal Environmental Quality: Results from the Mussel Watch Project*, NOAA Tech. Rep., Department of Commerce, Rockville, MD, 1995.)

Table 6.10-24 National Status and Trends Sites Ranking among the Highest 20 in 1986, 1987, and 1988 and Overall for Total DDT in Mussels (*Mytilus edulis, M. californianus*) and Oysters (*Crassostrea virginica*) from Various Estuarine and Coastal Marine Systems

Code	Location	State	Species	Ranking 1986	1987	1988	Overall	Significant Difference?	Trend
HRLB	Hudson/Raritan Estuary	NY	me	1t	7	10	5	yes	d
SPFP	San Pedro Harbor	CA	me	1t	4	1	2	no	no
PVRP	Palos Verdes	CA	me	1t	1	2	1	no	no
ABWJ	Anaheim Bay	CA	me	4	3	4	4	yes	no
SFDB	San Francisco Bay	CA	me	5	11t	∨	16	no	no
CBSP	Choctawhatchee Bay	FL	cv	6	2	3	3	no	no
BBAR	Buzzards Bay	MA	me	7t	∨	∨	∨	yes	d
NYSH	New York Bight	NJ	me	7t	19t	16t	14t	no	no
IBNJ	Imperial Beach	CA	me	9	10	7	10	no	no
NYSR	New York Bight	NJ	me	10	∨	∨	∨	no	no
LITN	Long Island Sound	NY	me	11	11t	∨	17	yes	no
HRUB	Hudson/Raritan Estuary	NY	me	12t	14t	8	11	no	no
CBCC	Chesapeake Bay	VA	cv	12t	∨	∨	∨	yes	d
SAWB	St. Andrew Bay	FL	cv	12t	∨	∨	∨	yes	no
SLSL	San Luis Obispo Bay	CA	mc	12t	∨	∨	∨	no	no
HRJB	Hudson/Raritan Estuary	NY	me	16t	∨	13	20	yes	no
DBBD	Delaware Bay	DE	cv	16t	8	∨	12	no	no
PDPD	Point Dume	CA	mc	18	6	12	9	no	no
LIMR	Long Island Sound	NY	me	19t	∨	∨	∨	no	no
MBCP	Mobile Bay	AL	cv	19t	∨	18t	∨	no	no
GBYC	Galveston Bay	TX	cv	19t	∨	∨	∨	no	no
MBSC	Monterey Bay	CA	mc	19t	∨	∨	∨	no	no
SFEM	San Francisco Bay	CA	me	—	5	9	7	—	—
MDSJ	Marina Del Rey	CA	me	∨	9	5	8	yes	i
DBAP	Delaware Bay	DE	cv	∨	13	∨	∨	no	no
BHDB	Boston Harbor	MA	me	∨	14t	∨	∨	no	no

(continued)

Table 6.10–24 National Status and Trends Sites Ranking among the Highest 20 in 1986, 1987, and 1988 and Overall for Total DDT in Mussels (*Mytilus edulis, M. californianus*) and Oysters (*Crassostrea virginica*) from Various Estuarine and Coastal Marine Systems (continued)

Code	Location	State	Species	Ranking 1986	Ranking 1987	Ranking 1988	Ranking Overall	Significant Difference?	Trend
NBWJ	Newport Beach	CA	mc	v	14t	v	v	no	no
SFSM	San Francisco Bay	CA	me	v	14t	v	v	no	no
SDHI	San Diego Bay	CA	me	v	15t	v	v	no	no
PGLP	Pacific Grove	CA	mc	v	15t	v	v	no	no
DBKI	Delaware Bay	DE	cv	v	19t	v	v	no	no
MBHI	Mobile Bay	AL	cv	—	—	6	6	—	—
OSBJ	Oceanside	CA	me	v	v	11	v	yes	i
MRPL	Mississippi River	LA	cv	—	—	14	13	—	—
GBSC	Galveston Bay	TX	cv	—	—	15	14t	—	—
APDB	Apalachicola Bay	FL	cv	v	v	16t	v	no	no
MSPB	Mississippi Sound	MS	cv	v	v	18t	v	yes	i
BRFS	Brazos River	TX	cv	—	—	18t	18t	—	—
SANM	San Miguel Island	CA	mc	—	—	18t	18t	—	—

Note: me = *Mytilus edulis*; mc = *Mytilus californianus*; cv = *Crassostrea virginica*; t = two or more concentrations were equal; d = decreasing trends; i = increasing trends.

Source: NOAA, A Summary of Data on Tissue Contamination from the First Three Years (1986–1988) of the Mussel Watch Project, NOAA Tech. Memo NOS OMA 49, National Oceanic and Atmospheric Administration, Rockville, MD, 1989.

Table 6.10–25 Median or Geometric Mean DDT Concentrations for Several National Survey Events

| Organism: Substrate | tDDT or DDE, ppm ww by Sampling Period | | | |
	1965–72	1972–75	1976–77	1984–86
Bivalves	0.024[1]		0.01[2]/0.001[3]	0.003[10]
Fish, whole juvenile		0.014[4]	ND	ND
Fish, muscle		0.110[5]	0.012[6]	
Fish, liver			0.220[6]	0.054[7]
Fish, whole F.W.	0.7–1.1[8]	0.4–0.6[8]	0.370[9]	

Note: See original source for reference material.

[1] From Butler (1973); median of 8180 site means composited from 7839 samples.
[2] From original data supporting Butler et al. (1978); median of 89 site means composited from 188 samples.
[3] From Farrington et al. (1981); median of 80 site values or site means.
[4] From original data supporting Butler and Schutzmann (1978); median of 144 site means composited from 1524 composites.
[5] From original data supporting Stout and Beezhold (1981) and Stout (1980); median of area or site means from samples.
[6] From original data supporting Butler (1978) and Sherwood (1982); median of 19 site means from samples.
[7] From original data supporting Zdanowicz et al. (1986), Malins et al. (1986), and Hanson et al. (1986); median of 42 site medians from 126 composites.
[8] From Schmitt et al. (1983).
[9] From Schmitt et al. (1985).
[10] Preliminary calculations from NOAA (1987).

Source: Mearns, A. J. et al., PCB and Chlorinated Pesticide Contamination in U.S. Fish and Shellfish: A Historical Assessment Report, NOAA Tech. Memo NOS OMA 39, Natural Oceanic and Atmospheric Administration, Seattle, WA, 1988.

Table 6.10–26 Relative Proportions of DDT Components in Fish and Other Organisms from North Atlantic

| Group | Components of Σ DDT (%) | | |
	p,p'-DDE	*p,p'*-DDD	*p,p'*-DDT
Bivalves	51	36	13
Crustacea	84	12	4
Groundfish	45	14	41
Pelagic fish	45	17	38

Source: Murty, A. S., *Toxicity of Pesticides to Fish,* Vol. 1, CRC Press, Boca Raton, FL, 1986, 50. With permission.

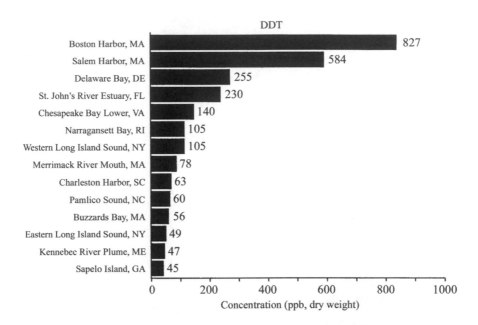

Figure 6.10–10 Concentrations of DDT in Atlantic Coast fish liver tissue sampled by the NOAA Status and Trends Program. (From Larsen, P. F., *Rev. Aquat. Sci.,* 6, 67, 1992. With permission.)

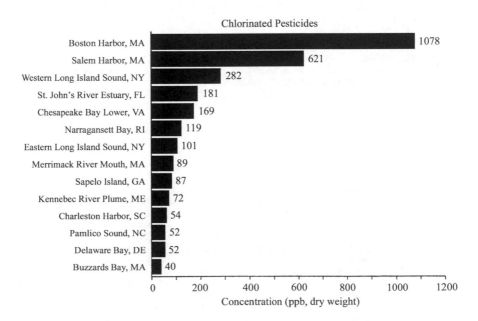

Figure 6.10–11 Concentrations of total chlorinated pesticides in Atlantic Coast fish liver tissue sampled by the NOAA Status and Trends Program. (From Larsen, P. F., *Rev. Aquat. Sci.,* 6, 67, 1992. With permission.)

Table 6.10–27   The Contamination of Various Species of Pelagic Seabirds by DDT, Its Metabolites, and PCBs

Species	Place of Capture (Place of Reproduction)	Tissues Analyzed	DDT and Metabolites (ppm)	PCBs (ppm)
Fulmarus glacialis	California (Alaska)	Whole bird	7.1	2.3
Puffinus creatopus	Mexico (Chile)	Whole bird	3.0	0.4
P. griseus	California (New Zealand)	Fats	11.3	1.1
		Fats	40.9	52.6
P. gravis	New Brunswick (Southern Atlantic)	Fats	70.9	104.3
Pterodroma cahow	Bermudas (same)	Whole bird	6.4	—
Oceanodroma leuchorhoea (Leach's petrel)	California (same)	Fats ex ovo	953	351
Oceanites oceanicus (Wilson's petrel)	New Brunswick (Antarctica)	Fats	199	697

Source: Ramade, F., in Aquatic Ecotoxicology: Fundamental Concepts and Methodologies, Boudou, A. and Ribeyre, F., Eds., CRC Press, Boca Raton, FL, 1989, 156. With permission.

Table 6.10–28   Representative Bioconcentration Factors (BCF) of Some Pesticides

Compound	Species	Conc. in Water	Duration of Exposure	BCF
DDT	Fathead minnow	0.5–2 μg/l	56–112 d	100,000
	Golden shiner	0.3 μg/l	15 d	100,000
	Green fish	0.11–0.33 μg/l	15 d	17,500
	Pinfish and Atlantic croaker	0.1–1 μg/l	15 d	10,000 to 38,000
	Daphnia magna	8–50 μg/l	24 h	16,000 to 23,000
	Salmo gairdneri	133–176 μg/l	84 d	21,300 to 51,300
Dieldrin	Sculpin	0.017–8.6 μg/l	32 d	300 to 11,000
	Guppy	0.8–4.3 μg/l	18 d	49,307
	Bluegill (static test)	1 μg/l	48 h	2441
	Bluegill (flowthrough test)	1.5 μg/l	48 h	1727
Heptachlor	Sheepshead minnow	6.5–21 μg/l	96 h	7400 to 21,300
	Pinfish	0.32–32 μg/l	96 h	3800 to 7700
	Spot	1.2–3.7 μg/l	96 h	3800 to 13,800
Mirex	Juvenile pinfish	25–46 μg/l	3 d	3800
Kepone	Sheepshead minnow juveniles	41–780 μg/l	21 d	2600
	Adult male	41–780 μg/l	21 d	7600
	Adult female	41–780 μg/l	21 d	5700
HCH	Pinfish	18.4–31.3 μg/l	4 d	218
	Sheepshead minnow	41.9–108.3 μg/l	4 d	490
	Guppy	10–1400 μg/l	24 h	500
Technical HCH	Pinfish, edible part	1.4–36 μg/l	24 h	500
	Pinfish, offal	1.4–36 μg/l	28 d	175
Chlordane	Goldfish	3.4 μg/l	4 d	67 to 162
	Sheepshead minnow	15–51 μg/l	4 d	12,600 to 18,700
	Pinfish	5.4–15.2	4 d	3000 to 7500
HCB	Killifish	160–380 μg/l	6.68 h	65 to 710
	Fathead minnow	—	—	16,200
	Green sunfish	—	—	21,900
	Rainbow trout	—	—	5500
Permethrin	Juvenile Atlantic salmon	1.4–12 μg/l	89 h	73
Cypermethrin	Juvenile Atlantic salmon	1.4–12 μg/l	96 h	3 to 7
Fenvalerate	Juvenile Atlantic salmon	1 μg/l	96 h	200

Table 6.10–28   Representative Bioconcentration Factors (BCF) of Some Pesticides (continued)

Compound	Species	Conc. in Water	Duration of Exposure	BCF
PCP	Trout	2 mg/l	24 h	100
	Killifish	57–120 µg/l	168 h	10 to 64
		100–610 µg/l	240 h	8 to 50
Trichlorophenol	*Poecilia* female	610 µg/l	36 h	12,180
	Poecilia male	350 µg/l	36 h	7000
Leptophos	Bluegill sunfish	240 µg/l	10 d	750
Fenitrothion	Killifish	800 µg/l	10 d	53
	Coho salmon underyearling	560 µg/l	24 h	16
Diazinon	Topmouth gudgeon	10 µg/l	7 d	152
	Silver crucian carp	10 µg/l	7 d	37
	Carp	10 µg/l	7 d	65
	Guppy	10 µg/l	7 d	18
Fluridone	Fathead minnow	140 mg/l	10 weeks	64
2,4-D	Bluegill sunfish	3 mg/l	8 d	1
2,4,5-T	Bluegill sunfish	3 µg/l	8 d	1
MCPA	Trout	10–100 mg/l	10–28 d	1
Fosamine ammonium	Channel catfish	1.1 mg/l	4 weeks	1
Hexamethyl phosphoramide	Sheepshead minnow	0.5 mg/l	28 d	1
Benthiocarb	Fathead minnow	28 µg/l	2.5 d	446 to 471
	Channel catfish	29 µg/l	3 d	120
	Bluegill	28 µg/l	5 d	91
	Longear sunfish	99 µg/l	1–5 d	280 to 300

Source: Murty, A. S., *Toxicity of Pesticides to Fish,* Vol. 1, CRC Press, Boca Raton, FL, 1986, 70. With permission.

Table 6.10–29   Bioaccumulation and Toxicity of Toxaphene in Estuarine Organisms

Species	96-h LC$_{50}$ (mg/l)	96-h BCF[a] (tissue/water)
Pink shrimp (*Penaeus duorarum*)	1.4	3100–20,600
Grass shrimp (*Palaemonetes pugio*)	4.4	3100–20,600
Sheepshead minnow (*Cyprinodon variegatus*)	1.1	400–1200
Pinfish (*Lagodon rhomboides*)	0.5	400–1200
Longnose killifish (*Fandulus similis*)	0.1–1.4[b]	4200–60,000 (whole body)

[a] BCF = bioconcentration factor.
[b] 28 days.

Source: Sergeant, D. B. and Onuska, F. I., in *Analysis of Trace Organics in the Aquatic Environment*, Afghan, B. K. and Chau, A. S. Y., Eds., CRC Press, Boca Raton, FL, 1989, 75. With permission.

Table 6.10–30 Summaries of Summed Concentrations of Three Chlordane Compounds (Σ *cis-* and *trans-*Chlordane, *cis-* and *trans-*Nonachlor, Oxychlordane, and Heptachlor) in Fish and Shellfish Collected in the Coastal and Estuarine Environment of the United States 1986–1987

Matrix	N	Σ Chlordane Range	Minimum Species	Minimum Location	Maximum Species	Maximum Location
Bottom-feeding fish (whole body)	40	6.91[b]–409	Red drum	So. Brunswick River, GA	Stingray	Colorado Lagoon, CA
Predatory fish (fillet)	8	6.94[b]–30.9	Spotted seatrout	North River, GA	Atlantic croaker	Houston Ship Channel, TX
Predatory fish (whole body)	8	7.50[b]–42.5	Sheepshead	North River, GA	Bluefish	Manhasset Bay, NY
Shellfish	6	7.50[b]–11.9	Softshell clam	Grays Harbor, WA	Shellfish (unidentified)	Lake Pontchartrain, LA

[a] Values in ng/g (ppb) wet weight.
[b] All five chlordane compound concentrations below quantitation limits; value shown reflects one half specified limits.

Source: Shigenaka, G., Chlordane in the Marine Environment of the United States: Review and Results from the National Status and Trends Program, NOAA Tech. Memo NOS OMA 55, National Oceanic and Atmospheric Administration, Seattle, WA, 1991.

Table 6.10–31 Ranges of Concentrations of Chlordane Compounds Measured in Tissues of Marine Mammals

Species	Tissue	Reporting Basis	Target Compounds	Range (ppb)
Harbor seal (*Phoca vitulina*)	Blubber	Wet	(not defined)	ND
Humpback whale (*Megaptera novaeangliae*)	Blubber	Wet	α-c	ND–200
Sperm whale (*Physeter catodon*)				ND–300
Dense-beaked whale (*Mesoplodon densirostris*)				100–300
Atlantic pilot whale (*Globicephala melaena*)				600–1400
Atlantic white-sided dolphin (*Lagenorhynchus acutus*)				ND
Saddleback dolphin (*Delphinus delphis*)				1200
Striped dolphin (*Stenella caeruleoalba*)				1400–2700
Pacific white-sided dolphin (*Lagenorhynchus obliquidens*)				5000
Pacific pilot whale (*Globicephala scammoni*)				ND
Grey seal (*Halichoerus gryphus*)	Blubber	Lipid	α, γ, oxy-c, *t*-n	10,000
Harbor seal (*Phoca vitulina*)	Liver	Wet	(chlordane)	<70–<100
			(heptachlor)	<20
	Brain		(chlordane)	<60
			(heptachlor)	<20
Harbor seal (*P. vitulina*)	Blubber	Lipid	*c-,t-*, oxy-c, *t*-n	500–5700
	Liver			2300
	Brain			940
White-beaked dolphin (*L. albirostris*)	Blubber			5400–11,300

Note: See original source for particular studies. ND = not determined.

Source: Shigenaka, G., Chlordane in the Marine Environment of the United States: Review and Results from the National Status and Trends Program. NOAA Tech. Memo NOS OMA 55, National Oceanic and Atmospheric Administration, Seattle, WA, 1991.

Table 6.10–32 Organochlorine Pesticides in Whales (Blubber)

Pesticide[a]	F-155[b]	F-155	F-155[c] Muscle	F-155[c] Liver	F-156	F-199	F-199	SE-200	SE-278
HCB	302	257	2.8	11.7	296	119	92.5	25.3	40.4
α-BHC	87.9	106	1.1	4.8	88.9	30.2	35.3	34.9	48.6
γ-BHC	13.2	13.5	0.19	0.31	12.9	4.3	4.3	5.9	8.0
β-BHC	22.0	22.6	0.81	10.5	19.9	7.6	6.1	4.7	6.7
Ochlor	48.8	54.5	0.85	1.8	46.5	23.3	19.9	10.4	13.5
Hepta epox	50.1	52.1	1.1	2.9	41.4	23.9	20.2	18.2	18.2
γ-Chlor					6.4	8.5	5.0		
T-Nona	232	284	4.5	7.0	214	116	80.5	34.8	51.0
α-Chlor	51.5	52.7	1.5	2.9	48.1	23.7	21.7	8.1	9.6
p,p´-DDE	1300	1540	19.2	32.6	1246	510	482	134	289
o,p´-DDD	150	167	3.7	15.4	126				
o,p´-DDT	692	743	10.0	1.4	585	204	159	60.4	110
p,p´-DDD	518	594	10.0	19.9	442	207	197	76.6	117
p,p´-DDT	437	680	5.3	5.5	494	164	139	95.2	201

[a] HCB = hexachlorobenzene; α-BHC = hexachlorocyclohexane, alpha isomer; γ-BHC = gamma isomer; β-BHC = beta isomer; Ochlor = oxychlordane; α-chlor = cis-chlordane; γ-chlor = trans-chlordane; Hepta epox = heptachlor epoxide; T-nona = trans nonachlor.
[b] See Table 3 legend of original source for whale description.
[c] Freeze-dried weight, all other samples are blubber.

Source: Lambertsen, R. H., in Biomarkers of Environmental Contamination, McCarthy, J. F. and Shugart, L. R., Eds., Lewis Publishers, Boca Raton, FL, 1990, 404. With permission.

Table 6.10–33 Organochlorine Pesticides in Whales (Concentrations Normalized to Lipids)

Pesticide[a]	F-155[b]	F-155	F-155 Muscle	F-155 Liver	F-156[c]	F-199[d]	F-199	SE-200[e]	SE-278[f]
HCB	396	257	55.1	68.5	366	147	115	30.9	48.8
α-BHC	115	106	21.6	28.3	110	37.4	44.1	42.5	58.7
γ-BHC	17.3	13.5	3.6	1.8	16.0	5.3	5.4	7.2	9.6
β-BHC	28.9	22.6	16.0	61.0	24.6	9.4	7.7	5.7	8.1
Ochlor	64.0	54.5	16.6	10.5	57.4	28.9	24.8	12.7	16.3
Hepta epox	65.7	52.1	21.7	17.1	51.1	29.6	25.2	22.2	22.0
γ-Chlor					7.9	10.6	6.2		
T-Nona	304	284	89.0	40.7	264	144	100	42.4	61.6
α-Chlor	67.6	52.7	28.7	16.6	59.4	29.4	27.1	9.9	11.7
p,p´-DDE	1710	1542	378	190	1540	632	602	163	349
o,p´-DDD	197	167	72.3	89.6	156				
o,p´-DDT	908	743	196	39.8	722	253	198	73.7	133
p,p´-DDD	680	594	196	116	547	257	246	93.5	141
p,p´-DDT	574	680	104	32.0	610	203	173	116	242

[a] See Table 2 of original source for full name of pesticides.
[b] Male fin whale 51 ft long.
[c] Male fin whale 53 ft long.
[d] Two-year-old female fin whale 57 ft long.
[e] Male sei whale 41 ft long.
[f] Eight-year-old female sei whale 42 ft long.

Source: Lambertsen, R. H., in Biomarkers of Environmental Contamination, McCarthy, J. F. and Shugart, L. R., Eds., Lewis Publishers, Boca Raton, FL, 1990, 405. With permission.

6.11 HEAVY METALS

Table 6.11–1 Trace Metals in Sediments from Selected Estuarine and Coastal Marine Systems in the United States (ppm)

Estuary	Chromium	Copper	Lead	Zinc	Cadmium	Silver	Mercury
Casco Bay, ME	92.10	16.97	29.13	76.27	0.15	0.09	0.12
Merrimack River, MA	41.15	6.47	23.25	35.75	0.07	0.05	0.08
Salem Harbor, MA	2296.67	95.07	186.33	238.00	5.87	0.88	1.19
Boston Harbor, MA	223.67	148.00	123.97	291.67	1.61	2.64	1.05
Buzzards Bay, MA	73.66	25.02	30.72	97.72	0.23	0.37	0.12
Narragansett Bay, RI	93.60	78.95	60.25	144.43	0.35	0.56	0.00
East Long Island Sound, NY	37.63	11.26	22.13	58.83	0.11	0.15	0.09
West Long Island Sound, NY	131.50	111.00	69.75	243.00	0.73	0.68	0.48
Raritan Bay, NJ	181.00	181.00	181.00	433.75	2.74	2.06	2.34
Delaware Bay, DE	27.76	8.34	15.04	49.66	0.24	0.11	0.09
Lower Chesapeake Bay, VA	58.50	11.32	15.70	66.23	0.38	0.08	0.10
Pamlico Sound, NC	79.67	14.13	30.67	102.67	0.33	0.09	0.11
Sapelo Sound, GA	51.80	5.93	16.00	38.33	0.09	0.02	0.03
St. Johns River, FL	37.67	9.77	26.00	67.67	0.18	0.11	0.07
Charlotte Harbor, FL	26.47	1.17	4.33	7.20	0.08	0.01	0.02
Tampa Bay, FL	23.70	4.97	4.67	9.10	0.15	0.08	0.03
Apalachicola Bay, FL	69.17	16.93	30.67	111.57	0.05	0.06	0.06
Mobile Bay, AL	93.00	17.40	29.67	161.00	0.11	0.11	0.12
Mississippi River Delta, LA	72.27	19.40	22.67	90.00	0.47	0.17	0.06
Barataria Bay, LA	52.07	10.50	18.33	59.33	0.19	0.09	0.05
Galveston Bay, TX	41.13	8.03	18.33	33.97	0.05	0.09	0.03
San Antonio Bay, TX	39.43	5.57	11.33	32.00	0.07	0.09	0.02
Corpus Christi Bay, TX	31.43	6.63	13.00	56.00	0.19	0.07	0.04
Lower Laguna Madre, TX	24.53	5.83	11.33	36.00	0.09	0.07	0.03
San Diego Harbor, CA	178.00	218.67	50.97	327.67	0.99	0.76	1.04
San Diego Bay, CA	49.70	7.67	11.61	58.67	0.04	0.76	0.04
Dana Point, CA	39.80	10.03	18.80	53.67	0.22	0.80	0.13
Seal Beach, CA	108.33	26.00	27.37	125.00	0.17	1.27	0.59
San Pedro Canyon, CA	106.50	31.33	17.33	118.33	1.17	1.20	0.32

(continued)

Table 6.11–1   Trace Metals in Sediments from Selected Estuarine and Coastal Marine Systems in the United States (ppm) (continued)

Estuary	Chromium	Copper	Lead	Zinc	Cadmium	Silver	Mercury
Santa Monica Bay, CA	53.53	10.53	33.37	46.67	0.18	0.51	0.01
San Francisco Bay, CA	1466.67	160.71	67.39	501.66	0.51	0.37	0.25
Bodega Bay, CA	246.33	0.06	2.17	38.33	0.18	1.74	0.14
Coos Bay, OR	110.30	1.47	4.65	32.00	0.62	0.31	0.11
Columbia River Mouth, OR/WA	29.53	17.00	15.90	107.67	0.86	2.14	0.25
Nisqually Reach, WA	118.07	13.33	24.57	105.33	0.68	2.62	0.32
Commencement Bay, WA	69.50	51.33	34.63	101.00	0.77	5.90	0.01
Elliott Bay, WA	114.37	96.00	20.23	166.00	0.84	1.18	0.11
Lutak Inlet, AK	58.27	26.67	15.90	180.33	0.96	0.09	0.24
Nahku Bay, AK	23.27	9.80	43.30	191.33	1.09	4.37	0.23
Charleston, SC	86.33	16.03	27.33	72.67	—	—	—

Source: Young, D. and Means, J., in National Status and Trends Program for Marine Environmental Quality, Progress Report on Preliminary Assessment of Findings of the Benthic Surveillance Project, 1984, National Oceanic and Atmospheric Administration, Rockville, MD, 1987; U.S. Geological Survey, National Water Summary, 1986.

Table 6.11–2 Average Concentrations of Metals in Sediments from 19 Estuaries in England Placed in Order of Decreasing Copper Concentration[a,b]

Site	Ag	As	Cd	Co	Cr	Cu	Fe	Hg	Mn	Ni	Pb	Se	Sn[c]	Zn
Restronguet Creek	3.76	1740[d]	1.53	21	32	2398	49,071	0.46	485	58	341	—	55.9	2821
Fal	1.37	56	0.78	9	28	648	28,063	0.20	272	23	150	—	39.5	750
Tamar	1.22	93	0.96	21	47	330	35,124	0.83	590	44	235	1.30	8.3	452
Gannel	4.13	174	1.35	26	24	150	25,420	0.08	649	38	2753	—	8.5	940
Tyne	1.55	24.8	2.17	11	46	92	28,206	0.92	395	34	187	1.23	5.4	421
Mersey	0.70	41.6	1.15	13	84	84	27,326	3.01	1169	29	124	0.30	8.3	379
Humber	0.42	49.8	0.48	16	77	54	35,203	0.55	1015	39	113	0.84	5.05	252
Medway	1.45	18.4	1.08	11	53	55	32,216	1.00	418	26	86	0.48	3.4	220
Poole	0.82	14.1	1.85	11	49	50	29,290	0.81	185	26	96	1.51	7.4	165
Severn	0.42	8.9	0.63	15	55	38	28,348	0.51	686	33	89	0.23	8.0	259
Hamble	0.16	18.4	0.34	10	37	31	28,132	0.43	241	19	56	0.41	3.9	105
Loughor	0.18	17.5	0.47	10	207	27	19,337	0.16	597	21	48	—	161	146
Dyfi	0.19	9.7	0.62	17	32	24	45,683	0.12	1127	33	166	0.20	0.98	212
Wyre	0.21	6.4	0.35	8	37	20	16,970	1.52	590	17	44	—	3.15	122
Avon	0.06	13.0	0.08	10	28	18	18,361	0.12	326	23	68	—	3.9	82
Teifi	0.09	10.6	0.17	10	29	13	30,280	0.04	684	23	25	0.16	1.14	87
Axe	0.13	4.8	0.17	7	27	12	14,004	0.20	248	14	26	—	1.39	76
Rother	0.17	12.4	0.13	6	29	11	15,648	0.09	259	15	20	0.18	0.62	46
Solway	0.07	6.4	0.23	6	30	7	14,816	0.03	577	17	25	0.11	0.40	59

[a] Concentrations expressed in μg/g dry weight.
[b] Data are for the <100 μm fraction of surface sediment following digestion in HNO_3.
[c] A large proportion of Sn in some samples occurs as cassiterite and is not dissolved in HNO_3 (fusion technique necessary).
[d] Figures in italics are the highest concentrations.

Source: Bryan, G. W. and Langston, W. J., *Environ. Pollut.*, 76, 89, 1992. With permission.

Table 6.11-3   Heavy Metal Concentrations (μg/g) in Contaminated Estuarine and Marine Sediments[a]

Metal	Baltic Sea[b] (various sources)	Bristol Channel/Severn Estuary, United Kingdom[c] (industry sewage)	Mersey Estuary, United Kingdom[d] (sewage, industry including chlor-alkali)	Los Angeles Outfall, CA[e] (sewage)	Derwent Estuary, Tasmania[f] (refinery, chlor-alkali)	Restronguet Creek, U.K.[c] (mining)	Port Pirie, Australia[g] (smelter)
As	—	8.0	71.0			2520 (13)	151 (1.0)
Cd	8.1 (<0.01)	1.1	3.9	66 (0.3)	862	1.2 (0.3)	267 (0.5)
Cu	283 (1.0)	54.0	144.0	940 (8.3)	>400	2540 (19)	122 (3.0)
Hg	9 (0.01)	0.48	6.2	5.4 (0.04)	1130	0.22 (0.12)	8.0
Ni	920 (1.0)	33.0	44.0	130 (9.7)	42	32 (28)	19.4 (12)
Pb	400 (2)	88.0	205.0	580 (6.1)	>1000	400 (2)	5270 (2)
Zn	2090 (6)	255.0	255.0	2900 (43)	>10,000	2090 (6)	16,667 (11)

[a] Maximum concentrations shown together with local background values (in parentheses), where given.
[b] Data from Brugman, L., Mar. Pollut. Bull., 12, 214, 1981.
[c] Data from Bryan, G. W. et al., J. Mar. Biol. Assoc. U.K., Pub. 4, 1985.
[d] Data from Langston, W. J., Estuarine Coastal Shelf Sci., 23, 239, 1986.
[e] Data from Mason, A. Z. and Simkiss, K., Exp. Cell Res., 139, 383, 1982.
[f] Data from Kojoma, Y. and Kagi, J. H. R., Trends Biochem. Sci., 3, 403, 1978.
[g] Data from Ward, T. J. et al., in Environmental Impacts of Smelters, Niragu, J. O., Ed., John Wiley & Sons, New York, 1984, 1.

Source: Langston, W. J., in Heavy Metals in the Marine Environment, Furness, R. W. and Rainbow, P. S., Eds., CRC Press, Boca Raton, FL, 1990, 115. With permission.

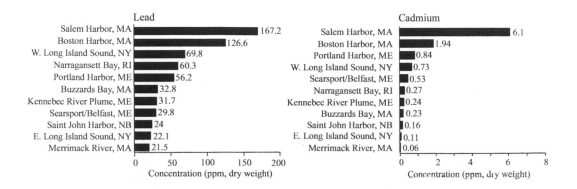

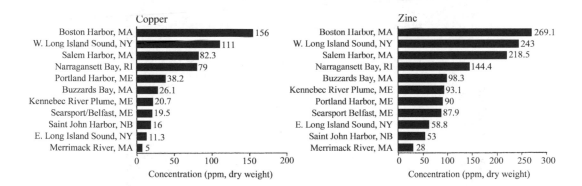

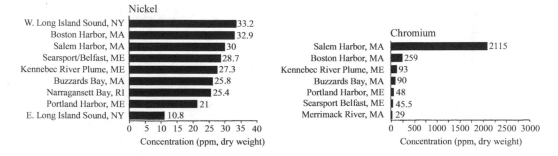

Figure 6.11–1 Concentrations of metals in northeastern U.S. coastal sediments as determined by the NOAA Status and Trends Program. (From Larsen, P. F., *Rev. Aquat. Sci.,* 6, 67, 1992. With permission.)

Table 6.11–4 Sources of Heavy Metals in Domestic Wastewater by Product Type

	Al	Sb	As	Be	Bi	Cd	Cr	Co	Cu	Fe	Pb	Mn	Hg	Mo	Ni	Se	Ag	Sn	Ti	V	Zn
Automotive products	X		X				X	X		X	X			X					X		X
Caulking compounds	X			X			X	X		X	X								X		X
Cleaners	X						X			X									X		X
Cosmetics	X			X	X	X		X	X	X		X	X		X	X	X	X	X		X
Disinfectants													X								
Driers	X																			X	X
Fillers	X																				X
Fire extinguishers	X						X			X											
Fuels	X		X	X							X	X									X
Pesticides	X		X			X	X		X	X	X	X	X	X							X
Inks	X								X					X					X		X
Lubricants	X			X			X				X			X							X
Medicine	X	X	X		X			X	X	X											X
Oils		X		X	X				X		X										X
Ointments	X		X	X	X		X	X	X	X	X	X	X								X
Paints	X						X	X		X	X	X	X						X		X
Photography	X												X		X	X	X	X			
Pigments	X	X	X	X	X	X	X	X	X	X	X	X	X		X	X		X	X		X
Polish	X			X					X								X		X		X
Powders	X									X	X										X
Preservatives					X					X											X
Suppositories												X									
Water treatment	X								X	X											X

Source: Stephenson, T., in *Heavy Metals in Wastewater and Sludge Treatment Processes*, Vol. 1, *Sources, Analysis, and Legislation*, Lester, J. N., Ed., CRC Press, Boca Raton, FL, 1987, 46. With permission.

Table 6.11-5   Heavy Metals in Wastewaters from Different Categories of Industries

	Al	Sb	As	Bi	Cd	Cr	Co	Cu	Fe	Pb	Mn	Hg	Mo	Ni	Se	Ag	Te	Tl	Sn
Metal Industries																			
Power plants (steam generation)						X													
Foundries—ferrous		X	X	X	X	X	X	X	X	X	X	X	X	X	X		X		X
Foundries—nonferrous	X	X	X	X	X	X		X		X	X	X			X	X			
Plating	X				X	X		X				X		X		X		X	
Chemical Industries																			
Cement and glass	X		X		X	X				X					X			X	
Organics and petrochemicals	X		X		X	X			X	X		X							X
Inorganic chemicals	X		X		X	X			X	X		X							X
Fertilizers			X		X	X		X	X	X				X					
Oil refining	X		X		X	X		X	X					X					
Others																			
Paper						X		X		X		X		X					
Leather						X													
Textiles		X				X													
Electronics		X						X				X			X		X		X

Source: Stephenson, T., in *Heavy Metals in Wastewater and Sludge Treatment Processes, Vol. 1, Sources, Analysis, and Legislation,* Lester, J. N., Ed., CRC Press, Boca Raton, FL, 1987, 51.

Table 6.11–6   Solubilities of Heavy Metals in Rivers

River	Sb	Cd	Cr	Co	Cu	Fe	Pb	Mn	Hg	Ni	Zn
				Heavy Metal Soluble Fraction (%)							
Ruhr, F.R.G.	—	100	96	100	74	56	62	69	—	—	86
Schuylkill, U.S.	—	21	15	—	36	—	5	—	—	42	33
Thames, U.K.	72	—	22	30	—	3	—	—	23	53	31
Yarra, Australia	—	80	—	—	75	83	58	—	—	—	90
Elbe, F.R.G.	—	22	—	—	50	4	—	69	—	—	48

Source: Stephenson, T., in Heavy Metals in Wastewater and Sludge Treatment Processes, Vol. 2, Treatment and Disposal, Lester, J. N., Ed., CRC Press, Boca Raton, FL, 1987, 74. With permission.

Table 6.11–7   Toxic Elements of Importance in Marine Pollution Based on Potential Supply and Toxicity, Listed in Order of Decreasing Toxicity[a]

Element	Rate of Mobilization (10^9 g/year)			D Toxicity (μg/l)	Relative Critical Index (km^3/year)	
	A Fossil Fuels (Human)	B River Flow (Natural)	C Total		A/D	C/D
Mercury	1.6	2.5	4.1	0.1	16,000	41,000
Cadmium	0.35	?	3.0	0.2	1,750	15,000
Silver	0.07	11	11.1	1	70	11,100
Nickel	3.7	169	164	2	1,350	82,000
Selenium	0.45	7.2	7.7	5	90	1,540
Lead	3.6	110	113.6	10	360	11,360
Copper	2.1	250	252.1	10	210	25,210
Chromium	1.5	200	201.5	10	150	20,150
Arsenic	0.7	72	72.7	10	70	7,270
Zinc	7	720	727	20	330	36,350
Manganese	7.0	250	257	20	350	12,850

[a] Equals the volume of seawater that would be contaminated annually to the indicated level of toxicity by the specified rates of addition, both by natural processes and anthropogenic activities.

Source: Ketchum, B. H., in Oceanography: The Past, Sears, M. and Merriman, D., Eds., Springer-Verlag, New York, 1980, 397. With permission.

Table 6.11-8 Heavy Metal Concentrations in Marine Fauna (μg/g dry wt)

Metal	Geometric Mean and Location	Phytoplankton	Algae	Mussels	Oysters	Gastropods	Crustaceans	Fish	Seals, Mammals
Arsenic	Geometric mean	—	20.0	15.0	10.0	20.0	30.0	10.0	
	Newfoundland	—	9.8–17 (b)	1.6–5	—	4.0–11.5	3.8–7.6	0.4–0.8	
	England	—	26.0–54 (b)	1.8–15	2.6–10.0	8.1–38.0	16.0	1.7–8.7	
	Greenland	—	36.0 (b)	14–17	—	—	63–80	14.7–307	
Cadmium	Geometric mean	2.0	0.5	2.0	10.0	6.0	1.0	0.2	
	Spain	—	0.8–4 (b)	0.5–8	2.9–3.5	1.1–9.0	0.7–32	<0.4–4.3	
	England	—	0.2–53 (b)	3.7–65	6–54	3.5–1.120	2.8–33	0.06–3.96+	2.2–11.6+
	Australia	—	—	4.2–83	9–174	2.8–30.0	—	0.05–0.4+	—
	Norway	—	1.0–13.0 (b)	1.9–140	—	0–51	1.9–7.0	<0.01–0.03+	
Copper	Geometric mean	7.0	15.0	10.0	100	60.0	70.0	3.0	
	Spain	—	5–26 (g)	6–14	120–435	5–50	110–435	<0.6–10.0	
	England	—	4–141 (b)	7–15	20–6480	0–1750	6–64+	0.5–14.6+	
	California	—	—	7–77	10–2100	3–177	(4–150)	(16–29.3)	14.5–386.0 (m)
	Norway	—	9–170 (g)	3–120	—	17–190	2–90	—	
Lead	Geometric mean	4.0	4.0	5.0	3.0	5.0	1.0	3.0	
	Spain	—	4–20 (g)	2–15	4–11	10–27	<1.2–11.0	<1.2–2.2	
	England	—	16.66 (g)	7–19	5–17	0.2–0.8	8.0	14–28	0.4+
	California	—	—	0.3–42.0	—	0.6–21.0	—	<0.001–5.3	0.3–34.2 (s)
	Norway	—	3–1200 (g)	2–3100	—	0–39	8.3	—	
Mercury	Geometric mean	0.17	0.15	0.4	0.4	0.2	0.4	0.4	0.6–103.0 (m)
	Hawaii	—	—	—	—	0–0.03	0.33–0.12	0.02–23.0	0.1–700.0 (s)
	California	0.2–5.3	<0.01–0.07+	—	—	<0.01–0.07+	0.02–0.04+	0.02–0.2	—
	Atlantic	—	<0.5–0.7+	<0.01–0.13+	0.02–180.0+	—	<0.05–0.6+	0.1–9.0	
	Mediterranean	—	—	0.25–0.4	—	0.1–3.5+	0.3–4.5+	0.1–29.8+	
	Australia	—	—	0.05–0.23+	1.5–8.2	0.32–0.65	—	0.3–16.5	0.1–106.0 (m)
	Norway	0.5–25.2	—	0.24–0.84	—	0.61	0.31–0.39	0.14–7.3	0.4–225.0 (s)
	England	—	<0.01–25.5 (g)	0.64–1.86	0.56–1.2	0.02–1.84	0.98	0.02–1.8	

(continued)

Table 6.11–8   Heavy Metal Concentrations in Marine Fauna (μg/g dry wt) (continued)

Metal	Geometric Mean and Location	Phytoplankton	Algae	Mussels	Oysters	Gastropods	Crustaceans	Fish	Seals, Mammals
Nickel	Geometric mean	3.0	3.0	3.0	1.0	2.0	1.0	1.0	
	England	—	4–33 (g,b)	5–12	2–174	8.8–12.3	1.1–12.3	0.5–10.6	
	California	—	—	3.3–20.0	—	1.8–18.5	—	—	
Silver	Geometric mean	0.2	0.2	0.3	—	1.0	0.4	0.1	
	California	—	—	0.7–46.0	—	0.4–10.7	—	0.1–1.2 (m)	
Zinc	Geometric mean	38.0	90.0	100	1700	200.0	80.0	80.0	
	South Africa	0.6–710.0	5.6+ (g)	73–113	400–886	12.0+	17.0+	3.2–7.2+	
	California	0.1–725.0	46–244	70–8430	1.7–288.0	—	—	78–875	
	Spain	—	63–345 (g)	190–370	310–920	60–120	79–330	21–220	
	Australia	—	—	170–1350	3740–38,700	56–1050	—	4–375	
	England	—	28–1240 (g)	12–779	1830–99,200	9.7–1500.0	36–82	2–342	
	Norway	—	20–2310 (g)	105–2370	—	87–2900	12–32	—	

Note: +, ppm wet weight; all other values in ppm dry weight; b, brown algae; g, green algae; m, mammals; s, seals.

Source: Förstner, U., in Chemistry and Biogeochemistry of Estuaries, Olausson, E. and Cato, I., Eds., John Wiley & Sons, Chichester, U.K., 1980, 307. With permission.

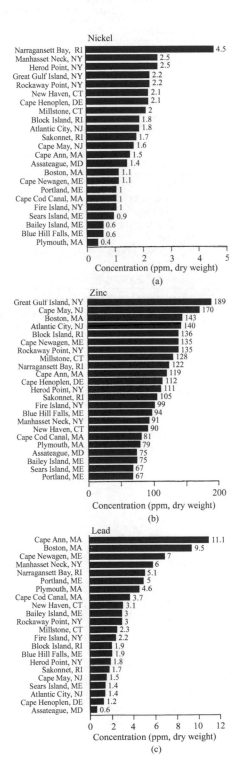

Figure 6.11–2 Concentrations of metals in mussels sampled in the northeastern United States by the USEPA Mussel Watch Program. (From Larsen, P. F., *Rev. Aquat. Sci.,* 6, 67, 1992. With permission.)

Table 6.11–9   Ranges of Typical Accumulated Concentrations of Zinc in
                Crustaceans and Bivalve Mollusks[a]

Crustaceans	Body Conc. Range
Barnacles	
Semibalanus balanoides	1220–113,250
Elminius modestus	4900–11,700
Balanus amphitrite	2726–11,990
Caridean Decapods	
Palaemon elegans	76–138
Pandalus montagui	119–214
Crangon crangon	56–174

Bivalve Mollusks	Soft Tissue Conc. Range
Oysters	
Ostrea edulis	660–3280
Crassostrea virginica	322–12,675
Saccostrea cucullata	430–8629
Mussels	
Mytilus edulis	14–500
Perna viridis	77–164
Septifer virgatus	74–116

[a] Expressed in μg/g dry weight.

Source: Rainbow. P. S., in *Ecotoxicology of Metals in Invertebrates,* Dallinger, R. and
Rainbow, P. S., Eds., Lewis Publishers, Boca Raton, FL, 1993, 3. With permission.

Table 6.11–10   Concentration of Copper, Zinc, and Cadmium in Subcellular Fractions from
                 Hepatopancreas of *Nassarius reticulatus* Exposed to Copper, Zinc, and
                 Cadmium in Sea Water

Fraction	Control (mean ± sd)	Cu-Exposed (mean ± sd)	Zn-Exposed (mean ± sd)	Cd-Exposed (mean ± sd)
Cu				
Mitochondrial	32.5 ± 11.0	52.2 ± 6.2[a]	66.1 ± 15.4[a]	8.4 ± 0.8[a]
Microsomal	10.3 ± 2.9	10.7 ± 3.5	13.3 ± 5.7	2.2 ± 0.3[a]
Cytosolic	5.1 ± 1.7	64.7 ± 9.3[a]	6.1 ± 1.9	2.5 ± 2.0
Zn				
Mitochondrial	109.0 ± 31.5	67.4 ± 15.5	188.2 ± 37.0[a]	18.0 ± 2.4[a]
Microsomal	17.2 ± 1.8	14.4 ± 6.1	26.9 ± 1.5	2.8 ± 1.0[a]
Cytosolic	747.3 ± 48.8	591.9 ± 34.9	1122.5 ± 162.5[a]	146.9 ± 30.2[a]
Cd				
Mitochondrial	0.22 ± 0.05	0.19 ± 0.04	0.21 ± 0.06	4.60 ± 1.38[a]
Microsomal	0.09 ± 0.03	0.05 ± 0.02	0.06 ± 0.01	1.10 ± 0.52[a]
Cytosolic	2.75 ± 0.32	2.41 ± 0.60	2.75 ± 0.95	36.35 ± 8.52[a]

Note: Each value is the mean of three pooled samples of eight individuals. All values in μg/g wet
        weight of original hepatopancreas.

[a] Values significantly different from control ($p < 0.05$, Dunnett's test).

Source: Kaland, T. et al., in *Ecotoxicology of Metals in Invertebrates,* Dallinger, R. and Rainbow, P. S.,
Eds., Lewis Publishers, Boca Raton, FL, 1993, 37. With permission.

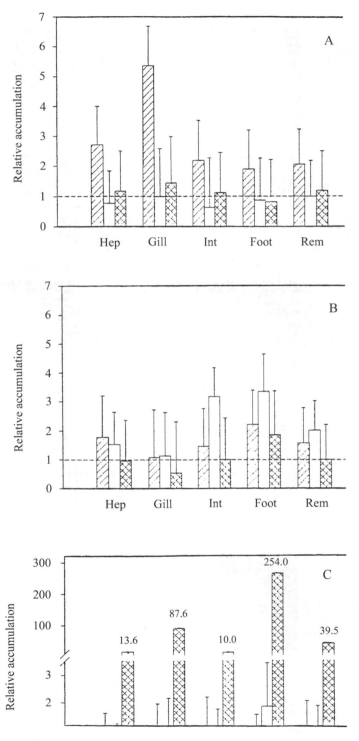

Figure 6.11–3 Accumulation of copper (diagonally hatched), zinc (blank), and cadmium (cross-hatched) in different organs of the marine gastropod *Nassarius reticulatus,* relative to control levels. The given values are summed concentrations from the subcellular fractions of each tissue. Hep = hepato-pancreas; Int = intestine; Rem = remainder. (A) Gastropods exposed to 50 μg/l Cu. (B) Gastropods exposed to 1.5 mg/l Zn. (C) Gastropods exposed to 0.9 mg/l Cd. Vertical lines denote one standard deviation. (From Kaland, T. et al., in *Ecotoxicology of Metals in Invertebrates,* Dallinger, R. and Rainbow, P. S., Eds., Lews Publishers, Boca Raton, FL, 1993, 37. With permission.)

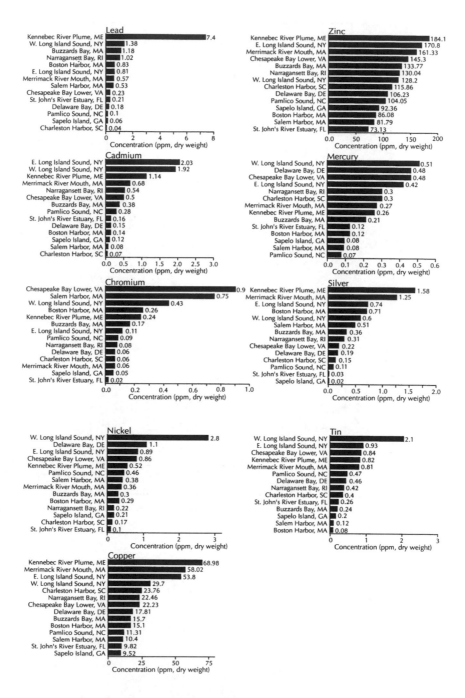

Figure 6.11–4 Concentrations of heavy metals in Atlantic Coast fish liver tissue sampled from various U.S. estuaries by the NOAA Status and Trends Program. (From Larsen, P. F., *Rev. Aquat. Sci.*, 6, 67–86, 1992. With permission.)

Table 6.11–11 Rankings on Four Geographic Scales of Metal Concentrations in Fish Livers from the Kennebec River Plume

Region (No. Sites)	Pb	Ag	Zn	Cu	Sn	Cd	Ni	Cr	Hg
Country (43)	1	3	4	10	15	18	18	18	22
East Coast (14)	1	1	1	1	4	3	5	5	7
New England (6)	1	1	1	1	1	3	1	3	3
Gulf of Maine (4)	1	1	1	1	1	1	1	3	2

Source: Larsen, P. F., *Rev. Aquat. Sci.,* 6, 67, 1992. With permission.

Table 6.11–12 Changes in Enzyme Activity Following Exposure of Fish to Heavy Metals

Chemical	Enzyme	Effect	Species	Duration of Exposure	Concentration	Organ
Pb, Hg	Alkaline phosphatase	↑	*Fundulus heteroclitus*	96 h	96-h LC_{50}	Liver
Cu, Cd	Alkaline phosphatase	NS	*F. heteroclitus*	96 h	96-h LC_{50}	Liver
Ag	Alkaline phosphatase	↓	*F. heteroclitus*	96 h	96-h LC_{50}	Liver
Pb, Cd, Cu, Hg	Acid phosphatase	↓	*F. heteroclitus*	96 h	96-h LC_{50}	Liver
Pb, Hg, Ag, Cd	Xanthine oxidase	↑	*F. heteroclitus*	96 h	96-h LC_{50}	Liver
Cu	Xanthine oxidase	↓	*F. heteroclitus*	96 h	96-h LC_{50}	Liver
Ag, Pb, Cu, Hg, Cd	Catalase	↓	*F. heteroclitus*	96 h	96-h LC_{50}	Liver
Cd, Pb, Cu, Ag, Hg	RNAase	↓	*F. heteroclitus*	96 h	96-h LC_{50}	Liver
Cr	Na/K-ATPase	↓	*Salmo gairdneri*	48 h	2.5 ppm	Kidney, intestine
	Na/K-ATPase	NS	*S. gairdneri*	48 h	2.5 ppm	Gill, liver
	Cyto, oxidase, succinic reductase, G-6-PO$_4$ dehydrogenase	NS	*S. gairdneri*	48 h	2.5 ppm	Several
Cd	Aspartate aminotransferase	↓	*Tautogolabrus*	96 h	3 and 24 ppm	Liver
	Aspartate aminotransferase	↓	*Tautogolabrus*	30 d	50–100 ppm	Liver
	Glucose-6-PO$_4$ dehydrogenase	↑	*Tautogolabrus*	30 d	50–100 ppm	Liver
	Leucine aminopeptidase	↓	*Pseudopleuronectes*	60 d	5–10 ppb	Kidney
	Carbonic anhydrase	↓	*Pseudopleuronectes*	60 d	5–10 ppb	Kidney
	Aspartate aminotransferase	↑↓	*Mugil cephalus*	1–4 d	96-h LC_{50}	Liver
	Aspartate aminotransferase	↑	*M. cephalus*	1–4 d	96-h LC_{50}	Heart, gill
	Alanine aminotransferase	↑	*M. cephalus*	1–4 d	96-h LC_{50}	Heart, gill
	Alanine aminotransferase	↓	*M. cephalus*	1–4 d	96-h LC_{50}	Liver
	Acid phosphatase	↓	*M. cephalus*	1–4 d	96-h LC_{50}	Heart, gill, liver
	Lactic dehydrogenase	↓	*M. cephalus*	1–4 d	96-h LC_{50}	Heart, gill, liver
	Ten enzymes	NS	*S. gairdneri* and *S. trutta*	2 weeks or 3 months		Several
	Malic dehydrogenase and propionyl-CoA-carboxylase	↓	Pacific Herring eggs		10 ppm	

Hg	Several	↓↑	*Channa punctatus*	15–60 d	3 ppb	Several
	Na/K-ATPase, Mg-ATPase	→	*Notopterus notopterus*	30 d	17–88 ppb	Gill, liver, kidney, brain
	Na/K-ATPase	→	*Channa punctatus*	30 d	17–88 ppb	Brain
	Succinic, lactic, and pyruvate dehydrogenases	→	*Ophiocephalus punctatus* and *Heteropneustes fossilis*	30 d	0.3 ppm	Liver, stomach, intestine and caeca
	Alkaline phosphatase	←	*O. punctatus*	30 d	0.3 ppm	Brain
	Acid phosphatase	→	*O. punctatus*	30 d	0.3 ppm	Brain
	Glucose-6-phosphatase, succinic, lactic and pyruvate dehydrogenase	→	*O. punctatus*	30 d	0.3 ppm	Brain
Pb, Hg	Delta aminolevulinic acid dehydrase	→	*F. heteroclitus*	14–14 d	0.8–10 ppm	Liver and kidney
Ag, Zn	Delta aminolevulinic acid dehydrase	←	*F. heteroclitus*	14 d	0.02–2.2 ppm	Liver
Pb	Delta aminolevulinic acid dehydrase	→	*S. gairdneri*	30 d	10–300 ppm	Erythrocytes, spleen, and distal kidney
Cu	Alkaline phosphatase	←	*O. punctatus*	24 h	5–7.5 ppm	Kidney
	Alkaline phosphatase	→	*O. punctatus*	24 h	7.5 ppm	Liver
	Acid phosphatase	←	*O. punctatus*	24 h	7.5	Liver and kidney

Note: When more than one chemical is listed in sequence, they are arranged in order of decreasing effect; NS = no significant change.

Source: Heath, A. G., *Water Pollution and Fish Physiology,* CRC Press, Boca Raton, FL, 1987. With permission.

Table 6.11–13   Effects of Tributyltin (TBT) on Marine and Estuarine Organisms

Species	Concentration of TBT in Water (ng/l as Sn)	Effect
Nucella lapillus, dogwhelk	1–10	Imposex, impaired reproduction
Crassostrea gigas, oyster[a]	8	Shell thickening
	20	Reduced growth, viability
Mytilus edulis, mussel[a]	40	Reduced viability
Venerupis decussata, clam[a]	40	Reduced growth, viability
Gammarus oceanicus, amphipod[a]	120	Reduced growth
Homarus americanus, lobster[a]	400	Reduced viability
Pavlova lutheri *Skeletonema costatum,* microalgae *Dunaliella tertiolecta*	40–400	Reduced growth

[a] Larvae.

Source: Langston, W. J., in *Heavy Metals in the Marine Environment,* Furness, R. W. and Rainbow, P. S., Eds., CRC Press, Boca Raton, FL, 1990, 117. With permission.

Table 6.11–14   Concentrations (ppm) of Heavy Metals in Aboveground Portions of *Spartina alterniflora*

Location	Cu	Pb	Hg	Mn	Zn	Cd
Massachusetts	3	2–26		48	11–31	0.06–0.21
Rhode Island	12–16	21–22			42–69	0.2–0.3
New Jersey	2–8	0.3–3	0.01–0.03	8–92	5–100	0.00–0.15
Virginia	2–5			35–140	12–23	
North Carolina	0.1–5	0.01–2	0.0–0.16	6–95	4–70	0.0–0.33
South Carolina	0.6–5	0.1–3	0.0–0.07	5–180	1–101	0.0–0.58
Georgia	0.8–8	0.4–55	0.01–1.13	30–77	0.4–64	0.0–1.14
Florida	1	1.5	0.01	39	14	0.06–0.018

Source: Nixon, S. W. and Lee, V., Wetlands and Water Quality: A Regional Review of Recent Research in the United States on the Role of Freshwater and Saltwater Wetlands as Sources, Sinks, and Transformers of Nitrogen, Phosphorus, and Various Heavy Metals, Tech. Rep. Y-86-2, U.S. Army Engineer Waterways Experimental Station, Vicksburg, MS, 1986.

Table 6.11–15   Several Effluents and Chemicals (Including Heavy Metals) Reported To Be More Toxic to Aquatic Plants Than to Faunal Species

Acrylates	Aldrin
Anionic surfactants	Dieldrin
Cationic surfactants	Endrin
Sodium salts	Chlordane
Acridine	2,4-D
Nickel	Potassium chlorate
Cadmium	Sodium tetraborate
Copper	Disodium hydrogen
Zinc	Hydrazine hydroxide
Arsenate	Industrial effluents
Chromium	Paper mill effluents
Glyphosate	Textile plant effluents
Organotin	Refinery plant effluents
Soil elutriates	Herbicide plant effluents
Potassium dichromate	Monochloroacetic acid
River water extracts	Chloramine
Polycationic polymers	Chloroacetaldehyde
Monobromoacetic acid	Dinitrotoluene
Phosphoric acid tributyl ester	Phenol
Phthalic acid dialyl ester	

Source: Klaine, S. J. and Lewis, M. A., in *Handbook of Ecotoxicology,* Hoffman, D. J. et al., Eds., Lewis Publishers, Boca Raton, FL, 1995, 198. With permission.

Table 6.11–16   Sublethal Effects of Metals — Growth

Species	Ag	As	Cd	Cu	Hg	Ni	Pb	Zn	Response
Phytoplankton									
Natural assemblage				0.3					Reduced ^{14}C fixation
				1.0					Reduced ^{14}C fixation
				10.0					Reduced ^{14}C fixation
Monochrysis lutheri		23	112	6.4	<6.0[a]	60[a]	20	20	Reduced growth
				21.6 (0.07 as Cu^{2+})					Reduced division
Natural assemblage					0.8				Reduced growth
					1.0				Reduced productivity
									Reduced photosynthesis
		5						15	Reduced growth
Macroalgae									
Laminaria saccharina									
Sporeling				10	0.5 (0.5)[a]			100	Reduced growth
Sporophyte				50	50 (5.0)[a]			1000	Reduced growth
Hydroids									
Campanularia flexuosa			195	14.3	1.6			740	Reduced growth
Mollusks									
Mytilus edulis	32		10	3	0.3	>200[b]	>200[b]	10	Reduced shell growth
Mercenaria mercenaria				16	15	5700			Reduced growth[c]
Crassostrea virginica	25			33	12	1200		195	Reduced growth[c]
Fish									
Pleuronectes platessa			5	10					Reduced growth

[a] No effect observed at this concentration.
[b] Methylmercury.
[c] For larvae: concentrations also represent LC$_{50}$ values (8 to 12 days).

Source: Langston, W. J., in *Heavy Metals in the Marine Environment*, Furness, R. W. and Rainbow, P. S., Eds., CRC Press, Boca Raton, FL, 1990, 107. With permission.

Table 6.11–17 Sublethal Effects of Metals — Morphology

Species	Metal Concentration (μg/l)									Response
	Ag	As	Cd	Cr	Cu	Hg	Ni	Pb	Se	Zn	
Hydroids											
Eirene viridula		300	100		10	3		300	3000	1500	Altered hydranth morphology[a]
Mollusks											
Crassostrea gigas	22	326	611	4538	5	7	349	476	>10,000	199	50% abnormal larvae
Mytilus edulis	14	>3000	1200	4469	6	6	891	758	>10,000	175	50% abnormal larvae
C. virginica	24					11				206	50% abnormal larvae
Fish											
Myoxocephalus quadricornis		32	0.5		0.8	0.1		1.2		5.3	Increase in vertebral deformities[b]

[a] Lowest reported threshold concentration.
[b] Metals applied as a mixture.

Source: Langston, W. J., in *Heavy Metals in the Marine Environment*, Furness, R. W. and Rainbow, P. S., Eds., CRC Press, Boca Raton, FL, 1990, 109. With permission.

Table 6.11–18 Sublethal Effects of Metals — Reproduction and Development

Species	Metal Concentration (μg/l)									Response
	Ag	As	Cd	Cr	Cu	Hg	Ni	Pb	Zn	
Macroalgae										
Champia parvula		60								Inhibition of sexual reproduction
Hydroids										
Campanularia flexuosa					0.05	0.01			500	Increase in gonozooid frequency[a]
Polychaetes										
Neanthes arenaceodentata			1000	50				3100	320	Reductions in reproduction
Capitella capitata			560	100				200	560	Reductions in reproduction
Ctenodrilus serratus			2500	50	100	50	500	1000	500	Reductions in reproduction
Bivalves										
Mytilus edulis					50					Development of oocytes suppressed
Spisula solidissima (germ cells)	9.5								200	Impaired embryogenesis
Crustaceans										
Pontoporeia affinis			5.5					4.9		Fecundity reduced
Rhithropanopeus harrisii			50						25	Hatch time increased
Tigriopus japonicus			44		6.4					Generation time doubled
Echinoderms										
Sea urchin eggs (various spp.)		1500	600	1000	10	10	600	1000	30	Fertilization and development arrested[a]
Fish										
Spring-spawning herring			5		10				10	Reduced fertilization
Fundulus heteroclitus						10				Reduced hatch
Leiostomus xanthurus (eggs)					0.064[b]					Reduced hatch
Menidia menidia (eggs)					0.025[b]					Reduced hatch

[a] Lowest reported threshold concentration.
[b] Calculated as free ion (Cu^{2+}).

Source: Langston, W. J., in *Heavy Metals in the Marine Environment,* Furness, R. W. and Rainbow, P. S., Eds., CRC Press, Boca Raton, FL, 1990, 111. With permission.

6.12 RADIOACTIVE WASTE

Table 6.12–1 Characteristics of Common Nuclear Radiations[a]

Radiation	Rest Mass	Charge	Typical Energy Range	Path Length Air	Path Length Solid	General Comments
α	4.00 amu	2+	4–10 MeV	5–10 cm	25–40 μm	Identical to ionized He nucleus
β (negatron)	5.48×10^4 amu 0.51 meV	—	0–4 MeV	0–1 m	0–1 cm	Identical to electron
Positron (β positive)	5.48×10^4 amu 0.51 meV	+	—	0–1 m	0–1 cm	Identical to electron except for charge
Neutron	1.0086 amu 939.55 meV	0	0–15 MeV	0–100 m	0–100 cm	Free half-life: 16 min
γ (e.m. photon)[a]	—	0	10 keV–3 MeV	0.1–10 m[4]	1 mm–1 m	Photons from nuclear transitions

[a] Exponential attenuation in the case of electromagnetic radiation.

Source: Eichholz, G. G., *Environmental Aspects of Nuclear Power,* Ann Arbor Science, Ann Arbor, MI, 1976. With permission.

Table 6.12–2 Oceanic Radiocarbon Inventories[a]

Source	Inventory (RCU)
Cosmogenic radiocarbon	
Fairhall et al.	1.94×10^4
Killough and Emanuel	2.00×10^4
Recommended value	1.97×10^4
Bomb-carbon (as of ~1972)	
Stuiver et al. (extrapolated)	310
Broecker et al.	303
Recommended value	303

Note: See original source for particular studies.
     RCU = radiocarbon units.

[a] Inventories are normalized ("recorrected") to $\delta^{13}C = 0$.

Source: Lassey, K. R. et al., *Rev. Aquat. Sci.,* 3, 117, 1990. With permission.

Table 6.12–3   Natural Levels of Radioactivity in Surface Sea Water

Radionuclide	Concentration (Bq/l)
Potassium-40	11.84
Tritium (^{3}H)	0.022–0.11
Rubidium-87	1.07
Uranium-234	0.05
Uranium-238	0.04
Carbon-14	0.007
Radium-228	$(0.0037–0.37) \times 10^{-2}$
Lead-210	$(0.037–0.25) \times 10^{-2}$
Uranium-235	0.18×10^{-2}
Radium-226	$(0.15–0.17) \times 10^{-2}$
Polonium-210	$(0.022–0.15) \times 10^{-2}$
Radon-222	0.07×10^{-2}
Thorium-228	$(0.007–0.11) \times 10^{-3}$
Thorium-230	$(0.022–0.05) \times 10^{-4}$
Thorium-232	$(0.004–0.29) \times 10^{-4}$

Source: Clark, R. B., *Marine Pollution*, 3rd ed., Clarendon Press, Oxford, 1992. With permission.

Table 6.12–4   Concentrations ($\times$ 10 Bq/l) of ^{210}Po and ^{210}Pb in Seawater

Sample (m)	^{210}Po	^{210}Pb
Surface water		
≤20	0.19–3.7	<0.37–5.0
Deep water		
500–1000	1.4–4.9	0.6–3.6
1000–2000	1.2–4.1	0.8–3.4
2000–3000	0.8–5.3	1.1–5.0
3000–4000	2.0–3.6	2.7–4.6
>4000	1.0–5.2	2.7–3.7

Source: Woodhead, D. S. and Pentreath, R. J., in *Wastes in the Ocean*, Vol. 3, *Radioactive Wastes and the Ocean,* Park, P. K. et al., Eds., John Wiley & Sons, New York, 1983, 134. With permission.

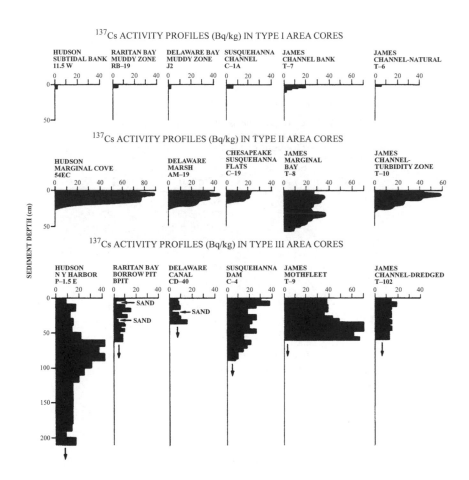

Figure 6.12–1 Cs profiles in estuarine sediments. Type I is typical of areas where the sediment surface is at present at or near a state of equilibrium with its respective wave, current, and flow regime. Type II is typical of marginal cove and mudflat areas where the sediment surface is approaching its equilibrium depth. Type III is typical of areas where the sediment surface is far below its equilibrium depth (such as forest areas on deltas) or areas that have been affected by human activities such as dredging or construction. (From Olsen, C.R. et. al., *Estuaries,* 16, 683, 1993. With permission.)

Table 6.12–5   Concentrations of ^{137}Cs and δ^{13}C in Bottom Sediments Collected along a Salinity Gradient of the Savannah River Estuary

Station	Salinity (%)	^{137}Cs[a] (Bq/kg)	δ^{13}C (%)
R-1	0	37.0 ± 0.6	−26.9
R-2	0	62.6 ± 0.7	−27.2
E-1	<5	12.4 ± 0.3	−25.6
E-2	7	13.2 ± 0.3	−22.2
E-3	10.9	16.0 ± 1.1	−22.4
E-4	13	13.7 ± 0.4	−20.9
E-5	13.9	7.6 ± 0.6	−20.7
E-6	14.3	0.9 ± 0.2	−20.8
E-7	24	0.6 ± 0.1	−22.0
M-1	>30	<0.4	−20.8
M-8	>30	<0.4	−20.4

[a] Statistical counting errors are expressed as one sigma.

Source: Olsen, C. R. et al., *Estuaries,* 16, 683, 1993. With permission.

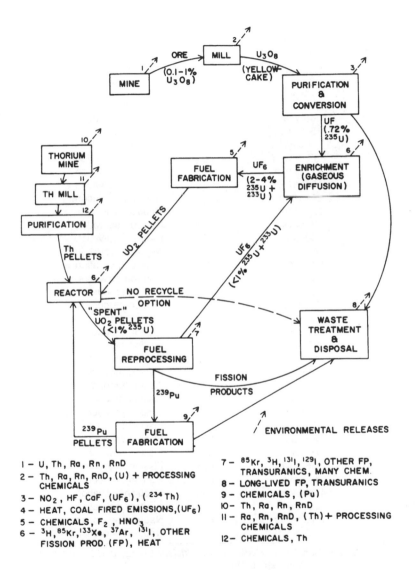

I – U, Th, Ra, Rn, RnD
2 – Th, Ra, Rn, RnD, (U) + PROCESSING
    CHEMICALS
3 – NO₂ , HF, CaF, (UF₆) , (²³⁴Th)
4 – HEAT, COAL FIRED EMISSIONS,(UF₆)
5 – CHEMICALS, F₂ , HNO₃
6 – ³H, ⁸⁵Kr, ¹³³Xe, ³⁷Ar, ¹³¹I, OTHER
    FISSION PROD. (FP), HEAT

7 – ⁸⁵Kr, ³H, ¹³¹I, ¹²⁹I, OTHER FP,
    TRANSURANICS, MANY CHEM.
8 – LONG-LIVED FP, TRANSURANICS
9 – CHEMICALS, (Pu)
10– Th, Ra, Rn, RnD
11– Ra, Rn, RnD, (Th)+ PROCESSING
    CHEMICALS
12– CHEMICALS, Th

Figure 6.12–2 Components of the nuclear fuel cycle, illustrating radioactive releases to the environment. (From Whicker, F. W. and Schultz, V., *Radioecology: Nuclear Energy and the Environment,* Vol. 1, CRC Press, Boca Raton, FL, 1982. With permission.)

Table 6.12–6   Radionuclides Generated by Nuclear Power Plants That Are of Potential
                Environmental Concern

Radionuclide	Half-Life	Radiation	Source	Element Analogue
^{3}H	12.3 years	β	Fission product, neutron activation	H
^{14}C	5568 years	β	Neutron activation	C
^{24}Na	15 hours	β, γ	Neutron activation	Na
^{32}P	14 days	β	Neutron activation	P
^{35}S	87 days	β	Neutron activation	S
^{41}Ar	110 minutes	β, γ	Neutron activation	—
^{45}Ca	164 days	β	Neutron activation	Ca
^{54}Mn	291 days	γ	Neutron activation	Mn
^{55}Fe	2.6 years	γ	Neutron activation	Fe
^{59}Fe	45 days	β, γ	Neutron activation	Fe
^{57}Co	270 days	γ	Neutron activation	Co
^{58}Co	71 days	β^+, γ	Neutron activation	Co
^{60}Co	5.2 years	β, γ	Neutron activation	Co
^{65}Zn	245 days	β^+, γ	Neutron activation	Zn
^{85}Kr	10 years	β, γ	Fission product	—
^{89}Sr	51 days	β	Fission product	Ca
^{90}Sr	28 years	β	Fission product	Ca
^{91}Y	58 days	β, γ	Fission product	—
^{95}Zr	65 days	β, γ	Fission product	—
^{103}Ru	40 days	β, γ	Fission product	—
^{106}Ru	1.0 years	β, γ	Fission product	—
^{129}I	1.7×10^7 years	β, γ	Fission product	I
^{131}I	8.1 days	β, γ	Fission product	I
^{134}Cs	2 years	β, γ	Fission product	K
^{137}Cs	27 years	β, γ	Fission product	K
^{140}Ba	12.8 days	β, γ	Fission product	Ca
^{143}Ce	33 hours	β, γ	Fission product	—
^{144}Ce	285 days	β, γ	Fission product	—
^{147}Nd	11 days	β, γ	Fission product	—
^{239}Pu	24,360 years	α, γ	Neutron activation	—
^{239}Np	2.3 days	β, γ	Neutron activation	—
^{241}Am	4770 years	α, γ	Neutron activation	—
^{242}Cm	163 days	α, γ	Neutron activation	—

Source: Whicker, F. W. and Schultz, V., *Radioecology: Nuclear Energy and the Environment,* Vol. 1, CRC Press, Boca Raton, FL, 1982. With permission.

RADIONUCLIDE PARTITIONING AMONG DIFFERENT PARTICULATE PHASES IN CONOWINGO RESERVOIR

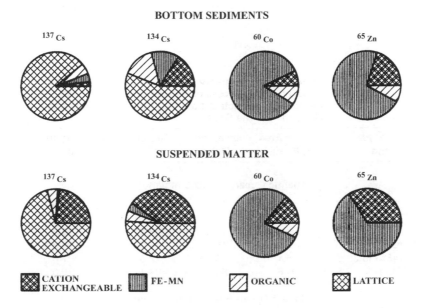

BOTTOM SEDIMENTS

^{137}Cs ^{134}Cs ^{60}Co ^{65}Zn

SUSPENDED MATTER

^{137}Cs ^{134}Cs ^{60}Co ^{65}Zn

CATION EXCHANGEABLE   FE-MN   ORGANIC   LATTICE

Figure 6.12–3 Radionuclide partitioning among different particulate phases in suspended matter and sediment samples collected in the Susquehanna River near the Peach Bottom Nuclear Power Station. (From Olsen, C. R. et al., *Estuaries,* 16, 683, 1993. With permission.)

Table 6.12–7   Bomb-Carbon Inventories According to Broecker et al.[a] for Mid-Latitude Atlantic and Pacific Oceans[b]

	Atlantic Ocean		Pacific Ocean	
Latitude Band	Col. Inventory (10^{12} atoms/m^2)	Inventory (RCU)	Col. Inventory (10^{12} atoms/m^2)	Inventory (RCU)
50°N–10°N	122	36.5	93	49.4
50°N–10°S	30	3.8	50	20.1
50°S–50°S	86	24.0	94	54.7
50°N–50°S	91	64.3	82	124.2

[a] Broecker, W. S. et al., *J. Geophys. Res.,* 90, 6953, 1985.
[b] All inventories estimated are as of 1972, and all are subject to 5% upward adjustment to compensate for an implicit fractionation correction. RCU = radiocarbon units.

Source: Lassey, K. R. et al., *Rev. Aquat. Sci.,* 3, 117, 1990. With permission.

Table 6.12–8   Bomb-Carbon Summary for Individual Ocean Regions
                Showing Either Excess or Deficient Inventories Relative to
                the Amount Expected If the CO_2 Invasion Rate Were
                Uniform over the Ocean[a]

Latitude Band	Water Area (10^{12} m²)	Inventory (RCU)	Input (RCU)	Inventory-Input[b] (RCU)
Atlantic Ocean (I = 22.3 mol/m²/year)				
80°N to 40°S	18.6	26.6	19.7	+6.9
40°N to 20°N	15.8	23.0	14.5	+8.5
20°N to 20°S	26.7	10.8	23.1	−12.3
20°S to 45°S	18.4	18.5	14.2	+4.3
45°S to 80°S	15.1	5.2	12.6	−7.4
80°N to 80°S	94.6	84.1	84.1	0.0
Indian Ocean (I = 19.4 mol/m²/year)				
25°N to 15°S	27.0	13.2	24.1	−10.9
15°S to 45°S	29.8	40.5	20.3	+20.2
45°S to 70°S	20.7	15.9	25.2	−9.3
25°N to 70°S	77.5	69.6	69.6	0.0
Pacific Ocean (I = 19.2 mol/m²/year)				
65°N to 40°N	15.1	7.3	13.4	−6.1
40°N to 15°N	35.0	35.9	27.8	+8.1
15°N to 10°S	50.0	23.7	39.1	−15.4
10°S to 55°S	63.0	61.3	43.6	+17.7
55°S to 80°S	13.8	6.6	10.9	−4.3
65°N to 80°S	176.9	134.8	134.8	0.0
World Ocean (I = 20.1 mol/m²/year)				
	349.0	288.5	288.5	0.0

[a] All inventories are estimated as of 1972 and are subject to 5% upward adjustment to compensate for implicit fractionation correction. RCU = radiocarbon units.

[b] The mean CO_2 invasion rate, I, is adjusted for each ocean and for the "World Ocean" so that ocean-average input matches inventory. This requires that, like the inventories, the invasion rate estimates are also subject to 5% upward adjustment, which when applied become I = 23.5, 20.4, 20.2, and 21.1 mol/m²/year for Atlantic, Indian, Pacific, and World Oceans, respectively.

Source: Lassey, K. R. et al., *Rev. Aquat. Sci.,* 3, 117, 1990. With permission.

Table 6.12–9   Estimated Number of Nuclear Explosions 16 July 1945 to 5 August 1963 (Signing of the Partial Test Ban Treaty)

Year	U.S. A	U.S. U	U.S.S.R. A	U.S.S.R. U	U.K. A	U.K. U	France A	France U	Total
1945	3	0							3
1946	2[a]	0							2
1947	0	0							0
1948	3	0							3
1949	0	0	1	0					1
1950	0	0	0	0					0
1951	15	1	2	0					18
1952	10	0	0	0	1	0			11
1953	11	0	4	0	2	0			17
1954	6	0	7	0	0	0			13
1955	17[a]	1	5[a]	0	0	0			23
1956	18	0	9	0	6	0			33
1957	27	5	15[a]	0	7	0			54
1958	62[b]	15	29	0	5	0			111
1949–58, exact years not available			18						18
1959	0	0	0	0	0	0			0[d]
1960	0	0	0	0	0	0	3	0	3[d]
1961	0	10	50[a]	1[c]	0	0	1	1	63[d]
1962	39[a]	57	43	1[c]	0	2	0	1	143
1 Jan to 5 Aug 1963	4	25	0	0	0	0	0	2	31
Total	217	114	183[e] (214)[f]	2[c]	21	2	4	4	547 (576)[f]

Note: A = atmospheric; U = underground.

[a] One of these tests was carried out underwater.

[b] Two of these tests were carried out underwater.

[c] Soviet information released in September 1990 did not confirm whether these were underground or atmospheric tests.

[d] The U.K., the U.S., and the former U.S.S.R. observed a moratorium on testing, November 1958 to September 1961.

[e] The total figure for Soviet atmospheric tests includes the 18 additional tests conducted in the period 1948–1958, the exact years for which are not available.

[f] The totals in brackets include the (probable atmospheric) explosions revealed by Soviet authorities in September 1990, the exact years for which have still not been announced. See *SIPRI Yearbook 1991*, p. 41 (full citation in original source). If the two tests in 1961 and 1962 (see note c) were atmospheric tests, this figure should read 216, under the column for atmospheric tests.

Source: Ferm, R., *World Armaments and Disarmament*, Appendix 6A, *SIPRI Yearbook 1993*, Oxford University Press, Oxford, 1993. With permission.

Table 6.12–10   Estimated Number of Nuclear Explosions 6 August 1963 to 31 December 1992

Year	U.S.[a] A	U.S.[a] U	U.S.S.R. A	U.S.S.R. U	U.K.[a] A	U.K.[a] U	France A	France U	China A	China U	India A	India U	Total
1963	0	15	0	0	0	0	0	1					16
1964	0	38	0	6	0	1	0	3	1	0			49
1965	0	36	0	10	0	1	0	4	1	0			52
1966	0	43	0	15	0	0	6	1	3	0			68
1967	0	34	0	17	0	0	3	0	2	0			56
1968	0	45[b]	0	15	0	0	5	0	1	0			66
1969	0	38	0	16	0	0	0	0	1	1			56
1970	0	35	0	17	0	0	8	0	1	0			61
1971	0	17	0	19	0	0	6	0	1	0			43
1972	0	18	0	22	0	0	3	0	2	0			45
1973	0	16[c]	0	14	0	0	5	0	1	0			36
1974	0	14	0	18	0	1	8	0	1	0	0	1	43
1975	0	20	0	15	0	0	0	2	0	1	0	0	38
1976	0	18	0	17	0	1	0	4	3	1	0	0	44
1977	0	19	0	18	0	0	0	8[d]	1	0	0	0	46
1978	0	17	0	27	0	2	0	8	2	1	0	0	57
1979	0	15	0	29	0	1	0	9	1	0	0	0	55
1980	0	14	0	21	0	3	0	13	1	0	0	0	52
1981	0	16	0	22	0	1	0	12	0	0	0	0	51
1982	0	18	0	32	0	1	0	6	0	1	0	0	58
1983	0	17	0	27	0	1	0	9	0	2	0	0	56
1984	0	17	0	29	0	2	0	8	0	2	0	0	58
1985	0	17	0	9[e]	0	1	0	8	0	0	0	0	35
1986	0	14	0	0[e]	0	1	0	8	0	0	0	0	23
1987	0	14	0	23	0	1	0	8	0	1	0	0	47
1988	0	14	0	17	0	0	0	8	0	1	0	0	40
1989	0	11	0	7	0	1	0	8	0	0	0	0	27
1990	0	8	0	1	0	1	0	6	0	2	0	0	18
1991	0	7	0	0	0	1	0	6	0	0	0	0	14
1992	0	6	0	0	0	0	0	0	0	2	0	0	8
Total	0	611	0	463 (500)[f]	0	21	44	140	23	15	0	1	1318 (1355)[f]

Note: A = atmospheric; U = underground.

[a] One of these tests was carried out underwater.
[b] Five devices used simultaneously in the same test are counted here as one explosion.
[c] Three devices used simultaneously in the same test are counted here as one explosion.
[d] Two of these tests may have been conducted in 1975 or 1976.
[e] The U.S.S.R. observed a unilateral moratorium on testing, August 1985 to February 1987.
[f] The totals in brackets include the explosions revealed by the Soviet authorities in September 1990, the exact years of which have still not been announced. See *SIPRI Yearbook 1991*, p. 41 (full citation in original source).

Source: Ferm, R., *World Armaments and Disarmament*. Appendix 6A, *SIPRI Yearbook 1993*, Oxford University Press, Oxford, 1993. With permission.

Table 6.12–11   Estimated Total Number of Nuclear Explosions 16 July 1945 to 31 December 1992

U.S.[a]	U.S.S.R.[b]	U.K.[a]	France	China	India	Total
942	648 (715)	44	192	38	1	1865 (1931)[b]

[a] All British tests from 1962 have been conducted jointly with the United States at the Nevada Test Site. Therefore, the number of U.S. tests is actually higher than indicated here.

[b] The figures in brackets for the former Soviet Union include additional tests announced by the Soviet authorities in September 1990 for the period 1949 to 1990. See *SIPRI Yearbook, 1991*, p. 41 (full citation in original source).

Source: Ferm, R., *World Armaments and Disarmament*, Appendix 6A, *SIPRI Yearbook 1993*, Oxford University Press, Oxford, 1993. With permission.

Table 6.12–12   Average and Range of Radioactivity in the North Atlantic Ocean in the Early 1970s Due to Radioactive Fallout from Nuclear Weapons Tests

Radioisotope	Radioactivity (pCi/l)	
	Average	Range
Tritium (^{0}H)	48	(31–74)
^{137}Cs	0.21	(0.03–0.80)
^{90}Sr	0.13	(0.02–0.50)
^{14}C	0.02	(0.01–0.04)
^{239}Pu		(0.0003–0.0012)

Source: Clark, R. B., *Marine Pollution*, 2nd ed., Clarendon Press, Oxford, 1989. With permission.

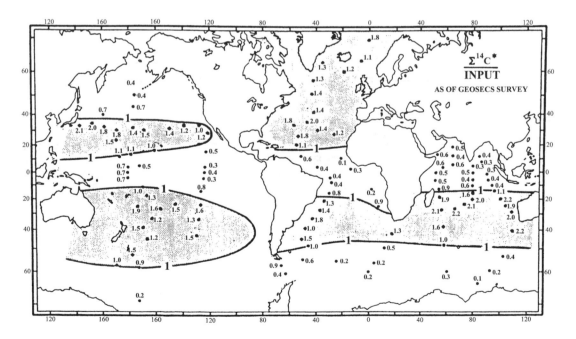

Figure 6.12–4 Map showing the ratio of water column inventory to net input of bomb radiocarbon for the stations occupied during the GEOSECS program, Regions with excess inventory over input are shaded. The ratio averaged over each of the three main oceans is unity. (From Broecker, W. S. et al., *J. Geophys. Res.*, 90, 6953, 1985. With permission.)

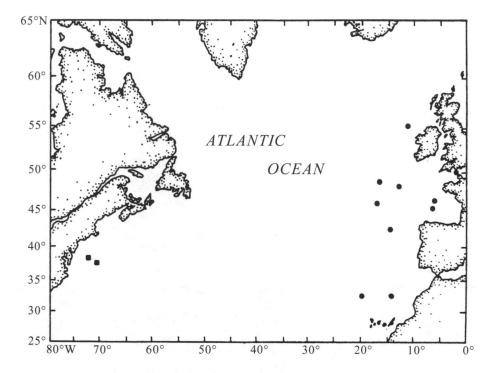

Figure 6.12–5 Radioactive solid waste disposal sites in the North Atlantic Ocean, 1946–1979. Darkened circles = European sites; darkened squares = U.S. sites. (Modified from Preston, A., in *Wastes in the Ocean*, Vol. 3, *Radioactive Wastes and the Ocean,* Park, P. K. et. al., Eds., John Wiley & Sons, New York, 1983, 107. With permission.)

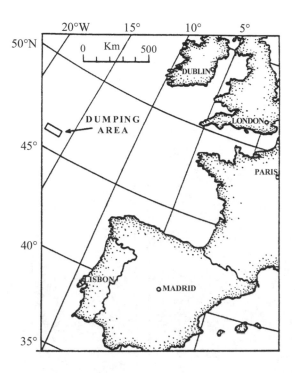

Figure 6.12–6 Location of the Northeast Atlantic low-level radioactive waste dumpsite area in the North Atlantic Ocean. (From Organization for Economic Cooperation and Development–Nuclear Energy Agency, Review of the Continued Suitability of the Dumping Site for Radioactive Waste in the Northeast Atlantic, Organization for Economic Cooperation and Development–Nuclear Energy Agency, Paris, 1980.)

Table 6.12–13 **Activity at 12 Radioactive Solid Waste Dumpsites in the North Atlantic Ocean, 1949 to 1979**

	Dumped Activity (Bq)	
	α	β–γ
Average per site[a]	3.7×10^{13}	2.6×10^{15}
Range per site[b]	$(1.1 \text{ to } 2.8) \times 10^{17}$	$(1.9 \text{ to } 3.7) \times 10^{17}$
Maximum Bq (per site per year)	5.2×10^{13}	3.5×10^{15}
Total for all 12 sites	4.8×10^{14}	3.1×10^{16}

[a] The sites used for more than 4 years.
[b] Range of years the sites were used was 1 to 14.

Source: Preston, A., in *Wastes in the Ocean,* Vol. 3, *Radioactive Wastes and the Ocean,* Park, P. K. et al., Eds., John Wiley & Sons, New York, 1983, 107. With permission.

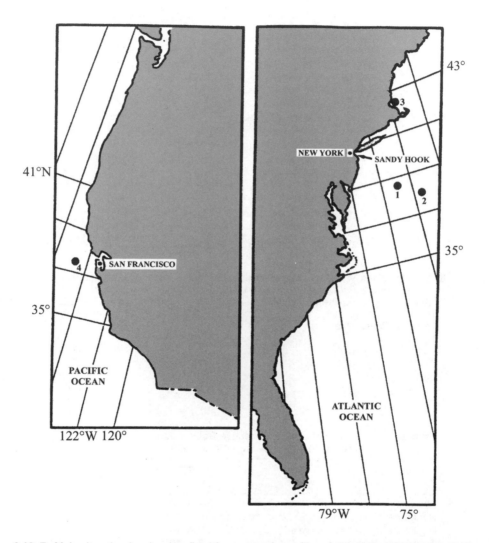

Figure 6.12–7 Major inactive low-level radioactive waste dumpsites of the United States (1) 2800-m site, (2) 3800-m site, (3) Massachusetts Bay site, and (4) Farallon Island site. (From U.S. General Accounting Office, Hazards of Post Low-Level Radioactive Waste Ocean Dumping Have Been Overemphasized, Report EMD-82–9, U.S. General Accounting Office, Washington, D.C., 1981.)

Table 6.12–14   U.S. Dumpsites That Have Received Packaged Radioactive Wastes

Distance from Land (km)	Central Coordinates	Depth (m)[a]	Activity (Bq)[b]	Number of Containers	Years Licensed
Pacific Ocean					
80.5 W of San Francisco	37°38′N:123°08′W	896–1700	5.4×10^{14}	47,500	1946–1970
32 NE of Honolulu	21°28′N:157°25′W	3500	3×10^{10}	39	1959–1960
483 N of Midway Island	34°58′N:174°52′W	5490	5.2×10^{11}	7	1960
56 SW of Port Hueneme	33°40′N:119°35′W	1830–1940	4×10^{12}	3114	1946–1962
370 W of California–Oregon border	42°12′N:129°31′W	3294	3.5×10^{10}	26	1955–1958
56W of California–Oregon border	42°04′N:125°01′W	4099	3×10^{9}	4	1960
306 NW of California–Oregon border	43°52′N:127°44′W	2928	3×10^{9}	2	1960
1600 WSW of Los Angeles	30°43′N:139°05′W	3660–4560	3.5×10^{10}	26	1955–1958
1290 SW of San Francisco	28°47′N:135°00′W	3477	4×10^{10}	29	1955–1960
322 W of San Diego	32°00′N:121°30′W	2210–3660	1.3×10^{12}	4415	1959–1962
1290 WNW of San Francisco	40°07′N:135°24′W	1830–1990	8×10^{9}	29	1960
564 NW of Cape Flattery	50°56′N:136°03′W	3294	3.6×10^{12}	1197	1958–1966
	52°25′N:140°12′W	3294	1×10^{12}	163	1962–1969
North Pacific	51°30′N:136°31′W	—	2×10^{10}	38	1946–1962
	52°05′N:140°00′W	—	2×10^{10}	41	1946–1962
	47°00′N:138°54′W	—	3.6×10^{12}	361	1946–1962
Atlantic Ocean					
Massachusetts Bay	42°25′N:70°35′W	92	9.0×10^{13}	4008	1952–1959
129 E of Cape Henry	36°56′N:74°23′W	1830–1967	3.2×10^{12}	843	1949–1967
225 SE of Sandy Hook	38°30′N:72°06′W	1830–2800	3.8×10^{15}	14,301	1951–1956 1959–1962
354 SE of Sandy Hook	37°50′N:70°35′W	1830–3800	7.8×10^{13}	14,500	1957–1959
350 E of Charleston	31°32′N:76°30′W	915–3660	2.3×10^{10}	119	1955–1962
Central Atlantic	36°20′N:43°49′N 45°00′W	3660–5289	1.8×10^{13}	432	1959–1960
Gulf of Mexico					
274 from New Orleans	27°14′N:89°33′W	1930	4×10^{11}	1	1958
402 from Appalachicola	25°40′N:85°17′W	3111	$7 \times 10^{-}$	78	1955–1957

[a] Dash denotes data not available.
[b] Activity given in estimated quantities at time of disposal.

Source: Mattson, R. J., Statement before the Subcommittee on Oceanography of the Committee on Merchant Marine and Fisheries, 20 November, U.S. House of Representatives, Washington, D.C., 1980.

Table 6.12–15   Radioactive Wastes Dumped at the Northeastern Atlantic
                 Dumpsite, 1967 to 1980

Year	Gross Weight (tons)	Approximate Radioactivity (Bq)[a]		
		α	β–γ	^{3}H
1967	10,900	9×10^{12}	2.81×10^{14}	—
1968	1700[b]	1.1×10^{13} [b]	7.0×10^{13}	—
1969	9180	1.9×10^{13}	8.55×10^{14}	—
1970	1700[b]	1.1×10^{13} [b]	7.0×10^{13}	—
1971	3970	2.3×10^{13}	4.15×10^{14} [c]	—
1972	4130	2.5×10^{13}	8.0×10^{14} [c]	—
1973	4350	2.7×10^{13}	4.67×10^{14} [c]	
1974	2270	1.6×10^{13}	—	3.7×10^{15}
1975	4470	2.9×10^{13}	1.13×10^{15}	1.10×10^{15}
1976	6770	3.3×10^{13}	1.20×10^{15}	7.8×10^{14}
1977	5600	3.5×10^{13}	1.34×10^{15}	1.18×10^{15}
1978	8040	4.1×10^{13}	1.59×10^{15}	1.56×10^{15}
1979	5400	5.2×10^{13}	1.52×10^{15}	1.57×10^{15}
1980	8400	7.0×10^{13}	4.67×10^{15}	3.87×10^{15}

[a] Dash denotes no information available.
[b] Assumed U.K. yearly average based on 5-year period.
[c] Includes ^{3}H.

Note: 1967 to 1979 data from Organization for Economic Cooperation and
Development–Nuclear Energy Agency, Review of the Continued Suitability
of the Dumping Site for Radioactive Waste in the Northeast Atlantic,
Organization for Economic Cooperation and Development–Nuclear
Energy Agency, Paris, 1980. 1980 data from Inter-Governmental Maritime
Consultative Organization. Report of the Fifth Consultative Meeting of
Contracting Parties to the Convention on the Prevention of Marine Pollu-
tion by Dumping of Wastes and Other Matter, Inter-Governmental Maritime
Consultative Organization, London, 1980.

Table 6.12–16   Summary of Radioactive Ocean-Dumping Operations, 1946 to 1979

Responsible Authority and Dates	Location	Details
United States (1946–1970)	Farallon Islands, Massachusetts Bay, off mid-Atlantic states	4.3×10^{15} Bq total in about 107,000 drums, mainly at these four Atlantic and Pacific Ocean sites
Japan (1955–1969)	Shallow, nearshore sites about 40 km from mouth of Tokyo Bay	
United Kingdom (pre-1967)	Deep areas of North Atlantic, southwest of England	1.8×10^{15} Bq (other western European countries also dumped during this period)
Republic of Korea (1968–1973)	Territorial sea	
Nuclear Energy Agency and its members (post-1967)	Northeastern Atlantic dumpsite	3.1×10^{15} Bq in 1979; total dumping in excess of 1.9×10^{16} Bq

Source: Modified from Finn, D. P., in *Wastes in the Ocean,* Vol. 3, *Radioactive Wastes and the Ocean,* Park,
P. K. et. al., Eds., John Wiley & Sons, New York, 1983, 65. With permission.

Table 6.12–17   Sources and Concentrations of Different Types of Radioactive Waste

Low-Level Waste

Low-level wastes are produced in large volumes by all the various medical, industrial, scientific, and military applications of radioactivity. They include contaminated solutions and solids, protective, cleaning, and decontamination materials, laboratory ware, and other equipment. They also include gases and liquids operationally discharged from power stations and other facilities. It has been estimated that during the period 1980 to 2000 about 3.6×10^6 m^3 of such wastes were produced, some of which was sufficiently low in activity to be directly discharged into the environment, either with or without prior dilution or chemical treatment. Typical maximum activity concentrations in low-level waste are 4 GBq t (alpha) and 12 GBq t (beta and gamma). Much low-level waste is currently disposed of by shallow burial in landfill sites, often with the co-disposal of other, nonradioactive, controlled wastes or by discharge into surface waters in rivers, lakes, estuaries, or coastal seas or by discharge into the atmosphere. If the environmental biophysicochemical behavior of the radionuclides in question and their possible pathways back to humans are well understood, then it is possible to make reliable estimates of the likely resultant doses of radioactivity to those most exposed in the population. If these doses are suitably low, then the disposal methods may be deemed to be acceptable. However, at the present time there are many uncertainties in the understanding of such behavior, pathways, and doses; nevertheless, the very large volumes of low-level waste being generated will, through lack of economically and environmentally viable alternatives, continue to be disposed of in these relatively uncontrolled ways.

Intermediate-Level Waste

Intermediate-level wastes are sufficiently active to prevent their direct discharge into the environment, with maximum specific activities of typically 2×10^{12} Bq/m^3 (α) and 2×10^{-14} Bq/m^3 (β and γ). They comprise much of the solid and liquid wastes generated during fuel reprocessing, residues from power station effluent plants, and wastes produced by the decommissioning of nuclear facilities. Very large quantities (~ 2000 t/year) of intermediate- and low-level wastes have been disposed of by dumping in deep ocean waters in the NE Atlantic. Although some authorities still consider this method of disposal to be the best practicable environmental option for these categories of waste, it is no longer practiced. Intermediate-level waste produced in the United Kingdom is now stored on land, mainly at Sellafield, awaiting further policy decisions.

High-Level Waste

High-level wastes mainly consist of spent fuel and its residues and very active liquids generated during fuel reprocessing. Typical maximum activities are 4×10^{14} Bq/m^3 (α) and 8×10^{16} Bq/m^3 (β and γ). At present such wastes generated in the United Kingdom are stored at Sellafield in storage ponds where it is proposed they will be vitrified prior to further storage (to allow the decay of shorter-lived nuclides) and final disposal in deep repositories. No such repository yet exists, but deep mines and boreholes on land and sea as well as other more exotic solutions including extraterrestrial disposal have all been proposed.

Source: Hewitt, C. N., in *Pollution: Causes, Effects, and Control,* 2nd ed., Harrison. R. M., Ed., Royal Society of Chemistry, Cambridge, 1990, 343. With permission.

Table 6.12–18   Some Fission Product Radionuclides of Potential Biological Importance

Radionuclide	Fission Yield (%)[a]	Radiation	Half-Life	Important Element Analogues
^{3}H	0.01	β	12 years	H
^{85}Kr	0.29	β, γ	10 years	—
^{90}Sr	5.77	β	28 years	Ca
^{89}Sr	4.79	β	51 days	Ca
^{137}Cs	6.15	β, γ	27 years	K
^{131}I	3.1	β, γ	8.1 days	I
^{129}I	0.9	β, γ	1.7×10^7 years	I
^{144}Ce[b]	6.0	β, γ	285 days	—
^{103}Ru[b]	3.0	β, γ	40 days	—
^{106}Ru[b]	0.38	β, γ	1.0 years	—
^{95}Zr[b]	6.2	β, γ	65 days	—
^{140}Ba[b]	6.32	β, γ	12.8 days	Ca
^{91}Y	5.4	β, γ	58 days	—
^{141}Ce[b]	5.7	β, γ	33 hours	—
^{147}Nd[b]	2.7	β, γ	11 days	—

[a] Based upon thermal neutron fission of ^{235}U.
[b] Decay to radioactive daughters.

Source: Whicker, F. W. and Schultz, V., *Radioecology: Nuclear Energy and the Environment,* Vol. 1, CRC Press, Boca Raton, FL, 1982. With permission.

Table 6.12–19   Estimates of Annual Doses (mrad/year) Received by Marine Organisms from Natural Sources of Radiation

Source	Taxonomic Group	Marine (20-m depth)
Cosmic	Phytoplankton	4.4
	Zooplankton	4.4
	Mollusca	4.4
	Crustacea	4.4
	Fish	4.4
Water	Phytoplankton	3.5
	Zooplankton	1.8
	Mollusca	0.9
	Crustacea	0.9
	Fish	0.9
Sediment (β+)	Phytoplankton	0
	Zooplankton	0
	Mollusca	27–324
	Crustacea	27–324
	Fish	0–324
Internal	Phytoplankton	17–64
	Zooplankton	23–138
	Mollusca	65–131
	Crustacea	69–188
	Fish	24–37
Sum of natural sources	Phytoplankton	25–72
	Zooplankton	29–168
	Mollusca	97–460
	Crustacea	101–517
	Fish	29–366

Source: Whicker, F. W. and Schultz, V., *Radioecology: Nuclear Energy and the Environment,* Vol. 1, CRC Press, Boca Raton, FL, 1982. With permission.

Table 6.12–20 Comparison of Annual Doses Received by Marine and Freshwater Organisms from Natural Sources of Radiation (mGy/year)

	Phytoplankton	Zooplankton	Mollusca	Crustacea	Fish
Freshwater Organisms					
Cosmic	0.24	0.24	0.19	0.19	0.19–0.24
Water	6.4×10^{-4}–0.54	9×10^{-5}–7.4×10^{-2}	4×10^{-5}–3.1×10^{-2}	4×10^{-5}–3.1×10^{-2}	4×10^{-5}–6.1×10^{-2}
Sediments ($\beta + \gamma$)	0	0	0.27–3.2	0.27–3.2	0–3.2
Internal	—	—	—	—	0.32–0.42
Total	0.24–0.78	0.24–0.31	0.46–3.5	0.46–3.5	0.51–4.0
Marine Organisms					
Cosmic	4.4×10^{-2}	4.4×10^{-2}	4.4×10^{-2}	4.4×10^{-2}	4.4×10^{-2}
Water	3.5×10^{-2}	1.8×10^{-2}	9×10^{-3}	9×10^{-3}	9×10^{-3}
Sediments ($\beta + \gamma$)	0	0	0–3.2	0.27–3.2	0–3.2
Internal	0.17–0.64	0.23–1.4	0.65–1.3	0.69–1.9	0.24–0.37
Total	0.24–0.72	0.29–1.7	0.97–4.6	1.0–5.2	0.29–3.7

Source: International Atomic Energy Agency, Effects of Ionizing Radiation on Aquatic Organisms and Ecosystems, Tech. Rep. Ser. No. 172, International Atomic Energy Agency, Vienna, 1976.

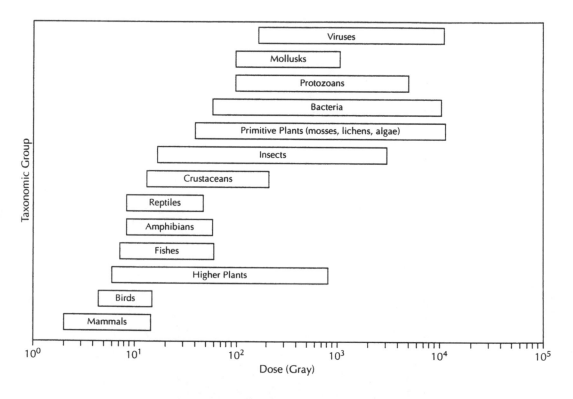

Figure 6.12–8   Ranges of acute lethal radiation doses to various taxonomic groups of organisms. (From Whicker, F. W. and Schultz, V., *Radioecology: Nuclear Energy and the Environment,* Vol. 1, CRC Press, Boca Raton, FL, 1982. With permission.)

6.13 DREDGING AND DREDGED MATERIAL DISPOSAL

Table 6.13–1   Types of Dredging Devices and Their Relationship to Sediment Type and Disposal Method

Dredge Type	Sediment Type	Disposal Conveyance
Mechanical devices		
Dipper dredge	Blasted rock	Vessel
Bucket dredge	Coarse-grain size	Vessel
Ladder dredge	Fine-grain size	Vessel
Agitation dredge	Mud, clay	Prevailing current
Hydraulic devices		
Agitation dredge	Mud, clay	Prevailing current
Hopper dredge	Fine-grain size	Vessel
Suction dredge	Soft mud, clay	Pipeline
Cutterhead dredge	Consolidated, coarse-grain size	Pipeline
Dustpan dredge	Sand	Pipeline
Sidecasting dredge	Fine-grain size	Short pipe

Sources: Kester, D. R. et al., in *Wastes in the Ocean,* Vol. 2, *Dredged Material Disposal in the Ocean,* Kester, D. R. et al., Eds., John Wiley & Sons, New York, 1983, 3. With permission.

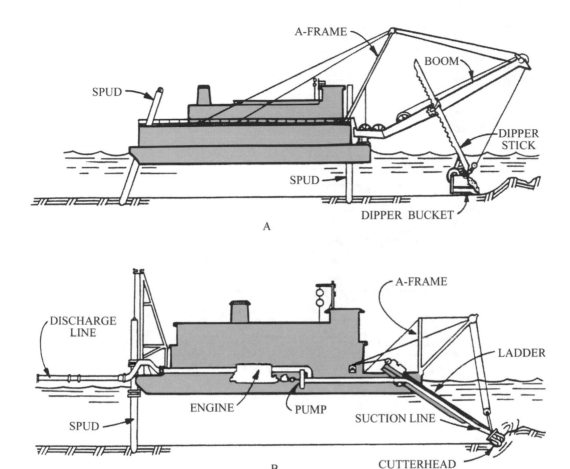

Figure 6.13–1 Two popular types of dredges: (A) bucket (mechanical) dredge; and (2) hydraulic (suction) type dredge. (From Clark, J. R., *Coastal Zone Management Handbook,* Lewis Publishers, Boca Raton, FL, 1996, 277. With permission.)

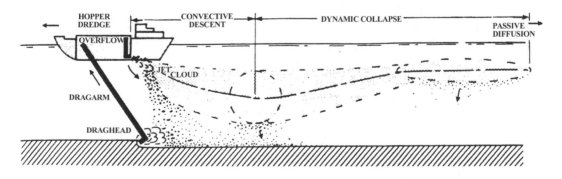

Figure 6.13–2 Hopper dredging operations in Chesapeake Bay showing an upper turbidity plume produced by overflow discharge and a near-bottom turbidity plume produced by draghead agitation and settling of particulates from the upper plume. The conceptual model depicts three transport phases for hopper overflow discharge: convective descent, dynamic collapse, and passive diffusion. (From Nichols, M. et al., *Environ. Geol. Water Sci.,* 15, 31, 1990. With permission.)

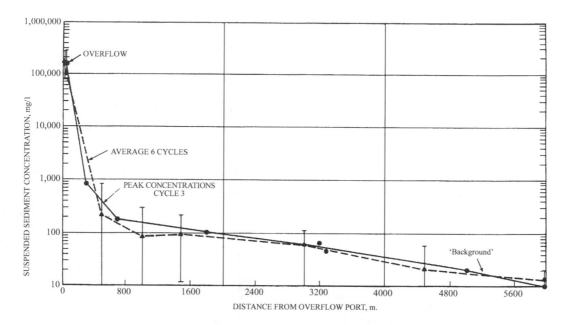

Figure 6.13–3   Dispersion curves for average peak suspended sediment concentrations at mid-depth (7 m) along the plume axis over six dredge cycles and for one dredge cycle (number 3) during hopper dredging operations in Chesapeake Bay. (From Nichols, M. et al., *Environ. Geol. Water Sci.,* 15, 31, 1990. With permission.)

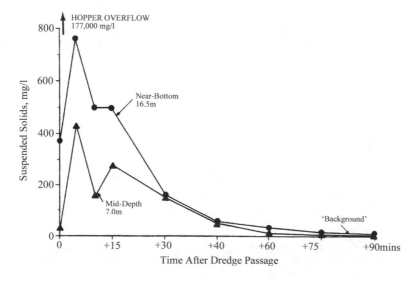

Figure 6.13–4   Temporal variations of average suspended sediment concentration in Chesapeake Bay at three fixed points in a plume to 90 min after passage of a hopper dredge. (From Nichols, M. et al., *Environ. Geol. Water Sci.,* 15, 31, 1990. With permission.)

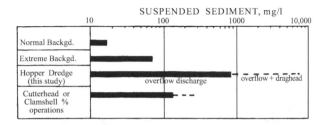

Figure 6.13–5 Comparison of suspended sediment concentration ranges for different background conditions in central Chesapeake Bay and different types of dredging operations. (From Nichols, M. et al., *Environ. Geol. Water Sci.,* 15, 31, 1990. With permission.)

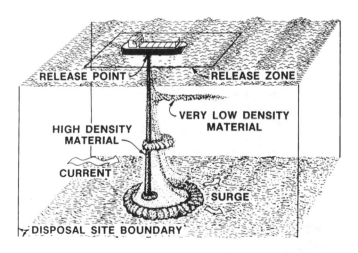

Figure 6.13–6 Sediment transport processes operating during open-water dredge disposal. (From Pequegnat, W. E. et al. *Procedural Guide for Designation Surveys of Ocean Dredged-Material Disposal Sites,* Tech. Rep. EL-81-1, U.S. Army Corps of Engineers, Washington, D.C., 1981.)

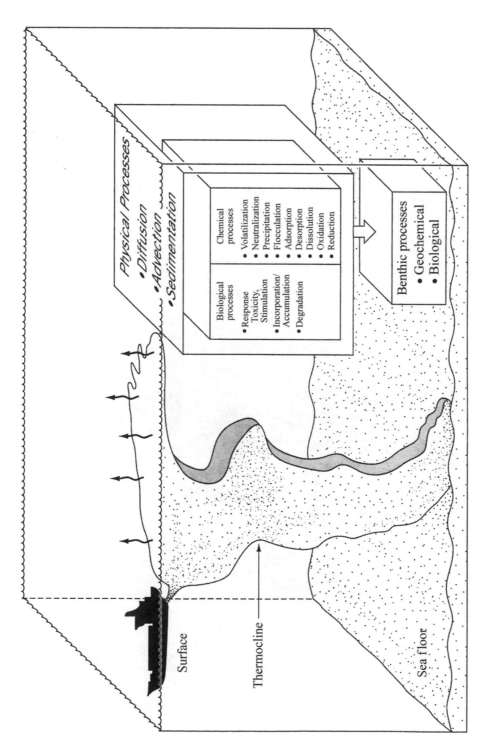

Figure 6.13-7 Biological, chemical, and physical processes affecting dredged material disposal at sea. (From Duedall, I. W. et al., Eds. *Wastes in the Ocean*, Vol. 1, Industrial and Sewage Wastes in the Ocean, John Wiley & Sons, New York, 1983, 3. With permission.)

Table 6.13–2 Summary of Field Studies of Dredged Material Behavior during Open-Water Disposal

Site	Site Characteristics		Dredged Sediment	Dredging/Disposal Characteristics				Sediment in Upper Water Column (% of original)
	Water Depth (m)	Bottom Currents (cm/s)		Dredge Type	Disposal Type	Typical Volume (cu/m)	Monitoring Technique/Device	
Long Island Sound	18–20	6–30	Silt-clay	Clamshell	Scow	900–2300	Transmissometer	1
Carquinez[a]	14	9–24	Silt-clay	Trailing suction hopper	Hopper	1000	Transmissometer and gravimetric	1–5
Ashtabula (Lake Erie)	15–18	0–21	Sandy silt	Trailing suction hopper	Hopper	690	Transmissometer and gravimetric	1[b]
New York Bight	26	6–24	Marine silt	Trailing suction hopper	Hopper	6000	Transmissometer and gravimetric	1[b]
Saybrook (Long Island Sound)	52	21–70	Marine silt	Clamshell	Scow	1100	Transmissometer and gravimetric	1[b]
Elliott Bay	67	0–21	Sandy silt	Clamshell	Scow	380–535	Transmissometer and gravimetric	1[b]
Rochester (Lake Ontario)	117–45	0–21	Riverine silt	Trailing suction hopper	Hopper	690	Transmissometer and gravimetric	1[b]
New York Bight	15–25	N/R	Silt-clay	Clamshell	Scow	1375–3000	Mass balance	3.7
Duwamish Waterway	20–21	6	Silt-clay	Clamshell	Scow	840	Gravimetric and mass balance	2–4

[a] Limited data at two additional sites included.
[b] Synthesis of all sites reported.

Source: Truitt, C. L., *J. Coastal Res.*, 4, 489, 1988. With permission.

Table 6.13–3   Priority Pollutants and 301(H) Pesticides of Concern in Dredged Material Disposal Operations

Structural Compound Class	PP[a]	Pollutant	Structural Compound Class	PP[a]	Pollutant
Phenols	65	Phenol	Phthalates	66	bis(2-ethylhexyl)phthalate
	34	2,4-Dimethylphenol		67	Butyl benzyl phthalate
Substituted phenols	21	2,4,6-Trichlorophenol		68	Di-n-butyl phthalate
	22	Para-chloro-meta-cresol		69	Di-n-octyl phthalate
	24	2-Chlorophenol		70	Diethyl phthalate
	31	2,4-Dichlorophenol		71	Dimethyl phthalate
	57	2-Nitrophenol	Polychlorinated	106	PCB-1242
	58	4-Nitrophenol	biphenyls (PCBs)	107	PCB-1254
	59	2,4-Dinitrophenol	as arochlors	108	PCB-1221
	60	4,6-Dinitro-o-cresol		109	PCB-1232
	64	Pentachlorophenol		110	PCB-1248
				111	PCB-1260
				112	PCB-1016
Organonitrogen compounds	5	Benzidine	Miscellaneous	129	TCDD (dioxin)
	28	3,3'-Dichlorobenzidine	oxygenated	54	Isophorone
	35	2,4-Dinitrotoluene	compounds		
	36	2,6-Dinitrotoluene			
	37	1,2-Diphenylhydrazine	Pesticides	89	Aldrin
	56	Nitrobenzene		90	Dieldrin
	61	N-Nitrosodimethylamine		91	Chlordane
	62	N-Nitrosodiphenylamine		92	DDT[b]
	63	N-Nitrosodiphenylamine		95	Endosulfan[c]
Low-molecular-weight	1	Acenaphthene		98	Endrin
polynuclear aromatic	55	Naphthalene		99	Endrin aldehyde
hydrocarbons (PAH)	77	Acenaphthylene		100	Heptachlor
	78	Anthracene		101	Heptachlor epoxide
	81	Phenanthrene		102	Alpha-hexachlorocyclohexane
	80	Fluorene		103	Beta-hexachlorocyclohexane
High-molecular-weight PAHs	39	Fluoranthene		104	Delta-hexachlorocyclohexane
	72	Benzo(a)anthracene		105	Gamma-hexachlorocyclohexane
	73	Benzo(a)pyrene		113	Toxaphene
				—	Mirex[d]
				—	Methoxychlor[d]

	74	Benzo(b)fluoranthene
	75	Benzo(k)fluoranthene
	76	Chrysene
	79	Benzo(ghi)perylene
	82	Dibenzo(a,h)anthracene
	83	Ideno(1,2,3-cd)pyrene
	84	Pyrene
Chlorinated aromatic hydrocarbons	8	1,2,4-Trichlorobenzene
	9	Hexachlorobenzene
	20	2-Chloronaphthalene
	25	1,2-Dichlorobenzene
	26	1,3-Dichlorobenzene
	27	1,4-Dichlorobenzene
Chlorinated aliphatic hydrocarbons	52	Hexachlorobutadiene
	12	Hexachloroethane
	53	Hexachlorocyclopentadiene
Halogenated ethers	18	bis(2-Chloroethyl)ether
	40	4-Chlorophenyl ether
	41	4-Bromophenyl ether
	42	bis(2-Chloroisopropyl)ether
	43	bis(2-Chloroethoxy)methane
Volatile halogenated alkenes	29	1,1-Dichloroethylene
	30	1,2-trans-Dichloroethylene
	33	trans-1,3-Dichloropropene
	33	cis-1,3-Dichloropropene
	85	Tetrachlorethene
	87	Trichlorethene
	88	Vinyl chloride
Volatile aromatic hydrocarbons	4	Benzene
	38	Ethylbenzene
	86	Toluene
Volatile chlorinated aromatic hydrocarbons	7	Chlorobenzene

	—	Parathion[e]
	—	Malathion[e]
	—	Guthion[e]
	—	Demeton[e]
Volatile halogenated alkanes	6	Tetrachloromethane
	10	1,2-Dichloroethane
	11	1,1,1-Trichloroethane
	13	1,1,-Dichloroethane
	14	1,1,2-Trichloroethane
	15	1,1,2,2-Tetrachloroethane
	16	Chloroethane
	23	Chloroform
	32	1,2-Dichloropropane
	44	Dichloromethane
	45	Chloromethane
	46	Bromomethane
	47	Bromoform
	48	Dichlorobromoethane
	49	Fluorotrichloromethane (removed)
	50	Dichlorodifluoromethane (removed)
	51	Chlorodibromomethane

(continued)

Table 6.13–3   Priority Pollutants and 301(H) Pesticides of Concern in Dredged Material Disposal Operations (continued)

Volatile unsaturated carbonyl compounds	2	Acrolein
Volatile ethers	3	Acrylonitrile
	19	2-Chlorethylvinylether
		Bis(chloromethyl)ether (removed)
Metals	114	Antimony
	115	Arsenic
	117	Beryllium
	118	Cadmium
	119	Chromium
	120	Copper
	122	Lead
	123	Mercury
	124	Nickel
	125	Selenium
	126	Silver
	127	Thallium
	128	Zinc
Miscellaneous	121	Cyanide
	116	Asbestos

a PP = priority pollutant.
b Includes DDT, DDD, and DDE.
c Includes *alpha*-endosulfan, *beta*-endosulfan, and endosulfan sulfate.
d Chlorinated 301(H) pesticides that are not on the priority pollutant list.
e Organophosphorus 301(H) pesticides that are not on the priority pollutant list.

Source: U.S. Environmental Protection Agency and U.S. Department of the Army, *Ecological Evaluation of Proposed Discharge of Dredged Material into Ocean Waters*, Tech. Rep., EPA Contract No. 68-C8 0105, U.S. Government Printing Office, Washington, D.C., 1990.

Table 6.13–4 Substances Controlled by the London Dumping Convention (LDC)[a]

ANNEX I

1. Organohalogen compounds.
2. Mercury and mercury compounds.
3. Cadmium and cadmium compounds.
4. Persistent plastics and other persistent synthetic materials, for example, netting and ropes, which may float or may remain in suspension in the sea in such a manner as to interfere materially with fishing, navigation, or other legitimate uses of the sea.
5. Crude oil and its wastes, refined petroleum products, petroleum, distilate residues, and any mixtures containing any of these, taken on board for the purpose of dumping.
6. **Radioactive wastes or other radioactive matter.**
7. Materials in whatever form (e.g., solids, liquids, semi-liquids, gases, or in a living state) produced for biological and chemical warfare.
8. **With the exception of paragraph 6 above,** the preceding paragraphs of this Annex do not apply to substances which are rapidly rendered harmless by physical, chemical, or biological processes in the sea provided they do not:

   (i) make edible marine organisms unpalatable, or

   (ii) endanger human health or that of domestic animals.

   The consultative procedure provided for under Article XIV should be followed by a Party if there is doubt about the harmlessness of the substance.
9. **Except for industrial waste as defined in paragraph 11 below,** this Annex does not apply to wastes or other materials (e.g., sewage sludge and dredged **material**) containing the matters referred to in paragraphs 1–5 above as trace contaminants. Such wastes shall be subject to the provisions of Annexes II and III as appropriate.

   Paragraph 6 does not apply to wastes or other materials (e.g., sewage sludge and dredged material) containing de minimis (exempt) levels of radioactivity as defined by the IAEA and adopted by the Contracting Parties. Unless otherwise prohibited by Annex I, such wastes shall be subject to the provisions of Annexes II and III as appropriate.
10. (a) **Incineration at sea of industrial waste, as defined in paragraph 11 below, and sewage sludge is prohibited.**

    (b) **The incineration at sea of any other wastes or other matter requires the issue of a special permit.**

    (c) **In the issue of special permits for incineration at sea, Contracting Parties shall apply regulations as are developed under this Convention.**

    (d) **For the purposes of this Annex:**

    (i) **"Marine incineration facility" means a vessel, platform, or other man-made structure operating for the purpose of incineration at sea.**

    (ii) **"Incineration at sea" mans the deliberate combustion of wastes or other matter on marine incineration facilities for the purpose of their thermal destruction. Activities incidental to the normal operation of vessels, platforms, or other man-made structures are excluded from the scope of this definition.**
11. **Industrial waste as from 1 January 1996.**

    For the purposes of this Annex:

    "Industrial waste" means waste materials generated by manufacturing or processing operations and does not apply to:

    (a) **Dredged material;**

    (b) **Sewage sludge;**

    (c) **Fish waste or organic materials resulting from industrial fish processing operations;**

    (d) **Vessels and platforms or other man-made structures at sea, provided that material capable of creating floating debris or otherwise contributing to pollution of the marine environment has been removed to the maximum extent;**

    (e) **Uncontaminated inert geological materials, the chemical constituents of which are unlikely to be released into the marine environment;**

    (f) **Uncontaminated organic materials of natural origin.**

    Dumping of wastes and other matter specified in subparagraphs (a)–(f) above shall be subject to all other provisions of Annex I, and to the provisions of Annexes II and III.

    This paragraph shall not apply to the radioactive wastes or any other radioactive matter referred to in paragraph 6 of this Annex.

Table 6.13–4   Substances Controlled by the London Dumping Convention (LDC)[a] (continued)

12.   Within 25 years from the date on which the amendment to paragraph 6 enters into force and
       at each 25-year interval thereafter, the Contracting Parties shall complete a scientific study
       relating to all radioactive wastes and other radioactive matter other than high level wastes or
       matter, taking into account such other factors as the Contracting Parties consider appropriate,
       and shall review the position of such substances on Annex I in accordance with the procedures
       set forth in Article XV.

ANNEX II

The following substances and materials requiring special care are listed for the purposes of Article VI(1)(a).
A.   Wastes containing significant amounts of the matters listed below:

      arsenic[b]
      beryllium[b]
      chromium[b]
      copper[b]
      lead
      nickel
      vanadium
      zinc
      organosilicon compounds
      cyanides
      fluorides
      pesticides and their by-products not covered in Annex I.

B.   Containers, scrap metal, and other bulky wastes liable to sink to the sea bottom which may present
      a serious obstacle to fishing or navigation.
C.   In the issue of secial permits for the incineration of substances and materials listed in this Annex, the
      Contracting Parties shall apply the Regulations for the Control of Incineration of Wastes and Other
      matter at Sea set forth in the Addendum to Annex I and take full account of the Technical guidelines
      on the Control of Incineration of Wastes and Other matter at Sea adopted by the Contracting Parties
      in consultation, to the extent specified in these Regulations and Guideliens.
D.   Materials which, though of a non-toxic nature, may become harmful due to the quantities in which
      they are dumped, or which are liable to seriously reduce amenities.

[a] Amendments of 1993 are indicated in bold.
[b] And its compounds.

Source: Final act of the London Dumping Convention, Annexes I and II, Office of the London Dumping
Convention, International Maritime Organization, London, 1972. Amended in 1993.

Index

C

hydrothermal and river fluxes of elements comparison,
100
in seawater, 46
in shelf vs. open sea-surface waters, 91
toxicity of, 792
Copper River, 429
Coral reefs
bacterial abundance in, 493–494
described, 459–460
dispersed oil effects on, 733
dissolved and particulate concentrations, tropical
systems, 686
energy zones, 590
macrobenthos densities, 556–557
meiobenthos densities, 550–551
nutrient concentrations, 151
predicted responses to global climate change, 669
productivity and P:R ratios, 592
protozoa abundance, 495–496
Coral Sea Basin, 360
Cormorant (*Phalacrocorax*), 769
Coronado canyon, 37, 41
Corpus Christi Bay, TX, U.S., 743, 785
Corsair canyon, 37, 41
Cory's shear water (*Calonectris diomedea*), 768
Coryphaenoides rupestris (roundnose grenadier), 635–636
Cosmogenic sediment, 291, 405
Costa Rica Rift, 357
Crabs, see *Cancer*
Crassostrea (oysters)
DDT status and trends, mussels and oysters, 777–778
larvae mortality rates, 546
PAH concentrations in, 745
PAH status and trends, 748–749
PCB concentrations status and trends, 762
Cretaceous period, 302
Crete canyon, 39, 43
Crevalle jack (*Caranx hippos*), 562
Crouch Estuary, England, 555
Crustaceans
cephalopods and, 462
described, 447, 470
natural source radiation comparisons, 825
natural source radiation estimates, 824
PAH concentrations in, 746
pollution effects on life cycle stages, 682
sublethal effects of heavy metals, 806
toxic concentrations of sewage sludge, 713
zinc accumulation in, 796
Ctenophora
cleavage patterns and larval forms, 541
percent carbon in, 477
Culvert equations flow measurement method, 251
Currents, coastal, see Coastal waves and currents
Cutthroat flow measurement method, 247
Cyclodiene pesticides, 760
Cynoscion nebulosus (spotted seatrout)
primary foods, 563
sublethal effects of petroleum, 732
Cynoscion regalis (weakfish)
feeding strategies, 562

primary foods, 563
Cypermethrin, 781
Cyperus spp., 534
Cyprinodon variegatus (minnow), 563
Cyreus articulatus, 527
Cystine, 113, 114

D

Dam crests flow measurement method, 250
Damodar River, 245
Dana Point, CA, U.S.
PAH concentrations, 743
trace metals in sediments, 785
Danube River
average sediment discharges to oceans, 429
runoff and sediment load, 655
Davies Lagoon, GBR, 151
Davies Reef, Australia, 551
DDD, 766
DDE, 766
DDT, see Dichlorodiphenyltrichloroethane
Decodon verticillatus, 523
Dee estuary, 208
Deep-ocean basin province
abyssal hills, 282
abyssal plains, 283
aseismic ridges, 283–284
deep-sea trenches, 284–285
described, 2–3
seamounts, 283
Deeps, major, 33
Deep-sea sediments, see also Sediments
authigenic, 290
biogenous
calcareous oozes, 288–289
siliceous oozes, 289
cosmogenic, 291
pelagic distribution, 289–290
terrigenous, 287
thickness of, 291
types overview, 286–287
volcanogenic, 291
Deep-sea trenches, 284–285
Deep temperature zone, 168
Dehydroascorbic acid, 112
Delaware Bay, DE, U.S.
PAH concentrations, 743
trace metals in sediments, 785
Delaware River, U.S., 555
Delgada canyon, 37, 41
Delta distribution worldwide, 430
Dengie Flats, England, 555
Dense-beaked whale (*Mesoplodon densirostris*), 783
Density
of the earth, 12
as function of temperature, 200
metric and U.S., 7
seawater properties, 168–169